'A very evocative novel that excels in its characterisations and depictions of life in Darwin'

'It's great to see local authors using the Australian landscape with such strength. Actor Matt Nable does this well.'

Townsville Bulletin

STILL

MATT NABLE

hachette
AUSTRALIA

hachette
AUSTRALIA

First published in Australia and New Zealand in 2021
by Hachette Australia
(an imprint of Hachette Australia Pty Limited)
Gadigal Country, Level 17, 207 Kent Street, Sydney NSW 2000
www.hachette.com.au

This edition published in 2022

Hachette Australia acknowledges and pays our respects to the past, present and
future Traditional Owners and Custodians of Country throughout Australia and
recognises the continuation of cultural, spiritual and educational practices of
Aboriginal and Torres Strait Islander peoples. Our head office is located on the
lands of the Gadigal people of the Eora Nation.

A catalogue record for this
book is available from the
National Library of Australia

ISBN: 978 0 7336 4840 3 (paperback)

Cover design by Luke Causby, Blue Cork
Front cover images courtesy Jiwa/AdobeStock and Kitti Tantibankul/Alamy Stock Photo
Author photograph by Sally Flegg
Typeset in Adobe Garamond Pro by Kirby Jones
Printed and bound in Great Britain by Clays Ltd, Elcograf S.p.A.

The paper this book is printed on is certified against the
Forest Stewardship Council® Standards. McPherson's Printing
Group holds FSC® chain of custody certification SA-COC-005379.
FSC® promotes environmentally responsible, socially beneficial
and economically viable management of the world's forests.

For my family, who by their existence lead from the dark and back into the light. I love you.

THE LONG TUFTS of spinifex curled over on a gust of warm wind. Whispered voices broke with a gravelled edge and the sounds of violence disturbed a brown snake resting in a tight coil on the corner of a steep embankment. The snake's head lifted, its tongue flickered and it looked at the shadowy figures, like a fighter adopting its stance. It unravelled itself and moved away, down the embankment into the large snarls of lantana and wild saltbush.

'Stand him up.' The voice came from a large broad-shouldered man, his shape caught briefly in the half-moon's light. The voice wasn't much more than a whisper, though considering where they were, it wouldn't have mattered had he yelled. The only sign of civilisation was the corona from the town's lights to the west of them and even it had been dulled by the ocean mist. In the darkness in front of the blockish end of a derelict machine-gun post, a slumped man was pulled up by his armpits. He stood, his face lifting from the shadows and into the light. His bottom lip was split in its centre and fell loosely either side of the gash.

'You were in the wrong place at the wrong time.'

The punch that followed struck the beaten man on the side of his jaw, the sound of bone against bone echoing through the concrete walls of the machine-gun post.

'Hit him again.'

The second punch hit him squarely on the side of his head. His knees dipped and he swayed, and though he tried to stay standing, he fell slowly onto his back.

The large man took a pistol held in his beltline and poked the barrel hard against the man's chest. 'Your troubles are over, mate.'

A gunshot rang out, and the ground shuddered underfoot. Colonies of fruit bats rustled in the canopies of casuarina trees close by and then took flight, their shadows hopping over the corpse.

'Shoot him again.' The gun was passed to another.

'He's already dead, though.'

'Do it. In the head.'

Another shot rang throughout the darkness.

The metallic tang of blood and the chemical spark of cordite mixed with the salty evening air. The snake was long gone.

CHAPTER 1

CHARLOTTE CLARK STOOD in her kitchen looking out the window above the sink at the row of weedy lots of land that were vacant and signposted for sale. She could hear the whirr of her husband's voice, and though she wasn't listening, she knew by the sounds that clipped his words that he was telling a story with fervour. She closed her eyes and remembered a time when his words and voice commanded her attention, and she'd wait for the climax of his tale, or for the declaration of his love. She had revelled in those three words, *I love you*. She wasn't sure when she'd stopped listening.

It was summer, 1963, and the humidity in Darwin sat still and thick over everything. In Nightcliff, where Charlotte lived, the humid air had rolled itself around the heat and made her every drawn breath laboured. It was the wet season and the afternoon storms were a reprieve Charlotte very much looked forward to. She loved the smells that signalled the weather on approach. The floral bouquets from her backyard garden, the last jasmine sprouts that had endured past spring and the tomato vines broadening their leaves to accept the rain. Even the town's garbage that was picked up by the wind at the front of the storm and thrown around in smelly gusts.

Looking out the window, she thought of her life and where she'd made it to. At twenty-three, with no children, she felt stuck. She'd left school five years previous, had abandoned a place at nurse's college to get married and start a family. But that hadn't happened. She'd fallen pregnant twice, both times miscarrying after twelve weeks. It had been hard. Somewhere in between she lost herself and also the connection to her husband. During the months after the last miscarriage, Charlotte wondered with some surrender if her body might not be made to carry a baby. That she may never become a mother. She had begun to think about reapplying to nurse's college. On a few occasions she steeled herself throughout the day, while washing clothes and preparing dinner, to broach the possibility with her husband. But she always faltered when he got home from work, either cranky or tired, and on more than one occasion too drunk to talk sense with. She had decided if she were to reapply it would be done in secret, and only if successful would she unfurl her ambition to her husband.

She felt restless, and as though her life were still. She found some joy in listening to the wireless as she folded clothes and cooked. The broadcasts sometimes brought news from places far removed from Nightcliff. Much of it from America. Charlotte listened, fascinated, the United States seemed so modern and robust, and moving so quickly toward uncharted experiences. The moon, *for goodness sake*. Charlotte wondered whether she could enjoy a place so rapid and busy. She liked the thought of one day visiting, to see a Christmas in the snow, to walk a street so far from where she knew; novel experiences that she could use to help her work out who she was. Without some adventure or challenge, she feared her identity may be close to complete.

At twenty-three, it bothered her that her entire life might only be lived in the spaces she could see in front of her. She didn't feel anywhere near complete. She wanted to learn, to talk about things that mattered, about important things. Politics and social issues. Too often in company when talking about such things, she found herself politely quiet and then on the margins of whatever followed. But she liked the thought that one day she'd be more vocal, more refined, and if she were asked why she stood where she did on an issue, she'd be able to respond with her own answers. Responses that were formed by her own thought, her own reckonings, and without parroting anything she'd heard someone else say. So far, she'd stayed quiet and still and mostly unseen. But her husband had noticed her, and after only a month of meeting, had focused on her completely. He'd talked and talked, mostly about himself and his family, but she'd never felt such attention. It was overwhelming and exquisite.

* * *

Charlotte looked down at her hands. Her fingernails were short, cut neatly so that small crescents of flesh protruded from them. She'd cut one of them too short and it stung beneath the nail. She put the finger in her mouth and felt a heat against her skin. She wondered immediately what her breath might smell like. She pulled the finger out and sniffed it. It smelt acidic and stale, and she ran herself a glass of water from the tap over the kitchen sink. She drank it quickly and then placed her sore finger back inside her mouth to feel the coolness.

She looked out the window again, past her ghostly reflection and to the sky. Clouds had begun to gather, but it was too late in the day for a storm. The forecast for the coming week had warned that precautions were necessary in case the storm building in the Arafura Sea strengthened and formed a cyclone. Charlotte, like most who'd lived in Darwin long enough, knew that a cyclone wasn't likely, and if it did form, then it was probably going to blow itself out before reaching land. She hadn't made a single preparation or given it any more thought. The warmth from the oven had risen, hit the ceiling and turned on itself, settling in an idle lump in the middle of the room and it made it hard for her to breathe. She could see the heat outside, vapour rolling in fuzzy waves across the bitumen street leading to a watery mirage. She looked at the window, at its corners where the fasteners had rusted through and been lapped by coats of heavy paint. It hadn't been opened in years. She wanted to smash through the glass and feel a gust of wind as proof it was just her life that was so stagnant in that moment and not the rest of the world.

'Charlotte, that pie ready?'

She turned away from the window, her head falling. About to answer, she was transfixed by the beads of sweat gathered between the fine hair on her forearm.

'Sweetheart?'

'It's comin'.'

She opened the oven, turned her head to the side and caught the squall of searing heat across her neck.

* * *

Bobby Clark sat at the table, held his plate to his mouth and licked at the last traces of gravy. Charlotte studied her husband. His dark brown hair looked black beside his ears where it was lank with sweat. The eyes she knew so well were sky blue, made brighter by the bronzed colour of his skin. His nose was flattened across its bridge, pushed slightly to one side, and whistled when he was out of wind or drunk.

She stared at his thick neck, it was thicker than when they'd first met, and when he spoke a knotty mass of veins rose and scurried like bolts of lightning. His rough-house look and love of drink had been shaped by his years of rodeo. She'd been charmed by his rugged swagger when they'd first met. She'd listened to his stories and learnt about Bobby starting rodeo as a six-year-old, bareback on bulky calves and tying goats, and by the time he was fourteen he was competing against men in saddle bronc riding. By sixteen he was riding bulls. His father and older brothers were national champions at steer wrestling and team roping. He'd spent his youth travelling through the Territory and into Queensland following the rodeo circuit. His stories of other places and the disparate people who occupied them had fascinated her.

Often the rodeo was part of an agricultural show and accompanied by a boxing tent. At a show in Gladstone in Queensland, Bobby's father offered him up to a young Aboriginal fighter who was part of Jim Sharman's boxing troupe. Bobby was twelve. He had his nose broken, and the last of his baby molars knocked loose. Charlotte was horrified that Bobby's father had pushed him forward and allowed such violence to attach itself to his son. She shuddered when she learnt the crowd showered both fighters with coins at the end of the contest and that, afterward, Bobby's father straightened his nose with the shaft of a tablespoon and bought him his first beer pulled from a draught tap. She never met Bobby's father. He'd died a year after that fight in a car accident while transporting young brumbies from North Queensland. Bobby had spoken to her about him and his passing. It was the first time she'd seen him cry. He didn't hide his pain with her, and his willingness to be vulnerable was a reason she fell in love with him.

Charlotte held the crockery dish out in front of her, the action unknowingly pushing her breasts to a heavy cleavage. The man next to her husband looked there until she placed the apple pie down on the table and stared at him long enough for his eyes to return to her face.

'Thank you, Charlotte.' Danny Lewis was a tall man, thickset with a rugby player's physique. A local policeman, he and Bobby drank at the same pub. Lewis enjoyed being in Bobby's presence, it nourished his ego to be mates with someone so authentically rough and tumble.

'She makes it from scratch.' Bobby smiled at his wife and tapped her gently on the backside.

Charlotte cut into the apple pie, smelt the stink of her underarm and hoped her husband and Danny Lewis were spared. She served them and then left for the kitchen.

Bobby leant closer to Lewis, lowered his voice and whispered, 'If ya don't like it, don't eat it. I'll have it. Just don't leave it on ya plate.'

Lewis nodded. 'It's a bit tart.'

'The apples aren't ripe. Not her fault.'

Bobby cut into his pie with the blunt edge of a fork, blew on it to cool it down. 'It's like eatin' fuckin' lemons.' Both men laughed as Charlotte came back into the room.

'Please don't swear.' Charlotte took her seat next to her husband.

Bobby looked at Lewis and with a glare encouraged him to finish what was left on his plate.

* * *

Later that evening, the men left the house and headed for Hotel Darwin, a pub on the harbour foreshore. They were already drunk and, before walking out the door, Bobby took Charlotte by the hand and led her to the bedroom. He thanked her for the meal and for the pie, and then kissed her deeply. Charlotte steeled herself to not pull away.

Later, she stood on the front porch smoking a cigarette, the warm breeze carrying a brackish waft from the Timor Sea. She took a deep breath and savoured the essence from the nearby beach, the salt water, the fishy odour from the vestiges of gutted whiting and pikey bream, and the bitter smack of rotting kelp that had washed in on a ripping southerly wind a week before. She straightened her elbow and looked, knowing they'd be there, the fine clusters of salt carried on the breeze that swept across the Timor's skin now come to rest on the ginger ends of hair across her forearms.

Standing there, Charlotte wondered, not without guilt, what another life might be like. With another man. In another place. As a nurse. Where she might end up. Whom she might become friends with and what kinds of people she would spend time with. Looking across the road to the vacant blocks of land, she waited for the cooler wind that was forecast just before midnight. She saw it first over the thick weedy lots across from her, the grass suddenly shifting in one direction. And then she felt it, across her arms and face, and billowing her dress. She closed her eyes and lifted the hem of her dress waist-high to let the breeze drift between her legs. It felt good.

She went to bed, knowing Bobby would be home soon. Even if sleep didn't come before that, she would pretend. He would be drunk, sloppy, and wanting sex. It would be fast and over quickly but she'd started to refuse him and she watched him wrestle with anger each time she did. She feared that his anger would turn into enquiry and suspicion. He would not want to know the truth. That she no longer loved him. Not the way or in the amount she thought was needed to remain married. She wished she could explain to him that she believed they got married too early. That expectation made her say yes. She knew he wouldn't understand, wouldn't listen. Women her age were expected to marry. To stifle their ambition. She'd done that, but the years had only made her more restless and her love for Bobby had waned. If he asked, would she be brave enough to say that, though she loved him, it wasn't enough? She wouldn't. She'd often wondered whether the women she knew who were the same age, and in similar circumstances, ever indulged in such thoughts of another life. She didn't believe they did. She'd listened to them, the sound of their voices, and watched as they smiled easily. They were happy, she'd decided. Right where they wanted to be.

* * *

Bobby arrived home just as Charlotte had drifted off to sleep. He woke her up and sat on the edge of the bed, crying, telling her how much he loved her, and that *this would be the year* they would have their baby. He lay beside her, mumbling through some laughter, though it was nothing she could interpret. She spoke softly to him, told him to *get some sleep*, and gently ran her fingers through his hair. Not a minute later he was asleep but Charlotte lay awake until morning.

CHAPTER 2

NED POTTER, A fishing rod resting loosely on his hip, looked north. The Timor Sea in front of him, bumpy and moving in all directions, was rebounding in torn crests off the weathered edges of the rock platform he stood on. His short sandy hair moved with the wind across the sharp part on the left side of his scalp. His light blue eyes shone, bouncing off golden ribbons of reflected morning glow that rolled over the swell. The colour of his skin looked more bronze than usual under the rising sun and above the russet water of the Timor. He was clenching his teeth tightly together in a pulse-like rhythm, something he did when concentrating or in deep thought.

At twenty-eight years of age, Ned was easy to look at. Handsome, taller than most, his body though not overly muscled was taut and lean. His thick hand, which was more palm than fingers, held the fishing rod lightly. He looked beyond the churn of the sea close to the rocks, and watched a collection of debris and rubbish that had been washed from the streets into the stormwater drains the day before now slowly heading to shore on the tide. He chewed on his lip as he shook his head. *Who'll clean that up?* That was Ned's thought while he stood there on the southern end of the East Point rock platform.

His thoughts turned to work and what was required for the day. Ned had been made a senior constable two years before. He'd studied hard to pass his exams and fought harder to gain the respect of the more senior policemen he was working with. In particular, Damien Clooney, who had been the oldest senior sergeant working in the Northern Territory Police Department. A returned infantry soldier from the Second World War, he'd served in the machine-gun battalion in New Guinea. Ned had attached himself to the older man, keen to learn, and had persisted through Clooney's apathy for getting to know him and reluctance to converse. Eventually, it was Clooney who gave up, saying, *Jesus fucking Christ, you're not goin' away, are you? Keep ya fuckin' ears open and less talk.* From that moment until Clooney retired, Ned spent most working hours with him. And he learnt. Clooney showed him how to manoeuvre through a stagnant investigation, pointed him toward the who and where to call upon favours, and demonstrated to him, sometimes in a violent manner, that some criminals were worth considerably more out of jail than what they were inside. Ned felt that his education under Clooney had him positioned as one of the Territory's most efficient investigators. It was a self-appraisal that Ned knew wasn't shared by some of the other senior policemen and certainly not by Senior Sergeant Joe Riley.

Ned had grown up in a big family, four brothers and two sisters, following Terry, their father, and his search for work during and post wartime. Ned was born while his father had worked at the Kent Brewery in Sydney. They'd lived in Redfern then, and when the wind blew the right way the sweet scent of fermenting alcohol blew into their old terrace house making it smell like a big apple pie. When his father grew tired of working indoors at the brewery, they moved to Coffs Harbour where he worked on the banana plantations. Two years later they moved further north to Murwillumbah to the cane fields where he drove heavy machinery. The Potter family landed in Darwin when Ned was twelve, where his father worked at Darwin Port and then bought a newsagency. He'd been a quiet man, made uncertain of himself and cloaked by disproportionate guilt due to his inability to serve during the war. A bacterial infection in his corneas had almost made him blind as a young boy and he had been forced to wear thick glasses for the rest of his life.

Ned's mother, Frances, had borne all six children before she was thirty and had never favoured any of them. She had no time, and praise and punishment were uniformly direct and moved on from quickly. Ned had been a good boy, the fourth born, and had looked after his younger brother and sister. In winter he'd slept in the same bed as they did until he was at high school. He told them stories to calm them when they were made afraid by their thoughts, and prayed with them for slumber without nightmares, or fever.

Ned's heart was good. His father had died when he was sixteen, and then three years later his mother had followed. During both periods, though distraught himself, he'd been a comfort for all of his siblings. He'd nursed them through their mourning, watched them carefully, rendering whatever help they needed. A hug. To be told it was going to be okay. To cook them dinner. To make them laugh.

* * *

He threaded his long shank hook with the bottom half of a school prawn and cast his last line. A moment later the lithe end of his rod quivered and then bent back on itself. He reeled as fast as he could, and just when he saw the red bream's colour flash through the dusky caramel water, his rod flicked forward and straightened. 'Bugger.' He walked home, the sun rising slowly, its heat melting the thin bands of stratus clouds cast from the cooler air moving across the sea at night. He turned into his street, a block back from the beach in the northern suburb of Casuarina in Darwin. Its name given to it by the abundance of casuarina trees that grew on the shores and banks of the beach. Ned's house was a small timber-clad cottage lifted up by rows of brick piers. He'd not long before painted the exterior, and had plans to tack another bedroom onto its end. When he got inside, his wife was asleep. He walked quietly to the bassinet at the foot of the bed and looked at his daughter. She had a drunkard's smile from a bosom full of milk. He leant in and kissed her forehead. Her eyes crossed, trying to focus, and Ned laughed at her silly look.

'You catch anything?'

'No.' Ned sat on the foot of the bed. 'You should go back to sleep. It's still early.'

'I had a dream. A bad one.'

'About what?'

'A cyclone.'

'It's clear out there.' Ned crawled up the length of the bed and settled next to his wife.

'Everything was flooded. I couldn't find her.'

'She's right over there. In her bassinet. Smilin' like you've got beer in those breasts of yours.'

Bonnie Potter was beautiful; long straight hair, darker than brown and black when it was wet. Her eyes were hazel, greenish in the light, her lips full. And her skin was brown and became darker when she'd been in the sun. People thought she was Italian, Aboriginal, and everything but what she was, which was pure Irish stock. Her parents were immigrants, her colour from the remnants of the Spanish Armada.

'I'm going to have a shower and go to work.' Ned leant over and kissed her on the forehead.

'What would you like for dinner?' Bonnie asked, her voice croaky from sleep.

'I was hoping fish.'

'I'll buy some. Fry it up.'

'And some beer. It's going to be hot today.'

'Okay.' Bonnie yawned and turned to her side to sleep some more.

'I'll see you tonight.' Ned leant over, kissed her cheek and then left for work.

* * *

Along the unsealed road leading to Tabletop Swamp, Ned always drove slowly. The Land Rover he'd been assigned was twenty years old and had been rebuilt from the axle up twice before. The terrain out of Darwin to the wetlands was severe, particularly during wet season when the ochre-coloured earth became saturated and turned to a clay muck that filled in tyre treads and stuck to the undercarriage of the truck, increasing its weight and compromising its handling. The steering became leaden, every gear change chewed through the box like cattle bone through a meat grinder, and the oil through the old engine boiled while it worked to keep the blunted wheels moving through the mire and across exposed mounds of ragged stone.

He often saw men on his patrols through the wetlands; sometimes alone, sometimes with a family. They were hunting, for kangaroo or pig, or on their way to a nearby billabong to fish and swim. He usually stopped to talk with them, enquired about their families and how they were, asked advice on the best waterholes to fish at and whether any crocodiles had been seen. One man he saw regularly was Michael Roberts. He hunted for kangaroo and fished by hand, something he'd shown Ned how to do. Ned looked into the reaches of the Darwin woollybutt and stringybark trees either side of him now, hoping to see Michael with his young son, mid-hunt or walking back through the bush with a catch of barramundi woven through a fish stringer.

Ned had his window down, but it did nothing to allay the choking humidity that kept him constantly thirsty and in a sweat. He travelled out this way routinely, always hoping to be back in the station before 3 pm to write a report, record who he'd seen, whom he'd spoken to, if anybody, and what condition the swamp was in and whether it had flooded.

He looked out over the wetlands, warm squalls of wind blowing rippling smears across the water's surface, and then long stretches of stagnant water reaching out to the knotty mangroves that stood from the water like wading bathers. Ned liked the tart smell of the swamp. It reminded him of his youth, long days spent on his father's tinny at the edge of the mangroves fishing for barramundi. His father would take a foam cooler full of beer, and Ned and his brothers were allowed two cans each, and one extra for whoever hauled in the prize fish, won not by its length, but by the width of its belly.

He wasn't ten minutes from the mouth of Tabletop Swamp when he saw two men standing by the side of the track. They turned his way when they heard the rumble of his vehicle, and then looked back toward the edge of the marshland. Ned stopped and got out.

'Dead,' one of the men said before Ned uttered a word.

Ned walked quickly and settled beside them, and the man who'd spoken pointed out past a small bed of swamp lilies. Ned followed the trajectory of his extended arm and saw it. The clothed back of a person, face down and swollen in a shallow edge of the swamp.

* * *

An hour later, Ned looked over the body that he and the two men had dragged from the shallow marshland and onto the side of the track. Ned knew the dead man, Ernie Clay, who had lived in the same suburb as him. While driving to work early of a morning, Ned had often seen him walking back from the beach with a cork reel and bucket of whatever he'd caught. Ernie was a tall man, broad across the shoulders and thin through the waist. Ned had spoken to him only on the odd occasion when they crossed paths, walking a nearby street, or at the small store they both shopped at from time to time. Ned had always thought Ernie to be a quiet man, had said as much to Bonnie. It was known that Ernie had been taken from his mother by the government at a young age and placed into a church-run mission. Bonnie had wondered how that may have affected him, torn from his family and dumped somewhere completely unfamiliar.

The dead man was barely recognisable. Ernie Clay's bottom lip was riven and white, his teeth uneven and broken, his nose bent and swollen, and there was a miasma of faeces where he lay. Ned got down on his haunches and looked closely at the body. There appeared to be a gunshot wound through the chest and another through Ernie's left temple.

'This is big trouble.'

Ned looked up, and one of the men looked down at him.

'Not for us, fella.' The man turned and walked away with his friend, following the track down toward the open mouth of Tabletop Swamp.

* * *

Ned radioed for an ambulance and, as he waited, watched the clouds above twist over themselves and thicken, like a block of dough rolled across sheets of flour, broadening and turning to stodge. Their colour changed as he watched, white no longer, they were deep grey, black in places and purple in the centre. They looked like the fresh bruises of pure violence, and with Ernie Clay dead in the mud next to Ned, he couldn't help heed the resemblance of the brutality building above and what lay at his feet. The storm was coming, the thunder clapped and echoed across the floodplain wetlands, scattering a colony of brolgas picking at sedge tubers in the shallows.

When the ambulance arrived, the rain had already stopped and the sun had broken through the dissolving clouds in long broad bands that hit the sodden earth and quickly cooked the still water. Its breath rose up, stinking and hot, and settled over Ned. He watched the two ambulance officers cover Ernie Clay's body with a white bedsheet, and lift him onto a gurney.

'What happened here?' one of them asked Ned as they pushed the gurney into the back of the ambulance.

'Don't know.'

'Well, from the look of him, he pissed someone off.' The officer closed the doors. 'One of his own, ya reckon?'

Ned raised his brow. 'What?'

Ned thought of the questions he'd asked himself while waiting for the ambulance. Race wasn't one he'd considered. 'No. I don't think so.'

A mountain of paperwork back at the station meant that Ned got home well after dark. Bonnie was asleep, curled up on their bed with her top half exposed, a single sheet tightly around the contour of her buttocks and bent legs. Even in that moment, after the horrors of his day, she looked desirable. He looked at his baby, asleep in her bassinet, and then back to Bonnie. He spoke quietly, making sure not to wake her. 'There's trouble, my love. I don't know just how bad. But it's bad.'

CHAPTER 3

THE POLICE STATION was two rooms, one for the senior sergeant, and the other for the officers who came and went from within the Territory. It was hot inside the station, without air conditioning the low ceilings squeezed the heat into every corner of the building. A resident king brown snake routinely slithered from the bushland behind the station to seek respite from the heat. It had found relief beneath the raised floor of the building, and every so often slid into the wall cavity and through the holes in the gyprock. Ned had twice discovered the snake asleep in a thick coil outside the toilet. The protocol within the station, effected by Senior Sergeant Riley, was to leave the snake alone and let it find its way back out when it was ready. Every morning, the first officer to the station had the task of searching for the snake, and then informing the incoming troops whether it was *in* or *out*.

Tacked onto the side of the building were the lock-up cells. They were small, double brick with a concrete floor. There was no ventilation in them apart from two air bricks high on the side walls. While Ned had been stationed in Darwin, three men had died in these cells. He'd never been present the mornings they were discovered and taken away to the morgue.

Ned was watching Danny Lewis load his pistol. His desk was across from him. Though Lewis was physically endowed and a capable policeman, Ned believed only a fraction of the stories he'd been told. Ned reckoned the truth lay somewhere between dividing the said story by four or five. They were always too fantastical, and too much. Lewis had been everywhere, beaten everybody, fucked everything. But Ned seemed to be on his own, the rest of the officers, and particularly Senior Sergeant Riley, liked him. They believed everything Lewis told them.

'You found him yesterday?' Lewis flicked his head at Ned.

'No. A couple of other fellas. I was just the first cop there.'

'They told me he stank worse than the swamp.' Lewis smiled and laughed through his nose.

'He'd been dead for hours.'

'He was shot?' Lewis holstered his pistol, put his hands on his hips and broadened his shoulders.

'Twice.'

Lewis took a breath and removed his hands from his hips. 'Well, he musta pissed off someone pretty good.'

'Yeah. Maybe.'

'You reckon he was killed there?' Lewis stood taller.

Ned took a moment, he had his thoughts on the question, but was reluctant to share them before speaking to Senior Sergeant Riley. 'I don't know.'

Ned turned back toward his desk and a moment later smelt the wake of Lewis's exit in the ironing aid holding his starched trousers and shirt tight.

'Potter.' Ned turned toward the voice and saw Senior Sergeant Joe Riley with his head poking around his office door. 'Get in here.'

Ned stood and walked into Riley's office.

'Take a seat.' Riley closed the door. 'You okay?'

'Yep. Fine.'

Riley sat at his desk and began to look over the photographs from the crime scene of the deceased Ernie Clay. Riley was fat, everywhere, the skin that made up his eyelids was flabby and stippled with loose wartish growths that Ned found difficult to look away from. He was snared looking at them while Riley glanced at the photographs.

'You know him?' Riley asked.

'Not well, but yes, sir.'

'Half-caste.'

Ned nodded. 'He was, sir.'

'Married to a white woman.'

'Yes.'

'That's one way to get out of a mission.'

Ned said nothing and Riley continued, 'I bet you didn't count on finding this?' Riley held up a photograph and laughed, it was a high-pitched natter, wheezy in its middle and incongruous with how he looked. Riley tossed the photograph onto his desk and pushed back in his seat. His collar tightened and his chin fell away and disappeared under a spool of red flesh.

'Any ideas on this?'

Ned straightened himself in his chair. 'Well, I think the body was possibly dumped there.'

'As opposed to the killing taking place there?'

'That's right, sir.'

'Why?'

'I was thinking that whoever did it possibly wanted the body found. There was no attempt to cover it up, bury it.'

'Might have left it for a croc to take.'

'No, sir, croc won't come up that distance. Too far from the mouth of the swamp.'

Riley tilted his head and smiled. He bared his crooked teeth, brown from the stain of tobacco.

'Tell me again where your wife gets that colour from?'

'The Spanish Armada. They got shipwrecked off the shores of Ireland in the sixteenth century. It comes from that. That's to say there was a Spanish man among her family back then.'

Riley folded his arms. 'All that time ago, hundreds of years, and still that colour comes through?'

'Yes, sir. It's common with the Irish. It's called Black Irish.'

'Well, it sure is colour.' Riley shifted forward quickly in his chair; his smile gone. He leant over his desk, and Ned could smell the cigarette he'd not long stubbed out as he spoke. 'I'm going to handle this personally. Make sure it's tidied up.'

Ned interrupted, 'Sir, I'd really like to be assigned this case. I found the body. I know some of his friends, I think they'd talk to me, I think –'

Riley cut him off, raised his voice and adjusted its timbre to intimidate. 'I don't give two fucks who you know, I'm handling it. It's done. Decided. Don't go lookin' around, don't go askin' questions. I'm on it. You understand?'

Ned nodded. 'Yes, sir.'

Riley pushed back again on his chair. 'You know you're doin' a good job, Potter.'

'Thank you, sir.'

'Good. Good. You can go.'

'Yes, sir.'

Ned went back to his seat, sat and looked down at his desk, at the yellow notepad written up in blue biro with the questions he was going to ask to investigate the death of Ernie Clay. He tore the sheet away from the red gummy glue that held the pages together at the top of the pad.

'What'd he say?' Lewis stood before him, his hands on his hips, chin lifted, his eyes narrowed.

Ned didn't look up. 'He said he was investigating it himself.'

'Smart.'

'Guess so.'

'He's got the Abos under control. Needs to stay that way.'

Ned considered a response, but just as the words found their order in his consciousness and the first letters formed in his mouth, he caught the bulky side of Riley in his peripheral vision and could tell he was listening. He took a breath, turned from Lewis and addressed Senior Sergeant Riley, 'Sir, if you don't mind I'd like to visit with Ernie Clay's wife?'

'Why?' Riley shifted his weight to one side. 'She's already been informed.'

'Just to see how she's coping. To let her know you're on the case.'

Riley glared at him. He could tell the senior sergeant wasn't certain whether the last comment he'd made was simple frankness, or disingenuousness. He followed up, 'To put her mind at ease, sir.'

Riley took a moment, his tongue poking and rolling across the insides of his cheek, tasting Ned's comments for intention. He flicked his head. 'Fine.'

'Thank you, sir.'

* * *

24

Ned parked across the road from the Clays' house. It was an old weatherboard shack standing off the ground on skinny stilts and with a small sheltered front veranda. He could see Martha Clay through the uncurtained windows. She was aproned and going about her jobs. Ned knew their story. Martha had known Ernie most of her life, she'd grown up across the street from the family where Ernie had been placed in Townsville. He was the only person of colour on the street. They had played together as children, and as they grew older they became good friends. Martha had kept their blossoming relationship from her parents, afraid of how they'd react. Eventually they were seen together. Word got back to Martha's parents and they told her to end the relationship. She moved to Darwin with Ernie instead and hadn't seen her parents since.

Ned got out of his car, walked quickly to the front door and knocked. Martha answered, her grief stuck to her face. Her eyelids sagged and small crescents of red flesh showed above them. Her mouth hung loosely, her gums and uneven teeth exposed. It was as if she'd pulled the skin and the flesh of her face downward to create a macabre caricature, and the form had remained deprived of the elasticity to right itself.

'Martha. Can I come in?'

She said nothing and let him past.

Ned sat on a sofa. Inside the smells seemed to alter. Cooking oil, cigarette tobacco and then dog, and where the floorboards split the redolence was sulphuric and shitty from the mud beneath the house. While Martha made iced tea, Ned looked up at the low ceiling dappled with mould. He wasn't sure how to begin. Martha entered with the tea in a clear jug, the ice cubes rattling against the glass. Ned smiled when she poured him a tall glass and then sat down opposite him. He took a long swallow. 'Wow, that's good tea.' He put his glass down on the table next to the jug and took an audible breath. 'I'm really very sorry, Martha.'

'Thank you.'

Ned made a considerate face, let it find its own way to an end and then asked, 'Do you have any idea why? Why someone would do that to Ernie?'

'No. Other than being what he was. Aboriginal.'

Ned nodded. 'So no one he was on the wrong side of?'

Martha raised her brow and upturned a corner of her mouth. She didn't need to say another word to make Ned feel that the question was both stupid and rhetorical. Ned succumbed and held up his hands. 'I'm just trying to help.'

'You investigating it?'

Ned took a moment, uncertain what his answer might provoke. 'No.'

Martha sat straighter. 'Why not?'

'Senior Sergeant Riley thinks it best he take control.'

'Does he now.'

'I'm just here to see how you are. How you're coping.'

Martha huffed laughter. 'No you're not.'

Ned plugged the dead air that followed with another mouthful of tea. As he drank, he thought of his next question and how to form it; how to make it sympathetic and less exploratory. She spoke while he was reaching forward to place his glass down on the table.

'They killed him because he saw.' Martha's mouth changed, her bottom lip pursed, her gums and teeth disappearing as she let her words free without restraint. 'That's why he's dead.'

A long silence followed as Ned tried to see through the ambiguity for the right question. Something that would confirm him as more than a dull-minded underling. The question, the only question he could find, sat on his tongue, and when the silence prompted Martha to stand, it raced out, like a child asking for the answer that ends an inflated tale conceived to scare. '*What* did he see?'

Martha glared at him, her voice louder and pitching higher. 'You think I'm gonna tell you that?'

From another room the disconnected beginnings of an infant's crying calmed Martha. She looked at Ned, her expression and posture forming a plea that accompanied her words. 'Please. Just let it be.'

The infant's crying became louder and Martha turned toward the noise and then back to Ned.

He stood. 'Thank you for the tea, Martha. If you do need anything, please let me know.'

'Thank you.'

* * *

On the way home, Ned stopped at the pub he drank at most afternoons. The Victoria Hotel. It was Darwin's oldest pub. Built in 1890 by Ellen Ryan, a wealthy landowner and mining lease magnate. Seven years after it was opened, it lost some of its roof to a cyclone known as the Great Hurricane. The storm killed twenty-eight people, sank ships and wiped out the town's pearling fleet. But it wasn't able to kill the pub. Accommodation on the second level had housed both Australian and United States troops during the Second World War. In 1941, with too much drink in them, the troops brawled inside and out of the hotel with such fury that the damage to windows and furniture took months to repair. Ned's father, Terry, had drunk there, and when Ned turned sixteen he took him to the public bar and bought him handles of Carlton Draught until he fell from his stool.

The bar Ned drank in was rectangular and long, the carpet on the floor was ruby red and had been soaked so often in spilt beer that it smelt like a stale schooner. In the wet season, during a downpour, the publican opened the windows to let in the relief, and the smell of baked tar cooling off was chopped up by the ceiling fans and flung to every corner of the pub. Ned loved that smell. A reminder of his childhood, riding pushbikes with his brothers when a storm hit, the roads slippery and allowing them to skid further.

The pub attracted a diverse bunch. The crocodile shooters and buffalo hunters arrived in the afternoons, the ochre dust of the Territory mixed with their sweat and settled over their bare arms and faces in a viscous grease. The mining prospectors drank in packs and spoke quietly, and the office workers and bankers crammed in every day at 5 pm. They were all hardworking people, friendly if not on occasion made stroppy by too much beer and the tropical heat. The conversations Ned had surreptitiously heard from all walks had been remarkably similar. Work-related complaining, stories from youth that were recycled and overblown, physical desires and the sexual contemplations of men that made him laugh. It was as if, when infected with three schooners or more, the capability of a man to fornicate with whomever he desired was immediately and without question no longer just possible but definite. And he heard a lot of bigoted rhetoric in regards to the local Aboriginal people.

* * *

Ned stood at the far end of the bar, his regular spot, and without having to ask or even gesture to the barman, a cold schooner of draught was served to him. 'Thank you.' Ned held the glass against his forehead, and then his cheek, and then brought the opening to his nose and took a long breath in. The first mouthful he let stay in there before swallowing, let it cool his tongue and the fizz tickle the insides of his cheeks. He swallowed and savoured the taste of the malt, the hop, and waited for the alcohol to untie his mind. He first felt it through his shoulders, a loosening of his posture, then across his neck, like the soft palm of a hand resting over it. Then the innards of his head. A sensation he enjoyed more and more each time it occurred. It was as if space had been cleared inside his mind, it felt lighter in there, his thoughts had room to move, not bumping into one another, not looking for places to hide. It was all much simpler when he drank.

But it had become worse over the last two years. The regularity with which he not only drank; but got drunk. He'd lose time, have to patch the night together in flashbacks that presented themselves arbitrarily. Those days after were often laden with anxiety, but what was starting to concern him was how that anxiety was giving way to apathy. He cared less and less what was at the bottom of those lapses in memory. Bonnie, the baby, work were all pushed aside. There was a self-destructive performance about it that he'd begun to crave. The low that followed and the energy he found to dig himself out of the hole again, to feel good about himself.

He'd seen the same behaviour in one of his older brothers. It had taken hold tightly by the time he was thirty-five, and by forty he'd become nomadic, his wife had left him and by last account he was down south in the Queensland cane fields. It worried Ned that he'd witnessed such a steep decline in his brother and wondered if he may be doomed toward a similar outcome. Maybe, he thought, such a destiny was woven into his DNA.

* * *

'What do you know, Senior Constable?' Katie Briggs, the wife of the publican, was a tall woman with broad shoulders and short cropped hair. Her cheeks dimpled when she smiled, and her teeth were bright and perfect. Her voice was deep and rasped, no doubt from her smoking, and it cut in and out through her laughter. Ned liked her.

'Not much. I don't know much, Katie.' He raised his glass and took another mouthful.

'You look troubled, Ned. You okay?'

'Work.'

'I heard you found that man out by the swamp.'

'I keep sayin', I was just the first cop there.'

'What's the story?'

'I don't know.' Ned drew in a long stretch of air, let it out through his mouth and when he smelt the beer on his breath his nostrils flared. 'No fuckin' clue.'

'You know him?'

'Not well.'

Katie leant over the bar, closer to Ned, and when she spoke he could smell cigarettes and rum on her breath. 'It's not good though, is it?'

'No. Not at all.'

Ned stood at his spot for an hour more, looked at his watch and contemplated going home.

'You want another one?' Katie had already taken the schooner glass from the fridge and had it under the draught tap ready to pull.

'Righto. One more.'

* * *

It was seven o'clock when Ned next looked at his watch. Katie had warned him when she served him his last beer, 'You got a baby at home, Ned. Go home.'

He chewed on Katie's suggestion, he knew she was right, but he couldn't help feeling aggrieved from being told what to do. Already halfway drunk, he didn't have the restraint to stop himself from indulging in the dark mood her comment had triggered. 'Sure. If you say so.' He finished his beer, nodded to Katie, and walked from his spot. He stopped by the front bar and bought a tall bottle of draught, intending to drink it at home. But when he got in his car, he opened the bottle, all the while thinking about what Ernie Clay might have seen to be shot in the head and then left in a shallow swamp to rot. He knew it must have been something bad. Ned wondered if there was a message to be gleaned from the cruelty of the murder, and the blatant positioning of the body. Perhaps a message to anybody Ernie had revealed information to.

As he drank, he remembered Martha Clay's lengthened face, the shape of her mouth, the colourless nature of her gums and the red crescents left atop her lower eyelids. He wondered after she'd seen her husband waterlogged and swollen, his head blown apart, whether her face would ever regain its flexibility and return to how it once was. He thought about her young son and if she'd tell him why his father was killed. Tell him the truth. What Ernie had seen.

Or was the threat of more violence going to stay with her forever, and so she'd never reveal the truth to anyone?

He started his car when he finished the bottle and drove to Hotel Darwin. It was a large hotel, with upstairs accommodation, and outside lawns that were always well kept and adorned with palm trees. It was known among locals as the 'Grand Old Duchess'. It had survived the Darwin bombings, and numerous cyclones, and from the mid-fifties had become a popular venue to watch live music. Ned had often found himself at the pub after more than enough; the days after spent sewing together the patchwork of memories infused with music and song.

He walked through the public bar to another saloon called the Green Room where the local artists performed. On the small stage was a tall, broad-shouldered blonde woman, her fringe cut neat and straight, the bulk of her hair held back by a white bow, the ends falling just short of her shoulders in thick hooks. Ned knew her. Kelly Dillon. Her athletic girth built from years of swimming, she'd been unlucky to miss out on a place in the Olympic team that had travelled to Rome in 1960. She was beautiful and now a local primary school teacher. And though married, she'd been known to stray.

On the stage with her were a young rockabilly on guitar and a thin percussionist with a red pompadour and newly etched tattoos on his forearms. Kelly Dillon's singing voice was huskier than when she spoke, and when she reached for higher notes the stretched words broke in parts and were reconnected with long raspy sections of vibrato. They played Dusty Springfield and Shirley Bassey songs and the red pompadour sang Elvis. It was a different crowd than the Victoria Hotel. The people in the Green Room were a younger lot, early twenties and couples eager to dance, though the patrons in the public bar were typically blue collar and almost exclusively male. It was where Joe Riley and Danny Lewis drank, and some of the other police officers from Ned's station.

Kelly Dillon and her trio took a break, and Ned walked through to the public bar. It was moderately filled, hazy with cigarette smoke that had risen to the ceiling and over time turned it a dirty yellow. He saw Riley and Lewis standing at one end of the horseshoe bar drinking schooners of dark ale. With them was Bobby Clark, still dressed in his Northern Territory Fire and Rescue Service garb.

Bobby and Joe Riley were close friends. They'd both been born and raised in the Territory, and though Riley was older, they'd formed a strong bond after Bobby's father had died. Bobby entered the Darwin Police Rotary Youth Club to box. Riley, a young senior constable, was an instructor, albeit one without any pugilistic credentials. Nevertheless, he became a kind of surrogate patriarch for Bobby.

Ned ordered a beer and, from where he stood at the curved middle of the bar, looked over toward them. Lewis saw him first, didn't acknowledge him but turned to Riley immediately after and said something close to his ear. Riley then found Ned, looked at him and then turned away. Ned was drunk and unsteady, and the barefaced snub was all that was needed to convince him the apathy among the police force would hinder an investigation into Ernie Clay's death.

'Fuck it.' He reached for the apex of the horseshoe bar, held it and steadied himself, before pulling forward to sling his body around its curve. He stumbled just before stopping in front of Riley. 'Senior Sergeant Riley.'

'Potter.'

Ned could smell Riley's aftershave, the same one he always wore, it was sweet and, though pleasant initially, Riley wore too much of it and it invariably became overpowering and distracting. 'Senior Constable Potter, sir.'

'What are you doin' here, Potter?' Riley shot out a knee and adjusted his cock.

'Drinking.'

'You're drunk.'

'Yep.'

'You rostered on tomorrow?'

'Yes, sir.'

'Maybe it's time to go home.'

Ned smiled at Riley. '*You* rostered on tomorrow?'

Riley took a beat. 'Yeah, I am.'

'Maybe you should go home too then. I could give you a ride.'

Riley straightened himself, lifted his chin and smiled. 'You're a mouthy little prick, aren't ya?'

'I can be, sir.'

'If you were under my command, I'd give ya a clip under the ear.' Bobby Clark said it without any nuance that might have suggested the comment was playful.

'No, thanks.' Ned's smile remained and he whipped it toward Bobby. 'You're a bit big for me.'

'He is mouthy, isn't he?' Bobby's eyes narrowed and moved up and down the length of Ned's torso, as though to measure him.

Riley stiffened his legs, widened his girth and adjusted his cock again, discernibly inflated by Bobby Clark's aggression aimed at Ned. 'Fuck off home, Potter. Or I'll smack you in the mouth.'

'Whoa.' Ned held up his hands. 'I'm not lookin' to be any trouble here. Just havin' a drink and thought I'd say hello.'

'Fuck off and drink somewhere else.' Bobby eyed Ned, his usually light blue eyes had turned silvery, deadened by the alcohol.

Ned's smile evened out and he felt a squirt of adrenalin loosen his legs and roil his stomach. 'Yeah, right.' He glared back at Bobby and Danny Lewis laughed.

'Is he gonna have a swing at ya, Bobby?'

'Way ya go then.' Bobby put his schooner of ale on the bar.

Ned took a step back and stumbled slightly.

'Nah, I didn't think so.' Bobby picked up his glass and continued drinking.

'You can be a cranky drinker, Bobby.' Ned steadied himself, finished off his beer and took another step backward. 'Time for me to go.'

'Got that right.' Bobby inhaled and held the air to deepen his breadth. 'Piss off.'

Ned stood still a moment, watched Bobby put his schooner back on the bar, and then turned and left.

* * *

When he got home, Bonnie was sitting on a chair in the kitchen breastfeeding the baby. She looked tired, her usually straight black hair was knotty and snarled around the clip she wore to hold it back from her face. Ned kissed her on the cheek.

'You smell.'

'Sorry.' He leant further over and kissed his daughter.

'Don't do that. Let her feed.'

'I'm drunk.'

'Yes, you are.'

35

'He saw something.' Ned went to the fridge, snapped the handle and pulled out a beer. 'I think it was a message. The murder.'

'What?'

'His wife, Martha, she said he saw something. She's spooked. She told me to forget about it. I don't know. Maybe the murderer was just sloppy. I just don't know.'

The baby squirmed and let go of Bonnie's nipple. She put her over her shoulder and gently rubbed her back until she burped and then vomited. Ned came with a tea towel to clean up the small mess on Bonnie's shoulder.

'What did he see?'

'She's not going to tell me that.' Ned opened his bottle of beer, took a mouthful, burped and held his chest. 'Heartburn.'

Bonnie attached their daughter to her other side. 'What are you going to do?'

Ned shrugged. 'Nothing. I've been told to leave it alone. Riley's taking over.'

Bonnie looked up at Ned from where she sat, studied him a moment before asking, 'You okay?'

'Yeah. I think so. I don't know.' Ned rubbed his forehead. 'I can still smell Ernie's body.' He lifted a shirt pocket of his police uniform and sniffed it. 'It's still everywhere, in everything.'

Bonnie looked down at the baby, its mouth attached to her nipple but still. She gently poked a finger in the soft fleshy skin beneath the baby's chin to wake her up and get her back feeding. She looked up at Ned, concerned but also unsure of what to say to offer him any comfort. 'You look tired. You should go to bed.'

'Yep. I should.' Ned kissed Bonnie and his daughter goodnight, took his bottle and left for the bedroom.

CHAPTER 4

BOBBY CLARK WAS still asleep when Charlotte left the house to go for a walk. It was routine for her, an hour's walk to the bus stop that was roughly halfway from her house to St Mary's Cathedral, where she attended mass every Sunday. She'd covered a plate of fried eggs and sausages in foil, and left it in the oven for Bobby. She'd boiled water, strained tea, and had the kettle covered in a woolly jacket to keep it hot. She was a little anxious that he'd be unhappy to find her gone when he woke, but she'd left early that Sunday morning for a reason. She had to go to confession. She was bothered, her mind had been incessantly spinning in circles all week by her thoughts.

She took off her shoes and walked her normal route, along the bitumen footpaths on the edges of the vacant lots of land that were overgrown and full of mosquitoes. The insects were prolific through the blocks of land, particularly of a morning, the ground still sodden from the storm the afternoon before, the stagnant water collecting in small puddles over the potholed clay floor, providing a perfect squalor for the mosquitoes to breed. Charlotte had to stop every so often and scratch where they'd bitten her. She enjoyed the relief from scratching the bites though, had done so since a child. Her mother had often told her to stop as she'd scratch her feet so furiously blood would be drawn.

***

When she arrived, she saw Father McKay's car parked in the grounds of the church. It was new, a brilliant light metallic green. She didn't know what brand it was, only that it had four round headlights, something she'd never seen before. Inside, the church smelt of the red cedar the timber pews and ceilings were cut from. The stained-glass windows were intricate, and the glass pieces held together by heavy lead borders. Along the side of one wall were the stations of the cross, the happenings carved from Kauri pine, lacquered in a dark satin finish and polished so that Christ shone beyond the other characters and props in the tableaux. The floor was charcoal slate and grouted with white cement so that it stood out from all the other furnishings.

Charlotte approached a statue of Mary beside the altar, her arms outstretched, her palms up. Charlotte wasn't aware of the significance of the gesture, though figured it had something to do with a promise of absolution. She knelt on the pew in front of it, crossed herself and prayed. She prayed to God for the strength to disclose her sins to Father McKay. While bowing her head, she sensed someone beside her. The pew groaned as they sat and Charlotte felt herself sink a touch lower. She heard the fidgeting of rosary beads and smelt jasmine. She glanced sideways and saw it was Kelly Dillon, the former swimmer, the schoolteacher and the woman who Bobby told her sang in the Green Room at Hotel

Darwin. Charlotte had seen Bobby looking at her during mass on Sundays. She didn't need to ask what he was thinking. She could see it in the shape of his mouth, his jaw set forward, his bottom teeth clamped over his upper row. Charlotte had seen that look at times when he was fucking her while drunk.

Kneeling there, Charlotte became distracted by what Kelly Dillon might be praying for. Maybe the same thing. For strength to tell Father McKay what she'd been guilty of. Charlotte crossed herself and stood. She looked down at Kelly Dillon and smiled politely.

'Off to confession?' Kelly whispered and turned one of the timber rosary beads between her thumb and forefinger. Charlotte thought it a strange question, and one she wasn't inviting with her smile. She certainly didn't want to get into a conversation with Kelly about her reconciliation.

'Yes.'

'Me too.'

'Oh. Okay.'

'It's weird though, isn't it?'

'I beg your pardon?' Charlotte heard the steps of someone else over the slate floor. She became anxious to get to the confessional box before more parishioners arrived.

'We all know Father McKay, but when we speak of our sins, we do it behind that mesh so we can't see him. Why is that?'

Charlotte spotted the newly arrived person kneeling at a pew at the front row of the church. She couldn't make out who it was, only that it was a woman with her head bowed in earnest. Kelly continued, her whisper growing louder, 'I feel very uncomfortable when I see him after my confession.' Her voice softened and the skin of her forehead pleated and raised concern. 'You don't think he tells anyone, do you?'

Charlotte had never considered that. Not for a moment. But now with Kelly Dillon looking up at her with such graveness, she felt the horrid spasm in her stomach that signalled her anxiety had shifted to panic.

'I hope not.' Kelly let out a nervous laugh through her nose.

'No, he doesn't tell anyone. He's not allowed to do that. He's a good man, Father McKay,' Charlotte said but she could tell Kelly was unconvinced.

Charlotte left her, walked to the middle of the church and knelt at the end of a row next to the confessional box. She could smell Father McKay as he approached. He always smelt strongly of body odour and Charlotte recognised it from the memories of her father. It was a spicy fetid smell, but as a young girl it had provided her with great comfort. It announced her father had returned from work safely. She liked that Father McKay smelt that way, it gave her something familiar and kind to associate the priest with.

She bowed her head and her eyes caught the hem of his robe and his shoes step into the confessional box. She took a breath, waited a moment, then stood and looked to the centre of the altar and blessed herself before a glazed ceramic crucifix. She entered the confessional and knelt. She could see the outline of Father McKay's face through the thick bronzed gauze window that separated them. She could smell the cigarette he'd just smoked. The corners of his moustache and the upper part of his beard were perennially stained yellow from nicotine. 'Bless me, Father, for I have sinned, it's been two weeks since my last confession.'

'And what sins do you have to confess?' Father McKay had a plangent way of speaking, though when dealing out penance his delivery was discernibly more dramatic, as though in those moments of assigning the measures for atonement, he was on stage and under lights.

'I have been lazy at times, Father. I've been tired and have found it easier to rest than to go about my housework.'

'Are you sick?'

'No, Father.'

'What else?'

'I have been riddled with thoughts of discontent. For my life. And I know I shouldn't.'

'No, indeed you shouldn't, but sometimes we can't see just how lucky we are. It's quite normal. But a sin, of course. What else?'

Charlotte took a breath, her next offerings were why she had come. She wasn't really sorry for her lethargy, nor for coveting another life. 'I've had thoughts of other men.'

'Hmmm.' Father McKay took a beat and Charlotte could hear him adjusting his vestments. 'Have you acted out on these thoughts?'

'Only on myself.'

'How many times?'

'Some days.'

'Hmmm. That has to stop.'

'Yes, Father.'

'It is the devil's work.'

'Yes, Father.'

'What else?'

'That is all, Father.'

Father McKay's voice deepened, 'For your penance, you need to recite twenty decades of the rosary, dwelling on your sins while you pray.'

'Yes, Father.'

'Now say your act of contrition.'

'Oh my God, I am heartily sorry for offending Thee, and I detest all my sins, because of Thy just punishments, but most of all because they offend Thee, my God, who art all good, and deserving of all my love. In the name of the father and the son and the holy ghost.' Charlotte made the sign of the cross.

'Amen,' Father McKay's voice overwhelmed her own.

* * *

When she opened the door, Kelly Dillon was kneeling in the same space she'd been while waiting for Father McKay. Charlotte avoided eye contact and moved toward the back of the church to complete her penance. After praying she went outside and waited for Bobby. She stood in the shade of the milkwood tree and watched the families, dressed in their best clothes, enter the church. Young boys wearing neckties and girls in long dresses. *Why?* She thought. *Why in such heat? To suffer for God. Again and again?* She admonished herself, resolute to keep her newly cleaned slate from all sin for as long as she could. Bobby was one of the last to arrive. He parked their car not far from where she was standing and walked over and kissed her.

'You get your breakfast and tea?'

'I did. Thank you, love. You go for a walk?'

'I did. It was nice. How are you feeling?'

'Bit dusty, love.' Bobby's words were soft, bashful, and then he made a face, and Charlotte recognised some embarrassment. 'I was babbling?'

Charlotte smiled. 'You were just drunk.'

'I didn't say anything stupid?'

Charlotte took his hand. 'No, darling. You said nice things.'

Bobby leant in and kissed her, and for a moment Charlotte felt like she hadn't in a long time. The moment was light, and she saw a glimmer of her husband's vulnerability once again.

***

During mass Charlotte kept a watch on Kelly Dillon. She was sombre the entire service and the last to get up from prayer after taking the host. Charlotte wondered what she might have confessed, why she appeared so repentant. The collection plate was passed through the congregation three times. Charlotte often wondered where that money went. She'd asked her mother once as a child, and her mother had told her that it went to the priest because they didn't get paid well enough to live *as God would like them to*. And that some of the money also went to the poor.

When mass was over, they drove to a local community hall a block back from the beach at Fannie Bay. Bobby was eager to get there, he told Charlotte he had some business to discuss with Joe Riley afterward. Charlotte read that to mean he was going to be drinking all afternoon, and soon after the morning tea would go to Hotel Darwin. After the pleasant interaction with Bobby before mass, she felt a little disappointed but quickly accounted for the rest of her day alone with baskets of laundry that needed doing and the novel she was a third of the way through. Then she'd prepare dinner, though it wasn't likely Bobby would be home to eat it straight from the oven.

The community hall was on a corner block two streets back from the beach. It was surrounded on one side of the road by elevated houses, many with a split-level storey, and next to it an old boxing gym beside a row of older cottages. Inside the hall the floors were hardwood timber, the walls clad with long strips of cypress pine that gave the space its distinct smell. While Charlotte drank tea, she watched one of the other men from the congregation speaking with Father McKay who was eating a sandwich. The man, who was taller, was leaning closely to Father McKay's ear. It was secretive, the way they were speaking. Charlotte felt her anxiety swell, the insides of her belly whined and fluttered, and she knew the blood beneath her cheeks was pooling as she felt her face heat up. The noise in her head was loud, and though she didn't pay attention to it, she knew what it was about. Kelly Dillon's concern, that Father McKay might tell others about the confessions he'd heard. There he was, whispering to another man. About what? That she'd been coveting another life? Desiring other men? And then pleasuring herself while indulging in the decadent scenarios she'd created. She watched the man listening to Father McKay, trying to read his mood. He laughed and patted the priest on the shoulder. Her relief was overwhelming, she felt her face cool and the tension across her shoulders loosen. She looked for Bobby and when they made eye contact, he smiled and waved, and then gestured to his wristwatch.

A minute later he left to go to the pub and Charlotte began her walk home. She took off her shoes to feel the cooked bitumen and small tarred pebbles that had loosened from the asphalt and now stuck between her toes. She followed the same path she'd walked earlier in the day, past the vacant lots of land that had since hardened from the sun. She walked slowly, enjoying the sting of the road, and thought about a scenario where someone had in fact learnt from Father McKay what her confessions had been about. And what consequences might follow. How it might spread through the community and find its way to Bobby. *Would he question her on the rumours? What would he do?* She wondered whether such a revelation might lead to a situation where she was alone. Free of her life. Although punished for her sins, she figured. She felt somehow deflated, as though that scenario might never be realised, a chance for a confrontation to begin the unravelling of her marriage.

CHAPTER 5

FATHER McKAY LEFT the community hall after mixing with his congregation. He drove back to his house, which stood a block back from the entrance to Darwin Harbour. His house was elevated on brick piers, clad in hardwood timber painted white with sky-blue gutter trims. It was newly built, and stood out as somewhat impressive from the rest of the houses in the street. When he'd first arrived in Darwin, he'd boarded at the vestry beside the church in the school grounds of the parish. He'd moved to the new house only a short time ago, and some within his congregation had gossiped among themselves on how a priest might be able to afford such an opulent dwelling. Some of them saw his relocation as immoral and decadent, and argued that a priest's way of life should only ever match the lesser members of his congregation. A *vestry*, they claimed, was where he was needed and belonged.

Inside, McKay went to the bedroom and unzipped a bag he'd taken from the car. He tipped the contents over his bed, the coins fell first and then the notes. Hundreds of bills, some evenly folded, others spread flat. He removed the coins and began sorting through the cash. A short time later he had three even stacks of money held together by rubber bands sitting on the bed. He left them there and showered, got dressed and then prayed in front of a cabinet with a mirror tacked to its front. He mumbled, blessing himself, and then recited the Our Father quickly and without pause. He looked at himself in the mirror when done, straightened his tie, rolled his neck through the collar of his shirt and then collected the money on the bed and left.

By the time he got to the public bar at Hotel Darwin, it was full. Bobby Clark and Joe Riley were there, and Danny Lewis, dressed in his police uniform, was in line at the bar. McKay settled next to Bobby and Riley.

'You wanna beer, Father?' Riley was red in the face, the skin just below his bottom lip yellow from the cigarettes he'd lit one after the other while drinking.

'No, I'll have vodka.'

Riley motioned to Lewis to fix the order. 'Tell me, what did Kelly Dillon have to say to you in confession this morning?' Riley laughed and knocked Bobby with his elbow. Father McKay frowned and looked at Riley as if to reprimand him. Riley huffed, pulled back on his cigarette and let out its waste as he spoke. 'Don't look at me like that, Father.' He took the priest by his arm and moved him out of earshot of Bobby Clark. 'Where's my money?'

McKay's shoulders narrowed and his brow fell, like a dog confronted by a pack leader, its tail involuntarily curling between its legs. 'I have it.'

'Well, don't leave here until you've given it to me. And do it carefully.' Riley looked furtively around the pub floor.

Danny Lewis returned from the bar and offered McKay his drink. He took it, waited until Lewis walked away and leant into Riley so he could be heard. 'What's happening with that investigation?'

'You don't need to worry about that, Father. I'm on it.' Riley took a mouthful from his glass of ale, looked away from the priest and across the bar to hint at his unwillingness to continue the conversation.

Father McKay took a step closer to Riley. 'What about the man who made the discovery?'

Riley looked the priest squarely in the eye and then checked the bar for where the mob's attention lay. He grabbed McKay hard enough by the upper arm so as to let him know it was a hostile gesture, and then leant in close to make certain he couldn't be heard by anyone except the priest. 'Do your fuckin' job, Father. Pray for the people and for yourself.'

McKay winced and pulled his arm away. Though rattled, he didn't completely give up the influence he held with God. 'Pray for yourself, Senior Sergeant Riley. God knows you need to.'

* * *

Mayor Landry arrived at the public bar shortly after Father McKay had started his third drink. By that time, the priest had handed over the three stacks of bills to Riley. Mayor Landry took up a position next to Riley and Bobby Clark. He was a tall man, over six feet, long limbed and with a narrow girth. He was always impeccably dressed, his necktie a perfect Windsor knot, his suits tailored, cut with just the right amount of space between himself and the jacket so it gave a permanently refined appearance. No matter how he shaped his body, while standing or sitting in the suit, he looked sophisticated. And he had an economy of movement that made him appear calm and unflappable. His face was long, his chin squared, and when he spoke only the bottom row of his teeth showed. His eyes were a brilliant blue, made brighter by his long dark lashes and tanned face. He was a good-looking man, spoilt by a comb-over hairstyle that he held down with an oily pomade.

Landry had been born and raised in Sydney, had come from a lineage of early settlers who'd arrived in Australia already wealthy. And they made more. His father and uncles were building contractors in Sydney's inner city, building government housing. He'd moved to the Territory five years after the war had ended, looking to expand the family's interests. He believed Darwin was ripe for investment and soon fell in love with the tropical, laidback lifestyle. He was also away from prying eyes in Darwin, away from his father and uncles. He was a lawyer by degree, but had never practised, and from an early age had showed interest in politics. He found Darwin lacking in an educated diplomatic voice and decided to run for Alderman of the Richardson Ward in 1955. He narrowly won, but by 1958 his popularity had grown beyond his ward. He'd found a way to get his voice on ABC radio, which broadcast through all four zones in Darwin. He spoke twice a week, on Monday and Friday afternoons, about Darwin's future and the potential for prosperity throughout the whole of the Territory. Tourism and mining, he spruiked, would one day make the Northern Territory the country's wealthiest region per capita. He spoke of housing booms and foreign investment, and of mass migrations from the other states that would serve to nourish the livelihoods of those already there. And he had a *plan*. And the right connections. And all of it was underpinned by a steadfast belief in God.

He was Catholic, and vocal about it, but his religion also served him another way. The Labor Party voters traditionally backed politicians who were Catholic, and Landry used every public forum he was afforded to express his beliefs. He attended mass every Sunday, and spoke with the congregation, and was often seen with the parish priest, Father McKay. He had grandiose political aspirations, and being Catholic was the cornerstone he intended to build his appeal among voters on. He wasn't an advocate of the White Australia Policy, which had prevented the immigration of non-European people, especially those of Asian origin. His dogma had little to do with him being a progressive in such matters, rather he saw the financial opportunities created with a multicultural population. In 1959 he ran for mayor and won easily. He was well liked and trusted, he knew how to win an audience by performance, when to pause, when to bend his face to the sentiment he was attempting to solicit. He could read the everyman without flaw, what they wanted to hear, when they wanted to be riled and when they needed to be flattered. He knew very well he only had to have people like him for them to forgive his backflips on policy or promises.

Joe Riley had often told him that he'd missed his calling as an actor. He and Riley were tight, through necessity for Landry. He needed support within the police force, both as advocates for his politics and also as attack dogs should his will and electoral plans be tested by community members. Riley revelled in the association. A constant handbag at mayoral functions and in photographs. To keep him on side and requisite to his orders, Landry arranged to pay Riley a cut from congregation collections. And when the task was unambiguously criminal and its motive and upshot needed to be concealed, he'd written fat cheques. Riley lived much better than any previous policeman in the Territory. For Landry, being mayor was only a brief stop. He had his eye on federal politics.

'How did you fare?' Landry asked the priest.

'Good enough I guess,' McKay answered quietly.

'Good.' Landry took a schooner of ale from Lewis. 'Thank you.' He turned back to the priest. 'Time to go.'

'What?' McKay asked with displeasure.

'No more drinking. Go home.'

* * *

Father McKay left soon after. He went home and lay down on his bed. In the seconds before dozing off with his thoughts rampant and without sense, he was bumped loose of imminent sleep by a door closing shut. He sat up and called out.

'Des?'

Mayor Landry entered the bedroom.

'You scared me.' McKay lay back down.

'Are you all right?' Mayor Landry sat on the bed next to him.

'Yes. Just tired.'

Landry took a breath. 'I've aligned myself with you.' He turned and looked at him. 'Do you know what that means?'

'Yes.' Father McKay's voice changed pitch. It became more solemn.

Landry looked down at the man lying flat on his back with his hands folded behind his head. McKay's eyes watered. 'Please, no.'

Landry's jawline tightened, his face flushed red.

'Please,' McKay begged.

Landry picked up McKay by his collar and stood him up at the edge of the bed. He pulled him forward as hard as he could until McKay's whole body was airborne. Landry kept his feet firmly planted and then swung through his hips and torso. He let go and McKay whipped into the mirrored cabinet beside them. Landry was on top of him a moment later. McKay whimpered and pleaded. Landry beat him with both his closed fists until the priest was unconscious.

When the assault finally finished, Landry was out of breath, his white shirt and suit jacket spattered with blood. Straddling McKay's torso with a soggy wheeze lagging through his laboured breathing, he fixed his hair, took the long pomaded straps that had fallen to one side of his face and whipped them across his naked skull. He pushed down firmly on the readjusted coiffure and then took a shard of broken mirror from the floor and looked at himself. Satisfied, he got off McKay and walked out of the room.

* * *

Landry went to his office, a large room at the back of his raised house that overlooked Darwin Harbour. He opened the louvred walls and let in the north-westerly breeze that brought with it a cooler temperature. The taupe-coloured Tasmanian oak floors were newly lacquered and shone even in the dim streetlight coming through the windows from outside. One of the walls was taken up by a bookshelf, stacked with law journals, novels and historical anthologies. Landry had read them all. The bookshelf was bare to begin with and he'd taken great pride in filling it. He was a voracious reader and believed adamantly that literature was the smartest means to becoming a well-rounded, properly authentic politician.

He took a block of ice from the small freezer he kept in his office, and struck it with an ice pick, breaking off thick shards that he then put in a heavy tumbler. He looked at the ice in the glass for a long time, until it began to melt. His mind played out scenarios stemming from the troubles he could see evolving from the politics of his job. He poured Irish whiskey over the ice and drank slowly. He settled on how to best deal with the problematic issues he could see in the weeks ahead. He then thought of the priest, and how he'd left him. It occurred to him that the assault on this occasion had been particularly vicious. He poured more whiskey over the ice, called to his wife to make him a fish sandwich, and then rang a number telling the person on the other end to report a robbery at the priest's address. And to call for an ambulance.

CHAPTER 6

WHEN CHARLOTTE GOT back to the house from the grocery store, Bobby was asleep on the lounge in front of the television. He was shirtless, his shorts unbuttoned and resting just below the coarse beginning of his pubic hair. One hand was flat across his chest, the other on his thigh. Charlotte glanced at him, walked by and caught the bleachy smell of semen. She put the lamb and mangoes she'd bought in the refrigerator, and then washed a bunch of carrots. She wondered for a moment what Bobby might have been masturbating to. Who? And what scenario he'd imagined. She wasn't upset, or repulsed, rather she felt guilt. That she hadn't been willing with her husband for weeks.

'That you?' Bobby's voice was rough, torn by sleep.

'Yep. Just getting dinner ready.' Charlotte heard him pushing himself from the lounge.

Bobby stood at the entrance to the kitchen, arms folded, leaning against the door jamb. 'Thought we might go to the pictures next week.'

'Yeah?'

'Yeah. You remember our first trip to the pictures?'

Charlotte could tell by the timbre of Bobby's voice that he was smiling. She turned from the sink, and looked at him. 'Yes. I remember.'

'You just looked so beautiful.'

'Did I?'

'Yep. Best-looking bird in the Territory.'

Charlotte could feel herself blush.

'I kissed you for the first time there.'

'I remember.'

'You always tasted so good.'

'Oh really?'

'Yeah.'

Bobby smiled, walked toward her and then kissed her gently on the lips. 'Just going outside for a while.'

Charlotte watched him out the door, guilt overwhelming her for her desires of another man, and that other life. She began peeling the carrots, and peered out the window, seeing Bobby in reflection, back to front, winding a tuft of chest hair into a long tassel. She felt light-headed at the sight, had to stop peeling the carrots and hold the edges of the kitchen sink to steady herself. It was an innocuous moment, but not dissimilar to others that had made her feel the same way over the years. Dizzy, and at times weak in the legs. Images she couldn't correspond with such physically potent reactions. She'd felt the same as a young girl when seeing her father blow his nose into a hanky and then look at the discarded waste. Another had been seeing her mother smell the length of a cigarette before she put it in her mouth and lit it. They were benign moments. But they all induced the same vertiginous corollary. Charlotte expected it may have had something to do with moments that were thoroughly without thought, actions whereby a person for just an instant becomes unaware of their surrounds and situation. As though invisible. They were moments not meant to be witnessed.

***

As she prepared the dinner, she heard the crack of a bull whip from outside. She saw Bobby, shirtless and bare-footed, looping a bull whip over his head, building momentum before pulling the thong straight by its stock. The crack echoed across the suburb and through the house. She smiled as she watched him and remembered the first time she'd seen him do it, showing off to her in the paddock at the back of his brother's house when they'd first started going out together. She watched him for a moment more and then busied herself with the meal. He came inside, showered and then they sat and ate together. She'd roasted lamb, baked potatoes, and boiled carrots and stalks of corn. Bobby sat across from her, pouring a king brown bottle of dinner ale into a chilled glass.

'You smell nice.' Charlotte cut into her lamb, poked it with a fork and began piling carrot and potato over it.

'It's a new aftershave.' Bobby was wearing a royal blue short-sleeved shirt and denim jeans, a large oval-shaped belt buckle and a pair of well-worn but polished cowboy boots.

'You going to the pub?'

'No. The show. I'm going to watch the rodeo.'

'Oh.'

Bobby looked across to Charlotte, and she dropped her head over the plate and began to organise her food ready for her next mouthful.

'Did you want to go?'

Charlotte smiled but kept her head down. 'No. It's okay.'

'You never liked the rodeo.'

'No. I know.'

'It's just men going.'

She looked up at Bobby, her smile broadened. 'I'm fine.'

* * *

Bobby washed the dishes and baking tray, dried them with a fresh tea towel and left. It was just before dusk when Charlotte stood on the front porch and measured the weather for the walk she was considering. The air was still, but the humidity that had clung to the afternoon dissipated as the remnant storm clouds dissolved. It was as though a blanket had been removed, allowing the wet air to escape and rise beyond the heights of where living things moved. Charlotte took a deep breath and took off, shoeless and wearing a light linen dress. She walked on the side of the road, the asphalt had cooled and the edges where the tar had become gooey in the heat had reset and looked like the hardened torrents of lava flow.

She arrived at the beach just on dusk, walked across a weedy embankment and onto the fine sand. Charlotte loved looking at the Timor Sea, the subtle changes in its colour depending on the sky or the wind. It could look muddy brown when it was overcast; other days when the sky was clear it looked sparkling turquoise and Charlotte could see the schools of mullet being chased by small sharks in the shallows. Sunsets were her favourite time to be looking over the Timor, long broad bands of brilliant orange sitting across the water. When the sun fell behind the horizon it stayed a caramel tone right up until night engulfed it. She stopped at the water's edge purposefully and waited for the rolling swell to crest and turn over into a small wave. As it broke and fell, its lip smacked against the shallows, its slag hissing and moving quickly toward Charlotte's feet.

'Ah. Beautiful.' Charlotte smiled through her words as the seawater rushed between her toes, rose over her feet and settled for a moment above her ankles before being dragged back out by the retreating tide. She looked up at the sky, the clouds vapour thin, as though they'd been stretched either side of the bumpy masses they'd become before the storm, their distended figures coloured in burnt orange from the radiance thrown by the dropping sun. She sat down on the sand and contemplated how, if she ran out of opportunities or courage to talk with Bobby about their marriage and how empty she felt, she might disappear. What the plan could be.

She thought about taking the bus from Darwin to Alice Springs. She could pack after Bobby had left for work and leave mid-morning. She'd connect on the train, buy a sleeping carriage ticket and travel all the way to Port Augusta in South Australia. From there, Melbourne or Sydney. She thought about life amid so many more people than she was used to. Not whom she'd become friends with but how? Without any introduction but her own.

She shovelled both hands into the sand and closed her fists, smiling with the thorough excitement her fear gave birth to. *She'd have to find a job. Fast. A place to live.* She nodded, as though ticking off each necessity, encouraging herself to keep moving forward with the imagining. She'd save money while applying to a nursing college. She stood up, happy with how her imaginings had so flawlessly played out.

* * *

On her way home she ran into Ned Potter, who was mid-run, sweating profusely and out of breath. He stopped, put his hands on his knees and leant forward.

'Hey, Charlotte.'

'Hello, Ned.' Charlotte craned her head toward Ned's bent posture. 'You okay?'

'Just unfit. Too much beer.' He stood upright and put his hands on his hips. 'How are you?'

'I'm okay, I'm good. Was just getting my feet wet.'

'Be careful of the box jellyfish. They're about at the moment, they've been flushed out of the mangroves by the swell.'

'Oh. I will be careful. How's your baby?'

'She's fantastic. Bit of a fever though.'

'I hope nothing too serious.'

'Just a cold. How's Bobby?'

'He's good. Off to the rodeo at the show.'

'Ah yes. Once a cowboy always a cowboy. Going there ourselves.'

'Oh. Well, enjoy.' Charlotte smiled through a tight mouth.

'I better keep going otherwise I'll cool down and seize up like an old engine.'

'Nice to see you, Ned.'

'You too, Charlotte.'

Ned smiled and took off running, and Charlotte watched him until he turned a street corner and disappeared. She, like most women, liked the look of Ned Potter.

* * *

When Charlotte got home, she poured herself a tall glass of beer and then sat out on the porch in a wicker chair she softened with a cushion.

She saw the first star appear and then brighten, as though it had popped through a stage curtain and taken a bow. The clouds south of her had begun to thicken and expand, and she could see them slowly rolling over themselves. Another storm was fomenting, and Charlotte felt the thickened air drag through her lungs as she breathed. She could smell the rain coming. She loved the smell. She loved the Territory storms. Their presence sat over summertime life, the talk that inevitably turned to cyclones. She'd been through some bad ones as a young girl, but it had been years since a severe storm had hit land while still gaining momentum. She recognised her enjoyment of the storms might have seemed somewhat strange. People had died in them, even ones without the strength and definition of a cyclone. She figured it was the interest a storm offered, the talk the days before on how it was tracking, how it was building, the estimated time of its advent. The boarding up of the houses, the construction of the sandbag flood levies. The imminence.

She finished her glass of beer, poured another one and got back to her imagining. A life away from where she felt so still. Would she find a man? Fall in love? She was very aware of her sexuality, and that she could feel insatiable at times. Though at the start of their relationship, she and Bobby had sex often, she'd never disclosed by either word or action the fullness of her desires.

The storm hit just after ten o'clock. The rain came down hard for an hour. She stayed on the porch until it stopped, and the humidity took hold again. She felt it first from the ground, the baked mud beneath the house that cooled and let out its stinking breath. As foul as a stink it was, she liked it. When she was a young girl, it was the smell that signalled it was safe to go back outside and play. She went back inside the house, poured herself another glass of beer, and turned on the wireless, hoping to hear Elvis.

CHAPTER 7

NED PUSHED THE pram slowly next to his wife. Bonnie had both her hands clasped around his elbow. They walked through an enclosure that was filled with people who were roaming through the different aspects of the agricultural show. The paddock was soft underground from the afternoon storm, and there were long broad lengths of displaced turf that had been thrown up by the hooves of livestock where they'd been unloaded and corralled. The whole show, end to end, was imbued with the odour of manure. Ned looked down to check the baby. 'She's asleep.'

'It's crazy, isn't it? All this noise, all these people and she can just nod off.' Bonnie held Ned's arm tighter. 'I just love her.' Then she kissed the thick muscle of Ned's forearm that swelled with his grip over the pram handles. They walked past the show yards and looked at the sheep and cattle being adjudicated to their breed specifications. Bonnie was more interested in the people who presented the animals to the judges, and the judges themselves. She pointed to one man who stood beside a white and silver Brahman bull. He was sweating through a thick denim shirt that was stretched tight around the bulbous middle of his belly, and while he leant down and adjusted the bull's gait for its show stance, a thick lump of muscle pushed past the collar of his shirt and sat high and bowed on the back of his neck.

Bonnie whispered in Ned's ear, 'He looks like he could have fathered that bull.' Ned laughed and Bonnie squeezed his arm to quieten him. 'Shhhh, he'll hear you.' She then pointed to one of the judges deliberating on the comb and wattle of a prized rooster. She was young, tall and, from what Bonnie could see, very attractive. 'She looks too pretty to be doing this. And too young.'

Ned looked down at her. 'What do you mean?'

Bonnie shrugged, pulled in closer to Ned and smiled through her words. 'I don't know. She just looks like she could be doing anything but that. Like a dancer or something. I mean, how do you get to be an expert on a rooster's feathers and the rubbery stuff on their heads and under their necks? How? And at that age? She's too young, surely.'

Ned laughed again, this time louder and one of the cocks being assessed startled and ran from its handler, crowing as it was chased from the judging ring and into the crowd. The young lady, whom Bonnie figured to be too pretty and young for such an eccentric interest, looked across to them and scowled. 'Shit, let's go.' Bonnie smothered her laugh by burying her nose and mouth into Ned.

They walked to a produce competition in the middle of the paddock, mangoes and melons laid out on trestles that were covered in sheets of butcher paper. They stayed and watched as three judges wearing white coats sniffed, gently squeezed and turned over a mango until one of them held it aloft and declared it the winner. 'You see, how do you get into that? A judge of mangoes.' Bonnie laughed, but quietly, and then dragged Ned away. 'That's enough of that.'

As they walked through the paddock, they could hear the sound of wood being chopped. The sound rang out in faint staccato, uneven and pitching in different tones depending on the speed of the woodcutter's chop and the accuracy and depth of his contact with the log. They followed the woody sounds and watched for an hour as men from the Territory competed against each other and those from parts of Queensland. They all wore singlets and long pants, and their shoes were the one brand of Dunlop Volleys that allowed the axemen grip to plant themselves firmly before twisting through their swing. They watched the single buck, and underhand, and during the standing block where the cutters stood on a short thick piece of wood and chopped a scarf in its centre. Bonnie had to look away, convinced one of them was going to cut their foot off with a mistimed swing.

She and Ned stopped by an ice-cream truck and bought a chocolate double cone that they shared while walking to the middle of the paddock where the rodeo ring had been set up. They sat down on the lowest rung of stepped seating and waited for the rough stock events to begin. Ned looked to the right and saw Bobby Clark with Joe Riley standing on the last raised step, drinking cans of beer. They were talking with a cowboy, his hat sitting high on his forehead, his chaps caked in long smears of red clay from where he'd slid across the rodeo floor while bulldogging a steer. Ned watched as the cowboy took off his hat and handed it to Bobby who put it on. Ned was aware of Bobby's celebrated rodeo past, it was impossible not to hear stories in Hotel Darwin about his rides and mishaps on top of bulls and broncos. *Tough* was always the word used just before the full stop on the story.

'Is that Sergeant Riley?' Bonnie gently rocked the pram.

'Yep. And Bobby Clark. And a cowboy.'

'I always liked cowboys.'

'Yeah?'

'I think it's the Cuban heel and buckle.'

Ned didn't reply, instead keeping an eye on Riley and Bobby.

'You okay?' Bonnie leant in and gently nudged him with her shoulder.

'Yeah. I'm fine.' Ned watched Bobby Clark hand the hat back to the cowboy and then a moment later they made eye contact. Ned and Bobby looked at each other well past the amount of time that would usually have been filled with some kind of polite acknowledgement. Ned looked away first and immediately wished he hadn't. He felt as though he'd lost in something. 'Dickhead,' he mumbled.

'Who?'

'Bobby Clark.'

'He's okay, isn't he?'

Ned shrugged. 'I don't know. Somethin' about him.'

'Is it because he used to be a cowboy?' Bonnie looked at Ned, playful. 'I'll buy you some boots and a buckle.'

Ned laughed through a closed mouth. 'And a hat.'

They stayed and watched the bronc riding and got through two cowboys tossed off Brahman bulls before the baby woke and needed to be fed. Bonnie took the pram and found a quieter spot by the produce stalls to feed. Ned was alone watching a cowboy trying to find a safe exit from his bull after holding on for the eight seconds required to receive a score.

'You ridden a bull, Potter?'

Ned looked behind from where the voice had come. Bobby Clark and Joe Riley stood on the step above, both drinking cans of beer. 'No. Never.'

'There's a novice's challenge later. You should go in it. They're just little steers.' Bobby smirked as he looked down at Ned.

'No, I'm all right. I'll need a brain.' Ned smiled and then turned back to the rodeo to catch the cowboy unfurl himself from his bull, land on his feet and raise his arms like a gymnast dismounting from some kind of apparatus.

'Not drinking today, Senior Constable?' Riley cupped his hands around the end of a cigarette to shield it from the wind as he lit it.

'No, not today, Senior Sergeant.'

'Well, that's good. You're not much of a drinker.' Riley pulled back on his smoke.

'None of us are, sir.' Ned didn't bother to turn back to look at him.

'What about the boxing tent, Potter? Put your hand up for that?' Bobby took a step down so he was on Ned's tread.

'Well, that's worse than rodeo. For your brain. I mean that's a sport where the sole purpose is to hit someone else in the head.' Ned looked across the paddock to the boxing troupe tent.

'That's not where it hurts the most when you get hit.' Bobby sat down beside Ned. 'Your gut's the worst. You get hit in the right place behind the ribs, you're fucked. You drop straight away. Can't breathe. Can't do anything but roll around on the fuckin' ground.'

'That right?' Ned turned his mouth upside down and nodded, then shrugged. 'Well, I wouldn't know, I've never been in a fight in my life.'

'How's that happen?' Riley took the step down a rung and the metal struts bracing the structure beneath whined and shifted under the transferred weight.

'Just not a fighter, I guess.'

'What about a blackfella? Never had a scrap with a blackfella in all your time here in the Territory?' Riley sat down on the other side of Ned, the tread bowed and the balance of the small platform shifted forward.

'No. Never.'

Bobby burped and blew his beery breath toward Ned with the words that followed, 'They can fuckin' fight, some of them.'

On the other side of Ned, Riley broke off the long trail of cigarette ash with a finger. 'Fast as fuck they are. No heart though.'

'Yeah, I don't get that.' Ned shifted on the rung and folded his arms. 'Colour of a man's skin doesn't have anything to do with whether he's willing or not in a fight.'

'Bullshit.' Bobby huffed, 'I've been fighting them since I was a kid. When it got real hard, not one of them enjoyed it.'

'Not much to enjoy though, is there?'

'You got an answer for everything, don't you, Potter?' Bobby shook his head and smiled, a gesture that he made certain let Ned know he was fed up. He looked across to Riley. 'Let's get another beer and head to the boxing tent.'

Ned spoke to Riley. 'Any leads on Ernie Clay's murder?'

Riley took a step off the platform and turned to face Ned. 'Not the time or place to be talking about that now, Potter.'

'I'm just asking.'

'Well, I'm just saying. Time and place.' Riley looked at his almost finished cigarette, as though contemplating the worth of one last pull. He flicked it over Ned's head and leant over his hip. 'But I'll tell you this, not certain it was murder at all.'

Ned felt his neck thicken as his head pulled back involuntarily in a wordless retort.

Riley followed up. 'Looks like it might have been suicide.'

'He was shot in two places … How can that be?'

Riley smiled. 'Not now, Potter. Your wife.' He threw his head across the seats. 'Mrs Potter.'

Ned turned and saw Bonnie walking toward them with the pram.

Riley and Bobby walked by Bonnie and continued to the middle of the paddock where the boxing tent stood.

Bonnie watched them walk past her and then turned back to her husband. Ned could feel his heartbeat through the vein across his temple that customarily filled with blood when he became upset or angry. He clenched his fists and felt the ends of his fingernails dig into the soft middle of his palms.

'What's wrong?' Bonnie glanced back to Riley and Bobby.

'Nothing.'

'Bullshit. Your vein is about to burst.'

Ned instinctively felt for it. He gently ran the fleshy end of a finger across its raised squiggled track. The baby let out a high-pitched grizzle and Bonnie began pushing the pram back and forth. 'So?'

'It's okay.' Ned stood up quickly, unfolded his fists and smiled at his wife. 'Dickheads. World's full of them. You wanna get a beer and go look at the boxing tent?'

'Does one go without the other?'

'Not in the Territory, love.'

* * *

Ned walked through the bar at the end of the paddock beside the bull and bronco pens. Above, three army marquee tops were held up by long hardwood poles, the floor was strewn with fresh hay and the temporary bars were long flat lengths of aluminium sitting over old timber barrelled kegs. It was mid-evening and inside it was filled with a mix of stud beef farmers and produce growers, the show breed crowd, and the bull riders who had been bucked and eliminated from the remainder of the competitions. The khaki-coloured roofs absorbed the sun and held its heat in the cloth for as long as possible before it pushed through the canvas and fell slowly over the patronage. The aroma was a stink of human perspiration, manure and beer-soaked hay. Ned politely worked his way through the crowd toward the bar, careful not to bump a beaten bull rider or produce grower disgruntled at losing to a mango with waxier skin. He ordered two cans of bitter, held them above his head and walked back out into the clear paddock. He handed a can to Bonnie and smiled. 'No place for a lady in there.'

'Please. I'm Irish, I'd fit right in.' Bonnie looked into the pram. 'She's out. For the night I reckon.'

'Well, let's go watch a couple of scraps.'

The sound of a bass drum thumping a slow beat grew louder and shook the unsteady tabletops of the food stalls they passed. The boxing tent was big, crested with three crowns. Unlike the bar marquee, it was enclosed by thick canvas flanks on all sides. Bonnie mused out loud, 'I wonder if my father ever did this?'

'What?'

'Boxed against one of these men.'

They stopped in front of a long makeshift stage at the front of the tent. They stood ten deep and looked up at the row of boxers. They stood still, some with robes, arms by their sides, their hands wrapped in gauze and bandage. They were all sizes, but mostly one colour. Ned counted silently. 'Ten of the twelve are Aboriginal boys.'

'Why so many?' Bonnie stood on her tiptoes to peer over a bull rider's brim.

'They're good at it.' Ned looked at Bonnie. 'Good at all sports.'

The boxers were all ages, the youngest looked also to be the lightest. Not much past boyhood. He stood on one end, barefoot, his slender legs were hairy and poked through a pair of long green satin boxing trunks that were held up over his waist with electrical tape. His shoulders were narrow but his neck thick, and when he folded his arms his biceps pushed out from where they rested on the back of his hands. They looked to belong to a much larger man. His hair was cropped short, close to his skull, his dark brown eyes shone in the light. His skin looked smooth and he was the darkest of the boxers on the stage.

At the other end of the stage was the troupe's heavyweight. He was well over six feet, long-boned, fair-haired and with fists that looked like small cannonballs. He was a Kanaka, a descendant of the Pacific Islanders who'd been coerced to work as indentured labourers in Australia. Ned knew many of them had been brought to North Queensland to work in the cane fields. The practice of the coercion had been named 'blackbirding'.

Ned pointed to the heavyweight. 'Look at the size of him.' He shielded his eyes from the spotlight to get a better view of the man standing in the middle. 'That's Michael.'

'What?'

'In the middle with the blue trunks. Michael Roberts.'

'Who's he?'

'You know. The fella I see sometimes out at Tabletop Swamp. He taught me how to fish for barra with my hands.'

'Oh.' Bonnie lifted herself higher by pulling up on the round of Ned's shoulder. 'You didn't tell me he was handsome.'

Ned looked at Michael Roberts as though through Bonnie's eyes. He stood close to six feet tall. His face was evenly shaped, his nose though quite broad was defined by its nostrils, which were distinct by how they fell at a steep angle, giving them the appearance of always being flared. His jawline was sharpened by lean knobs of muscle either side, and his eyes were green with flecks of hazel that shone like opals in the sun. His shoulders were broad, and his torso was hard.

'Looks like my body, doesn't it?' Ned nudged Bonnie with his elbow and smiled.

'Righto, here we go, ladies and gentlemen! I want takers for all my boys up here on the stage. You can win money here, gentlemen, all you have to do is last three rounds with any of my boys and I'll pay out double what you put on yourself.' Walking the length of the stage in front of the pugilists, an old rusted speaking trumpet held tight over his mouth, the promoter began the auction of his bouts. He was a short man, walked with a limp and wore an old magician's coat with long tails that reached down past the backsides of his knees. His voice was high-pitched and gravelly, he spoke quickly, and through the speaking trumpet his words lost their ends and it sounded almost as though he were singing. He auctioned off his fighters, walked them from the stage and pulled back a curtained door to the tent and everyone followed inside. Ned and Bonnie waited until most of the crowd had made their way in. They entered, pushing the pram, and found a spot in the middle of the tent ten rows back from the ring.

The crowd was loud, almost all of them men, and at one point during the second fight, the baby woke and Bonnie took her from the pram and held her tight against her front. They watched the young spindly lightweight with the big biceps and trunks held up by tape box a man twice his size. His opponent wore denim jeans and riding boots, he was shirtless, his upper body rounded with hard muscle and stippled by ginger freckles. He rarely got close to the young pug who was perpetual motion, in and out of range with an economic pivot from his back foot or a graceful roll of his shoulder. It lasted two rounds before the opponent fell onto the ring apron exhausted and bleeding from both nose and mouth. The promoter, who also acted as the referee, counted him out, raised his own boxer's arm and then instructed other members of the troupe to quickly collect on the betting pots they'd won. They saw the troupe's Kanaka heavyweight knock out a Queensland bull rider who'd been egged into the ring by his cowboy mates. They had to carry him out on a stretcher, though ten minutes later he was back in the tent drinking beer with his mates.

The second to last fight of the night saw Michael Roberts enter the ring wearing faded blue satin trunks with white strips and piping. His boxing boots were black and ankle high, and his torso was greasy with a sweat he'd worked up shadowboxing in the paddock waiting for his bout to be called. The gloves he wore were a brownish-maroon and the leather across the thumbs and fists was threadbare in some parts. He was introduced as Hurricane Roberts, and held up his hand and bowed to all corners of the crowd. A moment later Bobby Clark stepped through the ring ropes, which were held apart by Joe Riley. He was shirtless, shoeless and wildly cheered by the crowd when he was introduced as a *former rodeo champion and city fireman*. Bobby raised his arms, bounced on the balls of his feet and then threw a quick combination of punches through the cigarette smoke that filled the tent.

'This'll be interesting.' Ned shuffled forward to enhance his view.

'Who's gonna win?' Bonnie manoeuvred close beside Ned, the baby awake and alert, now turned on Bonnie's front so she could see out.

Ned raised his voice to be heard over the crowd. 'I don't know. Bobby Clark's a tough bastard.'

When the bell rang Michael moved forward slowly, his jabbing hand held low, his right hand across his chest, the glove open and resting beside the left flank of his jaw. Bobby Clark held his hands high and moved laterally, flicking out left jabs that Michael parried easily with the inside of his right glove.

Bobby smiled at him. 'Throw something, ya black bastard.'

Michael kept his chin tucked in behind the ball of his left shoulder.

'C'mon, Hurricane.' Bobby changed stance to southpaw, and Michael made an adjustment, moving further to his left.

Michael threw his first punches, a left hook off a straight one-two that landed high on Bobby's head. The crowd cheered and Bobby switched to an orthodox stance. 'You can't fuckin' punch.'

Michael gave no reaction to Bobby's taunting, his face as though set from a mould, his eyes narrowed, nostrils flared, and his mouth closed firmly, biting down on both rows of his mouthguard. A minute before the round ended, they entered into a wild exchange that pushed the crowd into bedlam. Both men landed solid blows, both of them wobbled on unsteady legs and, with the last punch Bobby threw, Michael dropped to the seat of his trunks. In Bobby's corner, Joe Riley washed his face down with an engorged sponge and offered instruction, moving his head side to side as though dodging punches. Ned watched and laughed. 'Look at Riley, giving him pointers. Like he's Sonny Liston.'

The second round was fast and willing, Bobby getting the better of most of it, boring forward and throwing windmilled punches that snuck past Michael's loose guard. Michael sat calmly on his stool at the end of the round, he refused water and took long deep breaths. Riley continued to encourage and coach Bobby Clark with his animated shadowboxing and pointed suggestions. Early in the third round, Michael was again dropped to the floor. It was a looping right that caught him on the left side of the temple. He staggered, and Bobby chased after him with wild punches until he fell. Riley sprang to his feet and pounded on the ring apron with a fist. Michael got to his feet, shook his head to clear the fog from the blow, and then regained his stance. Bobby, empowered by the crowd, moved in to finish it. But as he tore in without prudence or fear, he walked into a left hook that Michael whipped up from his hip. It landed flush on Bobby's jaw, his knees gave way immediately and he fell backward landing on his buttocks and then rolling onto the broad width of his shoulders. The promoter stood over him, counted very quickly to ten and Michael raised his arms as the winner. Bobby got to his feet and complained it was too quick a count. Riley stormed the ring and joined in on the objection, and quickly the crowd did the same. They began jeering, then chanting, 'Bullshit!' Ned turned to Bonnie and felt the hair lift from his scalp on one side. He ducked instinctively and watched as the beer can bounced off the ring floor, burst and then sprayed Michael's trunks.

'Time to get outta here.' Ned took the baby from Bonnie and they walked quickly from the tent.

* * *

Later that night, Bobby Clark and Joe Riley left the show and went to Hotel Darwin. It was thumping inside, the show-folk and their families, the bull riders and the out-of-towners mixed in among the locals. The buffalo hunters and croc trappers despised the annual event, the *riff-raff* that followed each other from show to show, dragged from one end of the Territory to the other by the hope of blue ribbons for their livestock and gold medals for their fruit. Every year on that weekend without exception, there was a fight at the pub. Two years earlier, a cowboy of some repute had brawled with a local pig hunter for more than an hour. The fight had spilled out onto the Esplanade and the police who had arrived to break it up and restore order stood by their Land Cruiser and watched with the rest of the crowd. Twice the men called a stalemate to take in water and wash away blood that had filled their mouths and flowed into their eyes from cuts above their browlines. It stopped only when the pig hunter's wife got between the men and turned on the cowboy. The police intervened and took the men away. The following day the same cowboy won the calf-roping and steer-wrestling events and then pitted himself against the big Kanaka heavyweight in the boxing tent. He lasted the full three rounds and the scrap was deemed so exhilarating by the crowd that they showered the ring with coins.

The upper rims of Bobby Clark's eye sockets were swollen, the flesh hung over the corners of both eyes and made it hard for him to see without lifting his brow. His nose was broken and fresh purple bruises had begun to colour in the soft skin above his cheekbones. Danny Lewis had joined them and they were drinking in their usual spot at one end of the horseshoe bar. Initially, Bobby was congratulated by many of the patrons, some of the cowboys he knew, and the locals who'd heard about but not seen the fight. It was a buffalo hunter Bobby knew who approached him and dug at the result, *Knocked out by an Abo, I heard.* Riley moved the hunter along before Bobby could respond in a manner that would have escalated the situation quickly. But Bobby stewed on the comment and when another local said something similar, he attempted an out-of-range punch that led to a messy wrestle with the local on the floor. Riley talked Bobby into going home just as Mayor Landry joined them. Danny Lewis walked Bobby out of the pub and, when they were gone, Riley turned to Landry with a grave look. 'We got a fuckin' problem.'

'What do you mean?' Landry took a packet of smokes from the top pocket of his shirt, took one out, put it in his mouth and continued to speak, the end of the cigarette jerking around in time with his clamped words. 'What's happened?'

'You know Lionel Frazier?'

'No.'

'He's a Pom, works at the school. He's seen something. He's been talking.'

'Seen what?' Landry lit his cigarette with a zippo lighter.

'Enough to make it news. Big news.' Riley gave Landry a look to make certain he understood the severity of the situation.

Landry pulled back on his smoke and held its withdrawal in his lungs for as long as he could. 'Who's he been speaking to?'

'He came to see me.'

'Fuck. What did you tell him?'

'That you'd go see him.'

'What?' Landry looked around the pub, suspicious. He leant into Riley. 'I'm not talking to him.'

'Well, then I'll have to get him to make a formal statement. That'll get reported to the press.'

'Fuck.'

'That's right.'

'Who else knows?'

'No one.'

Landry's head fell and he looked across the bar floor, the smoke from his cigarette let out through his nose. 'What's he done? This Pom, Frazier?'

Riley shrugged. 'Degenerate punter, been in the lock-up for drunk and disorderly a few times. One assault charge. Got into a fight with another drunk at the pub. Knocked his teeth out. That's it.'

Landry looked up. 'He's a pisshead?'

Riley let out a short phlegmy laugh. 'Compared to who? This is the Territory.'

CHAPTER 8

IT WAS DUSK the next day when Mayor Landry knocked on the door of the small, elevated house behind an overgrown front lawn. The iron gate he'd walked through was unhinged and the small concrete path leading to the front door was cracked and lifted by the roots of wild weeds and wrongly planted trees. Landry could smell dog shit, and before anyone could answer the door, he checked the soles of both shoes. The door opened and Leila Frazier stood before him. She was not much taller than five feet, and squat. Her dark skin was mottled over her hands and arms with asymmetrical patches of white. Landry looked directly at them.

'Vitiligo.' When she spoke, her bottom lip showed its inside; it too was discoloured in spots, the dark pigment replaced by large pinkish shapes that looked like islands sitting over water on a map. 'Comes on when I get stressed.'

'Well, I'm sorry to hear that. Does it hurt?' Landry's intrigue was genuine, it looked like the lady standing before him had begun to turn white.

'No, I can't feel a thing.'

'I'm Desmond Landry. The mayor.'

'Yes, I know who you are.'

'Senior Sergeant Riley would have told you I was coming by.'

'Told my husband.'

'Okay then. May I come in?'

Leila didn't reply, just opened the door wider and stepped to the side to give Landry room to enter. Inside, it was hot and smelt of boiling vegetables and frying fish. Landry looked over the threadbare furniture while Leila led him through to the kitchen. There, at the stove hotplates, turning crumbed flounder over a shallow covering of butter was Lionel Frazier. He was a short thickset man, his round face reddened by both the sun and constant drinking.

Landry had done some homework before arriving. Nearly twenty years older than his wife, Lionel had come to Australia from Cumbria in the north of England after the Second World War. He'd travelled with his first wife, but she'd passed away with cancer two years after they'd arrived. He'd married Leila, who was Aboriginal and Papua New Guinean, when she was just seventeen. It had been made uncomfortable for him in public at times after he and Leila had wed. Lionel worked as a groundsman and cleaner at the St Mary's Catholic School in town. His Cumbrian accent was often parroted by the young students at the school when they encountered him mowing the lawns or scrubbing the toilets. His life was simple, spent mostly with his wife. The weekends he bet on the horses, and once a week he played cards illegally at a gambling house. How he fared, made the difference between a week of jug wine or beer.

Landry put out his hand to shake. 'Desmond Landry.'

Lionel shook his hand and looked him directly in the eye. 'Lionel Frazier.'

'Would you like something to drink, Mayor Landry?' Leila asked softly.

'Oh. Well … what do you have?'

'Iced water, milk.'

Landry smiled at them both. 'What about a beer? For both me and Lionel.' It was clear Landry was there to charm, his smile and good looks had always served him well with his constituents, though he wasn't after a vote this time.

'Okay then. I'll get two beers.'

'Thank you, Leila.'

* * *

They sat on old deck chairs on the back porch overlooking a small yard that was much better kept than the front. The lawn was mown, the small acacia shrubs were tended to and the fencing was newly painted. Landry commented, 'Like a different place out here to the front.'

'I spend time out the back. I'll get to the front one day.' Lionel wiped his forehead with the back of his hand.

Landry took a full swallow from his bottle. 'Ah, that's nice, Leila. Very cold. It's the only way to drink it in the Territory.' Landry didn't get a response of any kind from either of them, and so he got down to the reason he was there.

'Okay, Lionel. What exactly did you see?'

Lionel took a mouthful from his bottle and thought a moment. He straightened himself and leant forward over his knees. 'Look, I'm not sure why you're here, Mayor. I told the police and they didn't do nothin' and so I went and saw 'em again. Seems to me it's their problem now, and they don't want to deal with it.'

Landry put the beer bottle down between his feet. 'Well, you see, I'm your elected official, I'm here because I want to help, but I just need to know exactly what we're talking about.'

'The police would have told you.' Lionel's voice was matter-of-fact and his expression showed frustration.

'Yes, they've told me what you said may have happened. But are you sure?'

'Yes. I am.' Lionel sat back in his chair.

Landry did the same and looked across at Lionel. 'Maybe you made it up?' Landry's smile faded, his posture and the tenor in his voice turning accusatory.

Lionel, not bothered by it, answered back quickly, 'Why would I do that?'

'I don't know. Were you having trouble at the school with those in power? The headmaster?'

Lionel turned to Leila and shook his head. 'No. What I saw is what I saw. Why don't you go and talk to the parents? I told them too.'

Landry's carriage stiffened and he adjusted the hair across his scalp. 'Lionel, you're an alcoholic. Everyone in town knows that. You've been locked up before because of it. And you've been convicted of assault. Now I know that has nothing to do with this, though it will if you're brought before a court if this goes that far. And the defence will say that you're a drunk and that you were probably drunk on the day you say you saw this thing happen. And then they may say that you're not a credible witness because you're a criminal.' Landry's voice flavoured the statement so that it might be read as somewhat sympathetic. 'A lawyer would exploit that. I'd hate to see that happen.'

Lionel glared at Landry, his contempt made certain by a quiet huff he tied with a shake of his head. 'You can leave, Mayor Landry.'

Landry glared back at Lionel, and then smiled. 'Well, if you say so … I was hoping it may have been, you know, something else.' He took the beer from between his legs and finished what was left with one swallow. 'Ahhhh. That was good. Thank you for the beer.' Landry stood up and shook hands with Lionel and Leila. 'Lionel, just out of curiosity, aside from the parents, did you tell anyone else about what you saw?'

'Just the police.'

'Are you sure? Because if the police are to move on this then keeping it between you and them is imperative. People start talking, it becomes a rumour, becomes a Chinese whisper that takes a whole other narrative. Do you understand?' Landry held his hands together as if to sincerely implore the necessity of keeping what Lionel had seen a secret.

Lionel glanced very quickly at Leila, and though Landry saw the look, he didn't acknowledge it.

'Yes, I understand.'

'That's very good to hear.' Landry smiled and Leila walked him out. As he passed through the living room, he noticed a young boy, somewhere between eight and nine years of age, sitting on the ragged end of a couch playing with an old set of yellowing knuckle bones. He looked up at Landry, his eyes were bright blue and glimmering under a dimly lit ceiling light bulb. His mouth was open, and he was missing a row of baby teeth.

'You've got beautiful eyes for a brown boy, don't you?' Landry kept walking to the front door and the boy smiled.

* * *

Landry drove straight to Hotel Darwin. He called Riley and another man, Jack Taylor, and told them to meet him there. Taylor was a brute of a man. Well over six feet and nearly seventeen stone. He had a short crop of blond hair, fairish skin and when he spoke or smiled he showed the missing teeth in the top row of his molars. Taylor was pure muscle for Landry and somewhat of a last resort. He'd worked for Landry's family back in Sydney resolving pay disputes and limiting union interference. Landry had brought him north, paid him weekly and set him up rent free in a bungalow on the Darwin River.

Taylor had spent ten years in Sydney's Long Bay Jail for second degree murder and grievous bodily harm. He'd been involved in a fight outside a pub in the city, killed a man and put another in a coma. Landry had said to Riley on more than one occasion that *Taylor was born bad*, and had to be *managed* to keep his propensity for violence *in check*. When they arrived, Landry was noticeably nervous, his cheeks were beet red, his face shiny with the kind of perspiration that never developed into beads or drops of sweat, but a perennial film that, no matter how often Landry wiped it away, presented again moments later.

'How'd it go?' Riley ordered a drink with his eyes at the barman.

'We've got a big fuckin' problem.' Landry coughed into his hand, then signalled the barman for another beer. 'He's not walkin' away.'

'You offer him money?' Riley said it quietly.

Landry wiped a palm across his comb-over and tried to quieten his voice by sending the words through gritted teeth. 'Do you think I have a never-ending bank account? I told you, he isn't walking away. Money won't matter.'

Some others in the bar looked toward Landry, all very aware of who he was. He composed himself, straightened his tie and ran the insides of both thumbs under his belt and lifted his trousers. 'I think he spoke. He told someone else.'

'Fuck.' Riley looked at Jack Taylor.

'Find out who he's closest to and clean it the fuck up. But don't …' Landry stopped and glared at Taylor. 'Scare 'em. That's it.'

Taylor frowned, and with a pitch in his voice that didn't marry with his frame, asked, 'Scared enough they won't speak?'

Landry nodded, and then turned to Riley. 'And put someone on Frazier. He's a pisshead. Pissheads talk when they're pissed. Have him followed.'

Landry straightened his tie, finished his glass of beer in a mouthful and walked from the bar.

CHAPTER 9

CHARLOTTE HAD RISEN before dawn, taken the car and driven the six or so miles to Lee Point. She was on the beach just as the high point of the sun peeped past the horizon. Brightened by its light, the sky fanned out in a tri-colour wedge of orange and pink and faded blue. She walked to the tideline with a bucket, a set of pliers and an old stocking full of pilchards that she began sweeping across the sand. It was a technique for catching beachworms her father had taught her. The stocking filled with rotting pilchards was called a 'stinky', and was used to lure the greenhead worms from beneath the sand.

Charlotte planted her feet firmly, gently swayed the stinky just above a receding wave, and when a greenhead emerged enticed by the whiff, she clamped the pliers just below its head and pulled it from the sand. She dragged ten worms from the beach just as the bottom of the sun lifted past the horizon.

Later that afternoon, on low tide and just before dusk, she walked to the beach with a can of beer, an old cork fishing line and a small tub of greenheads. She stopped in the water just as her ankles were covered, and then threaded a long shank hook with a small piece of beachworm. She let out a good length of fishing line from the cork reel, spun it quickly as though preparing a lasso to loop around the forequarters and neck of a buck, and then let it go, the line whizzing from the reel carried by the weight of the sinker to a spot out past the small shallow break. In fifteen minutes she had six sand whiting, all long and thick through the flanks, which made for good filleting.

Back at home, Charlotte cleaned the fish and cut lean fillets either side of the spines. She floured and fried them in a shallow pan of oil and served them with scalloped potatoes and fresh lemon. It was Bobby's favourite food and they sat at the table together and ate.

Bobby was quiet and more than once Charlotte asked if he was okay. He'd been in a bad mood since the weekend, after he'd come home from the show. Charlotte had tried to fuss over his swollen eyes and broken nose, but he'd refused her suggestion of ice and offerings of help. When she asked what had happened, he told her only that he'd been boxing in the show tent. It wasn't uncommon; most years when the show came to town, Bobby had put his hand up to fight. But he'd never come home looking the way he did, or in a mood that she determined was from him perhaps having lost.

Not long after they'd finished eating, Danny Lewis knocked on the front door and, without stepping inside, left with Bobby. Her husband had thanked her for dinner, kissed her and left the house quickly.

Charlotte cleaned up, had a shower and went out again not long after. She looked forward to the one night every week she spent with her father at the home he'd been admitted to two years earlier. Dennis Hale was a large man and big everywhere. He stood six feet two inches tall, and in his prime weighed over fifteen stone. Back then his neck was bulky, and his shoulders sloped to rounded knobs of muscle that filled out whatever shirt he was wearing. Even as he'd grown older, he'd held onto the shape of his younger physique, albeit now softer and without the separation of muscle. His dementia had come early for his age, and had grown severe quickly. Over a period of eighteen months his mind had deteriorated to the point where he'd become lost driving to places he'd known for years. He repeated himself incessantly, asked the same questions over and over and forgot who he was on a daily basis.

Charlotte's mother had died many years before the illness took hold. Her father had struggled to come to terms with the unexpected loss of his wife. He drank heavily, became a recluse and had attempted suicide by taking an overdose of paracetamol. Charlotte had found him collapsed and semi-conscious in his bathroom. But the year before the dementia had reared, he'd been much better. He'd stopped drinking and had given up smoking.

Charlotte visited every week but Bobby had only visited twice. Once on the day he was admitted, the other for his birthday. He'd told Charlotte he didn't like to be *around all the craziness*. Charlotte tried to explain to him what dementia was, and how, to the best of her knowledge, it ravaged a person's mind. How it stole memories, and then gave them back in pieces arbitrarily. How it could come on very quickly and leave a person confused to the point of sheer panic. She described it to him as *cruel*. Bobby sympathised with her father's condition, but added with a mind so *soured*, he was *better off dead*. Though she'd preferred Bobby come with her on occasion, she did enjoy the drive by herself and often took the longest route to and from seeing her father. Lately she'd been fantasising about not returning at all.

* * *

At the home, her father was confined to his room and a small recreational area inside. There was no air conditioning, but instead rows of propeller-sized fans in the hallways. They were set at high speed, making it hard to hear anything over the noise of the whirring blades. Everything smelt of mildew and boiling vegetables. The walls were dank from the humidity, and the carpets were perennially soggy from the mopped-up flooding of previous storms and cyclones. The water that was forced in by the winds could never be completely wiped dry. It was common for homes and buildings in the Territory to be in a permanently damp state.

That night, Charlotte arrived just before dark. Her father was sitting in the recreational area drinking a tall glass of milk. The man next to him was asleep in a chair, dribbling. She watched her father take a handkerchief from his trouser pocket and wipe clean the man's chin. He didn't recognise her initially when she said hello to him. She talked to him however, about her fishing, and the chance of a cyclone later in the month, which she'd heard about while watching the evening news. A little while later, back in his room, he stumbled upon a long stream of clarity. She was sitting on a seat beside him as he lay on his bed.

'How's Bobby?'

Charlotte tried not to overdo her keenness to answer. But there was always a desperation to get as much said as possible before the switch was turned off and the lucid awareness and presence of her father's mind would be gone again. It could happen mid-sentence. It could happen so quickly after a moment he'd look at her with such familiarity that she stumbled trying to resolve how he could be lost so fast to the fog.

'He's okay.'

'He treating you all right?'

'Yes. Always, Dad.'

'Just asking. He was always quiet with me. But how are you, my darling girl?'

'I'm good, Dad.'

'You happy?'

Charlotte shifted in her seat. 'Am I happy?'

'Yes. Are you?'

Charlotte felt the sting of emotion that involuntarily showed in her eyes. He father saw it and reached for her hand. 'You get but one life, darlin'. That's all.'

Charlotte couldn't stop a tear from splashing across her cheek and she burrowed through her handbag for a handkerchief.

'Hey. Look at me.' Her father squeezed her hand. Charlotte wiped her face with the handkerchief and looked directly at him. 'I love you.'

'Thank you, Dad.' She leant forward and kissed his hand. In the short silence that followed, her father lost his way, he entered the fog again and looked down at his hand clasped tightly by hers. She let his hand go and watched him gently rest it over his chest.

'Goodbye, Dad.' She got up from the chair, stood over him and kissed him on the forehead.

* * *

In the car park of the nursing home she sat and cried, before driving home the longest way she knew. She took a detour down a road she'd never been before. The sealed track diminished mile by mile until it was just loose gravel and muddied shoulders. It led her out to a mangrove system on the banks of a small swamp. A thick fog rested across the wetland, so dense and grey it looked like a storm about to open up three feet over the water. Charlotte would have usually been made nervous by the surrounds, the blackness, the lurking shadows of the mangroves that split the light from the small crescent moon and hopped across her car bonnet. Panic would have come soon after. But she felt none of that. Instead she drove on and searched for the pure truth of how she felt. Way past knowing she was unhappy, she mined into the why's and how's of her life, shifted away the concessions and the reconciliations she'd made that covered the truthful reasons for her unhappiness. It was her marriage. She conceded she'd given up too much of herself for it. Her ambition was redundant inside it, her curiosity futile. Her future all boxed up together and wrapped tightly in her life's presumed evolution. *To a quite unremarkable death*, she concluded.

She drove on for ten minutes until the swamp broadened and the mangroves became thicker. She stopped her car on the muddy shoulder closest to the swamp and got out. She looked over the water and into the distance at the distorted mangrove branches that were just shapes, reaching for the water like the gnarled arms of a storybook monster. She didn't hear a sound until the hand was around her mouth.

'Shhhh, shhhh.'

Charlotte tried to scream but her breath was squashed by the strength of the man's grip.

'Please, help me.' The voice was panicked, terrified. 'I'm not going to hurt you.' He slowly removed his hand from Charlotte's mouth and took a step away from her. 'I need your help, I'm hurt.'

Before Charlotte turned around, she saw a gust of wind sweep over the swamp and spoil the black slate of still water. The moonlight bounced off the disturbance and she caught the glowing eyes of a crocodile just before they sank beneath the water. She faced the man, the blackness of his face darkened further where it was bloodied. From his skull, down both cheeks and into his mouth.

'They tried to kill me.' His jaw was distended, broken, and the points of his words were missing.

Charlotte remained silent. And still.

'Please, they're looking for me. Take me somewhere.'

'Who are you?' Charlotte said it in a whisper.

'No one. Just a man. A good man, I promise.'

'What's your name?'

'Michael. Michael Roberts.'

Charlotte had never seen him before, had never heard the name.

'What happened?'

'Please, just take me to somewhere safe.'

Charlotte saw there was more bleeding from his torso. 'You need a hospital.'

'No.' Michael raised his voice and Charlotte flinched. 'I'm sorry, I'm sorry. I can't go to a hospital, not here. They're going to kill me.'

'I can take you home and call the police.'

Michael reached for her, looking for leverage to hold himself up. 'Please, no. No police.'

'Have you hurt someone?'

'No!'

Charlotte recoiled at the reply.

'I'm sorry, but I need help. They're out there somewhere looking for me.'

Charlotte made her decision quickly. 'Okay, get in the car.'

Michael got in the back, he groaned and yelped, and then settled with his back against the door and feet laid out over the bench seat. Charlotte turned the car around and drove back the way she'd come.

'Are you okay?'

'My leg, something is wrong with my leg.'

Charlotte thought about taking Michael home and asking Bobby to help her with the situation, but she was deterred by the questions he'd ask of her. Why she was where she was, so far from town, in a spot that only people wanting to be clandestine would go? She looked back at Michael, his eyes closed, his breathing shallow and laboured. There was an option.

When they got back onto the sealed road, she drove to an old property her father owned that was twenty-five miles from Darwin. He'd planned to retire there, farm a small head of cattle and fish the estuaries nearby. But he'd never had the chance. The property was enclosed by a decaying timber boundary and a single dilapidated barn sat to one side of the fence line.

* * *

Before she returned home, she got into the back seat of the car where Michael had lain, and cleaned his blood from the leather with a rag she'd found in the barn and wet from a bore beside a row of old stables.

When she got home, the house was dark and she could see that Bobby hadn't returned. She took off her blood-stained clothes and hid them behind a brick pier beneath the house. She showered and went to bed, wondering whether or not Michael would still be alive when she returned to the barn. He'd passed out not long after she laid him over a crude mattress she'd made from the coarse remnants of a bale of hay. She'd stemmed the bleeding from his abdomen the best she could, stuffed a handkerchief into the wound and then tied the cardigan she'd worn around his torso as tightly as she could manage. His ankle was broken, and she'd made a splint from a fallen fence paling, securing it with one of her socks. His jaw she didn't know what to do with.

She wondered how she'd get back to the barn to tend to him, the lies she'd have to tell Bobby. How to get access to the car when she needed it? At least until Michael was stabilised. He'd need to be bathed and the wounds cleaned as often as possible to begin with. Her head became messy with how it could all come undone. How he'd die. And then how to handle that. Bury him? Keep it a secret? If the body was found where would that lead? If someone stumbled across the barn and found Michael, how would that play out? What would Bobby do if he found out she'd been harbouring another man and nursing him back to health? An Aboriginal man. Though she was afraid, she was determined. She had a purpose.

CHAPTER 10

NED SAT WITH his eldest brother, Fraser, on the back porch to his home that overlooked a narrow slice of the Adelaide River, seventy miles south of Darwin. Fraser was six years older than Ned, taller and thicker, and rudimentary when it came to living his life. His wife had left him three years earlier, she'd gone back to her home town of Townsville in North Queensland. She couldn't get to like the Territory enough to stay, and Fraser would never leave. They'd met while he was stationed at the Royal Australian Airforce base in Townsville. Though Fraser didn't dislike it there, he missed the inland estuaries and bush of the Territory, the red dirt and the slower pace of life. Most of all he missed the river fishing.

With his wife gone and without children he spent his days as a mechanic in Darwin. As soon as the day finished, he drove the hour and a half back to his house, and by dusk he was in his small aluminium boat out on the river fishing until well after dark. Most nights he had a fresh catch of barra and mangrove jack. He rarely had guests over to his house, and when he did, they could often

94

become uncomfortable because of Fraser's quiet way. He seldom asked questions and so unless there was a thread of conversation he was engaged and interested in, it could very quickly become mute. His family could sit with him through the silence only because they were used to it and expected nothing less. He drank only beer and only Carlton Draught. He drank evenly through the week and more on the weekends, and Ned often wondered if he was ever sober enough to feel a hangover. They both had a can tonight, and Ned was feeling the knots of discontent about his job beginning to loosen.

'No rain today.' Fraser looked skyward and though the clouds were dark, he was sure. 'Too cool on the ground here.'

'Storms all next week they say.' Ned finished his can and reached for another in the foam esky at their feet that was packed with crushed ice.

'How's Bonnie?'

'She's good.'

'The baby?'

'Good. Still no name.'

'What do you call her?'

'Sweetheart. Darlin'. That type of stuff.'

'Well, you best get onto that.'

'Yep. Bonnie's left it to me to decide.'

'Brave woman, that one.'

Fraser's eyes narrowed. 'There's my croc. Comes by this time every afternoon. Been here for the last year.'

Ned didn't ask where it was, he wanted to find it himself. To show his brother he hadn't lost any of the skill identifying the signs of where the croc would be. In the silence as he looked for it, Fraser smiled and let loose a tiny laugh through his nose.

'Fuck off. I'll find it.' Ned was smiling with him. 'Oh, shit, he is a big one.'

'It's a she. Long for a cow, but still a cow.'

Ned sat forward and looked closer. 'You sure about that? Big snout.'

Five minutes later they were on the water in Fraser's boat drifting on the momentum of the cut motor, the croc swimming slowly in front of them.

'Mate, I think it's a male.' Ned looked over the side of the boat.

'It's too skinny being that long. That was male it'd be twelve inches broader across its belly and it'd have turned and had a go at us.'

Ned sat down, reached into the esky and pulled out a can of Carlton Draught. 'Okay, it's a female.'

'Yep. Just a big well-fed one. I've named her Marilyn.' Fraser smiled from the corner of his mouth which he'd always done.

'As in Monroe?'

'I still can't believe she's gone.'

'Yeah, sounded fishy to me.' Ned pulled the ring from his can and took a swallow. 'Girls like that, that age? They don't just die havin' a fuckin' snooze. Who the fuck would know with the Yanks. She was fucking Kennedy, wasn't she?'

'Both of 'em I read somewhere.'

'Well, if someone up high didn't want that out, what do ya do?'

'I like to think she just had a snooze and didn't wake up.' Fraser smiled at Ned exposing the ends of his top row of teeth.

* * *

They sat opposite each other as the boat drifted out of the narrow part of the river and into a roomier stretch where the water ran quicker.

'How's work at the garage?'

'Same as it was yesterday, same as it'll be tomorrow. What about you?'

'Well, it's never the same, but it is. Shit happens, but always gets handled the same way. It never gets finished properly.'

'Jesus, that's not gonna work out for you then, mate.' Fraser laughed, he knew Ned well, his principle to follow through on things had been a staple from a child onward. It was a trait Ned's brothers and sisters had relied upon while growing up together. Often to keep them out of trouble. Ned needed only be asked once to do something, and it'd be done. Many times, his siblings would take advantage of his thoroughness and coerce him into finishing their own chores. It worked easy enough if they threatened Ned that without his help they'd all be in serious trouble. Truth was, Ned liked finishing things. To see them through. And whether it be a chore, his own or his siblings, or a book he didn't particularly like, or an investigation, there was a satisfaction he craved by having finished it. It was as though he couldn't put a task to rest knowing he hadn't completed it. The fact he'd never actually been assigned to investigate Ernie Clay's death made it somewhat easier to let the investigation go.

'You heard about the man found out by Tabletop Swamp?'

'Everyone heard about that, Ned.'

'I found him. Well, I was the first cop there.'

'Yeah, I know that too.'

'How?'

'When people expect you to say nothing, they forget you're about. I walk through this town fuckin' invisible. I hear everything.'

Ned smiled. He adored how his brother was able to make sense of people, how he read them so intricately. 'So who'd you hear it off?'

'I was down by the fire station, I asked to use their hydrant and hose to wash the belly of my truck. It was caked with swamp mud and suffocatin' the exhaust. It was that blue-eyed brutish cowboy, Bobby Clark.'

Ned smiled, looked over the river and laughed. 'That man. I was only saying to Bonnie there's somethin' about him I don't like.'

Fraser smiled. 'He's not your type of bloke, Ned.'

'What's that mean?'

'He's full of himself. You've never liked those kinds, mate.'

Ned huffed. 'Yeah, maybe.'

'What's his wife's name?'

'Charlotte.'

'That's right. He was raggin' on her pretty good too. Saying she wouldn't give it up anymore.' Fraser took a mouthful from his can and spat it out over the river. 'Fuckin' warm.' He took another one from the esky and opened it. 'That won't end well.' Fraser took a long swallow from his can and then stood and ripped the motor's pull cord.

* * *

Ned stayed the night at Fraser's house, and just after dawn walked along the bank of the Adelaide River to an inlet that curled sharply away from the main body of water. Once he arrived, he checked the marshy scrub above the tideline for croc slides and gathered vegetation that might have been a nest hiding eggs. When he considered it safe, he took off his T-shirt and entered the small inlet in just his shorts. His aim was to catch a barramundi with his hands, something he would have thought impossible the year before. But at the end of the last dry season, he'd seen Michael Roberts wading waist deep in a small billabong not far from the dirt road near Tabletop Swamp. Concerned for his safety, Ned approached Michael and asked him what he was doing. Michael replied, 'Hand fishing.' Ned watched, fascinated, as Michael slowly walked across the muddy floor of the billabong, feeling for rocks and fallen logs with his feet and legs. And then he'd stopped still, smiled at Ned and quickly disappeared under the water. Ned grew anxious at the amount of time he was submerged, and when the surface of the water broke from the struggle beneath, he considered diving in and attempting a rescue. A moment later, Michael emerged laughing, holding a thickset barra by the gills. 'Got him.' Michael threw the fish on the riverbank and while it snapped its body side to side desperately trying to find water, he began his process again. All told, Ned watched him pull four barramundi from the billabong with his bare hands. While Michael threaded the fish through a stringer made of old nylon cord, he explained to Ned how to hand fish. He told him that barra liked hiding between rocks and mangrove roots and in holes, and if you were *quiet and soft enough*, it was possible to flush them from where they were hiding and corner them in shallower water. 'Then,' he said, 'you fight with him.'

Ned had been to the same spot twice before and had caught nothing, though he'd been overwhelmed by thoughts of a crocodile lurking below, slowly creeping along the riverbed, making its way toward him, readying itself to pull him beneath the water, jam him under a tree root and then come back to eat him after he'd softened. On both those occasions, the macabre scenario had gotten the better of him and he'd left the billabong quickly, running along the riverbed, his thighs burning, his knees high enough to break the water and give off the type of sound that encouraged Ned to believe he was being chased. He'd screamed as he reached the riverbank, and then a moment later laughed when considering what someone might have thought had they just had seen what he'd done.

Now Ned kept his arms out of the water and spotted a craggy narrowing alcove in the shoreline that was shadowed by a knotty mangrove. *I can corner something there*, he supposed. He began walking slowly toward the bank, slipped off a clayish shelf to a reedy bottom and stumbled. 'Fuck.' He took a breath, continued moving, the consistency of the riverbed changing with each step, at times his feet so deeply sunk in the mud he felt trapped. His lower legs brushed by the soft blades of the bulrush reeds, his hands gently floating above the river's skin.

Two metres from the shoreline he stubbed a toe on the gnarled root of the mangrove and stopped. He lifted his feet over the thick stems and searched for a wedge of mud between the twisted root structure of the tree. As he planted his feet, he felt the smooth flank of something brush by the inside of his calf. 'Fuck.' Ned stayed still, quickly ran a diagnostic of what it might have been. *Not a croc. Not a snake. A fish.* He moved another step forward and felt the spiny ends of a barramundi's dorsal fin across the top side of one of his feet. A moment later, just in front of him, the silvery body of the fish broke the water and he could see it dart toward the shoreline. He took two more steps and then felt the full length of the fish brush past his ankle. 'Jesus Christ.' He stood still, smiling, both alarmed and excited at the size of the fish. 'All right, where'd you go?' He felt the riverbed vibrate and a brown muck rose to the surface.

Ned pushed off the bottom, curled his arms and torso toward the water and dived for the riverbed. He felt blindly over the mud, the mangrove root and between the stalks of the bulrush reeds. He could feel the water moving around his arms and across the middle of his abdomen, the current kicked up by the barramundi's panicked search for an unobstructed path to deeper water. Ned followed the swirling wake of its retreat and reached down into a deeper chasm of water that was bounded either side by tree roots. He felt its mouth, its hard lips and the first rows of fine villiform teeth. He reached further along the side of its head, looking for a gill to cup his hand through. The fish turned and plumes and coils of dislodged mud shot quickly from the hollow and hit him squarely in the face. Momentarily blinded, he pulled back his arm, and when he reached back into the hole, he felt the fish push past him and away into open water. He rose from the bottom and quickly turned around, the course of the runaway barramundi scored by a broadening rippled arrowhead across the surface of billabong.

* * *

Ned walked back to his brother's house, showered and began the track back to Darwin. While driving he thought of the fish, whether it had felt fear being cornered and chased, and whether it would remember the encounter so as to keep it from swimming that part of the billabong again. *It's a fuckin' fish, Ned, they don't remember things.* He shook his head, smiled to himself and wondered what people might think of him had they somehow been given access to his thoughts. But there was a resentful feeling after the initial thrill of the encounter. One he couldn't shift on the drive home. He felt that he'd been beaten by the fish, and he pictured it smiling beneath the water, laughing at him as it swam away. *Fuck you, Ned.* He resolved to try again, to win, to catch a barramundi by hand.

CHAPTER 11

BONNIE HELD A basket of freshly washed clothes and sheets, their weight causing her to lean back and even the load as she walked. She put the basket down and began hanging the washing on the clothesline. The sun was mid-sky and the heat came first from where she stood, through the earth and across the weedy lawn. Her legs were spotted with small oval beads of sweat, made misty in their centre from an oily softening cream she'd applied earlier that morning.

'Hey there.'

Bonnie turned. Ned stood, fishing rod and bucket in hand. 'How'd you go?'

'Nothing.'

She smirked. 'You know I've heard all these stories from you and your brothers. How good at fishing you are. And you just keep comin' home with nothin' but sunburn.'

'Well … one got away. A big one, too.'

'Yeah, yeah.'

Ned walked over to her and held her from behind. She pegged a petticoat on the clothesline and then rested her arms over his and peered into his face.

'Have the day off,' she whispered.

'Mmmm.' He kissed the corner of her mouth.

'Honestly.'

'And what would we do?'

'Go on a picnic on the beach. Then put the baby to sleep. And make love all afternoon.'

'All afternoon? Really? Would it be just me, because all afternoon is a long time, my sweetheart.'

Bonnie swayed her hips and bumped Ned to the side. She turned to face him. 'C'mon. Stay home with me.'

'I can't.'

Bonnie reached for him, dropped her arms over his shoulders and grinned. 'You can do whatever you want, Ned Potter.'

Ned smiled back, tilted his head, a little uncertain. 'I don't know what that means.'

'It means … whatever you want.'

Ned straightened his look and put his hands over hers. He kissed her and then spoke quietly. 'Would you ever consider leaving here?'

Bonnie pulled away to get a better look at the expression that accompanied his question. 'Wow. That was a mood changer, Potter.' The piece of skin between her eyebrows pinched and scored two deep lines that rose up and stopped just short of the middle of her forehead.

'Would you? Go somewhere else?' He looked directly into her eyes.

Bonnie could read he was being solemn. 'Is this about Ernie Clay?'

'I don't know. I just wonder, would it be different in a bigger city?'

'Different how?'

Ned took a laboured breath. 'I don't know.'

Bonnie smiled and let out a small laugh. 'Jesus, you don't know much, do you? Come on. Stay home with me.'

He kissed her. 'I gotta get to work.'

'Okay … but know what you just turned down.' Bonnie winked at him.

They laughed together and Ned left her at the clothesline to get dressed for work.

* * *

Ned didn't go to the station, and instead drove out along the back roads toward the outskirts of Darwin. He was still thinking about the barramundi and how to even the score. As the asphalt on the road's shoulder loosened and the dust thrown up by the Land Cruiser's tyres reduced his visibility, he began thinking about what he'd asked Bonnie. *Would you ever consider leaving here?* It had come from nowhere. He'd never contemplated leaving the Territory, not from discontent or wonder of another life somewhere else.

Ned felt a swell of melancholy pass by him that momentarily softened his frame and loosened his muscles. He recognised the sensation as the precursor to the thoughts that would follow. History, though pushed to a corner of his mind, he couldn't completely cover. Unlike other memories or considerations that waited patiently in his brain to be replayed or listened to, this history was recalcitrant and noisy. Like a misbehaving school child posturing for attention. It put its hand up to be answered when it was quiet, when Ned ran out of those inane thoughts he often supposed would have him either friendless or committed if relayed to another person. It was the recollection of his father's death. How he'd found him motionless in the backyard one afternoon during wet season. A storm had just passed, and Ned had come from the house to look for the small floodplain frogs that were customarily flushed out into open areas after heavy rain. He used them for bait to catch barramundi and after a downpour their backyard was usually hopping with them. He saw his father in the middle of the yard, flat on his stomach next to the new push-reel lawnmower he'd bought just the day before. Ned turned him over quickly, his glasses askew across his face, one of the lenses dislodged and broken, its sharp edge embedded high on a cheekbone. Ned shouted at him to wake up, slapped him across the face when he didn't respond, and when his mother and two of his brothers arrived by his side, Ned was blowing full breaths of air into his father's mouth. He'd been dead for an hour. Eager to use the new lawnmower, Terry Potter had begun to mow the lawn before the storm hit. He'd collapsed with only two small strips left to mow, just as the wind had picked up and the front of the storm released its first fat drops over his backyard. It was a memory that troubled Ned both while awake and asleep, the dream often amplified by the sound of croaking frogs.

Ned shook away the memory and continued down the narrow road in the middle of the swampy land. He reached forward to close the vent that was letting in the humidity from outside, the air so full of moisture that the leather seats had begun to sweat with condensation. In that moment, with his eyes not on the road, a scampering wild pig hit the grille of the Land Cruiser, bounced onto the bonnet and through the windscreen. On top of

Ned. He braked as firmly as he could, the vehicle locking up and sliding across to the opposite side of the road and into the edge of marshland. All he could smell was the pig shit, though he could taste his own blood, the coppery tang mixed with his saliva.

The boar wasn't fully grown, no more than sixty pounds, and the brunt of its momentum had been absorbed across the grille and windscreen. Still, Ned was hurt. His nose felt numb and, when he touched it, he could immediately tell it was broken. The pig was still alive, its snout and head at rest on his lap. As he looked down on it, its nostrils torn apart, blood coming from its ears, its front legs twisted and broken, he couldn't neglect the peculiar nature of the events of his morning. The barra and now the pig.

He pushed the boar off his lap, it squealed in pain and then shit itself again. Ned knew he had to kill it. He got out of the truck and dragged it by its hind quarters across the front seat and onto the road. It rolled to its side, its breathing obscured and wet, struggling to cope with the blood that was building up internally. Ned moved the truck to the side of the road, the wheel alignment skewed so severely he wasn't sure it'd be drivable back to the station. He cleaned his face with a handkerchief, and then took his revolver out from its holster. He checked the chamber for rounds, then looked for any oncoming traffic. He stood next to the boar, its meaty jowl ripped from under its eye and lying limp on the road. Ned held the revolver against the middle of its head.

'I'm sorry, pig.' He fired once, the boar stiffened and rolled to its back, blood spraying across Ned's lower arms and over the dirt beside where he stood.

He felt his face again, the numbness thawing and giving way to a throbbing. His heart was still beating quickly. He looked at the boar, and then his surrounds. *Where to bury it?* He wasn't

going to leave the carcass to rot in the sun on the road, the smell
would become rancid and the dingoes and wedge-tailed eagles
would come from miles away to scavenge and fight over it. They'd
probably get hit by another car or lorry that came by. He thought
about dumping the carcass in the swamp as a free meal for a croc,
but that was illegal, and didn't sit well with him. But it was just so
hot. And the thought of dragging the dead pig over marshland to
drier footing with his nose bleeding and broken, and then to dig
a hole three feet deep to be sure the carcass wouldn't be dug up
or uncovered by a storm … It was almost too much to grasp and
follow through with. It'd be dark before he got back to the truck.
He looked at the swampland next to him, the stodginess of the
underfoot, the viscosity of the bush, the stagnant water that pooled
in large holes that he just knew he'd fall into. *Fuck.* 'I should have
stayed home with Bonnie. What a fucking idiot.' He opened the
back of his car and took out a small shovel.

* * *

By the time Ned got through the marshland and to drier ground,
he was wet through with perspiration, his shoes sodden, and the
boar blackened and heavier from the mud he'd dragged it through.
He sat down next to the pig, the urge to lie flat too potent to deny.
He positioned himself, feet stretched out, his hands resting gently
on his chest and his head relaxed on the belly of the pig. He closed
his eyes and a moment later he was asleep.

When he woke, his eyes didn't open as wide as they usually
did. The swelling from his broken nose had spread under and over
his eyes. He looked through his compromised outlook at the sky.
It had darkened, the clouds had begun to roll over themselves,

gathering the humidity until the air inside them cooled enough to release the pressure. Rain. Lots of it. Ned could see it coming. He got off the pig and began digging.

The first foot was simple enough, soft soil that was displaced easily and he could throw from the shovel's blade. Beyond that it was hard. The soil was wet and stuck to the shovel, and the deeper he got the more water seeped up from underneath. The walls kept collapsing and filling in the hole. It was dusk before he dragged the pig into the grave. The water at the bottom of the hole submerged half its body. Ned filled it in as quickly as he could and then belted down the earth with the base of the shovel. Just as he finished, thunder rumbled to the side of him, the storm ready to burst over the swamp. He began walking, the swelling around his eyes heavy.

The rain started to fall with slow drops that were evenly spaced. Ned stopped, angled his head to the sky, opened his mouth and invited the rain in. He swallowed and could taste the vapour from the cooked tar in the bitumen that had risen up off the road. The volume of water increased quickly, and Ned had to turn his head from the sky to stave off the sting in the rain. He pushed forward, to the road and his truck.

Ten minutes later, he had to rest, his thighs burning, every step an effort to pull from the mud. More than once he'd toppled over. He sat on a felled eucalypt stump and rested his legs on a hillock of clay. He lifted his head again and drank directly from the sky. He swallowed and then looked out over the marshland. It was flooding, the road would be un-drivable for hours. He took his shovel and poked at the small hill of mud his legs rested on. His mind was cavernous, as though given a reprieve, instead concentrating on dispersing the lactic acid built up in his muscles and tissue and ligaments.

Ned didn't recognise the hand at first. It looked like a tree root, could have been just that given the proximity it was to the eucalypt stump he was sitting on. It wasn't until the rain washed away the mud over the fingernails that he knew it was a body.

* * *

It was pitch black by the time he'd uncovered both bodies. They had been buried on top of each other in a grave that wasn't more than three feet deep. The bodies were swollen and there were signs of decomposition. Their skin had begun to mottle with large clusters of discoloured patching. One of the men was big, tall and thickset; the other short and rotund. Ned couldn't smell as a result of his broken nose blocking his airway, but supposed by their decaying state that they'd stink. They were both clothed, their shirts and trousers caked in swamp muck so thick it was impossible to tell what was blood-stained or mud. Ned could tell though that both men had been beaten about the face, and both had been shot in the head. He looked closely at their faces and could immediately tell one of them was Lionel Frazier. The other, the larger man, he couldn't place.

Ned laid them beside each other, took off his shirt and placed it across their faces. He couldn't leave them. A mob of dingoes would sniff them out, or a drove of pigs. They'd eat them to nothing. A croc could cross the road and find them if it got the whiff. It'd drag them back into the swamp. Wedge them under a fallen tree. They'd never be found again. He sat against the stump, got as comfortable as he could and closed his eyes.

CHAPTER 12

NED WOKE AT dawn. The congestion in his nose had cleared a little and he could smell. The rain had stopped hours before and the marshland had begun to warm, its stink from the algae, fungi and bacteria living in the pools of stagnate water was overwhelming. If the bodies stank, it wasn't yet discernible over the stench of the swamp. Ned thought about dragging the bodies the rest of the way back to the road. But they were both heavy men. Too heavy. He moved as fast as he could back to the truck and radioed the station. He asked if Bonnie could be contacted and told that he was safe and well.

***

By midday the clouds had begun to gather over the swamp. The storm was going to come early. Gathered at the site was a television reporter with a cameraman at his side, a paperman from the *Northern Territory News* and most of the police officers from the town station. Bobby Clark was also there with a fire truck and small brigade. Ned stood away from the bodies, watched as they were photographed and prodded, and at one point dragged out of the sun to stop them blistering. Senior Sergeant Riley hadn't spoken to him. He'd looked at him, but Ned couldn't tell his mood. Not long after, Mayor Landry arrived. He looked rattled. His comb-over unfinished, as though rushed, his bald patch left uncovered at its base. And his face was ashen when every other man present was red from the sun and heat.

'You sleep out here?' Bobby Clark's shirt was wet through with sweat. 'Why? They're dead already?'

Ned could smell Bobby's breath, it smelt the same as the swamp, acidic and shitty.

'Dingoes, crocs.'

'Well, it's a fuckin' mess now, Potter.' Bobby motioned toward Landry.

Ned, exhausted, was powerless to filter his thoughts. 'How inconvenient.'

Bobby raised his brow. 'You're a smart arse, Potter.'

'Yep. You've said that before.'

Bobby smiled, shook his head and walked away, turning back to glare at Ned.

'You the one that found 'em?'

Ned turned from watching Bobby Clark. 'Yes, sir.'

'Ron Thompson, Northern Territory Coroner's Office.'

'Ned Potter.' Ned shook his hand.

Thompson was short and plump. His hands were particularly portly, and soft, his bespectacled face wrought in a constant state of deliberation. His fingernails were trimmed exactly, and there was a discernible economy about the way he spoke and the way he moved. He got down to his haunches and looked across the marshland toward both bodies. 'Someone got really lazy. They couldn't be bothered to drag them any further. Or they weren't strong enough.'

'I know one of them.'

'That right? What'd he do wrong?'

Ned shrugged and shook his head.

Thompson stood. 'Well, they didn't deserve this.'

'Gunshot?'

'I don't know.' Thompson shook his head, removed his glasses and cleaned them on the sleeve of his shirt. 'I can't imagine the type of person who does this and then goes about their life.'

Ned looked around, at the police, the firemen, the news reporter and paperman. 'They're among us. Somewhere.'

'I fuckin' hate this place.' Thompson walked away leaving Ned alone. Ned turned back toward the swamp and begun to dwell on what Thompson had said. Thompson had implied *murderers.* Ned knew of cruel people, either through stories or from his own observations of violent behaviour. Conduct he suspected was only a suggestion of what some people were capable of. But to *murder* someone and bury them? Ned felt uneasy as he watched Thompson squat beside both bodies, pulling back the shirt on one of them, poking the engorged flesh with the butt of a pen. Ned walked toward Thompson, settled beside him and looked over the bodies again.

'That's Lionel Frazier.' Ned pointed to the body.

'The white fella?'

'Yep.'

Thompson looked over the body of the larger man. 'He's a Kanaka.'

'What?'

113

'The big one here.' Thompson nodded at the larger corpse next to Lionel Frazier.

'I know him.' Ned's eyes widened. 'Well, I know who is. He's a boxer, he was with the tent at the show.'

Thompson bowed his head, and rubbed his brow with the back of his hand. 'Looks like he got the worst of it.'

'Can we get a word? I understand you're the policeman who made the discovery.' The news reporter held a microphone with a bright blue wind gag at its top. He wore a brown suit, had a neatly trimmed but thick moustache, and was followed by a cameraman who was complaining about the swamp mud sticking to his shoes. 'It's just for local.' The reporter held his bottom lip over the moustache to mop up the perspiration that was quickly filling it.

Ned looked around. He spotted Riley speaking with Mayor Landry away from the throng. He watched them closely. Landry stood with his hands in his pockets, but his posture and the speed with which his mouth was gobbing words suggested that he was doing all he could to appear calm.

'Please, just a few words.'

Ned turned back to the reporter just as the man's bottom lip again reached for his moustache.

'Okay.'

'Great! Let's go. What's your name?'

'Ned Potter.'

The reporter looked into the camera lens, and in the reflection adjusted his hair and straightened his necktie. He pulled Ned in close to his flank, and asked the cameraman, 'How's that?' The cameraman raised a thumb. 'Okay, in three, two, one.' The reporter began, 'We're here about fifteen miles south-west of Darwin, on the edge of a swamp, the scene of the grisly discovery of two dead men made by the man standing next to me, police officer Ned Potter. Mr Potter, what can you tell us about the dead men and how you came to find them?'

Ned cleared his throat and glanced toward Riley and Landry who were still talking. 'I hit a pig with my car, I came inland to bury it and stumbled across a shallow grave.'

'Have the men been murdered?'

'I don't know what happened to them.'

'I've heard here today that they were beaten.'

'They were dead, they were covered in mud. Like I said, I don't know any more than that.'

'What's your hunch on what happened?'

Ned took a moment. He knew his response, but the one that sat on the end of his tongue would have implications for him if voiced. 'I think they were.' He stopped. 'I think they were in the wrong place at the wrong time.'

'And they were killed because of that?'

'I can't say that. I can say they're dead, and they didn't die in a nice manner.'

'Thank you, Officer Potter.'

Ned walked away from the reporter, who continued to chew through his reportage. He felt good about his response. He knew there'd be trouble though. He stopped at the edge of the activity and watched how it was all evolving. The reporter was now trying to get a word on camera from Ron Thompson, though he was plainly dismissive. The fire brigade was clearing the brush surrounding the grave, and the paperman was folding over a full page of written observations on his notepad as he approached Mayor Landry.

'What were you doin' out here, Potter?' Riley approached quickly.

'A patrol. My job. I hit a boar and came into the marshland to bury it.'

Riley looked around at the scene. 'Why didn't you dump it in the fuckin' swamp?'

'It's illegal.'

'This is a mess! We got the paper here, the fuckin' TV. Jesus.'

'I woulda thought that'd be a good thing. More eyes on this the better chance we have of catching who's responsible.'

'You think, do ya? Wrong, Potter. All this attention is gonna make whoever did this clamp up like a poked arsehole. Or they're gonna run.' Riley looked at the bodies. 'Lionel fuckin' Frazier. Pisspot. And the other fella. He's some kind of an Abo.' Riley shook his head. 'He'll have a record, you watch.' He reached for the top pocket of his shirt, pulled out a packet of cigarettes, tipped it upside down and tapped its bottom edge. 'Fuck!' He threw the empty packet on the ground. 'Go home, Potter. You're way overtime.'

'I'm going to stay, sir.'

'You're off duty!' Riley raised his voice, and Ned watched a bead of sweat run from his forehead into his eye. 'Fuck!' Riley squinted, stung from the perspiration.

Ned considered an argument, but only for a second. He was tired, filthy and he wanted to see Bonnie and his daughter. And he knew by Riley's reaction, and the people at the crime scene, that the deaths weren't going to be dealt with in the same way Ernie Clay's had been. He was going to be able to investigate. Word would spread quickly. Scrutiny would be demanded by the media. It was a shit storm now. And there had to be two sides. By Riley's displeasure, Ned suspected some kind of cover-up may be attempted. If he hadn't stayed with the bodies and reported his discovery the night before, it may have been already in motion. But it was too big now. Riley was hobbled. Ned didn't have the clues as to what had happened to Lionel Frazier and the big Kanaka troupe boxer, but he had a hunch that Ernie Clay's death, and the pushback on its investigation, might be somehow tied to the new murders.

* * *

By the time he got home, Bonnie knew all about his discovery. She'd been watching the news on television just before he'd arrived home. She hugged him, and he held his daughter before showering. Afterward he sat on the end of his bed, a towel covering his waist. Bonnie entered. 'She's down.'

'Thank you for doing that. I'm exhausted.'

'Did the pig die?'

'What?'

'You said on TV you hit a pig.'

'I had to kill it.'

She kissed his cheek. 'I told you. You should have stayed home with me yesterday.'

'What?'

'We could have made love all day.'

'That was yesterday we were talking about that?'

'Yes.'

'Jesus Christ, that seems like a week ago.'

Bonnie sat down beside him. 'You looked very handsome on TV. Even with your broken nose. Made you look like a boxer.'

'Thank you.'

'What happens now?'

'Now I'm going to find out what happened. They can't cover it up. They can't stop me.'

Bonnie was worried, though.

Ned was sound asleep in their bed not long after dark. She lay next to him. Even in his sleep he frowned. His eyeballs scurried beneath their lids. She wondered what was playing out in his dream. She ran her fingers through his hair and gently spoke to him. 'Shhh. It's okay, Ned. I'm here. I'm with you. I'm always with you. I love you.'

CHAPTER 13

MAYOR LANDRY SAT behind the desk in his office, the colour in his face had returned and his hair was restructured so that no bald patch could be seen. Standing in front of him, Senior Sergeant Riley looked troubled, his width narrowed by the position of his shoulders, which were pinned high up and close to his ears. Landry looked directly at him. 'Someone got away?'

'Yes. He ran.'

'Fuck! Well, where is he?'

'I don't know. I wasn't there.' The tail end of Riley's declaration softened and could barely be heard.

'Jesus fucking Christ! I told you and that fuckin' ape Taylor. No bodies.'

'It must have got out of hand.'

'No shit, Senior Sergeant.'

'He wouldn't have survived.'

'Well, where the fuck is the body?' Landry snapped.

'Wherever he hid. He would have bled out.'

'How do you know?'

'I was told. Taylor.'

'You want to hope you haven't dug us all a fucking grave.' Landry's head fell in his hands.

'What about the parents?' Riley placed his hands on his hips.

'I've taken care of that. I told you I would.' Landry looked past Riley and through the window to a row of prawn trawlers moored in Darwin Harbour. 'We should have gone to sea with them.'

'Potter worries me.' Riley took his hands from his hips and folded his arms. 'I'll deal with him tomorrow. But we're accountable now. It's out. Every fucking state in the country will know about this in a day or so. Spotlight's gonna be bright here.'

'Find someone, Riley. And fast.' Landry stood from his chair. 'You know what I mean?'

Riley raised his brow. 'That might take a while.'

Landry raised his voice. 'We haven't got a while, this town will be crawling with news people from here to fuckin' Timbuktu. And they'll want answers. We feed them now. We don't and this is gonna get bigger by the fuckin' day. And we'll all be dragged into it. Mark my fuckin' words. Am I clear?'

Riley replied quietly, 'Yes. We're clear.'

'Keep me informed.' Landry walked from behind his desk, opened the office door and ushered Riley out. Not long after he drove to Darwin Hospital. Father McKay was asleep when he got there. Landry stood over the bed.

'He's been having nightmares.' Landry turned and a young nurse moved toward McKay. 'Wakes up screaming.'

'Right.' Landry watched her take his pulse.

'He rambles in prayer too. Guess that'd be proper for a priest. Kind of normal.'

'Yeah, well. Not sure God helps all of us.'

'It's awful good of you to come visit, Mayor Landry. You've been his only visitor aside from one or two older ladies from his parish.'

Landry looked down at the priest. 'Is he getting better?'

'Much. He was in a bad way when he came in.' The nurse placed a thermometer under the priest's armpit and waited. 'I know I shouldn't be asking this, but those two men found in the swamp. Were they murdered?'

Landry looked over McKay, at the cut on his cheek that looked too tightly closed with sutures. 'I don't know.'

'I saw an officer on television say he thinks they were.'

'He doesn't know anything. No one does. Not yet.'

'I'm sure there's some kind of a story for why they're dead.' She took the thermometer from McKay's armpit and held it to the ceiling light. 'Normal.'

She smiled at Landry as she walked from the room. He watched her out and then closed the door behind and went back to the priest's side. He looked down the length of his body, the shape it made beneath the covers, the pointy end of his feet. When he looked back up, McKay's eyes were open and focused on him.

'Go back to sleep.' The priest shook his head and Landry raised his eyebrows as a threat. 'Go to sleep.'

The priest reluctantly closed his eyes.

'I'll see you tomorrow.'

The priest listened for the sound of Landry's exit. And then opened his eyes and began to cry.

* * *

After he finished his shift, Bobby Clark went to the pub and by the time he got home, he was half drunk and so tired he could barely speak. Charlotte made a fuss of him, had his dinner ready on the table beside a cold beer, and afterward served ice-cream with apple pie.

She urged him to go to bed and then watched over him until he fell asleep. She shoved him, clapped her hands beside his ear and pinched the soft skin of his underarm. He didn't flinch. Charlotte had hidden a box of fresh dressing and pain relief tablets behind one of the brick piers that raised the house. She'd also prepared chicken sandwiches, a bowl of fruit and had filled a half-gallon flagon with cold water. She didn't turn the car headlights on until after she'd turned the corner of her street and was completely out of sight from the house.

When she got to the barn, Michael's eyes were closed, and his skin pallid. She dropped to her knees quickly and rested her head over his chest. It rose and fell, but his breathing was shallow. She didn't bother to wake him as she began bathing the wound on his abdomen, and then released the splint and re-secured it with a fresh bandage and clean piece of timber she'd pulled from a new fence built two houses down from her own. He woke while she was cleaning the cuts on his face.

'Where am I?' Michael spoke, still unable to form his words completely from the broken jaw that hung loosely to one side.

'You're safe but you've been badly injured.'

Michael tried to lift his head to look down at his torso.

'Don't move. Just rest.'

'When was it? When you brought me here?'

'A week ago. I've been back twice, tended to your wounds, and you've taken small amounts of water. You were delirious from the infection. You were barely awake.'

'I can't remember. Am I okay?'

122

Charlotte soaked the flannel she was using to clean his face in the bowl of water next to her. She wrung it out. 'Yes, you're going to be okay. I'll look after you. Your jaw will heal on its own.'

'They're gonna be looking for me.'

Charlotte took a cotton bud from the box she'd bought and dug into one of the cuts over his eye.

'Oewww.'

'Sorry, it's still full of swamp mud. If I don't clean it, it's going to turn septic.'

'My ankle.'

'It's broken, but I set it the best I could and it's in a splint.'

'You a nurse?'

'No. My mother was. She taught me a lot.'

'What's your name?'

'You've asked me a few times.' Charlotte smiled.

'Sorry I can't remember.'

'Charlotte.'

'I'm Michael.'

Charlotte looked down at him and directly into his eyes. 'Pleased to meet you. I'm truly sorry this has happened to you.'

'There's two other men.'

Charlotte soaked the flannel again. Silent.

'They'll be dead.'

'Yes. They've been found. I'm sorry.'

Michael looked stunned and shifted so he sat more upright. 'Where?'

'Not far from where you were.'

'Who found them?'

'A police officer.'

Michael took a deep breath and then lay all the way back down. 'Is it safe here?'

'Yes. I promise you.'

Charlotte took a moment before broaching the next subject.

'Have you been to the toilet?'

'Just water.'

'I'll dig a hole.' She pointed over to the opposite barn wall twenty feet away. 'Can you make it there?'

Michael looked over to the wall. He smiled. 'I guess I'll have to. I'll manage. I can drag myself backward I think.'

* * *

Charlotte left twenty minutes later, after she watched Michael eat and drink what he could. She helped him stand and then balanced him while he relieved himself into an old water jug she'd brought from home. She gave him two pain relief tablets and left four more. She told him she'd be back the following evening, though she didn't know how she was going to manage the lie to make that happen. She didn't yet know what the lie was going to be.

Driving home, she thought about scenarios that Bobby might agree to. To go see her father again. There was an evening mass every night she could say she wanted to attend. She could say she needed to see a doctor. There'd be questions on whatever she chose to lie about.

She turned away from the noisy mistruths and drifted into a reminiscence of her childhood. Though she cared for her father now, it had been tumultuous growing up with him. When he drank, he'd at times be violent with her mother. She'd seen him hit her. One of her earliest memories was watching her father on his knees, his mouth over her mother's as she lay still on the floor. It was only years later she recognised it to be resuscitation. She'd never brought it up with him. Or her mother. She didn't want to know why her revival had been necessary.

Her mother had been sad for as long as Charlotte could remember. She'd always appeared tired, and some weeks never got out of bed. It was then her father was at his most gentle with both of them. There were times when her mother was in hospital due to her melancholy. Her father would pack Charlotte's lunch, get her off to school and prepare dinner. Never did she hear him raise his voice during those times.

One Christmas afternoon, Charlotte had found her mother in her bedroom looking at a photograph of a baby. Charlotte supposed it was of her, but when she asked, her mother told her it was her sister. It was a frank response, leaving no space for it to be interpreted as a joke or a playful beginning to a silly conversation they might have. She told her that her sister had been born two years before her. That she had Down syndrome. And that they had sent her to a care facility under the recommendation of a doctor. Then told other family and friends it had been a stillborn birth. Her mother told her that she'd been heavily pregnant with Charlotte when her sister had died at the facility. The explanation had been respiratory failure. Many of Charlotte's questions about her mother's state were answered in the revelation.

Her mother died before her fortieth birthday. She had taken an overdose of codeine, slipped into a coma and never woke.

CHAPTER 14

'YOUR LEG LOOKS better today.' Charlotte carefully tightened the bandage around the timber splint. 'The swelling is going down.'

The colour in Michael's face was returning, the ashen shade of his skin had lifted and the yellowness of his eyeballs had softened.

'Why are you helping me?'

Charlotte didn't have an answer ready; she hadn't thought of her help being any more than what a decent person should do. 'Because you would have died.'

'There are people around here who would've let me do just that.' Michael winced as Charlotte lifted his broken leg to wrap the bandage beneath it. 'You said the other men had been found?'

'Yes.'

Michael turned his head to one side and looked over the scrappy decaying edges of the barn wall. 'What's happening with that?'

'There's been people from all over. TV people.' She lifted his shirt and looked at the wound on his abdomen. 'What happened here?'

'I must have been knifed. I didn't feel it though.'

'Your leg?'

'I did that runnin'. It got caught in mud and I twisted.' Michael moved on quickly. 'What's police doin'?'

'I don't know.'

He looked down at Charlotte as she pulled away the soiled dressing over his stomach. 'You married?'

'Yes.'

'You got kids?'

'No.'

'Where's your husband?'

Charlotte soaked a cloth in a bowl of antiseptic water she'd mixed. 'He's at work.'

'What's he do?'

She gently bathed the wound. 'You really need sutures for this.' She could see part of his intestine; it was dark red, which she knew was a good sign as it meant blood was still flowing through it. 'He just works odd jobs.'

'Fixin' things?'

'Yes.'

Michael lifted his head and looked down at his exposed wound. 'Are you from the Territory?'

'Yes.'

'You like it?'

'Some of it.'

'Which part?'

'The bush. The beach.'

'You fish?'

'I love to fish.'

'Yeah, me too.'

Charlotte smiled at Michael and then changed course. 'What about you? You married?'

'No. I had a woman but she died.'

'I'm sorry.'

'That's okay. She had some kind of cancer. In her blood. Took her quick. Months and she was gone. It's been two years.'

'Do you have children?'

'I have a little boy. He's eight.'

'Where is he?' Charlotte immediately felt anxious. The muscles through her neck tightened and she could feel her spine straighten. 'Sorry, I didn't mean to ask that, it just popped out. You don't have to tell me anything.'

Michael looked at her and she could feel his wariness. 'It's okay.'

Charlotte changed her position so she was more upright and on her knees. In the quiet that followed she began a new dressing and Michael drifted off to sleep. She looked over his body. His broad shoulders and the clear definition of his clavicles that angularly speared to a point at the top of his chest. She noted the size of his hands. They were muscular, like the rest of his body, forks and scurries of thick veins pushed out from under his skin. She supposed his grip would be strong. She looked down to his stomach, only partially covered by his shirt that she'd lifted to bathe his wound. She stopped at his navel and closed her eyes. The conflict she felt was quickly overwhelmed by her sense of starved intimacy. She peered down to the bony points of his hip bones, to the course trail of pubic hair breaching the rim of his trousers. She could see it beneath, limp and fallen to one side. She looked at it a long time and imagined herself reaching forward and touching it, pulling it out of his pants and stroking it until it was full of blood and hard.

She looked away from Michael and stood quickly.

* * *

Before she drove home, she left enough food and water to sustain him for a few days. She wasn't sure when she might be able to get back.

She drove slowly. She'd told Bobby that she was helping Father McKay and others at the parish chapel to clean the mildew from the pews. It was a job she'd done before and would take hours. Driving home, she switched off the car lights as she turned into her street, and then cut the engine when she knew she had enough momentum to glide into the curb space beside the house. She did this whenever the opportunity presented itself. There was a peculiar comfort to being unheard, not seen, as though she were sneaking through life unnoticed.

She saw the lights in the house were on. She stopped the car and looked into the window of a lit room. Bobby walked into the frame, a bottle of beer held close on his hip. She wasn't in any rush to go inside, and she was comfortable, even satisfied to wait in the car until Bobby went to bed. Charlotte stayed in the car until the lights in the house went out. She tried to be as quiet as she could when she entered. The kitchen was strewn with empty bottles of beer. She thought about cleaning it all up, but the tinkering and clanging of glass would be too loud and perhaps wake Bobby. She got into bed, and could smell soap on Bobby from his shower. She turned away from him, held the edges of her pillow tight and stayed awake until dawn, wondering about the messy sum of her life and where it may end. Her loveless marriage. The harbouring of another man.

* * *

She was out of bed before Bobby woke and cooked him breakfast. Fried eggs and sausages, and she squeezed a jug of orange juice and half filled it with cubes of ice. He emerged from the bedroom not long after she'd set the food out on the table.

'Looks wonderful.' Bobby sat, pushed his chair closer to the table and began to eat his sausages, his mouth open to cool the meat as he tossed it side to side. Charlotte watched, disgusted. He looked like a dog thrown a piece of scalding brisket, barely chewing it before swallowing.

'You clean those pews up?'

'Excuse me?'

'Last night, at the church?'

'Yes. We did. I'm going to see my father tonight. If that's okay?'

Bobby looked up from his breakfast. 'Again?'

'Yes, he's not well.'

Bobby nodded and went back to his food. 'Okay. Maybe we can go out tomorrow night?'

Booby looked back up from his food when Charlotte didn't respond.

She quickly found a smile. 'Sure.'

'You okay?'

'Yeah. Just a bit worried about my dad.'

'Yeah. Poor bastard.' Bobby shook his head and went back to eating.

CHAPTER 15

NED SAT ACROSS from Senior Sergeant Riley in the waiting room outside Mayor Landry's office. They didn't speak. Ned didn't even look at Riley but could feel his glare. And he could hear his tongue running across his gums, loosening the remains of what he'd just eaten. Riley shifted in his seat and made a sound as though he were in pain.

'Come in.' Landry poked his head through the office door.

'After you.' Riley stayed seated and Ned got off his chair and walked into the office.

They both sat opposite Landry's desk. The walls were decorated with framed photographs of Landry standing opposite other luminaries. There was a photo with him beside Australian Prime Minister Robert Menzies, and another of him shaking hands with Donald Bradman. Landry lit a cigarette and sat at his desk.

'Ned Potter.'

'Yes, sir.'

Landry flattened his comb-over and spat the loosened tobacco leaves from his cigarette. Ned watched them land in a tiny wet cluster on the table.

'Two dead men.'

'Yes, sir.'

'Did you know them?'

'Lionel Frazier, I knew of him. The other I'd seen. He was a tent boxer.'

Landry glanced at Riley, and then picked up a sheet of paper from his desk and read, 'Clarry Tallis. That's the other bloke. Big fucking Kanaka.' Landry held out the sheet of paper, inviting Ned to take it. 'Read it.'

Ned took the piece of paper and began to read while Landry rattled off parts of the rap sheet. 'Assault, theft, intoxication, illegal gambling. He should have been in jail.'

Ned looked up. 'Maybe. But he didn't deserve what he got.'

Landry pushed forward. 'And what did you know of Lionel Frazier?'

'He's a Pom. He worked as a groundsman and cleaner at one of the local schools. Like I said, I knew of him, but didn't know him.'

'How's that?'

Ned took a moment, then shrugged in a kind of surrender. 'I arrested him. For public drunkenness.'

Landry smiled. 'There ya go. He was a pisspot. So they were both criminals.'

'So the law says,' Ned replied evenly.

Landry sat forward, his cigarette delicately between his index and middle finger. 'Son, we have a real problem. The whole fucking country has its eyes on us, and we need to give them some answers. Make some arrests.'

'Yes, sir. I agree.' Ned sounded encouraged.

'What do you think?' Landry leant back in his chair.

'What do I think?'

'You found 'em.'

'And then you got on TV and told the country what you thought happened.' Riley did nothing to disguise his caustic tone.

'Is it my case?'

Landry and Riley looked at one another.

'What do you know?' Landry broke the blackened trail of ash from his cigarette with his middle finger.

'Well, we know they were beaten. And shot. Possibly post-mortem.'

'You're not a fuckin' coroner, Potter, you don't know that.' Riley threw the comment at Ned with such force that he ran out of breath on the last two words.

'Well, it was similar to what happened to Ernie Clay. Coroner thinks he may have been shot post-mortem.'

Landry peeped over at Riley.

'Jesus Christ, Potter,' Riley said. 'One has nothing to do with the other. I told you, Ernie Clay looks like he done himself in, these two could have come to grief any hundred different ways. Tallis was a violent prick and a gambler and Frazier a pisshead punter as well. They could have owed money to fuck knows who.' Riley's face was red and he'd broken a sweat.

'Well, we'll find out soon enough from the coroner.' Ned stayed firm.

'Okay, okay. Look.' Landry stood. 'Potter, we want to make an arrest. We want to look good here. It's important. I don't want the nation's media coming up here and makin' a whole big shit storm over the murder of two criminals. And as much as you might not like it, that's what they were. Fucking felons. And this, as Senior Sergeant Riley pointed out, could have been done by anybody.'

'So what do you want me to do?'

Landry and Riley looked at each other. 'This was done by a couple of blokes that had come into town for the show.' Landry sat back down and lit another cigarette. 'They're carnival people. Hustlers. Gamblers. Both have been in jail before. Theft, assault, public drunkenness. List goes on. They're violent men.'

'Both Tallis and Frazier gambled. We know that. It's quite sad, takin' money from their own families they don't have to take.' Riley did his best to sound sympathetic.

'Tallis and Frazier were seen with these men at a gambling house. They got into debt and couldn't pay. It got ugly.' Landry pawed at his comb-over.

'I don't believe that, sir. In fact, that's complete bullshit.'

'It's goddamn what happened!' Riley sprang to his feet and stood over Ned.

'Sit down!' Landry pointed at Riley, genuinely angry, his frustration incongruous with his usual appeasing disposition. Ned recognised it.

'Can I ask who these men are? The carnival folk?' Ned said.

'They're part of the boxing troupe.' Landry looked away from Ned to a nowhere spot in the office.

It stayed silent for longer than Landry and Riley were comfortable with, but they waited it out, until Ned spoke again.

'You can't do this.'

'You'll get to bring 'em in. You'll get the credit for the arrests. The whole investigation and the speed of the apprehension will all be awarded to you.' Landry smiled.

'I'll make you a plaque. So you can hang it in the office over your desk.' Riley smiled at Ned and then winked.

The inside of Ned's head felt light; the skin of his scalp tingled from the middle of his skull to beside his ears on both sides. It was a sensation he'd never experienced. He looked at both Landry and Riley as the feeling slowly dissipated and his head grew heavier. Until the weight overwhelmed him and his head fell onto his chest.

'You okay?' Landry smirked. 'You havin' a turn or something?'

'No.' Ned looked at the floor. At the grey carpet, his shoes and up to his socks that were revealed by the raised hem of his trousers as he sat. He looked at the pale colour of his skin on his lower legs, showing between his socks and pants, and at the patterned indentations left from where the socks had been sitting at one point. 'I can't do it.'

Ned heard Riley shift and mutter something.

'Well, you should reconsider that. This could be an incredible opportunity for your career.' Landry stubbed out a barely sucked cigarette and lit another immediately.

Ned looked up at them. 'This is wrong.'

'This is the Territory, Potter.' Landry's voice changed, its timbre deepened.

Riley, empowered, took it as an opportunity to stand.

'Can I ask, where are these men?' Ned looked back down at the floor.

'We have 'em.'

'How so fast? I only found the bodies a week ago.'

'The suspects stayed after the show left. They were picked up by two officers at the same gambling house they were seen with Tallis and Frazier. They were questioned and gave up some information. We got a touch lucky on this, Potter.' Landry tried on a smile.

'I can't believe this.' Ned shook his head. 'This is fucking bullshit.' He looked them both directly in the eye.

Landry's smile evened out. 'You have a day to make up your mind.'

Ned dropped his head; he could see the buttons of Riley's shirt holding in his gut, pulled hard against their fastening holes. Like they were choking. It made Ned feel nauseous. He stood without looking at either of them and walked out of the office.

* * *

He drove to the Victoria Hotel, and then sat in his car in conflict as to whether to do it. Whether to begin drinking and let it take him where it would. *Fuck it.* He got out, went inside and sat at his regular place. Katie Briggs had a cold schooner of beer for him not a minute later.

'You look like hell, Ned Potter.' She leant over from her side of the bar. Ned could smell the sweetness of tobacco on her breath.

'Shit of a day.'

'Had some news people in here last night. They were from Queensland. Lit up, the lot of 'em. They're gonna be here a while they said. Good for business.'

Ned took a lazy mouthful from his glass. 'They won't be here more than a few days.'

Katie smirked and leant in closer. 'What do you know, Ned?'

'I don't know a fuckin' thing, Katie.'

* * *

When Ned got home it was well past midnight and Bonnie was sitting at the table in the dining room drinking a beer with her father.

'Hey.' Ned smiled.

'You got a young wife and young daughter here.' Bonnie's father still held the curls and the cadence of his Irish accent. 'Pissin' up and not getting home at a reasonable hour, that's no good.'

Ned's instinct was to defend himself, but he looked at Bonnie. The whites of her eyes were red from crying and the skin underneath them was furrowed and dark grey. Her forehead looked longer with her hair pulled back tightly, and her nose looked broader. Her mouth was loose, and the length between her bottom lip and the end of her chin looked shorter. It was a face she'd not presented before, not that Ned could remember. He sat opposite her.

'I'm sorry. I had a bad day at work and needed to drink my thoughts away.'

'What happened?'

'They're gonna string up two men, say they did it. It's bullshit.'

'I thought you said you'd be able to investigate.'

'Nope. They're offerin' me the chance to bring the men in though.' Ned rubbed his eyes with the heels of both palms. 'They'll give me the credit for the arrests.'

Bonnie looked at her father in a way that signalled there was going to be a problem.

'Then take the credit.' Graham lit a cigarette, pulled back hard on its end and then gulped, ingesting all of the tar and nicotine in the smoke, filling his lungs until it burnt inside and he had to let it out. He blew the smoke over Bonnie's head toward an open window.

'They didn't do it.' The words fell loosely from Ned's mouth.

Graham nodded, as if to acknowledge and accept Ned's position. 'You want a beer?'

'Yes, please.'

Graham stood and walked to the fridge. He was a tallish man for his time. Just over six feet. His shoulders were broad and round, but he was slight through his breadth. Looked at from the side, he appeared slender. He had large hands, thick long fingers and bumpy knuckles that dipped and rose in the wrong places, squashed and broken from bare-knuckle fighting as a young man in Ireland. He wasn't dark though. Not like Bonnie. The Spanish had come from her mother.

Graham had come to the Australia with his young wife before the war. They'd sailed from Dublin and ended up in Sydney where Graham had cousins. He worked in a bar at Marrickville and, when the war broke out, he moved to find work as a mechanic. He and his wife went to Melbourne, and then, at the end of a cold winter, decided to move somewhere warmer. Graham had always held a fascination for the Territory. The ochre-coloured earth, the beauty of Ayers Rock, the immense gorges and untouched bushland. There wasn't anything in Sydney, or Melbourne, that seemed novel. Brown stone buildings, cobbled streets and too many people. Not unlike Dublin. But Darwin, *Fucking crocodiles, can you believe that*, he told his wife. *Now that's different.* Not long after, his brother Callum followed him, but the stifling humidity was too suffocating and he moved south to Brisbane.

'Where did you go?' Bonnie's voice was split with exhaustion.

'Just to the pub. Publican shut the doors and kept it open for a few of us. I'm sorry. Like I said, it was a shit day.' He reached for Bonnie's hand, took it and gently stroked it.

'Just … you need to take care of yourself, Ned. And us.' Bonnie squeezed his hand.

'Yes. I know.'

Ned slept off his inebriation. But it was disturbed and tortured sleep. He heard police sirens, saw unfamiliar faces against the bloody cloth of his closed eyelids. He dreamt in disconnected threads that were indecipherable, landscapes and scenarios changing arbitrarily. When he woke mid-morning, the bed was sodden with sweat where he'd been lying. He rolled onto his back and stayed still, feeling for a hangover. He was thirsty, but his head wasn't aching nor his stomach agitated. He took a deep breath and got stuck dwelling on his dreams. The people he'd never seen before in them were so vividly and exactly constructed. *What the fuck is that about?* he thought. *Who are they?*

He got up and showered, dressed and drove to the Fannie Bay Gaol where he asked to speak to the two men being held on suspicion for the murder of Clarry Tallis and Lionel Frazier. He told the young watchman he was the investigating police officer and the one who'd found the bodies. When he got to the cell, both men were asleep. They both woke when the iron gate was pulled open. They looked at each other, eyes wide. Escape, their first thought, their first contemplation. Ned saw it.

'Take it easy, boys.' He stepped into the cell. He turned to the watchman and signalled for him to close them in and leave.

'I'm Senior Constable Ned Potter.' Ned stood firm before them. Both men sat on the edge of their cots.

'And you are?'

'Fucked.' It was the larger of the two who answered. Taller and thicker set. And lighter in colour, his eyes greenish, his voice soft but resonant. Ned looked at him hard, and then the smaller man next to him. It was clear both men had Indigenous blood. 'I've seen you two before. You were with the boxing troupe.'

The larger man answered, 'That's right.'

'What's your name?' Ned smiled at him.

'Dell.'

'And you?'

'Andrew.' Andrew was older, balding through the middle of his scalp. The hair either side of the barren patch was tightly curled and unkept.

'Dell and Andrew.' Ned laughed, an attempt to put them at ease. 'Good names. Where you from?'

'North Queensland.' Dell rested his elbows on his knees and looked down at the floor.

'Okay. How long you been in Darwin?'

'Since the troupe came in.' Dell looked up.

'The troupe left, why did you stay?' Ned delivered the question in a prosaic fashion and without any suspicion attached.

'To fish. Gamble.'

'Yeah?'

'Yeah.'

'What do you guys play?'

'Cards.'

'Blackjack?'

'Sometimes.'

'What else?'

'Four card poker.'

'I never played that one. You roll dice. Craps?'

'No.'

Ned took a breath. 'Why are you here?'

'No one told us nothin' yet. We got picked up at a gamblin' house for bettin' and bein' drunk. But we weren't. Not pissed anyway.'

'They're gonna frame us for the murder of those two men.' Andrew stood up from his cot, agitated. 'We knew Clarry well. He boxed with us. He was our mate.' Fear was scrambled through his words and the high-pitched timbre of his voice.

'Hey, hey, take it easy. Sit down. It's okay. Please just relax.' Ned moved a step closer to the men.

Andrew sat back on his bed, looked at Dell and then back to Ned. 'We didn't kill nobody.'

'Why do you think you got blamed for these murders.'

Both men looked at each other. Dell shook his head. Ned stayed quiet. He felt the withdrawal of both men, their silent contract bound and understood by the other.

'Did you know the other man? Lionel Frazier?'

Dell shot Andrew a look. Again to stay quiet.

'Dell?' Ned shifted his focus.

'We didn't know him.'

'At all?'

Dell looked back down at the floor. 'No. First time we saw him was at the card game we were playin'.'

'You speak to him?'

'Everybody speaks to each other.'

'Anyone else there that night? Anyone you've seen since?'

Dell looked across at Andrew.

'Couple of white guys.' Andrew ran a hand through one side of his wild hair. He was nervous. 'They were there when we got pinched two days ago.'

'You mean policemen?' Ned sat straighter.

'Yeah.'

'Same guys who arrested you?'

Andrew continued, 'They didn't put the cuffs on, but they were there. They pointed us out.'

'Shut up, Andrew. We're not sayin' anythin' else.' Dell folded his arms, lifted his head slightly.

Ned waited in the dead air. He looked at Andrew with an expression to let him know he wanted him to continue.

'We're done.' Dell pushed himself to the head of the bed and lay down. Andrew looked at Ned, scratched the bald middle of his scalp and then pulled at both ends of his hair either side of it. He did it over and over again, the faintest of moans escaping his mouth.

'Go back to sleep, Andrew.' Dell's tone clearly made it a command not a suggestion.

Andrew crawled to the head of cot and lay down as he had been told. Ned sat and waited. Dell fell quickly into sleep, a bass-toned snore that was felt through the concrete floor and walls, satisfying Ned his senses had been turned off. Ned could hear Andrew breathing quickly and could see the rise and fall of his chest.

'You scared, Andrew?'

'I'm not speaking anymore.'

'Dell is asleep.'

Ned watched as Andrew slowly turned to his side and looked at Dell.

'He's asleep. He's snoring. You hear that?'

'I don't hear very good. Got burst eardrums from boxing.'

'Did these men, the ones who were murdered, did they owe you money?'

'No.'

'Did anything happen at the card game? Any fights? Arguments? Anything like that?' Ned kept his volume not much past a whisper.

'No.'

Ned looked over at Dell, his sleep interrupted by a gasp for air. He then flipped quickly to his side facing away from them. Ned waited until Dell's snoring built momentum again and he could feel the rumble under his feet. 'Did you hear anything there? Any stories. Something you might think would get someone in trouble if it got out.'

Andrew rolled onto his back and pulled at his hair again, and then moved to his stomach.

'Andrew?'

Andrew lifted his head from the mattress. 'I'm not sayin' anything else.'

A minute later Ned signalled to the watchman from behind the cell bars. When the gate opened, Dell woke and sat up, the same expression, the same contemplation of escape.

* * *

Ned drove back out by Tabletop Swamp where he'd found Ernie Clay in a shallow bog. He got out of his car and walked to the edge of the marshland. He thought back to the conversation he'd had with Martha Clay. She'd said they'd *killed him because he saw*. And then she asked him to leave it be. Dell and Andrew didn't see anything, but Ned thought they may have heard something. He didn't know what though. *Had they heard who killed Ernie Clay? Who killed Clarry Tallis and Lionel Frazier? Or had they heard why they were killed? Did they know what Ernie Clay had seen? Or were they just the nearest and most accessible to pin it on? Or,* Ned thought, *perhaps they did do it.*

* * *

He got home on dark. Kissed Bonnie on the cheek while she stood over the stove frying fish, and then went into the nursery to look down over his daughter in her bassinet. She was asleep with her arms raised either side of her, as though in surrender. Her head was turned to one side, her cheek covered with tiny clusters of milk pimples turning her flesh red. He ran his forefinger across the irritations to check their heat. She was cool. Dried sweat held her wisps of blonde hair together in pointy ribbons that settled over her ears and face. Her bottom lip was turned slightly inside out, her mouth open. Ned smiled, touched her bottom lip with the point of his finger. She stirred and Ned pulled his finger away. He laughed when he watched her mouth searching blindly for the end of his finger. He couldn't help himself. He reached down again and let her take its end. She sucked hard, her eyes opening.

'What's your name?' Ned whispered, the end of his finger tickling, his daughter pulling harder to find milk.

'Who are you?' He took his finger from her mouth and her eyes stayed open. It took a moment for her to focus, and when she did, she smiled. Ned laughed. 'There you are.' He buried his nose beneath her tiny chin and took a deep breath. He pulled back and looked at her. 'You smell like roses. What has Mummy rubbed on you, eh?' He did the same thing again and took a deeper breath, then looked at her and gave her the tip of his finger. 'Rose Potter. That sounds like a nice name. Shall we ask Mum?'

CHAPTER 16

NED SAT ACROSS from Ron Thompson. The coroner's office was nothing more than a half partition wall in the corner of the small morgue. Ned could see the stacks of mortuary fridges, three high and eight deep. Thompson was on the phone chewing through a litany of medical speak. Ned had switched off after Thompson began explaining how *the urethra had been split*. He looked at the mortuary fridges and considered who might be inside them. The bodies of men and women, perhaps children, allowed by their families to be taken away and cut open to determine how they met their end. It seemed so impersonal. A stranger performing the autopsy. Ron Thompson. And usually done with the help of others. He wondered what the discussion might be around the opened body while they dissected and dismembered it. Jokes? Conversation about their planned holidays, or conflict with wives or girlfriends? Or banter that might be crass and aimed at the shape and condition of these dead people. But they weren't people anymore, Ned reasoned, they were bodies, corpses. Cadavers. And while the families of these dead mourned, the dead's bodies, their vessels, were prone in a fridge waiting for autopsy or burial. Or a furnace.

'Got ya blokes on the slab over here.'

Ned turned to Thompson, then motioned to the mortuary fridges.

'They full?'

'Yep.'

'Jesus Christ.'

Thompson looked over at them. 'Seventy-five per cent black.'

'Why?'

'No money for hospital. No money for medicine. They die of flu, chest infection, pneumonia. Simple shit that gets fixed with tablets or an injection.'

'Kids in there?'

'Two. An infant and a three-year-old. Both dead from measles.'

'Fuck.'

'Your boys though, they didn't die from measles.' Thompson stood up. 'Come and I'll explain.'

As they walked, Thompson fired questions at Ned. 'When you found them, what did you see?'

'Not much. They were caked in swamp mud. I could barely make out their faces. I saw what you saw when you got there.'

'They dressed them.' Thompson raised his glasses higher on the bridge of his nose.

'What?'

'What they did to them, they did it while they were shirtless. Then they dressed them.'

'Why?'

'I assume they hoped the clothes would cover the stench until they rotted. That's all I can come up with. Come and have a look.'

Clarry Tallis and Lionel Frazier were laid flat out next to each other on separate stainless-steel tables. The area around them was thick with a smell of pickles. Ned covered his mouth and nose. 'What's that smell?'

'Formaldehyde.'

Frazier had a single gunshot wound to the back of his head and another through his chest. His torso was mottled with bruises and his nose and jaw were visibly broken. His septum was bent and squashed to one side and his lower mandible hung loosely, his bottom row of teeth separated and his gum line split at the point of fracture. Thompson put on rubber gloves and the slapping sound of taut rubber rebounding off the thick concrete walls made Ned's head ring.

'Frazier got off okay. No stab wounds. The gunshot to the chest is how he died. It severed his aorta. He bled out. The shot to the back of his head was post-mortem.'

'Same as Ernie Clay.'

'And same as Clarry Tallis.'

Ned looked over the body of Clarry Tallis. His torso was punctured with three stab wounds, the flesh white inside and the skin on the outer was outlined by deep bruising, closer in colour to black than purple. There was a gash just beneath the fold of his pectoral muscle that was wider and looked deeper than the others. 'That what killed him?' Ned pointed to the wound.

'You'd think so, but no. That was post-mortem.' Thompson pointed at the gunshot hole in place of Tallis's left eye. 'And it wasn't that either. Also post-mortem. He died …' Thompson took a breath, hooked his arms under Tallis's mid-back and upper thighs, and rolled him over.

Ned took a step back. 'Fuck.'

Thompson looked at Clarry Tallis's back, his face chewed up in horror at the savagery that had been left. There were long cords of distended flesh that had opened up in the miring swamp humidity the morning the bodies had been found. The flaying was at all angles and there was hardly a wound that wasn't cut by another lash from another direction. His back looked like the carving of a roadmap with intersections and wide carriageways.

'This killed him.' Thompson took a step back from the table. 'Sixty-two times. That's how many lashings there are. In some places it's down to the bone, the backside of his ribs. And beyond. His lungs, both of them, were punctured. He suffocated.'

Ned stood speechless.

Thompson took off his rubber gloves and placed them on the table next to Frazier.

'What was he whipped with?'

'There were fragments of leather all over his back, inside the wounds. Whatever was used was thick and heavy.'

'Fuckin' animals.' Ned gritted his teeth, a kind of tick that overcame him when he was angry. His brothers would deliberately tease him when he was younger until the tick showed itself and they'd laugh and call him a *bulldog*.

'You got any ideas?' Thompson undid the top button of his shirt and loosened his tie.

'I don't know the kind of person who's capable of this.' Ned swallowed and could taste the pickly essence of formaldehyde.

Thompson looked over his glasses at Ned. 'Stinks of real hate. Something this violent. This abhorrent. They shot them both in the head post-mortem. And they stabbed Tallis post-mortem.'

'Does that mean something?'

Thompson took his glasses off and began cleaning them with a handkerchief from his trouser pocket. 'I studied behavioural science before I did pathology and pre-med. It's a pack type behaviour. The men are dead; someone, usually a subordinate, feels like they have to contribute above and beyond to earn their stripes, so to speak. My guess would be that's what happened.'

'To earn respect?'

'As disgraceful as it is to associate the word respect to an act like this? Yes.'

'But why? To do this to a person. Whatever these men did, it doesn't add up to how they died.' Ned found himself staring at the back of Clarry Tallis. The opened lashings blurred into a fuzzy mix of purple and white colours.

* * *

That evening Ned ate dinner and nursed baby Rose to sleep. He hardly spoke a word to Bonnie. She could tell he was troubled and was anxious that he might drink. She asked him not to if he was at all considering it. Ned bit his tongue, but it was difficult, his anger had gathered momentum during the day, until it had consumed his every thought by dusk. He was playing out scenarios. Bonnie's request that he refrain from drinking wouldn't have usually unsettled the influence he had over his temper. But it had been an extraordinary day. He had seen things inflicted upon humans that he'd never be able to unsee. It would always be there, the trauma of seeing it, the assumptions and suppositions of how the slaughter played out, the undeniable and certain terror of those men, what they might have been thinking during such an ordeal. The last moments before death. And the images of them dead and broken and torn would be presented in his mind's eye whenever the trauma chose.

As much as he felt like a drink, he refrained. He went to bed early, drifted off to sleep and dreamt wildly. The dreams were violent and illogical, he fought with his father, yelling at one another in a foreign language. He saw the pig he'd run over, scampering through the reedy knots of the swampland, a chortle rather than a grunt being pushed through its snout. It was as though it were laughing.

CHAPTER 17

CHARLOTTE HAD FINISHED bathing Michael's wounds, had tightened the splint on his leg, and she'd eaten with him. She'd made roast chicken sandwiches with lettuce, and made certain the chicken had been pulled apart into thin strands so that Michael was able to chew without too much pain from his jaw. And she'd bought him two bottles of soft drink. He was midway through the second one, when he asked her again, 'Who's your husband?'

Charlotte was reluctant to speak Bobby's name. To have it included in the conversation and the moments she was enjoying with Michael. 'Doesn't matter.'

Michael studied her, could see her averseness to answer and moved on. 'The soft drink is nice.'

Charlotte smiled at him and then gently asked, 'Your boy?'

'Yes?'

'You must miss him?'

'Yeah. All the time.'

She noticed Michael's chin quiver and she decided to stop asking, worried where it might lead, to him closing up and becoming quiet. An end to the pleasure she was experiencing while talking to him.

'What about your other family?'

'Mum and Dad are dead. Two brothers. One here. One in Brisbane.'

'They'll know you're missing?'

'By now, yeah.'

'Do you want them to know you're okay?'

'No!' Michael's voice lowered and he lengthened the word until it finished with a gravelled quaver, like the tail end of a tenor's note sung in vibrato.

Charlotte's whole body flinched.

'I'm sorry,' he said, 'I didn't mean to say it like I did. Didn't mean to scare you. If someone knows, anyone, they'll talk. Won't be able to help themselves with such good news. And we all drink. Too much. It'll slip by and the wrong person's gonna find out … but thank you for askin'. Comes with a lot of courage to help me out like this.' He smiled at her and extended his hand.

Charlotte looked at it, smiled back and very gently took it. Only for a moment, but it was enough for her to feel as though she'd won some trust.

* * *

She watched him go off to sleep, collected the bottles and drove out from the barn. When she got home, Bobby was watching television. She was quiet, hoping for as few questions as possible. But he was quiet too, and it was Charlotte who felt compelled, part by paranoia, part by habit, to ask, 'How was work?'

'Good. Bit quiet.'

'Okay. Well, I'm going to bed.'

'How was your dad?'

Charlotte stopped her advance to the bedroom. 'He was good. Remembered who I was the whole visit.'

Bobby let out a huff covered with some laughter. 'Silly ol' bastard.'

'He said to say hello.'

'Bullshit, love. He never really liked me.' Bobby turned from the television to Charlotte. He was smiling. 'It's time we had that baby.'

Charlotte's stomach turned in on itself, she felt light-headed, as though she'd stood up too quickly after being prone for a long time. She wasn't expecting this declaration tonight. It was as though her whole body had registered and then rejected what he'd put forward. The idea of sex. Her body had told her, *No, we're not doing that.*

'What do ya think?'

'Yes ... But we've tried.'

'We try again. And again, until it works.' Bobby sounded energised, even determined. 'Well?'

'Okay.'

Bobby's smile broadened. 'You need to go see the doctor again, find out when your eggs are gonna be ripe.'

'Okay.'

Bobby turned from her and back to the television.

Charlotte left the room and stopped in the hallway leading to the bedrooms and bathroom. She leant forward, her forehead resting on the wall. She could smell the lemon-coloured paint, and the mud from beneath the house that was rising up through the split and rotting floorboards. She thought again about just disappearing from her life. Seriously and without skipping past the actualities of what such a vanishing would lead to. A police search. And how long Bobby would look for her and what might prompt him to stop. *Time? Or another woman? Maybe*, she thought, *he'd never stop.* There were obstacles in the way of her new and imagined life. And there was also the reality that she couldn't leave town while her father was in care. She continued into the bedroom, lay on her bed fully clothed, closed her eyes and remembered the feel of Michael's hand when he'd taken hers.

CHAPTER 18

NED WOKE UP in the morning before dawn and told Bonnie he was going fishing. He took a rod and a tub of frozen school prawns and walked to Casuarina Beach. He arrived just as the sun was breaching the horizon, the sky above it mottled by skinny layers of pink and orange cloud, and over that the blackness of night fading to shades of dark blue. He stood at the edge of the shoreline, the water still, not a breath of wind, the tide immobile. It was rare to catch it this way. It would only stay still for a minute, maybe seconds, before it began moving in the opposite direction. Ned loved to look over the stillwater when he caught it. He was used to the large tides of the Territory constantly moving. At times it made him anxious, the sea in a constant drag either side of itself, as though it couldn't settle and take a moment to relax, just to be still and calm. For the creatures underneath to have respite from battling against the current, to move freely on their own steam instead of being pushed along at a pace that probably made a fish nervous. Ned imagined a fish with its eyes wider than normal, too tired to swim against the current, instead letting it take them, trying to manoeuvre through reedy dark holes that housed predators. At times, the whole Territory felt like that to Ned. If you weren't big enough then you'd tire of the struggle and eventually be eaten. A croc or a shark. Or one of the fat white men made plump by the hundreds of thousands of fish battling the tides. *Still water*, he thought. That's what the place needed more of.

He threaded a shank hook with the middle part of a prawn that was still part frozen. He cast out over the water and a moment later the tide turned and the water rose above his feet and scurried in a bubbly rush up the beach. Holding his rod loosely against his hip, he thought of Dell and Andrew, still in jail without having been charged. But today was the day.

He replayed what he'd told Riley and Mayor Landry, that he couldn't do it. That he wouldn't walk those men into an ambush of media. He'd said it without an alternative, a plan to do something else. He wasn't in the position of power to release them, he didn't have any other suspects, and if he was honest with himself, he didn't know for certain they didn't do it. He didn't believe for a minute they did, but he couldn't prove that, and so in the realm of possibility, it was in fact a possibility. He thought about asking Riley and Landry for an extra day to come up with something else, but he had nothing. He thought about lying, saying he'd found the weapon used to split open the back of Clarry Tallis. That he had it hidden. But it was all fanciful imagining that he wasn't going to follow through on. They'd made up their minds and if he wasn't going to present Dell and Andrew to the town later that morning, they'd get someone else to do it and find a way to push him to the side.

They'd offered it to him only because he'd found the bodies, had spoken to the press and expressed his opinion that they were dead from *being in the wrong place at the wrong time*. They needed to put him back out there, have him say it was over and that, *yes*, he'd been right, it was a murder but they'd found those responsible. It'd get closed quickly, the national press would leave, and perhaps not return for the trial. Dell and Andrew weren't a big story. They were both convicted criminals who were involved in illegal gambling. What was news was what Ned supposed. That Ernie Clay's murder was connected. These men all knew something. Ernie, Clarry and Lionel. And Dell and Andrew were going to pay for what those men knew.

With no other course of action to set the men free, Ned settled on doing what he'd been offered by Landry and Riley. He thought that, given the opportunity to see them again, he could perhaps drill for information on what they both might have been keeping quiet on. Anything that might offer a clue as to why Ernie, Clarry and Lionel had been killed. And he'd continue to dig on his own time if need be.

He looked over the Timor Sea, the sun lifting higher by the minute, the blackness of pre-dawn gone and the sky now cloudless and made soft orange by the sun.

* * *

Dell and Andrew stood beside each other, handcuffed. Ned stood in front of them.

'Where are we goin'?' Andrew's eyes had widened since Ned last saw him, and his tight curly hair had been shaved so it sat against his skull either side of his bald patch.

'You're being charged with the murder of Lionel Frazier and Clarry Tallis.'

'No shit.' Dell shook his head. 'This is bullshit.'

'They're gonna hang us.' Andrew shuffled on the spot and closed his eyes tightly. 'I need to shit.'

'Hold it in.' Ned sounded cold, though he felt sick, about to walk them out in front of media and a small crowd. There was an indulgent kind of pageantry about it all that was backward. It was like the town was about to burn a witch, or hang the accused in the town square, sell tickets to it, and drink beer and cheer when they heard their necks break. Ned wanted to drink, to anaesthetise himself from the noise that was building to a crescendo in his head. *You're weak, you're nothing but words, this is wrong, you know it's wrong.*

'Potter. The good senior constable.' Riley was smiling as he entered the jail. Ned couldn't bear to look at him. Riley pushed up close to him and Ned felt the solid roundness of Riley's paunch against his forearm. 'You're doing the right thing, Potter,' he whispered in Ned's ear. Landry walked in, shook Riley's hand and then walked toward Dell and Andrew. He stopped a foot short of them, looked them up and down and then turned to Ned, who was still beside them.

'Good work, Senior Constable Potter.' Landry then raised his chin and glared at Dell. 'Do you have a family?'

'Yeah.' Dell stood tall, his face stern, his skin shiny with a film of sweat.

'And how are they going to manage with you in prison for life, huh? Or dead by hanging?'

'They'll be okay. Always have.'

Landry raised his brow at the tone of Dell's reply. 'Well, that's a position they wouldn't be in if you'd decided on an honest life. Am I right?'

Dell looked Landry square in the eye. Made no attempt to cloak his contempt and made certain his words were drawn out and as caustic as he could manage. 'Fuck you, cunt.'

Landry looked over at Riley for him to do something. He took the baton from a holster on his hip and rapped Dell hard across the backside of his thighs. He dropped to his knees, but in silence. Ned bent over and helped him back to his feet. 'Leave him be.'

Riley threaded his baton back through its enclosure.

Landry then turned to Andrew. 'And what about you? Have a family?'

Andrew shuffled on the spot again, his eyes closing tightly. He looked like a child having a tantrum.

'I asked you a question, son?'

Ned smelt it first and looked away. 'Jesus Christ.' The words came softly from his mouth and he could feel the skin across his forehead fold into a wavy stack.

'I'm sorry.' Andrew kept his eyes closed.

Landry smelt it then and took a step back. 'You dirty bastard.'

The stink reached Riley and he took his baton to Andrew's legs. He fell to the ground and began to cry. Dell looked down over him. 'It's okay, Andrew. Get up.'

'I wanna go home!' Andrew looked up at Dell, his face overwhelmed with fear.

Ned hated himself. Passionately. In that moment he wanted to step out of his own flesh and run away to somewhere no one would ever find him. But he stood there, watching a man so consumed by fright and panic that he'd shit his own pants.

'Christ almighty, clean him up.' Riley walked away with Landry back to the jail entrance.

* * *

Ned waited in the bathroom while an uncuffed Andrew cleaned himself up.

'My undies?'

'Leave them in the toilet. Someone will take care of that.'

'I'm sorry.' Andrew walked out of the toilet, his shoulders held high, narrowing his frame, his hands held tightly against his body. Everything about him, the contracted frame, his cowed expression. It was shame. It broke Ned's heart to see it. A man, who he believed innocent, emasculated and humiliated to the degree where he felt shame of himself.

'Wash your hands.'

Andrew turned on a tap and rubbed his hands quickly around a worn cake of soap. Ned watched him, he was thorough, rubbing the webbing of both palms against the other, washing the front sinewy sides of his hands.

'Okay, Andrew. That's enough.' Ned tore a piece of paper from the dispenser beside the sink and handed it to Andrew.

'Thank you.'

Ned looked around the bathroom quickly to check they were alone and out of earshot of anyone else. 'Is there anything you can tell me? Anything at all? Anything Dell doesn't want you to say? Because this is it, Andrew. You're going to be charged with the first-degree murder of two men.'

Andrew dried his hands thoroughly.

'Anything?' Ned pressed, his desperation cutting through the question so it sounded like he was pleading.

Andrew took a moment and tossed the paper he'd dried his hands with into a small bin. 'The white fella saw somethin'. He was pissed and told Clarry. That's what we heard before we found out they were killed. Before they picked us up.'

'What did they see?'

'I don't know.'

'Hurry up, Potter, get this boy squared away and get out here.' Riley tapped on the door. 'Now! C'mon, let's go.'

Ned opened the door for Andrew and motioned him to go through.

* * *

Waiting outside were the press from almost every state in the country. Riley led Ned, Dell and Andrew out. He was smiling, answering questions on the run as they were fired by newspaper men and TV reporters like rounds from a Gatling gun. It was rapid and excitable, Dell and Andrew blinking and momentarily blinded by the popping of camera flashes. Ned helped them into a police wagon, and it drove away, sirens blaring, as if to announce to all it passed that inside were the culprits. The murderers. That the job was done. The press converged on Ned, Riley and Landry.

'This is who you wanna talk to. Senior Constable Potter. Found the bodies and then the men responsible.' Landry put an arm across Ned's shoulder.

'How did you find them, Senior Constable Potter?'

Ned couldn't see where in the media scrum the question had come from. 'Ah, we just followed through on some leads. Ended up gettin' a bit lucky.' Ned looked at Landry, self-loathing overwhelming him for parroting how Landry had described the unfurling of the arrests to him only days before.

'Do they deserve the death penalty, Senior Constable Potter?'

Ned looked at the reporter as though to admonish him for asking the question. 'I don't know. I'm not a judge or jury.'

'But you saw what these men did. It was brutal, isn't that true?'

Ned looked over the small crowd that had gathered. Landry watched him closely and when he didn't answer, he did it for him. 'They'll get what they deserve, you can count on the judicial system to do just that.'

Ned continued looking over the crowd. There was no outrage, no family members of Lionel Frazier or Clarry Tallis shouting at the accused, baying for retribution.

'Senior Constable Potter, do you believe you have made Darwin a safer place?'

'Of course he has.' Landry didn't wait for Ned to respond and a moment later Ned turned and walked away from the media to a corner beside the jail. He watched Landry continue, and Riley began to field questions. He looked past them, and when he did, he saw Martha Clay just as she was turning to walk away. They caught each other's eye before she moved off. Ned thought about following her, but instead watched her closely, wondering if she'd turn around again to see where he might be. Whether he was following her. He waited, and just as he was about to turn away himself, she swung slowly and looked at him squarely. Involuntarily, he waved.

* * *

Ned didn't go back to the station to watch Dell and Andrew being formally charged. He went straight to the Victoria Hotel and shoved the thoughts of upsetting his wife somewhere where they wouldn't become a story and then a scenario of consequence. It was so crowded. In his mind. Alcohol would deliver a reprieve, an opportunity for him to be present, to turn his head noise down.

It was not long after midday. Outside, the heat had begun to sweat as cumulonimbus clouds over the Timor gathered and suffocated the dryness of the sun. There was a storm coming. Ned could smell it, the sharp stank of petroleum oil boiling in the road tar made its way through every split in the bar's floorboards, every worn-through crevice in the windowsills and panes. Katie Briggs was wearing a summer dress that turned transparent when hit by the shards of sunlight coming through the windows. Ned watched her pouring beer, her weight on one side of her hip, a buttock pushed out, round and right before him. She looked over at him and smiled, changed the weight of her posture and set a glass of beer on the bar for another customer. She walked over to him. 'Ned Potter. What do ya know?'

'Not a thing.'

'You want a beer?'

'And a shot of vodka'

Katie raised an eyebrow. 'You okay?'

'No. Not really.'

'You want to talk about it?'

'No. Not really.'

Katie nodded, turned and dipped to her haunches, opening a bar fridge. Ned watched her; her thighs splayed as she reached for a frosted schooner glass. He thought about sex with her, and how her thighs would feel over his crotch while he fucked her. He could feel an indifference for life overcoming him. He couldn't bear the thought of himself. Impotent. Cowardly. Nothing. Self-destruction was not only appealing, it was deserved. Cheating on his wife, fucking Katie Briggs, *might* be essential to begin the unravelling, the annihilation of his life.

'There ya go.' She placed the full glass on the bar.

'And the shot.'

'Oh yeah.' She smiled from the corner of her mouth.

* * *

An hour into Ned's stay, a man pulled up a stool and sat to his left. He was short, his hair fair and neatly combed, his nose narrow, his shoulders rolled over his chest, his hands trembling slightly. Ned watched him order a double Scotch straight in a short glass. Between mouthfuls his head fell between his forefinger and thumb and rested there. Ned, buzzed by the beer and vodka, didn't think at all before saying, 'Someone's always got it worse than us, mate.'

The man turned to Ned, and it was then he saw that he was crying. 'Shit, I'm sorry.'

The man's head fell back to its groove in his hand, and he pulled back through his nose on the saliva and snot that had come with his quietened sobbing. 'It's okay.' He lifted his head and took a mouthful of his Scotch. 'Just havin' a bad day.'

'We all have 'em.'

The man sat upright, took a handkerchief from his trouser pocket and wiped his eyes. Ned extended his hand. 'Ned Potter.'

The man turned and looked directly at him, and Ned recognised some kind of an appeal for help in the shape of his face. 'I'm David O'Shea.' He took Ned's hand and shook it.

'What do you do here in Darwin, David?'

'I've got a store. Boots and leather. Bags. What about you? You're a cop?' David pointed at Ned's uniform.

Ned nodded, and David took a long look at him and then threw his head back in recognition. 'Yeah, I saw you on TV, right?'

'Maybe.'

David turned toward the bar. 'They were murdered? Those men in the swamp?'

'Yep.'

David looked at Ned, his eyes half closed and swollen from crying. 'And you caught 'em, huh? The killers?'

'Yeah. I caught 'em.'

'Well, this is a celebration then.' David signalled to Katie Briggs. She walked over, her eyes firmly on Ned. 'Another round on me, this man here caught the men responsible for those murders.'

'That right?' Katie pressed Ned.

'If he says so.'

'You don't seem too happy about that, Ned.' Katie waited for a response but got nothing except Ned's dead glare. She left to fix the drinks.

'What about you, David? Why were you cryin'?'

David slumped forward to face the mirror over the bar, its reflection interrupted by fishing trophies and saloon clutter that had accrued over years and years. 'I sold out. I sold my little boy out. I abandoned him.' He turned back to Ned. 'I failed him.' He began crying again.

Ned watched carefully, David's head falling back between his forefinger and thumb. He probed carefully. 'What happened?'

'I can't talk about it.'

'Sure ya can.'

'No! I can't!' David's face turned red, his cheeks trembled and spittle flew from the corners of his mouth. He held his breath and made an ungodly sound that was twisted by agony, pitching high and then low, as though his voice was in panic, scrambling for somewhere safe to hide.

'Okay.' Ned tried to calm him.

'I can't tell anyone.' David lifted his head and stood quickly. 'I have to go.' He turned and walked out, and Ned watched him through the bar window break into a run while crossing the road.

He looked over to Katie who'd been watching it unfold. 'You seen him before?'

'Last couple months. He's been here most days.'

'He tell you anythin'?'

'I got bit and pieces. What I can gather, his son was beat up or somethin'.'

'Said he sold out.'

'I don't know what that means. He comes here, gets drunk, cries and talks to himself and that's how I know what I know.'

Ned looked back out the window to see whether he might be loitering close by. He had a hunch and wanted to talk to David O'Shea some more.

'So, you found those men, huh? The murderers.' Katie leant over her side of the bar. Ned could smell her, her cigarettes and perfume minced together.

'No, I didn't find 'em. I just turned 'em over to be charged.'

'Did they do it?'

'No. They didn't.'

'You're sure?'

'Yep. I am.' He took a mouthful from his glass. 'You look particularly pretty today.' Ned said it flatly, without a smile.

'You're on a path to no good, Ned Potter.' Katie said it slowly. But she looked him squarely in the eye. 'You're married. So am I.'

'Yeah. Happily most days.'

Katie paused, her brow furrowed. 'He's away.'

'Is he?'

They looked at one another, wordless, until a patron down the bar whistled at Katie. Ned, now present, his mind clear of self-loathing and concern for any consequence, sat straighter on his stool. His stomach fluttered, the alcohol now taking him completely, there was no pause for thought, no questions allowed.

* * *

After closing, Katie closed the doors and rang out her till, and then sat with Ned drinking at the bar. It wasn't long before they began to talk freely without the sieve that was used when they were both sober.

'So, who do you think murdered these men, Ned?'

'I don't know. Not the two men I walked out into a fuckin' ambush of press.'

'Then who?'

Ned thought for a moment on the question. 'I don't know.'

'Then why couldn't these men have done it?'

Ned thought some more, but he was drunk and he struggled to find the pieces that he believed might exonerate Dell and Andrew. 'I'm drunk.'

Katie smiled. 'You don't know any more than I do about who did this.'

Ned bristled to defend himself. 'It wasn't them. It's a conspiracy. They saw somethin'. A man was whipped to death. A black man wouldn't do that to another black man.'

'Of course. Has to be a white man to do that.' Katie huffed with laughter.

Ned looked at her and then pulled his head back sharply. 'You a bigot, Katie?'

'No. No more than you.'

Ned pointed his finger at her. 'Hey, I'm no fuckin' bigot. No racist.'

Katie looked at him with calm. 'You got any black friends, Ned? Real friends. People you'd have over for dinner?'

Ned didn't need to think to have his answer. He shifted on his stool. 'So what?'

'Why not?'

'Do you?'

Katie shook her head. 'No. Never have. I don't hate 'em, I just don't know any of 'em too well.'

Ned sat quiet.

'It's okay, Ned. To feel that way.'

'What way?'

'That we're different.'

Ned closed his eyes tightly and watched, on the back of his eyelids, the first rotations of what would quickly become dizziness. He opened his eyes and looked at Katie. 'We're not. Different. Everyone's the same.'

Katie smiled. 'You're smarter than that, Ned. And you don't believe that.'

The subject changed and they got to talking about their past. Former girlfriends and boyfriends. Their parents and siblings. They laughed and at one point Katie cried retelling the story of her father's passing. When they stopped drinking it wasn't long before dawn. Katie led him upstairs to the unit she lived in, and when she poured him a glass of water, he thought about kissing her. Without thinking his words came quickly, 'I need to go.'

Katie handed him the glass of water, took a step forward and he could feel her breath across his chest.

'I'm going.' Ned turned from her, opened the front door and walked out.

CHAPTER 19

BOBBY THRUST FROM behind, Charlotte's head lay over the pillow. He talked, but she couldn't understand a word of it. She had her wrists close to her ears, and so all sound was muffled. She could hear herself breathing, could smell her own breath. She felt nothing down there but filled. There was nothing sexual for her about it. Bobby thrust harder, groaned and then climaxed. He rolled onto his back immediately and pulled a sheet over his waist. 'My god. That was good. Can you get me a drink of water, please?'

Charlotte didn't answer, she got out of bed, wiped herself with the tissue that was on the bedside table and walked out of the room. She wondered what was happening inside her. Millions upon millions of his sperm swimming in a race to find her eggs. To bulldoze their way through and fertilise. Full of his traits, different shades of his likeness, the best and very worst parts of him in indiscriminate amounts. All determined to imbue as much of him as they could in partnership with her DNA. She came back with a glass of water, stood over him naked and handed it to him.

'Thank you.' Bobby took a long swallow and then handed her back the glass. 'Did you?'

'No.'

'How come?'

'I don't know.'

'Do you want to do it again, later?'

'Maybe.'

'I like it when you have one.' Bobby smiled up at her. 'Lot of stuff went in there. I've been savin' that up.'

Charlotte felt nauseous as he said it, and she caught the odour of semen on her body.

'Ten days. That's what the doctor says, right? Ripe for ten days?'

'Yes.'

'Shit. I dunno if I got that in me.' Bobby laughed. 'Might have to dress you up in a costume or somethin'.' He laughed harder until his delight turned over into a coughing fit and he reached for the glass of water from Charlotte.

* * *

Bobby left for work an hour later, picked up by a junior driving the truck. Charlotte drove out to her father's barn to tend to Michael. She hadn't seen him for three days and was worried about him. It felt good. To be so concerned for someone. She arrived and redressed his stomach wound, got him to his feet, and watched him hobble around, all the while smiling at him. She ate sandwiches with him and drank iced water with slices of lemon she'd made before leaving. After eating they sat opposite each other, Michael up against the barn wall on a blanket, and Charlotte cross-legged on the decomposing hay. Charlotte felt much more relaxed than her previous visits. She'd felt Michael hand over some trust.

He rested his head against the wall, took a deep breath as though he'd finished a day at work and was now ready to relax. He looked directly at Charlotte.

'Thank you. Again. You have saved my life.'

'Yes.'

Michael smiled at her. 'You're very … nice, aren't ya?'

'I guess, I am.'

'You believe in God?'

'Yes, I do.' She waited a moment, unsure whether to ask. 'Do you?'

She could feel in the silence that followed that Michael was deliberating, searching for the truth of what he actually did believe. Charlotte saw discernible moments of contemplation, perhaps of a question he hadn't really answered truthfully before. 'I don't know.' His eyes widened and amplified his agnostic conclusion. 'I really don't know.'

'Do you go to church?'

'Nah. Never.'

'What makes you unsure? Of a God.'

'People.'

Charlotte thought a moment on Michael's answer and then smiled at him. 'That's a good answer. And a good reason.'

Michael finished his water, placed it down on the blanket and lifted himself straighter against the wall. 'How's your husband?'

Charlotte shrugged. 'Are you sure you don't want your boy to know you're okay?'

Charlotte saw his response begin to shape his mouth, as though words were ready to be voiced. But he stopped. He folded his arms and looked at Charlotte carefully. For her part she never looked away, she never broke eye contact. It was an instinctual reaction. Her body was aware of the stakes in the moment. 'I can do that for you. I'd like to do that.'

Michael didn't say a word, but he didn't say no. They spent the next hour talking about the music they liked to listen to, the television shows they loved to watch. It was the kind of material used on a date to assuage the initial awkwardness that came with talking. The entire way home as she drove, she smiled.

* * *

Before she returned to the house, she stopped by her grocer to buy produce for dinner. She was going to make rissoles and gravy with a potato and pumpkin mash. It was comfort food, memories of her childhood when her mother was in good spirits. They'd all sit down together to eat. She remembered on those nights wishing so very hard that it could stay that way.

On her way to the grocer she walked past a row of still growing fig trees. The trunks were as round as her body, and the branches just starting to thicken enough so a child could safely begin to climb them. Against one of the trunks, slumped and staring ahead into nothing, was Ned Potter. She looked closer to make certain it was him. She altered her line and made her way toward him. 'Ned?' She stopped a few feet short of where he sat, uncertain whether he'd heard her. 'Ned?' she said louder.

Ned broke from his glare, turned slightly and looked up at her. 'Charlotte Clark.' He smiled.

'Are you okay?' She knelt so she was eye level with him.

'Yeah, I'm just takin' a rest.' Ned shook his head and ran his hands either side of the part in his hair that barely remained.

'Okay.' Charlotte stood, bemused.

Ned took a deep breath, held it and then stood slowly. 'Jesus.'

'You okay?'

'Yeah … too much to drink. How are you anyway?'

'I'm fine. Just about to do some shoppin' for dinner.'

'Right.'

There was a long silence, Charlotte not sure what to follow up with and Ned concerned by how he must have looked. Still drunk, in police uniform and smelling putrid. He could smell his body odour all over himself. He wondered if she could too.

'Oh well. Nice to see you, Ned.'

'You too.'

She took the first step to walk away but then stopped and said, 'Oh, I saw that you caught those men. I watched you on television when the bodies were found and then yesterday.'

Ned tucked in his shirt. 'Yeah. I caught 'em.' He closed his eyes. 'Job well done, Ned Potter.' Ned smiled at her though Charlotte could hear the self-mocking tone in his voice. 'Well, you better go and get your things for dinner. Bobby will be ravenous after a day at work.'

She smiled back. 'Bye then.'

'See ya, Charlotte.'

* * *

Ned watched her walk inside the grocer and then turned and looked across the other side of the road. Three blocks away he could see the roof of Hotel Darwin. He shielded his eyes from the

174

sun and walked toward the pub. He entered, sat at the bar, ordered a beer and drank it quickly. By his last swallow the alcohol had already settled his thoughts. It was all just a little brighter. He'd go home after a few more, explain to Bonnie what had happened the day before, the horrible instance of walking two men he believed innocent into a pit of reporters and cameras. He'd tell her how impotent he felt, how stupid he was for the bluster aimed at Riley and Landry, telling them he wouldn't do it. The night spent talking with Katie Briggs, thinking of infidelity, he could hide away in a part of his mind never to be revisited. He ordered another beer and finished it just as quickly, and he felt the insides of his head lighten, as though the clutter in there, the immoral thoughts, the painful memories of the past, all got swept away into a corner leaving room for other thoughts. Optimism could flourish, and a state of mind that said it *would all be okay*, could roam freely. That's why he drank. That's what it allowed him.

He ordered another and with a distorted rosier outlook, began thinking about how he could continue to investigate the murders without being shut down. The trial for Dell and Andrew would be over as quickly as possible. They had no money for a defence or a lawyer who'd dig beneath the charges. *Say you did it and they might not hang you.* The defence would come from the town, paid for by the taxpayer, the great majority of whom would be outraged by a lengthy trial of two men with prior convictions accused of murdering two already convicted men. Landry had set it up well. Immediately after the discovery of the bodies he'd fed the press the information that Lionel Frazier and Clarry Tallis were convicted criminals. Now with the two accused processed and charged, Ned knew the information about their criminal past would be placed in the media's hands too. It was all prepared for an open and shut case. Done away with as quickly as possible. Ned knew also that his best opportunity to investigate further was after the verdict was handed down. No one would be watching nor contemplating that he was still on the case. His thoughts turned to Bonnie and Rose. He should be getting home. He didn't know the time but figured it was mid-afternoon by the light coming through the windows. It was dull light, covered over by clouds that Ned could smell had rain in them. He heard the strum of an acoustic guitar and walked into the Green Room where a young man with wolfish sideburns and a lady wearing a pink satin jacket were on stage. He played the acoustic guitar and she sang. By that time Ned had dispelled any thought of going home. He thought of Bonnie only momentarily, but never allowed the consideration to get out of control where he'd become stuck there. *She would be in bed, Rose too.* He'd be home before it was too dark.

* * *

When Ned woke on the floor in his living room it was early morning. Graham, Bonnie's father, was sitting on the couch in front of him. Ned closed his eyes, relieved that he'd made it home.

'Bonnie and the little one aren't here.' Graham's voice was flat and matter-of-fact.

Ned lifted his head from the floor, opened his eyes again and saw the fuzzy shapes of Graham's legs, one folded over the other. 'What did you say?'

'Your family. They're not here.' Graham's Irish brogue sounded thicker and more drawn out when he spoke in an even tone.

'Where are they?' Ned lifted himself onto his elbows.

'They're with me. You don't deserve them right at the moment.'

Ned let his elbows collapse and he fell hard onto the back of his head.

'Where were you?'

'I was out. Drinkin'.'

'Where?'

Ned took a breath and covered his eyes with the backsides of both hands. 'The pub.'

'For two days and a night?'

Ned thought about that, did the sum of daylight and night sky he'd seen and remembered. 'I guess so.'

'You think that's appropriate for a man with a young wife and daughter?'

'I don't know.'

'You don't know? Stand up.'

Ned heard the change in Graham's voice. He was commanding him. He stood slowly and smelt the alcohol on his own breath, the thick sweet vapour that was indistinct. Not beer, not rum, or vodka, it was a fume all its own.

'What else were you doin'?'

'What?'

'Where did you sleep?'

Ned stood silent, Graham's eyes unblinking and set firmly on his. 'I didn't.'

Graham studied Ned for only a moment. 'Take your pants off.' He looked down at Ned's crotch.

'What? I'm not takin' my pants off.'

'Take your fuckin' pants off now!' Graham's eyes were lit, the browns of his irises brightening to a copper tint that made him look doggish.

'Why?' Ned took a step back.

'Just do it, son.'

Ned undid his belt, then his trousers and stepped out of them.

'Your underwear.'

'No.' Ned made his response as defiant as he could. Regardless of his behaviour, he felt at least justified in saying no to being stripped naked.

'I'm not interested in the size of your cock, boy. Take 'em off.' Graham took a step forward and Ned noticed Graham's right hand was clenched. 'Take 'em off, or we're gonna have an incident here. And believe me, son, it won't end well for you.'

Ned didn't dispute that, he'd heard so many stories from Bonnie about her father's scraps and how they ended poorly for the other man, or men. Ned pulled his underwear down to his ankles and stood naked in front of his father-in-law. He didn't know what was next, Graham wasn't looking at his penis, he was studying Ned more, his head cocked to the side. He then straightened up, and his expression changed from inquisitive to semblances of hope and warmth, as though he were on Ned's side somehow. He walked slowly over to Ned, stopped less than a foot away and then dropped to his haunches. Ned looked down in horror and then disbelief. Graham had his nose in his pubic hair. A moment later he stood eye to eye with him.

'I can't smell cunt. You're clean.'

Ned's forehead caved to a frown and his eyes closed.

Graham took half a step back and looked down at Ned's cock. He then threw his arm quickly at Ned's crotch and took a fistful of all of it, cock, balls and hair. He squeezed it hard and Ned's knees gave way. 'Don't you fuckin' fall over on me. Stand up.'

Ned winced and righted himself best he could. Graham was nose to nose with him and Ned could smell the whiskey mixed with coffee on his breath, and, underneath that, the cigarettes and something garlicky.

'You don't do this to my little girl, you understand?'

Graham squeezed tighter and Ned yelped in pain, 'Please!'

Graham let go, took two steps back and then turned away. Ned collapsed in pain, his underwear around his ankles, his penis shrunken and hidden among his tangles of pubic hair. Spittle shot from between his clamped lips as he tried to balance the pain by holding his breath and groaning. Graham sat back down on the lounge.

'You're fuckin' pathetic. Look at you.' He took a soft packet of cigarettes from the top pocket of his shirt and tapped one out. 'I've got one daughter. I love her more than I love her mammy. And you'll love your daughter more than you love Bonnie. It's just the way it is with fathers and daughters.'

Ned reached for his underwear, pulling them to his waist.

'Men are not saints.' Graham lit his cigarette and pulled back hard. He leant over his knees and looked down at Ned who had managed to sit upright. 'You see, I believe in Jesus Christ, the man who walked the earth as told to us in the new testament. The stories that went before that, the old testament? It's shite. Noah's Ark, Adam and Eve. We don't come from two white people in a garden eating fruit and talkin' to a fuckin' snake. We came from the apes. And do you know what the strongest instinct a male primate has?'

'No.'

'To fuck. To lay his seed. We're apes. You. And me. All men. Bein' with one woman? It's hard. But you married my daughter. So while I understand your problem, I couldn't give a fuck if you're King Kong. Keep your cock in your trousers.' Graham stood up and extended his hand.

Ned, uncertain, and trying to make sense of the sermon Graham had delivered, reached up and took his hand. Graham pulled him to his feet. Ned felt emasculated, completely. But also released from the guilt of his thoughts. He also knew that wasn't the moral way to be feeling. A thumping comprehension of his situation fell on top of him, he felt heavier, laden. He wasn't released from anything. Not with Bonnie's father. Not ever. Not deed nor thought.

'Every man likes a drink. I won't deny you that. That's not my place. You've never hit her, never been violent. But be a man. A fuckin' man. And come home.' Graham turned and headed for the front door.

'Are they coming back?'

'Talk to your wife.'

CHAPTER 20

OUTSIDE ON HIS back veranda, David O'Shea sat with his legs overhanging the small timber deck. The yard in front of him was covered by a tight, newly mown couch grass. He could smell the freshly cut lawn, the newly cropped blades of grass letting out their chemical defences as a first aid against the injuries inflicted from the lawnmower. He loved the smell and often enjoyed a cold bottle of beer after he'd finished. He looked over the lawn, its even layer and sharpened edges, the lighter shade of green and the precision he'd mown around the garden bed and small shrubs. Mowing the lawn was a necessity, it was a task he attached to the order of his life. The house was to be clean. The car washed. His clothes ironed for work. His hair neatly cut. The mown lawn was the bow he tied around it all. It was all of his life moving in the same direction, all stable and just the way it should be. With those routines complete, he could find the space he needed to cope with the other parts of his life. His wife who placed God above all else, and who had begun to view him as a sinner of mortal repercussion. She'd caught him masturbating and supposed the next step was adultery. And his two boys, five and seven, whom he could see being indoctrinated by his wife for a lifetime of serving God. He didn't want that for either of them. He wanted them to know that it was their own choice to believe or not. That hell didn't await them if they chose to question it all. It was hard finding any room around the praying and the preaching to get to his boys and explain that some of it was to be discarded as just story, and only a point to aim their moral compass toward. He believed if he couldn't get to them at this early age and enlighten them about what he knew to be true, then the propaganda would be too fearfully programmed in them; that to look another way, to question, to exercise their objectivity, would be lost forever. And then their life would be restrained by the company of only those who'd been reared the same way and followed the same dogma.

He was sitting on the edge of the deck watching his eldest boy, Aaron, on the lawn picking up clippings and smelling them. He was a small boy for his age, with sandy-coloured hair that was parted neatly to the side and cut similarly to his father's. David smiled as he watched his son, and felt his eyes sting as they filled with tears. Aaron lay on his back and rested his small hands on his chest, and David wondered with great concern what he might be thinking. He could remember his thoughts in quiet moments at the same age. They were anxiety ridden, worry for his older brother who was sick. It was the first time he'd heard the word cancer. He remembered thinking what heaven would be like for his brother if he died. Would it be as it had been explained to him? With angels and long rows of comfortable beds, where all those who'd died and had gained entry slept? Would his brother see their uncle who'd died in the war? Or was their uncle going to hell? His mother had told him that his uncle had probably killed other men. By David's reckoning, back then, that was murder and something that was most certainly a sin to damn someone to hell. He remembered how he'd imagined hell, it was all burning, one great big fire with the devil's face shooting through the flames with a pitchfork and a distended smile.

He was hoping Aaron might be thinking about something peaceful, perhaps swimming in a creek on a hot day, or something fun, bouncing on a trampoline and remembering the feeling of falling, to be weightless while his stomach dropped and he tingled all the way from his toes to the tips of his ears. David had done both with him. Aaron turned onto his stomach and lay his head to the side over the grass. David could see that his eyes were open. They moved and Aaron blinked, and then his son's eyes focused on something David couldn't see himself. The blinking stopped, and David recognised that Aaron had fallen into a gaze with no register of what he was looking at. It made David incredibly uneasy.

'Hey.'

Aaron's eyes shifted toward his father and he sat up.

'You okay?'

'Yeah.' Aaron picked at the grass.

'You want to go for a swim?'

'No.'

David pushed himself off the veranda and onto the lawn. He walked over to Aaron and sat down beside him. 'What are you thinking about lyin' down here on the grass?'

'I dunno.'

'You don't look too happy.' David put his arm around his son.

'I'm okay.'

'You sure about that?'

'Yeah.'

David stood up and looked back toward his house. An uneasy feeling overwhelmed him when he looked underneath the veranda. There were long tangled weeds he could see in silhouette, shooting up and bending at their ends on the underside of the floor. They looked like some kind of creature trying to force their way inside. He felt the order of his life tip to the side, like being in a boat and hit by an unseen wave. He suddenly felt unsteady on his legs.

* * *

Later that evening, after he put his two sons to bed and his wife retired to their bedroom to read, David drove his car to town. He drove with his windows down, and the chatter from the streets floated through the warm wind and into his car. He parked close to Hotel Darwin and went inside where he heard the riffs of slide guitar blues coming from the Green Room.

He had learnt classical guitar as a young boy, but always preferred the blues. He had one acoustic guitar at his house, but rarely got to play anything but three chord hymns. He'd bought albums by Roy Orbison, Johnny Cash, Elvis Presley and BB King. But inside the house they were only played late at night or when his wife was out.

Inside the Green Room he ordered a Scotch neat and thought through the sequence of duties he needed to tend to so that order could be restored. The sight of wild weed beneath the veranda had flung everything into confusion. First job was to billhook the wild weed. The more he drank, the better he felt and the easier his life fell into an organised queue. He was about to leave the bar when Mayor Landry walked in. David watched him being seated close to the stage by the hotel manager. Landry's hair was particularly precise, some extra grown length on its longest side allowing him to cover his bald spot almost completely. The lady he was with was not his wife, David knew that from the photos he'd seen of Landry and his wife that were a constant feature in the *Northern Territory News*. This lady was much younger than her, was taller and more buxom, and she looked to David as though she could be European. He ordered another drink and moved closer to the stage, only two tables from Landry. His inebriated thoughts gathered and began to team up against him. They called him weak and a coward, they dared him to challenge his wife and then laughed at his action plan. *You'll never do that!* He looked over at Landry and the woman he was with, and without consciously thinking, he approached them. He put his scotch on their table, and looked Landry squarely in the eye. It took Landry a moment to recognise him, and when he did, he scowled. 'What do you want?'

David couldn't hear what Landry said beneath the music, could only see the shape of his mouth change as the words were pushed out with a discernible irritation. David leant in closer. 'What?'

'What do you want?'

'I don't want your money.' David pulled back so he could see Landry's reaction clearly.

Landry stood. 'Come outside with me.'

He took David's arm just above his elbow and forced him through the crowd, knocking over a table on the way to the exit. On the street outside the pub he walked David further, around a corner, away from any people and where the sounds of music were blunted by the thick backside of the brick building. 'What the fuck did you say to me?' Landry pushed David against the wall and stood over him.

'Keep your money. I don't want it.' David's words were stretched and unfinished, dragging through the alcohol. 'Fuck you.'

Landry took a step back from him. 'We had a deal.'

'Not with me.'

Landry checked if anyone was around, and then stepped forward, close enough that David could smell the beer on his breath when he growled at him, 'Take the money. Or leave the Territory.' Landry walked away, around the edge of the pub and back toward the entry.

David walked aimlessly, he thought about continuing to drink somewhere else, but he felt sick, like his innards were being rolled like bread dough through a beater. The glands beneath the soft edges of his jawline squirted something bitter and he vomited over the footpath. He wiped his mouth and kept walking, with no plan, no route. He had no thought, however, of going home.

When he got to the shoreline of Nightcliff Beach, the sun hadn't breached the horizon, but the sky had begun to brighten. It was clear but for a low stratus cloud that was so thin it could have been mistaken for ocean mist. He sat down and looked over the Timor. The water was retreating quickly, the slag of every small wave sucked back further into the sea by the tide. The air was still, the water looked like a giant sheet of glass withdrawing from the beach toward the horizon. A prawn trawler chugged with the current out to sea, its hopper empty, its steely arms folded upright. David looked at the trawler and watched two deckhands standing at the stern, their arms resting over the grab rail. He wondered what life might be like on one of those boats. He knew that, depending on where they were fishing, the crew could stay aboard for days, even weeks on end. *What kind of a life would that be?* How would the order he craved fit into a job like that? What would be the necessities he'd require to organise and settle over his existence? Sitting there on the sand, he liked the idea of his life being contained on a boat, isolated from the intangibles he couldn't see coming, intangibles that would always be happening onshore. Occurrences that would meddle with the tidiness of his life. A car accident, a flood. A crime. He watched the trawler until it was out of sight and then stood. He looked over the Timor, took off his clothes, and then walked slowly toward the retreating tide.

CHAPTER 21

'WHAT'S HIS NAME?'

'Marcus.'

'What's he look like?' Charlotte sat cross-legged on a blanket she'd laid out.

'More like his mum.'

'What did she look like?'

'You're just full of questions, aren't ya?' Michael laughed, the colour in his face had permanently returned to a healthy hue.

'I'm sorry.'

'No, it's fine. I like to talk about them. She was pretty. Tall and skinny.'

'You must miss her.'

'Every day. Gone too soon, eh?'

Charlotte shifted her position, uncrossed her legs and she saw Michael peep at the gap that momentarily opened between her thighs. It felt good. She settled on her side. 'I could tell him, Michael. I'd be careful. I could bring him to see you.'

Michael looked at her a moment and then out beyond the barn doors Charlotte had left open. The paddock was overgrown with wild grass and weed, but it was green, and the unfettered sun and blue sky made everything look brighter. The dirt at the edges of the paddocks was red, and the water that had puddled in the potholes after rainfall looked blue, like the ocean.

'They'll be after him.' Michael looked back to Charlotte.

'Who?'

'Government. They already tried to take him off me when his mum died. Wanted to put him in a mission station. I took off with him. Joined the tent boxin'. But we come back here a lot and stay with our people. They'll have him. But I don't know for how long.'

Charlotte sat straighter. 'Where is he?'

Michael looked at her, his manner stern, a warning planted behind his eyes. 'No one can know.'

'Okay.'

* * *

The rest of the afternoon they talked openly. Michael about his childhood, his mother and father and his two brothers. How they'd moved to the Territory from North Queensland as his father looked for work. His dad had signed up for the army midway through the Second World War. He'd served in an infantry battalion in New Guinea and been behind a fellow soldier who had stepped on a mine. He lost his left arm from just above his elbow. Michael talked about how, while working clearing forests in North Queensland, he'd become his father's left arm. He was no more than ten years of age, never two steps behind his father, keeping cool from the violent heat in his shadow. His father swung an axe, its head the thickest the haft could hold without splintering while chopping into the stalks of ribbonwood trees. Even with one arm, Michael told her of how his father was precise with his chopping, of his lazy long stroke that the other men admired and tried to emulate with both arms. *Nah, they couldn't do it. Dad made it look easy, eh?*

When the work dried up, they moved north to the Territory and his father worked on the melon plantations. It was in the Territory that his father had taught Michael and his brothers to hunt, and how to fish by hand. And he told Charlotte about his father's perennial sadness, and that he couldn't remember more than a few occasions where he saw him smile. It was like a coat of paint he couldn't wash off. He told her about his own chequered career as a boxer. That at sixteen he'd travelled to Sydney to fight as a professional and had trained with his older cousins in a gym at Redfern that he said smelt like an old boxing glove. He explained to her that he and his cousins would congregate on one of the wharves on Sydney Harbour and fight thirty second scraps, against other men to show enough to get on the card. He'd started off good, but needed more money, so took some dives to get paid better.

Charlotte listened for long periods without saying a word, but imagining the scenarios that Michael explained. They were new offerings of a life she'd never known or contemplated. Like paintings, full of colour and thick texture, and when Michael paused to conjure his memories so he could best explain them, Charlotte wondered what it all might smell like. The forests, the tents and shacks he grew up in, the trains and railroads his family moved from place to place on. She told Michael about her own father and mother. Without thinking, she offered up information and stories she'd never told anyone before. She felt exhilarated while sitting across from him. She'd never felt anything so gratifying. Would never have expected nor thought it possible.

* * *

She left just before dark. With a plan. Michael had told her where his boy lived, and how to approach him. He told her Marcus was wary of people and didn't trust a woman any more than he did a man. He had given her some information that only he and his son knew. Once she'd established it was his son, she was to discreetly tell him what Michael had told her.

She got home and began dinner. Smiling the whole time, she peeled potatoes and stuffed the small chicken with seasoned breadcrumbs. Putting the chicken in the oven, she thought about Ned Potter and how she'd seen him sitting under the fig tree. She remembered how he'd smelt of alcohol and that the whole encounter was so out of step with the interactions she'd had with him in the past. *I hope he's okay*, she thought.

* * *

Bobby got home just as Charlotte was setting the table. He'd brought along Danny Lewis, and both of them were already on their way to being drunk. They all sat at the table, and Bobby was especially chirpy about something that seasoned his every observation and response with a tone that made Charlotte suspicious. *What's he so happy about?* Toward the end of eating dinner, Charlotte, without thinking too much about what she was going to say, said, 'I saw Ned Potter yesterday. He was drunk, I think.'

Bobby and Lewis glanced at one another. 'Where did you see him?' Bobby said it as matter-of-fact as he could.

'He was underneath one of the new figs near the grocer.'

'Doin' what?'

'He was just sittin' there.'

Bobby huffed. 'He's turnin' into a drunk, that man. I seen him a few times myself at the pub. Mouthy little prick he is.'

Some silence followed and then Charlotte continued, 'He caught the men who did those murders. I saw that on TV.'

Bobby huffed. 'He couldn't catch a cold. He found the dead men, that's all. He hit a pig, dragged it through the swamp to bury it. The bodies were fifty feet from him. Can you believe the chances of that?' Bobby swabbed a piece of bread through the gravy left on his plate. 'Dumb luck.' He stuffed the piece of bread in his mouth and shook his head.

Charlotte wasn't sure what to make of what he'd said. And though she had an urge to follow up, she didn't. She watched him chew his food and wipe the remnants of gravy on the side of his cheek with the back of his hand. It was another innocuous moment that made her light-headed. She got up when she finished her dinner, served them both banana with ice-cream and bread pudding. She then washed the dishes and cleaned the kitchen, collected the carrot and potato peelings left in the sink and scrubbed the inside of the oven. She then asked her husband if it would be okay if she went to the bedroom to rest. She told him she wasn't feeling well. He was polite, and told her *he'd be there soon*. She knew what was coming, her *eggs were ripe*, and he seemed more determined than ever that they conceive.

* * *

Later that evening, after Bobby had come to the bedroom and she'd had sex with him, she went outside onto the front porch to get some air. The moon was full, and across the vacant lots of land in front of her, a wedge-shaped corridor of light fanned out over the overgrown and uneven grassland. She could see rabbits darting in and out of the light, looking for cockroaches and caterpillars or newly hatched snakes. Standing there on the porch, she felt not a breath of wind. It was still. So stagnant that she could hear the sloshy collapse of small waves breaking over the sand on the beach. She raised her chin and tilted her head toward the sound. She smiled. She didn't feel stuck in the stillness of the climate like she had done before. She felt as though she were moving through it, unshackled and gaining momentum.

CHAPTER 22

BONNIE RETURNED HOME after staying at her father's house for three nights. She and Ned had spoken on the phone, but it was uncomfortable and there were long moments of silence. Ned, stuck in the guilt of his actions, found it hard to ask her questions that would show he was a decent man. Questions about Rose's milk pimples, about Bonnie's sore breasts from feeding. He did tell her about how he'd walked Dell and Andrew straight into the pack of media. Something he'd sworn not to. How he felt impotent at work. Bonnie sympathised with him but told him she'd prefer he didn't drink so much. Ned agreed. Bonnie asked him what had transpired between himself and her father. Ned said little, but Bonnie knew her father would have made his position clear, and perhaps there'd have been violence. Bonnie knew her father very well.

When she'd been a young girl of ten, playing hide and seek at her friend's house with a bunch of other girls, the father of her friend had come across her concealed in one of the rooms. He gagged her with a sock, tied her hands together with a belt and locked her there. She could hear the other girls playing, laughing, screaming with fright when found. She listened to them all leave, one by one, until it was quiet. She never heard anyone ask for her. The door opened not long after. The father walked in, stood over and looked at her for a long time. She was terrified, had wet her pants. He squatted beside her, gritted his teeth, called her a *half-caste*, and told her that, though he should, he wasn't *going to kill her*. But when she was older, he was going to *rape* her. Before he untied her and pushed her out a window, he told her *never to set foot in the house again*. Bonnie went home and told her father immediately. He held her, calmed her crying and gently told her to have a shower.

A year later, her friend's father was found dead on Nightcliff Beach, his skull fractured, his face barely recognisable from the beating. Bonnie only learnt of what had happened years later. While dating Ned, she'd come home late to find her father drinking in the space under their stilted house with his two brothers who had come to the Territory on holiday. They were merry, asking where she'd been, asking about Ned. The eldest brother, Callum, quipped in a still heavy Irish brogue, *Jesus fuckin' Christ I hope he's a decent man. I don't want to make another trip*. The brothers laughed, but her father didn't. He just looked at her, not for long, but it was unapologetic and matter of fact. And before he looked away he shrugged at her. She understood it completely, *what did you expect me to do* was what he told her with his gesture. She'd never told Ned.

* * *

Bonnie and Rose were asleep before eight o'clock and Ned left to go to the Victoria Hotel. He was nervous while walking there. He had no idea what he was going to say to Katie Briggs. He wanted to say in some way how tempted he was, but was afraid what that might lead to. He was hoping she'd see it the same way, and not be looking to somehow build on where they'd finished. When he got there, she smiled at him while serving another customer and then made her way to him.

'Ned Potter.' She flattened her lips and made them a straight line. It was a mannerism that Ned had used himself to contain a smile from breaking free.

'Katie Briggs. How are you?' She placed a schooner of beer on the bar. Ned looked at it, he'd intended to not drink. She saw his reluctance and pulled it away, and her smile broke free from her tightened mouth. 'Just a coke.'

'You got it. You okay?'

'Yeah. I'm okay.'

Katie leant in. 'I had a really good time the other night. But I'm glad you went home.' And then she paused and looked at Ned. 'But that can't happen again. You drink here, and it stays here.'

'Yes, ma'am.' Katie winked at him and went to the fridge to get his bottle of coke.

Ned had gone to the Victoria Hotel not just to talk to Katie Briggs and stem whatever might grow out of the intimacy they'd shared that evening. He was hoping to see the man who'd been there last time. David O'Shea. He'd told Ned he'd *sold my little boy out*, and though the memory Ned had of the encounter was dim, he hadn't forgotten the suspicion the conversation had alerted in him. When Katie came back to serve him, he asked, 'That fella been back?'

'David?'

'Yeah.'

'Haven't seen him since he was here last with you.'

Ned looked disappointed. He thought about what his next move might be. He was fearful now that, outside the banal traffic misdemeanours and petty crimes, he would never be allowed to examine anything autonomously. He needed to follow up, to dig, even if it were little by little while the mundane immediacy of his work took precedence. He had no idea where to find David O'Shea, he could check the telephone book, and police records, but he didn't hold much hope they'd provide him with information on David's whereabouts. The phone book for Darwin was unfinished, thousands of names had not been entered, and David O'Shea hadn't struck him as an individual whose life might be detailed by a litany of crimes in a police record. He thought about going to Fannie Bay Gaol, where Dell and Andrew were being kept before their trial, but that would alert Riley. There was paperwork to be authorised and the records kept of who came and went and who'd they'd seen. He reflected on the look Martha Clay had given him after he'd waited to see if she'd turn back toward him after he'd accompanied Dell and Andrew out of the jail. *Why was she there? What did that look mean?*

* * *

Walking back to his car, Ned passed the local Catholic church and saw the priest closing its large doors. Father McKay. He was threading a chain through the chapel door's nickel handles and padlocked it, and then stepped into the light thrown down from the moon. He looked directly at Ned, his face had mottled bruising on his cheeks and above his eyes, and he walked down the stairs with a limp and grimaced in pain.

'Hey, Father.' Ned bent his frame as he walked toward Father McKay, as though to look under a sheet covering something that was to be hidden. The priest barely lifted his head.

'Hello.'

'How are you?' McKay had nowhere to go and so stopped and looked up at Ned, his face now completely lit by the streetlights. 'Jesus.'

'It looks much worse than it is.' McKay smiled.

'What happened?'

'I had a fall. From the stairs in my house. Too much to drink, I think.' McKay looked away, his beard overgrown at the sides of his face so his cheeks looked rounder than they were. 'I'd best get home.'

He didn't wait for a response from Ned, he didn't look up, he walked around him and toward the darkness of the streets. Ned watched him disappear. He didn't believe for a moment that the priest had fallen. He could see there had been fists used, that the bruising wasn't scraped with abrasion that would indicate a fall down a flight of stairs. And he didn't believe that Father McKay had been involved in a fair and square fight. He'd been assaulted by someone. Perhaps for something he'd done, or as a warning. Ned wondered whether Father McKay had seen the same things Ernie Clay and Lionel Frazier had. What Clarry Tallis had heard. *Maybe*, he thought, *he'd been afforded a warning they hadn't*.

Ned went home and got into bed next to Bonnie. She woke and he tucked in tightly behind her and gently stroked her cheek with the back of his hand.

'What did my father say to you?' Bonnie's voice was croaky from sleep.

Ned thought quickly. 'I told you. To behave and not drink as much. What did he tell you he said?'

'He didn't tell me anything. He just said he'd seen you.'

Ned stopped stroking her face, the image of her father with his face buried in his pubic hair swamped his thought. 'And he told me I needed to be a better father, and a better husband.'

Bonnie flipped over so she was facing him. 'Where were you? The night you didn't come home?'

'I was drinking.'

'The whole time? With who? Another lady?'

Ned could feel the lies lining up through his throat. They were all weak. Made worse by him knowing she'd believe whatever he told her. He was aware she just needed to hear an explanation from him. 'Yes, just drinking. And no, not with a lady. Other men. Looking for a drink, that's all.'

Bonnie looked at him, her eyes almost black in the dim light. Ned recognised the doubt in the shape of her browline, it was inclined and similar to how it would bend if she were hopeful of something.

'I love you.' Ned ran the tip of his index finger along her brow and it straightened.

'I love you too.' She kissed him and then rolled back over.

Ned pulled her in close and held her tight again.

* * *

The next morning when Ned arrived at work, he saw an older man and a young boy in Senior Sergeant Riley's office. The boy sat while the older man stood. Ned could see Riley leaning back on his chair, could hear the drone of his voice through the thinly glazed windows of his office. The man motioned to the boy next to him and put a hand gently atop his head. Ned sat at his desk and continued to watch, Riley's voice rising at different points and the drone giving way to words that could be heard. *Fuck, fault* were words Ned made out. The older man took the hand of the young boy and they walked out. The little boy was long-limbed, his hair straight and bleached blond by the sun. He looked at Ned on the way out, and Ned smiled at him, and for an instant thought he recognised him. Riley walked to the doorway of his office and watched them leave. Ned could see very well that Riley was irritated. Spurred on by the fear of other tedious tasks, he got up and walked over to Riley. 'Who were they?'

'None of your fuckin' business.'

Ned smiled at Riley, pleased with himself for having provoked the reply.

* * *

Ned waited an hour, continued the monthly report he was close to finishing, and when Riley left the station to get lunch, he walked across to a young constable who'd only just joined the force and was responsible for the registration of all visitors.

'Hey, mate.' Ned smiled.

The young constable smiled back, his toothy grin made more obvious by the narrow shape of his face. 'Senior Constable Potter.'

'So who was the man and boy in Riley's office?'

'Um, they were …' The young constable shuffled some paperwork on his desk revealing a register book. He opened it and read aloud, 'Timothy Mitchell and Marcus Roberts. But I don't know who was who.' He looked up at Ned.

'Thanks, mate.' Ned winked and walked away. He searched both names for a police record and found Timothy Mitchell had been booked for assault and had served twelve months in Fannie Bay Gaol.

Ned drove to the western shore of Darwin Harbour to the Delissaville Aboriginal Mission. He got out of his car and walked along the hardened red dirt track leading into the settlement. There were rows of canvas tents pitched with slim timber rafters, their roofs made from long sheets of corrugated iron that were in various conditions of rust. The men looked at him warily and the young children scurried to their mothers and clung to their sides. Ned tried to slacken his stature and smile warmly, to make himself as unthreatening as possible. He looked across the faces and tried to place Timothy Mitchell, but many of the men turned away when he made eye contact with them. It was at the second to last tent along the stretch that he saw the young boy he'd seen at the police station. He was sitting on the ground outside the tent, an old Sherrin football between his long legs. He held a piece of sharp shale in one hand, running its edge along the length of the football, scoring deep cuts through its leather. Ned stopped in front of him. 'Hey, mate.'

The boy looked up, his eyes widened and he dropped the rock. 'It's okay.' Ned spoke softly, 'I'm just lookin' around.' The boy's shoulders loosened. 'What are you doin' with the footy?'

'I'm makin' it sticky.'

Ned looked at the football and the long scored cuts through its husk. 'So you can catch it better?'

'Yeah.'

Ned smiled and looked at the boy closely, another twinge of recognition flashed before him. 'You must be Marcus. That right?'

'Yes.' His voice was high pitched and slow. 'You a policeman?' The boy pointed to the badge on Ned's chest.

'I am. Is Timothy here?'

'No.'

'And where would he be?'

Marcus didn't reply; his eyes widened further and he stood up.

'It's okay, Marcus. I saw you both today at the police station. I was just wondering why you were there.'

Marcus stayed silent and Ned took off the police badge that was pinned to his shirt over his chest. He handed it to Marcus. 'See that. Northern Territory Police.' Marcus nodded and gave it back to Ned. 'You don't have to say anything if you don't want. We can wait until Timothy comes back if you like. My name is Senior Constable Potter. But you can just call me Ned. Okay?'

Marcus nodded and then spoke, 'My dad's gone.'

'What do you mean?'

'We can't find him.'

'Okay. How long has he been gone?'

'Lots of days. We were at the station because we told the police.' Marcus stepped forward, his eyes showing hope. 'Are you gonna find him? We're supposed to be back with the boxing tent a long way from here.'

Ned smiled. 'I can look for him if you want? What's his name?'

'Michael Roberts.'

Ned stood silent for a moment, and then his smile grew wider. 'I know your dad. I've seen you before. Fishing with him out near Tabletop Swamp. I knew I recognised you.'

Marcus's eyes filled with emotion. 'Can you find him for me? I don't want to get taken away to another home.'

'I can certainly try, son.' Ned paused and then lowered himself so he was eye level with the boy. 'Can you keep a secret?'

Marcus nodded.

'Okay, this is our secret. You don't tell anybody I was here. And I promise I'll try and find your dad, okay?'

'Thank you.'

* * *

Ned didn't go back to the station, instead he took the long drive out to the site where he'd discovered the bodies. He thought the whole time of Michael Roberts and their sporadic encounters. The day Michael showed him how to trap barra and fish them out from waterholes with his hands. And of the last time he'd seen him with the boxing troupe fighting Bobby Clark. He stopped his Land Cruiser in the same spot he'd parked after hitting the pig, took the same shovel, and then walked through the marshland to the shallow grave site. The hole had been left unfilled and there was now weed growing up from its muddy bottom. Ned looked down at it, and then across at the peaty backcloth either side of him. He was looking for disturbed earth, something revealing the locality of another grave. Where, Ned figured, he'd find Michael Roberts. He dug at two spots where the earth looked like it had been moved. It was hard excavation, his shovel often becoming stuck. When he pulled it out it made a wettish dragging sound, like a plunger slowly pulled from its suction. He dug four feet at both locations but found nothing.

He was wet through from perspiration when he got back to his truck, and so thirsty he considered drinking the bottle of distilled water that was under the back seat and there in case the battery began to falter. He didn't and instead stayed thirsty on the long drive back to town until he got to Hotel Darwin. He entered, ordered a schooner and sat at the middle of the horseshoe bar hoping to see Senior Sergeant Riley. It was Bobby Clark who arrived first, his fireman's uniform and one side of his face covered in black soot. He saw Ned, lifted his head in recognition and sat where he usually did. Ned watched Bobby closely, he looked tired and the speed of his drinking suggested he was in a hurry to get the hit of alcohol. Ned waited until Bobby finished his glass of Old, walked to the end of the bar and sat beside him. 'You look rooted. I'll buy you a beer.'

'It's all right, I get me own.'

'Nah, my shout.' Ned signalled the barman. 'Schooner of Old and schooner of Carlton.' He turned to Bobby. 'You been in the wars today?'

'Just back-burnin'.'

The barman slid over the schooners. Ned held his up. 'Cheers.'

'Yeah.' Bobby took two long swallows and emptied half his glass. 'My missus said she saw you.'

'Oh yeah?'

'Under a fig near the grocer. Said you were pissed.' Bobby smiled. 'And that you stank.'

Ned shrugged. 'Well a couple days on the drink'll have anyone drunk and smelly.' Ned smiled back, took a sip from his schooner and watched as Bobby Clark turned away from him and square to his front.

'I saw you fight.'

Bobby turned sharply. 'It was a fast count, they fuckin' dudded me.'

'Well, it was a great fight. I thought you had it.'

'I did have it.' Bobby turned away.

Ned contemplated what he was about to say, whether it might lead to him being assaulted.

'Black bastard put his hands in the air like he'd won a world title.' Bobby didn't bother looking at Ned when he said it.

'You know he's missing? Michael Roberts.' Ned sat tighter on his stool.

'That right?'

'Yeah. For a while now I think.'

'Oh well. He'll turn up. They all go walkabout, don't they?' Bobby glanced sideways at Ned without moving his head.

'I guess.'

They drank in silence and before Ned finished his beer, Danny Lewis and Joe Riley arrived and took up their spots next to Bobby. Riley looked at Ned and then Bobby, it was a confused, wary contemplation that Ned recognised.

'Potter.'

'Senior Sergeant. You want a beer?'

'I'll get my own. What are you doin' here?' Riley reached into his top pocket and pulled out his packet of cigarettes.

'Just havin' a beer. Saw Bobby, thought I'd say hello.'

'Right.' Riley lit up.

Ned sat straighter, pulled his shoulders back and winced. 'Hey, did you know Michael Roberts was missing?'

Riley's eyes narrowed through the rising smoke he'd just exhaled. 'You listen to me, Senior Constable Potter, and you listen good. We've done everything we can to make you look good with the arrests of those men. And instead of being gracious, which you should be, you're spending your time digging around in other people's business. My business. Leave it alone now.'

Ned glared back at Riley, pulled the corners of his mouth downward and nodded. 'If you say so.'

'I fuckin' say so!' Riley growled and took a step forward.

Ned took a step back, looked at both Bobby Clark and Danny Lewis. 'What a cranky fuckin' bunch.'

'Fuck off, Potter.' Bobby stood from his stool.

'What? You gonna belt me, Bobby?'

Bobby positioned his feet as though ready to fight, his left foot forward.

'That nose healed yet?'

Bobby swung at Ned from where he stood, the straight right hand falling short without Ned having to move from it. Riley moved quickly to hold Bobby's advance. 'Fuck off before you get a hidin', Potter.'

Ned turned and walked out of the pub without saying another word, but he felt like a winner. If the whole interaction between himself, Bobby and Riley had been seen by a crowd and judged by a referee, his victory would have been unanimous.

CHAPTER 23

CHARLOTTE CAUGHT A bus that stopped not far from the Delissaville Aboriginal Mission. Michael had drawn a rough floorplan of the mission on the barn floor, and had shown her the position of the tent he and his son had been staying in. He said there would be lots of children there, and so had given her a very specific description of what his son looked like. With a smile, he said it was a *sure thing* his son would be *kicking a football around*. He told her there was a position on the western side where she could see the housing without going into the mission. *Have a look from there.*

When Charlotte got off the bus, she walked to the spot Michael had mentioned. It wasn't far from the harbour shoreline and close enough to the housing that she could make out faces, though not discernibly enough to identify them accurately. She looked past the tents to the patch of grassless red dirt where a group of young boys were kicking a football, their voices and laughter cutting through the muggy air, lyrically dancing past her. *That's got to be him.* Charlotte smiled. The boy she watched was long-limbed and skinny, his straight hair bleached by the sun. He took a mark and howled and Charlotte laughed, and a moment later the boy looked her way.

'Shit.' Charlotte turned away quickly and walked back to the bus stop. On the way home, all Charlotte could think about was what might happen to Marcus if he was not reunited with his father. All of the scenarios she contemplated were dire and ended with Marcus on the wrong side of the outcome. As troubling as her conclusions were, it felt good to be worried that way. A maternal bone she'd never felt ache before. She couldn't wait to see Michael and tell him she'd seen his son, to see his reaction.

* * *

When she arrived home, Bobby was home from work and quiet. He'd been that way for the previous two days and though Charlotte wondered what might be at play, she hadn't asked. She watched him closely as he sat on the lounge in front of the television.

'What are you watching?' she said it so he'd hear the smile through her words.

'Just the news.'

'Anything interesting happening in the world?'

'They're all goin' apeshit in America.'

'What do you mean?'

'There's a riot down in the south. Police against the blacks.' Bobby sat forward. 'Can you get me a beer, love?'

'Sure.' Charlotte went to the fridge and brought back a bottle of ale for Bobby. She handed it to him and sat down beside him on the lounge.

'Jesus.' Charlotte's mouth twisted and her hand involuntarily settled across it. On the television they watched the footage of rioting that had been unfolding in Alabama in the United States. Police were lashing out at young black men and women with batons, and cars and houses had been set on fire.

'What's happening?' Charlotte felt uneasy.

Bobby shrugged. 'Someone wants desegregation. Look like that'll work to you?' Bobby shook his head. 'Just leave it as it is. Over there and here.'

'What do you mean?' Charlotte looked across at her husband.

'You know what I mean. We have our place, they have theirs. It's like that all over the world.'

'But that can change, surely?'

Bobby huffed laughter. 'How many Abo friends do you have?'

Charlotte's eyes widened with a sudden burst of excitement at the chance to talk about Michael. Her mouth opened, and she saw Bobby intrigued by her reaction. Her eyes narrowed and she said nothing.

'Neither do I.'

***

Charlotte followed the story with interest over the following days, listening to radio broadcasts and watching the news that had the unrest front and centre. She learnt the riot had been sparked by members of the Ku Klux Klan who were unhappy about the announcement of the Birmingham Truce Agreement that was to introduce partial desegregation. Many of the high-ranking Klansmen had assembled in Bessemer, Alabama, for a rally. In response to the announcement, the church house of AD King, the brother of Martin Luther King Jnr, was blown up along with a motel where King Jnr and others had been staying. The black community, who had been celebrating the announcement of the agreement, assembled in great numbers after the bombings. What Charlotte had seen on the television was what had followed.

***

She and Bobby spoke about the troubles over dinner for the next few nights. He said President Kennedy had acted the right way by using the military and cited that three black men had stabbed a white police officer in the ribs, and that they *should be hung in public for doing it*. Bobby seemed energised by all of it, the riot, the uprising of the black man and the defence of the white establishment. Charlotte did her best to fight through her husband's myopic opinions but was inevitably drowned out by his raised voice. When she manoeuvred the discussion in her favour by citing his own hypocrisies over treatment of people both black and white, they ended their last discussion with Bobby saying that, *the Territory is different to anywhere, and what our government does protects them from themselves.*

Charlotte went to bed early that evening and lay awake worried about Michael Roberts. He'd been alone for two days and though she'd left him ample water, he'd not have eaten for most of that time. She was worried he might think that she'd abandoned him. That he might have tried to leave and look for refuge somewhere else. A place where he may be turned over to the police. She drifted off to sleep and dreamt about her mother. She was in a house she didn't know, her mother in a bedroom breastfeeding a baby. Her mother was crying, and the baby kept pulling away from her nipple. Charlotte saw herself as a grown woman, a similar age to her mother. She walked over and tried to help, but her mother yelled at her to stay away and told her the baby was okay. She woke the next morning to Bobby's erection pushing between her buttocks. He growled as he thrust harder and she could tell his noise was pushed through a smile.

'I don't feel well.' Charlotte edged away from him. 'Tonight. I'll be better tonight.'

Bobby shoved himself away from her, turned over and swore beneath his breath. Charlotte contemplated giving in to his craving, to appease him and temper what suspicion might grow from her lack of interest. She felt sexual, but not for her husband. She got out of bed, walked to the bathroom and locked the door. She faced the mirror and looked at herself. Her breasts were full and sat firmly. She took note of the new ginger-coloured freckle on her left side. She lifted her long hair up, held it for a moment, then let it go and watched it fall across her face in ribbons. She felt one of her breasts, gently sweeping her hand across her nipple. It filled with blood quickly and she watched her areola contract and deepen in colour. She closed her eyes and thought about Michael Roberts and how his hands might feel across her breasts. What his open mouth and tongue across her nipple might arouse in her. She opened her eyes, pulled her hand away from her body and felt between her legs. It was wet and sticky, and she could smell herself.

* * *

She made Bobby breakfast. When he came to eat, he was sullen and answered her questions with clipped words that were roughened by his sleep. Charlotte felt nervous and wished she'd submitted to his interest. He left when a car horn sounded from the street outside. When she asked him when he'd be back, he didn't reply. She had access to the car, but for how long she didn't know. Her insides fluttered and she could smell the tart fragrance of her own breath, which she recognised came with being nervous or excited. She made a decision, energised by the risk of going to see Michael without a lie to explain away her whereabouts if Bobby returned looking to use the car, or wanting to spend time with her.

As she drove out to the barn she tempered the uncomfortable threads of guilt she'd felt earlier in the morning for not having had sex with her husband, and the fear that he might suspect her lack of interest as the outcome of cheating. Her anxiety dissipated and she was left with only the anticipation of seeing Michael. She'd packed medical supplies, bandages, antiseptic, and plenty of food and water. And she'd also filled a small foam cooler with ice and six bottles of lager.

When she got to the barn, she pulled open the door and Michael was standing only a metre from her. She was startled and let out a noise that made Michael laugh.

'You just sounded like a dog yelping.'

Michael limped toward her and gently took the basket of food Charlotte had hooked over her elbow.

She looked at his broken ankle, still in a splint. 'Where were you going just now?'

'Just the door. I have been walking as much as I can the last couple of days. Getting as strong as I can.'

'You thinking of making a run for it?' Charlotte said it so it could be read as jocular, but beneath her inference, hiding, was her fear that she may return one day and he'd be gone.

'No. I wouldn't run out on you. Not after what you've done for me.'

Charlotte felt a relief envelop her, so generous that she could feel herself lighten. Her shoulders lifted and the arches of both feet pushed away from the soles of her shoes. She could feel the blood rushing to her cheeks as she blushed and smiled. 'Well, you look better.'

She laid down a blanket beside Michael's makeshift bed and they both sat. They ate sandwiches, mango and apple and then opened the beer. After his first mouthful, Michael closed his eyes, lifted his head at the barn's gabled roof and laughed. 'Shit. A white woman giving me a beer. No one's ever gonna believe that.' He looked across at Charlotte, his grin lifting the flesh around his cheekbones to two knobby circles.

Charlotte smiled back. 'I wasn't sure what sort of beer to buy. My husband drinks ale or Old, which I don't like, so I went for this.'

'Any beer is good beer. It all does what we want it to do, eh?' Michael shrugged. 'Being affected by grog is always going to have its good happy bits.'

'I guess you're right.'

'It's what happens after those bits when we all drink too much that it goes wobbly. But that first taste? Like a cord snapped across your shoulders to make you all loose, and you feel that relaxin' feelin'. That's pretty good.'

'Yeah, it sure is.'

Midway through her second bottle, Charlotte felt the effects of the alcohol first in her cheeks, they warmed, and she knew they'd have reddened. Michael was almost finished his third, when he asked, 'Did you see my son?'

'Yes, I saw him. I didn't make any contact, like you said, but I watched him from a distance at the place you told me about.'

Michael took a long labouring breath and his eyes began to well. 'How did he look?'

'He looked just as you said. Tall, skinny. Kickin' a footy.' Charlotte let loose a laugh. 'He looked very handsome. Just like his father.' Charlotte looked away when Michael held eye contact with her; she knew she was blushing but it was hard to feel the sensation that came with it with her cheeks already warmed by the beer.

A moment of quiet passed and she asked softly, 'Can I talk to him next time? Tell him you're safe. Make a plan to bring him to you.'

'You have to be careful. My people will be watchin' him.'

'I will, I promise.'

'Okay.'

They sat quietly for a moment. Michael held up his bottle of beer, waving it side to side through a narrow sunbeam that had split through the barn roof. 'What do you tell your husband? When you come here?'

'I lie.'

Michael turned to her. 'What's he like?'

Charlotte took a moment to answer, weighing how much honesty to respond with. 'He's a man. Man's man sort of bloke.'

'Everywhere up here.'

'Yep.'

'So what makes him a man?'

Charlotte shrugged. 'He was a cowboy. A bull rider. He acts like a man. Thinks like a man.'

'A white man,' Michael said without inflection so it couldn't be mistaken for a question.

'Yes. He does.'

'Not his fault. Learn what you're taught. We all do.'

Charlotte looked at Michael a long time in the silence that followed, and then said it quickly and frankly, 'You might know who he is?'

Michael turned to her. 'Yeah?'

'Bobby Clark.'

Michael's brow furrowed and he looked away from her.

Charlotte absorbed his reaction and then laughed through a tight mouth. 'You do know him.'

'Yeah, I know him.' Michael didn't turn back to her. 'He's a man, eh?'

Charlotte could hear the dislike in Michael's voice. She didn't reply, afraid it would lead to an uncomfortable end to their day. Instead she opened another beer for them both, and they leant back on the barn wall. He rested his free arm across his lower abdomen and made a soft fist. Charlotte looked at the thick veins that darted through the rear of his forearm. In a thought she didn't invite, she wondered whether his penis might also hold the same vascular form under its skin. She dismissed the reflection quickly, though didn't feel the uncomfortable prickle of guilt that normally followed.

'I'll be better soon. My ankle is strong. If you can bring my son to me, I could leave with him during the night. Catch a train.' Michael looked at Charlotte, his eyes brightened, his mouth ajar, his frown pinched tightly scoring two deep lines either side of his eyebrows. Charlotte recognised his hope. It was the first time she'd seen it. And it presented like a child's hope for something unattainable. A present for Christmas a parent couldn't afford, the hope that a lost loved one was still alive.

'Yes. I can do that.'

'It's gotta be soon. Someone's gonna find me here. Some time.'

Charlotte's head dropped to the blanket and her eyes stung. 'I know.'

They spoke for the next hour about how to manage the escape from Darwin. What date, what time of day, and where to. Michael said Sydney where he had cousins. By the time Charlotte left to go home they'd made their plan. She cried from the moment she drove out from the barn until she turned into her street.

CHAPTER 24

EARLY IN THE morning, just after dawn, Ned got a phone call from a young constable asking him to go directly to Darwin Harbour. When he arrived, the constable directed him to a fishing trawler that was lashed to the side of a pylon. Two men in their thirties stood in the boat, both were unshaven and barefoot, both sinewy and underfed.

'What have you got here?' Ned settled by the pylon.

'Dead fella. In the boat.' The accent had a Queensland twang, and the fisherman spoke from the side of his mouth.

Ned climbed aboard. On the deck was the uncovered body of a man, naked and bloated, the flesh discoloured, and in parts open from where prawns and crabs had begun to feed. Ned looked at the face, and though it was swollen and sheet white, he could tell straight away that it was David O'Shea. He cupped a palm, covered his nose to soften the smell, and then got off the boat.

* * *

David O'Shea had been found in a trawling lane several miles north of Nightcliff Beach. Ned made sure he was at the morgue when Ron Thompson first viewed the body. It didn't take Thompson long to determine that O'Shea had drowned. Ned pressed him on whether there might have been foul play, whether it had been a forced drowning. But there were no indications that suggested anything other than he'd taken a swim, and then been dragged by the tide to a spot he couldn't make it back to shore from.

'The Timor takes more people than any body of water in this country.' Thompson covered the corpse, took off his latex gloves and pointed to the stack of mortuary fridges. 'There's one in there. A little boy from a mission. Mother turned her back a moment, and he was gone. They shouldn't be swimming this time of the year anyway, fuckin' crocs and box jellyfish everywhere.' Thompson looked over David O'Shea. 'It's a miracle he wasn't eaten or stung.'

'He was found naked.'

Thompson raised an eyebrow. 'Well, clothes can fall away, but not likely unless they were threadbare to begin with.'

'So, he entered the water naked?' Ned looked over at the covered body.

'Yep. Almost certainly.'

Ned looked up at Thompson. 'It was suicide.'

'It was drowning, I can't know what his intentions were when he entered the water and I don't know why he was naked.'

'How long had he been in the water?'

'A few days at most. Anyone been reported missin'?'

'This is the Territory, Ron, people come here to go missin'.' Ned didn't tell Thompson he knew who the dead man was, he wasn't going to tell anyone that. 'Thank you, Ron.'

* * *

Driving back to the station, Ned thought back on the night he'd seen David O'Shea at the Victoria Hotel. And what he'd said. *I sold my little boy out.* He remembered how upset he was, how desperate his self-loathing sounded. There was nothing for Ned to do but the paperwork on a drowning. But he was going to follow up, talk with O'Shea's family and delicately prod to see if there was any merit in his suspicion that he had suicided.

Two days later the body of David O'Shea was formally identified by his wife. It was a front-page story in the *Northern Territory News*. Ned got to the O'Shea residence just on dusk. The humidity throughout the day had been suffocating, rain had fallen in small bursts from broken lumps of storm clouds, but no sooner had it stopped than the sun shone through again baking the wet roads and earth, sending bands of sodden steam into every living space. Ned had changed his shirt twice during the day, and his socks were wet through from the toes to the end cuffs. He craved a beer as he walked up the stairs and onto the porch of the small house elevated by brick piers. His mouth was dry, and he could tell from the heat of both his tongue and the fleshy insides it touched that his breath would smell sulphuric. He knocked on the door and then turned back toward the coastline he could see through the weeping foliage of casuarina trees. He looked out onto the Timor for a moment, it was smooth, not a breath of wind to push the rows of tiny waves that rose and collapsed on themselves. Ned raised his hand, spread his fingers and felt for moving air. There was nothing. 'Still,' he said quietly to himself.

'Can I help you?' The voice was soft, medium-pitched, and Ned could tell it had been made uneven from sleep.

He turned from the sea and looked at Cassandra O'Shea. Her eyes were bright blue, the skin beneath them sagging from tiredness. She was brown freckled across her face, her lips were full and looked drained of blood, as though she were about to faint.

'I'm Senior Constable Ned Potter. I'm the man who responded to the call about the discovery of your husband's body.'

'Oh. Of course. Um, please come inside.'

* * *

Inside it was dark, there wasn't a light on in the entire house and, with the sun falling outside, Ned could barely see two steps ahead of himself. The first thing he properly noticed was a crucifix hanging on the wall in the room Cassandra led him to.

'I'm sorry. Could you turn on a light, I'm having trouble seeing.' Ned smiled at her, his hands held together, close to his torso so as to be as congenial and unthreatening as possible.

Cassandra didn't say a word but turned on a light.

'Thank you.'

'Please sit down.'

Cassandra sat on a single lounge chair that faced a television. Ned looked around for the best place to sit and face her. There was nothing, only a longer lounge that stood beside where Cassandra had planted herself. He sat down as close to her as he could.

'This is a lovely home.' Ned looked around, it was neat, new carpet had been laid and he could smell the fibre. 'Smells like new carpet.'

'Yes, David laid it himself only last month. It's very soft.'

'Yes, it looks it. And I love the smell of new carpet, well the smell of new anythin' really.' He smiled at Cassandra and then quickly looked around the room. There were two bookshelves

against the furthest wall, both full. And every wall was adorned
with a crucifix.

'Do you go to church, Senior Constable Potter?' Cassandra
positioned herself so she could get a straighter look at Ned.

'I go, yes.'

'Daily?'

'No. Not daily. Um … some Sundays, Easter, Christmas.'

'Do you believe in God?'

'Yes. I do.'

'I mean really believe? That He's up there? Looking over us all?
Protecting the good? Listening to our prayers?'

'Mum?'

Cassandra stood quickly and Ned turned to the sound of the
voice. In the doorway stood a young boy, his sandy-coloured hair
falling over his eyes and beside his cheeks in long thick ribbons
held together by sweat. He ran his small hand gently across his
bare torso, as though tickling himself.

'What is it?' Cassandra walked to him.

'I had another bad dream.'

Ned was drawn to the young boy's shorts. They were sodden on
one side from where he'd wet himself.

'It's okay. Go with your brother and run a bath and I'll be with
you in a minute.' Cassandra turned the young boy around and
gently pushed him from the doorway and quickly out of sight.

'Is that your son?'

'Yes. My eldest. That's Aaron.' Cassandra stood in the doorway
where the young boy had been. 'If you could come back another
time that would be better.'

Ned stood. 'Of course. I just wanted to make sure you were
okay. I have some questions. I can ask them another time.'

'We spoke to the mayor. It was a lie. The mayor was very helpful. I don't have anything more to say. So, if you could please leave us.'

Ned nodded and smiled back at her. 'Of course.'

* * *

Ned fought his desire to think as logically as he could. He weighed the urge against the trouble he might find, but in the end it was all overwhelmed by the choking humidity that was so viscous Ned imagined opening a hole through it with his hands and poking his head into the space to take a breath of cool moving air. It had given him pleasure to imagine a similar thought when he was a boy, to summon the air moving across his face, to fill his mouth and then his lungs. He thought about what Cassandra O'Shea had said, that *we* had spoken to the mayor. *About what?* Ned wondered. It was unusual for Landry to be talking with members of the general public. And it sounded as though he'd assisted the O'Sheas somehow. He'd been *very helpful*, Cassandra had said. It didn't make sense. What puzzled Ned most was what she'd said in between those things. That it was a lie. *A lie about what?* He pushed the query to one side and moved on, though David O'Shea was another name he could now throw at Riley to gauge whether any dots were there to be joined.

While he drove to the Victoria Hotel, he remembered young Marcus Roberts and the forlorn look he'd given Ned when he'd asked if Ned would be able to find his father. Ned played out the versions of what may have happened to Michael and what was most likely. The most logical resolutions were the ones where Michael was dead. Perhaps, Ned thought, his body had been taken somewhere else to be buried. In that case he'd never be found. Ned thought about how improbable his discovery of Clarry Tallis and

Lionel Frazier in those shallow graves had been. The probability of finding Michael buried somewhere else was minute. He entertained the possibility that Michael may have escaped. He was a strong man and a fighter, and would have been able to overpower two or possibly three men. If that were the case, and if he wasn't injured too badly, then he was gone. He was a bushman and hunter. He'd never be found. Ned hoped that was what had happened. That Michael was making his way south through Kakadu, fishing with his hands for barramundi, hidden in the scrub and sleeping in the shade during the day while moving at night.

* * *

When he arrived at the Victoria Hotel it was full. The croc shooters, buffalo hunters and melon farmers mixed with the white-collar crew who'd allowed themselves an early mark due to the suffocating humidity. Ned politely made his way through the crowd toward the bar and ordered a schooner. He took it outside and stood on the footpath under the pub's awning. It was less crowded, and even in the soppy stillness, it was cooler and easier to breathe. The chatter from inside burst onto the veranda every time the doors opened to let out another patron. It was a noise built layer by layer, infused with the hums of alcohol. There was laughter and words spoken through grins, and the belly of arguments that squawked momentarily over the messy harmony and the clatter of glass. Ned loved the sound of a pub. He smiled and thought of his father, and the first time he'd sat and drank draught beer with him in the same hotel.

'Ned.'

Ned turned and standing in front of him, a glass of beer in hand, was Martha Clay. He almost didn't recognise her. Her face was narrower, the dimples through her cheeks deeper and visible without her smiling. Her bottom lip had tightened and no longer hung loose, and her eyes, though darker, paradoxically shone brighter. She looked healthy. She wore a loose summer dress, and the shoes she had on gave her some more height.

'Martha.' He smiled. 'What brings you here?'

'The same thing that brings everyone here. The fuckin' heat.'

'That's the truth. How are you?'

'I'm okay.'

Ned looked her up and down and smiled. 'Well, you look beautiful.'

'Thank you.'

He hesitated, and then stepped in closer to her. 'Has anything happened? Have you heard anything from Riley?'

'Nothing other than they're still investigating. What have you heard?'

Ned wasn't going to tell her Riley was angling to pin Ernie's death on suicide. 'I was told to keep out of it.'

Martha shook her head. 'The whole thing stinks.'

'Yeah.'

'I saw you at Fannie Bay Gaol. When you walked out those two men.'

'Yes.' Ned felt shame pass through his body, it was as if he shrank before her: his shoulders narrowed and slumped, the breadth of his chest squeezed inward and his legs bent at the knees.

'They didn't do it. They didn't kill Lionel Frazier and the other fella.'

'No. They didn't. Why were you there?'

'I wanted to see them. I wanted to see how they walked, what their faces looked like. Like I said, they didn't do it.'

She paused a moment, and Ned sensed she was deliberating whether to disclose what was on her mind. 'Ernie had a job before he was killed. Part-time. Lionel Frazier had got it for him. They worked together.'

Ned looked at Martha and just as the first sounds of a question left his mouth, a man appeared by her side. He was broad shouldered, his nose flattened, and his fingers nearly made it all the way around the shaft of the schooner glass he was holding. It looked as though he were choking it.

'Who's the copper?'

'This is Ned Potter. He found Ernie. Ned, this is my brother, Troy. He's up from Townsville to help me out. I'm going to be moving back there.'

'Right. Well, g'day, Troy.' Ned extended his hand.

Troy looked at it and then back to his sister.

'It's okay. He's okay.'

Troy shook Ned's hand quickly.

'Just give us a minute.' Martha smiled at her brother and he walked away to give them some space.

'He looks pissed off.'

'He was the only one in my family who spoke to Ernie. The only one who kept in contact with me.'

'I'm sorry, Martha.'

Martha looked him squarely in the eye. 'Lionel Frazier? He saw what Ernie saw. You understand?'

'Yes. Can I just –'

Martha interrupted him, 'That's it. I'm not saying anything else.' And she walked to the far end of the veranda toward her brother.

CHAPTER 25

'WHAT BUSINESS YOU got with Mrs O'Shea, Potter?'

Mayor Landry's office smelt of tobacco and sweet aftershave so Ned knew Riley had not long left there. Landry was sweating, his comb-over wet and lank, with large uncovered patches in between where his hair had gathered in thick bands. Ned looked at the bald spots, they were pale and shedding flaky bits of skin.

'I was the officer investigating the drowning of her husband.' Ned placed his hands behind his back and lifted his chin. 'It's my job. I was just following up, sir.'

'He drowned, Potter, that came directly from the coroner.' Landry lit a cigarette and sat forward over his desk. 'Why the hell would you need to see his wife?'

'Well, sir, I ran into David O'Shea not long before he drowned and he was a mess.'

'Meaning what, Potter?'

'Meaning he was upset. He was ramblin'.'

Landry cut Ned off. 'He was a drunk. Did you know that?'

'No, sir.'

'Well, he was.' Landry stubbed out his barely smoked cigarette and stood. He walked to the window and looked out. 'What did she say? Mrs O'Shea.'

Ned looked at Landry's hardly sucked cigarette in the ashtray, the paper split, tobacco spewing from its white tube, the yellow filter wet from Landry's mouth. *Landry was nervous*, Ned thought, he was agitated and unable to settle.

'She didn't say much at all. She asked if I believed in God. And then her young boy needed assistance and she asked me to leave.'

Landry walked from the window, sat back down behind his desk and lit another cigarette. 'Did she mention me?'

'No.' Ned's lie was well timed, without hesitation, and bereft of any signals that might alert Landry.

'I only ask because I helped her out with some issues she was having.'

'That right?' Ned nodded and then asked, as though it were incidental, 'What issues were those?'

'That's none of your business. But I'll tell you so as to make certain there's no further need for you to be callin' on her. Her husband was also a gambler. She has been a solid contributor to one of the Catholic parishes and was upset she couldn't continue to pass on her good fortune like she had been. She spoke to the priest and the priest spoke to me. I helped her out, cleared his debt.' Landry stood again, this time with confidence, his anxiety seemingly gone.

'That's mighty kind of you, Mayor.'

'Well, it's the least I can do for such a complete believer.' Landry followed with nothing but a smile at Ned. It was self-assured and completely without humility. 'You can go.'

'Okay.' Ned hesitated. 'Can I just ask a couple of questions?'

'Go ahead.'

'Um, who would be the priest at that church?'

Landry smiled. 'Does it matter?'

'Well, I guess not. Just my investigative instincts leading me somewhere.'

'Anything else?'

'Why did you bring me in here?'

'I beg your pardon?'

'Why would you be worried I was talking to Mrs O'Shea? Her husband's gambling and her contributions to the church aren't concerns of mine. I don't know the lady. I don't see how those might be a matter of concern for anyone but the O'Sheas. The only thing I get out of this, Mayor Landry, is that you seemed worried that she might have mentioned your name. And if it is as you say it is, the mayor helping out one of the churchgoers, I don't see why you wouldn't want that somehow broadcast. After all, we're all voters.' Ned stood still, his face an overplayed expression of curiosity. It was purposeful and there to make Landry uncomfortable. Landry walked to Ned.

'You know, Potter, I've done as much as I can to help you. I gave you those two scalps.' A fleck of tobacco shot from Landry's mouth and landed on Ned's chin. 'And they took the plea we offered. You should come to the sentencing. Speak to the press. Tell them what a good job you did. It'd be good for the town to have people hear that on the news. Read it in the newspaper. You should be grateful.'

'What are their names, Mayor?' Ned wiped the tobacco from his chin.

Landry turned away from him.

'Dell Sanders and Andrew Liston.' Ned followed Landry. 'That's their names. The ones goin' to jail for nothin'.'

Landry sat back down in his chair. 'Maybe it's time you moved on from here. Being as ungrateful as you are.'

'To where? I love the Territory.'

'Do yourself a kindness, son. Stay away from Mrs O'Shea.' Landry lifted his brow to reiterate the threat. 'Now get out.'

'Yes, Mayor.'

When Ned returned to the station, Riley fed him an arrogant grin from the doorway of his office. Ned watched him take his belt at the sides and pull his pants up higher.

'You'll choke yourself, Sergeant, if you pull those pants any higher.' He winked at Riley as he walked past and sat at his desk. When he looked back to where Riley had been standing, he'd gone. Ned felt as though he was winning at something. And yet he didn't see any way he could claim a victory. He had them unsettled, that was clear, but all he had was a suspicion that there was a connection in the murders of Clay, Tallis and Frazier. He didn't know why Landry was interested in David O'Shea, and he didn't know where Michael Roberts was, and couldn't be sure he'd been with Frazier or Tallis when they'd been murdered. But he did have the connection now that Ernie Clay had worked for or with Lionel Frazier. He was going to follow up that and also, despite what Landry had said, Cassandra O'Shea. But indirectly.

* * *

Ned made his way to St Mary's Cathedral. It was a large Catholic parish, and though he didn't know where Landry worshipped, it seemed like the obvious place to enquire. Ned had long stopped going to mass. He'd been brought up as Protestant, and even as a young boy, had been baffled by the disparities between Catholicism and Anglicanism. They both had a crucifix of Christ over the altar, both believed that he'd walked the earth, and they read from the same bible. From what he'd learnt later from reading, the Protestants had started their own religion because Henry the Eighth had requested an annulment of his marriage from Pope Clement the Seventh, and was denied. They also believed that the bread and wine offered up during mass was only a representation of Christ. The Catholics, he read, believed that, during the mass, the bread and wine was altered by miracle into the actual flesh and blood of the saviour. *Bullshit, all of it*, was how Ned had come to settle over religion.

He knocked on the front door to the parish vestry and Father McKay answered and stood before him. He'd healed since Ned had last seen him walking from the church in the evening. His chipped teeth had been capped, the bruising under his eyes and across his nose had dissolved, and he'd trimmed his beard so his face looked leaner.

'Father McKay. How are you?' Ned offered his hand and McKay shook it.

'I'm very well, thank you.' He took a moment to study Ned. 'Is there anything wrong?'

'No, I'm just following up on something.'

'Do I know you?'

'I'm Ned Potter. I last saw you after you'd had that fall.'

McKay looked confused and then found his recollection. 'Ah yes. Of course. Um, so how can I help you?'

'Just a simple question, Father. We came across a body not too long ago in the Timor. David O'Shea. A drowning it appears. His wife, Cassandra O'Shea, does she attend your parish for mass durin' the week or on Sundays?'

McKay brought his forefinger and thumb to his chin. 'O'Shea, you said?'

'Yes, Cassandra.'

He shook his head and then looked at Ned, eyes widened, mouth open and down-turned before replying. 'Maybe. It's quite a big congregation. I don't know all of them.'

'I'm sure you'd remember her, she contributes quite a bit.' Ned waited for a reaction from the priest but got nothing that roused any suggestion of collusion. Ned smiled. 'Well, maybe it's another parish. Thank you for your time, Father.'

* * *

Ned called two other churches in the town area, but neither parish priest knew of a Cassandra O'Shea. When he returned to the station, Landry was in Riley's office. He walked slowly to his desk, expecting to be called in. The request never came, though an hour later, Landry left Riley's office without looking in Ned's direction.

He got home just on dusk and when he walked into the house, Bonnie's father was sitting at the kitchen table smoking. Ned felt nervous energy tighten his chest, and then cascade into his stomach, making it swirl. His mind had jumped to the last encounter with Graham, when he'd buried his head in his crotch.

'Hey.'

Ned turned and Bonnie stood with Rose on her hip. Her eyes were red. 'What's wrong?' Ned immediately braced himself for news someone had died.

'Someone was here.' She began to cry, and Ned reached for Rose and took her from Bonnie's side.

'What do you mean?'

'A thug.' Cigarette smoke billowed from Graham's nose as he stood. 'Someone came to scare her. She called me and I came over.'

'What?' Ned reached for Bonnie and she tucked into the side opposite where he held Rose.

'You pissed some people off it seems.' Graham walked over to Ned. 'They sent someone to make sure you stop what it is you're doing.'

Ned stood quietly.

'What are you doing?' Bonnie asked, her nose running.

'My job. Who was here?' Ned's tone took a turn toward anger.

'A man. I've never seen him before.'

'What'd he look like?'

'Big, cropped hair.'

'What colour hair?'

'Blond.'

Ned thought of the men he knew that fitted the rudimentary description. 'What did he say?'

'Tell your husband to stop his line of enquiry.'

'Into what?'

'He didn't say.'

'He say anything else?'

Bonnie looked to her father.

'What?' Ned raised his voice.

'He said that someone would likely go missing if you continue.' Graham folded his arms, the old tattoos over his biceps spreading further than they once had, dissolved of all colour but bottle green.

'As in me?' Ned shook his head. 'It's bluster, Bonnie. Don't worry about it.'

'What if it's not?' Bonnie pulled hard up through her nose, her crying making her words quiver.

'They're not going to get rid of me. All I'm doing is my job.'

'I want to leave this place.' Bonnie turned and walked from the room.

Ned looked at Graham. 'There's nothin' to worry about.'

'That may be so. But what you're not considering is that the threat may not be aimed at you. It could be her. Or the child. I won't stand by and watch that happen.'

Ned hadn't ever considered that Bonnie and Rose might be used as a way to stop his interference. But he felt uneasy.

* * *

Ned fed Rose a bottle and nursed her to sleep. He put her down in her crib and then checked in on Bonnie, who was asleep in their bedroom. He kissed her on the forehead and went back out into the kitchen, took a bottle of beer from the fridge and joined Graham on the front porch. They leant over the timber balustrade and looked out onto the street. There was a faint smell of cooked tar and petrol. The moon was big and burnt orange, still lit by the fallen sun.

'Do you know why the moon appears so big like that?' Graham pointed to the moon with his cigarette held between his middle and index fingers.

'No. I've wondered why though.'

'It's an optical illusion that causes the moon to appear larger near the horizon than it does up in the sky.'

'Why?'

'Fucked if I know. It just does.' Graham swigged the last mouthful from his beer bottle. 'Some things just are, son. Like this place. The Territory. It's not for everyone.'

'What about over in Ireland? What was that like?'

'I loved Ireland growing up. Where I lived it was farmland. It was like an adventure every day. Fuckin' around and gettin' into mischief. But you never had to look over your shoulder. Not then. We hadn't long finished fightin' the Brits to become a free state. No one had any money in the country, but there was a sense of bein' free.' Graham smiled as he looked over the moonlit street. 'It was simple there.'

Ned smiled with him; he liked the way Graham made life back *there* sound. 'Would you ever go back?'

'No. There's goin' to be trouble there. I know men there, family.' He paused and stubbed out his cigarette on the balustrade. 'It's not far off. And it'll be brutal. Fuck the British.'

Graham lit another cigarette; his smile had gone. His anxiety was palpable and it made Ned apprehensive about asking any more questions.

'What are you goin' to do about this?' Graham flipped around so his elbows were resting on the balustrade.

Ned stayed facing the street. 'I don't know.'

'Well, if someone comes past again and makes a threat, I'll be takin' matters into my own hands.' Graham walked back inside and left Ned alone.

He stayed on the porch for another hour, deliberating on his next move. He didn't want Bonnie or Graham to be more concerned than they needed to be, but he was bothered by what they'd told him. He couldn't fit the description of the man with anyone. He thought about Mayor Landry in Riley's office, and if that meeting may have been the seed of what followed later in the day. He'd left Landry's office earlier that morning having been told it was perhaps time to move on. *Maybe*, he thought, Landry had stewed on their conversation and decided that a threat might pressure him to consider leaving. To bring his wife into the scenario where she'd become frightened and squeeze the idea of leaving to keep the family safe. *Fuck 'em*, Ned thought.

* * *

The next morning Ned walked into Riley's office and closed the door.

'What the fuck do you think you're doin'?' Riley stood from his chair, immediately combative. 'Get out.'

'Someone came by my house. Threatened my wife. Said I should quit doin' what I'm doin'.'

'That so.' Riley showed no signs either way of knowing or not.

'Big buzz cut, blond guy.'

'Well, Potter, I don't know anything about it, but I wouldn't for one second waste time hiring some thug to make a threat.' Riley walked around his desk and fronted Ned. 'If I wanted to threaten you, I'd do it in front of you like I am now.'

Ned nodded. 'Okay.'

'Anything else?'

'Anythin' happens to my wife or child, I'll kill whoever is responsible. From the hand that does it to the brain that puts it together.'

Riley laughed, turned from Ned and walked back to his desk. He continued to laugh; it was sickly and wheezing and quickly turned to a cough that chopped up the phlegm from his lungs and threw it up into his mouth. Ned watched him swallow it. Riley took a breath and sighed. 'Oh fuck, that was good. You're a funny man, Potter. And I will say this. Ballsy. Now get the fuck out.'

Ned stood, emasculated. He felt smaller than when he'd walked into the office. Riley was still laughing at him, and he wished he were someone else. Ned Potter was just a pest. That's all. A man they'd manipulated to arrest innocent men. A man they would shut down.

CHAPTER 26

CHARLOTTE WATCHED FROM the same place she'd hidden before. This time, Marcus walked the red dirt path leading him out of the mission. He was barefoot with a football in one hand and a bucket in another. Charlotte scampered quickly from her spot, skirted the boundary of the mission and fell in behind Marcus as he walked toward the beach.

She stayed a good distance away, and though his stride was lazy, his gait was long and made it hard for Charlotte to keep up. She quickened her pace and could feel beads of sweat gathering on her top lip. She mopped them away with her bottom lip and tasted the salt. She watched as Marcus turned sharply from the trodden dirt path toward the beach, through a row of casuarina trees and over copses of saltbush. She could see the length of his body shortening as he hopped down the soft sandy decline leading to the water. She took off her shoes and followed, but made her own path and stopped at the summit of a small dune that gave her an unfettered view of Marcus at the water's edge.

He held a battered old roll of cork with a spool of dark green fishing line. Charlotte watched him bait a hook with a prawn. He let out some of the line and swung it above his head like a lasso, faster and faster until the line blurred and then became invisible. Charlotte could hear the line cutting through the air. He let it go, and his baited hook landed about a hundred feet from where he stood.

Charlotte looked back toward the mission. She couldn't see it through the fluffy tree canopies and the knotty stalks of saltbush, and she couldn't hear anything but the sound of the small waves collapsing on the shore. She walked down the small sandbank and approached Marcus slowly. She stopped just before the tideline where he'd left his football, and spoke gently, 'Marcus.' The word nowhere loud enough for the boy to hear. 'Marcus Roberts.'

He turned quickly, dropping his fishing cork, the length of his body tightening, as though preparing to run. 'Who are you?'

'My name is Charlotte Clark. I know where your father is.'

Marcus's eyes narrowed, and Charlotte could see him balancing what he'd just been told and by whom. *A white woman in a powder-blue dress with red hair.* He ran toward her, scooped up his football in one hand and ran back toward the mission. Charlotte's first instinct was to chase him. She overturned it though, and instead walked slowly to where Marcus had dropped his fishing reel. She looked out along the trajectory of the fishing line and instantly felt a strong pull against the reel.

'Ooohh.' It tugged again and then the fishing line ran from its spool. She watched the line quickly come away from the cork, loop by loop, and then took hold of the line and stopped the fish's run.

'Reel it in.' The voice came from just behind her and was high pitched.

'Okay.' Charlotte began winding the line back onto the cork, circle by circle.

'Let it run again.'

'I beg your pardon?'

'Let the line free again. Need to tire him out. It's big.' The voice had come closer.

'Okay then.' Charlotte let the line free and watched it unravelling from the cork as the fish ran again.

'That's enough.'

Charlotte turned around quickly and saw Marcus standing at the tideline, the football tucked under his arm. 'Do you want to reel it in?'

'No. You do it.'

Charlotte stopped the fish's retreat and began reeling it in. It breached the surface of the water twice, and both times Marcus let out a kind of cheer. Charlotte smiled the whole way fighting with the fish, and by the time she brought it to shore, Marcus was standing beside her. Charlotte looked down at the thick bronzed flanks and spiny rays of the fish. 'It's a mangrove jack.' She smiled at Marcus.

'How'd ya know that?'

'I fish. All the time. Haven't caught one of these in a while though.'

'It's 'cause of the bait. Jacks love prawns, but you gotta keep the shell on or they'll pull it off the hook.' Marcus dropped his football, got to his haunches and took the hook from the jack's mouth. 'I'll fry him tonight for dinner.' He put the fish in the bucket he'd left behind when he'd run, and then looked up at Charlotte, his uncertainty back.

'It's okay. Please don't run again.'

Marcus stood up. 'What's his name? Me dad's.'

'Michael. Roberts.'

'Where is he?'

'He's safe. He wants to see you.'

'What happened?'

Charlotte thought for a moment how to reply. 'He can tell you. But he's okay.'

Marcus looked at her, only a small part of his caution let go. 'Who are you? To him?'

'I just found him. He was injured. I helped him get better.'

'Why?'

'Because it's the right thing to do.'

Marcus said nothing, but Charlotte felt he believed her.

'I can take you to him.'

'When?'

'Tomorrow. At night. I can come and collect you and drive you there.'

'Can't you just tell me where he is? I'll find it.' Marcus's suspicion ran through the length of his question; he did nothing to bury it or even tip it slightly so it might be read as just a convenience for him to go alone.

'It's miles away. I have to take you. And you can't tell anyone you're going, and after, you can't tell anyone you know where he is. That was said to me by your father.' Charlotte paused and then took a breath. 'He told me to tell you something only you and he knew.'

Marcus narrowed his eyes. 'What?'

'Before your mother died of cancer, she told you that you were her reason for fighting so hard to stay alive.'

Marcus turned from Charlotte and looked over the Timor. His eyes began to water and tears fell and slipped down his cheeks. He never made a sound. He wiped his face with his palms and looked back at Charlotte.

'What time?'

'I'll meet you here at six o'clock. The car will be parked somewhere close by and we'll walk to it.'

'Okay.' Marcus put out his hand which took Charlotte by surprise. She looked at it a moment, and just long enough that Marcus's instinct for wariness was alerted again and he began to retract his hand. Charlotte reached quickly and took it. She held it and looked into his eyes. 'You can trust me, Marcus. I'll prove that to you.' She shook his hand and smiled, and he nodded subtly at her.

* * *

When she got home, she prepared one of Bobby's favourite dishes, T-bone steak with spinach and roast potatoes. She cleaned the house, vacuumed the carpet, mopped the floors, dusted shelves, disinfected the toilet and scrubbed the bath. She wasn't sure whether Bobby would notice her work, but it was another piece of her plan, along with the meal, that would hopefully soften him for the request she was going to present. She needed the car. Going to the beach the next evening and telling Marcus she couldn't follow through wasn't an option. Any trust she'd established would dissolve right then.

She was also going to initiate sex with Bobby, and hoped that act, along with the clean house, the meal and a bright disposition would be enough to confidently ask for the car knowing the answer would be yes.

When Bobby got home his clothes were covered in the ash and embers from a house fire he'd been called to extinguish. His face was reddened from sunburn and his eyes looked lighter than usual, the blueness almost turned to white. It gave him an exotic kind of look, and Charlotte had often thought the colour change made him irrefutably handsome. He showered and made a comment on the cleanliness of the house without being prompted to notice. Charlotte served dinner and sat with him while they ate. She asked about his day and the fire, and listened to him talk quietly about what had happened. He told her that there had been children trapped inside and that he'd gone into the house and pulled them out. He said it humbly without boast or hyperbole, and said that he didn't know if he'd be able to carry on as a fireman if he'd seen *those children burn. That's tragic and somethin' I don't think I'd recover from.* Charlotte felt guilty. 'You're a good man, Bobby.'

He looked at her, nodded and raised his brow. 'Sometimes.'

She asked for the car when they'd finished eating sweets, and Bobby nodded in reply and said nothing else. He went to bed early without a drink, and when she came into the bedroom he was fast asleep. She lay next to him and wondered whether, if she tried, *really tried,* a life with Bobby could be fulfilling. She conceded to herself she hadn't been an assertive lover, and had stolen time from Bobby to be in the company of another man. And she was about to do it again, when she knew that the right thing to do as a wife was to be with him. If she could shift the reverie of her invented lives and avenues of escape, and just *exist in the moment,* then maybe she could be free to live with what was in front of her. She dozed off to sleep with the possibility losing its thread and her mind chasing the commitments of the next day and what lay ahead.

CHAPTER 27

NED SAT ON a stool at the Victoria Hotel. It was just after three o'clock on a Saturday afternoon, and the humidity from outside seeped into the bar from every open nook and broken part of the building. Up through the floorboards and through the brickwork joints that had eroded, leaving stacks of blocks on top of unsteady beds of mortar. Ned asked Katie Briggs to turn up the fans she'd placed at either end of the bar, but the extra torque made it worse, the hot wet air chopped up and thrown too quickly at the customers. She turned them back down and offered respite by saying that air conditioning was to be in by the middle of the next month.

Ned had spent the morning and early afternoon with Bonnie and Rose shopping. Bonnie had wanted to buy a new dress for herself and a swimsuit for Rose. They were planning on a holiday in the middle of May to North Queensland. The box jellyfish would have moved out into deeper water and the beaches would be open. They'd swim during the day and then relax in the house they were looking to rent not far from the town centre. As Ned sat in the soggy mire of humidity, his schooner of beer almost finished and warm, he wished he was on holiday already. Away from Darwin and the events that he was measuring himself against and had him locked in a state of unease. Perhaps a move to another town might be a way to get out from under his self-loathing. Somewhere he could begin fresh instead of chasing unfinished business. He was tired of being hauled into Riley and Landry's offices. He felt as though he was being told to stay *still*, not for a moment, but forever while he continued to work here as a policeman.

'Another one?' Katie wiped the sweat from her forehead with a small bar towel.

'It won't stay cold long enough.'

'Yeah? Drink it faster.'

'I suppose I could do that.' Ned finished his glass with a single gulp and ground up his face in reaction to the tepid beer. 'Jesus, not even a bubble left in it.'

Katie took his empty schooner glass and pulled a bottle of beer from an esky stacked with ice. 'This will stay colder. The fridges are about to go bust.'

'Thank you.' Ned took a long swallow, his bottle half-finished when he lowered it and burped into the soft edge of a fist. 'That is cold.'

'Be careful, Senior Constable, that's a cracking pace.' Katie left him with a smile and walked to the other end of the bar to serve another customer.

* * *

An hour later, Ned could feel the weight of the troubles resting on his shoulders begin to lighten. He wasn't free of them but was aware that, after a few more beers, they'd be anaesthetised.

He wasn't certain yet if he was going to head down the path of complete emancipation.

An older man, Trey Bushell, sat down beside him. Ned knew of him from the pub and from stories he'd been told by his father. Bushell and Ned's father were roughly the same age and had worked together at one point at Darwin Port. Bushell had been a quiet man after returning from the war. He'd served in the Pacific and was held as a prisoner in a Singapore camp. Ned's father had told him that Bushell was *twisted from the capture*, and that *he was unstable*. He'd told Ned stories from his time on the port, where Bushell would fight bareknuckle behind the docks against whomever the man holding the money offered him. Big money was being bet and Ned's father never saw Bushell lose. On one occasion Bushell's nose was so badly broken that the cartilage forming the bridge was exposed and split through its middle. *Bushell*, Ned's father said, *never showed a sign of pain let alone discomfort*.

Bushell was of average height, not particularly well muscled and looked anything but intimidating. His nose was flattened and was the only reference to his brawling, otherwise he could have passed for an accountant or a clerk. His hair was now bluish grey and neatly combed, and held in place by a good amount of Brylcreem. His eyes were light brown with hazel specks spattered through the ring closest to his pupils. His teeth were off-white, though straight, and only the bottom row showed when he talked. Ned had, on occasion, had conversations with him while at the pub. But they were nothing of substance, and it was always Ned who was left with the chore of moving the dialogue forward. He looked across at Trey Bushell and deliberated on whether to bother starting a discussion he knew would be tedious. The alcohol in his blood however, as it often did, tickled his compassionate and optimistic traits.

'Hey, Trey. What do you know, mate?' Ned turned on his stool so he was facing Trey Bushell.

'The same as yesterday. The day before that. And the year before that.'

'Same same, hey?'

'Yep.' Bushell took a mouthful of his drink, a whiskey and ice filled to the top of a seven-ounce glass.

Ned searched, as he knew he would have to, for the next question. As he did, a draft of hot air blew past him in the wake of another customer and brought his attention back to how chokingly hot it was inside. Instantly he didn't have the energy to continue with inane questions for Trey Bushell's consideration.

'Okay then.' He turned back to the bar.

'You look like your dad.' Bushell sat straighter.

Ned, surprised, turned to him. 'Yeah? Most people say I look like my mother.'

'She was pretty.'

'Yes, she was.'

Bushell grimaced and reached for his knee.

'You okay?'

'Knees and hips. Can't hardly get outta bed some mornings. The heat though, it's good for the joints. If I lived any further south I'd be bedridden.'

It was the most Ned had heard Trey Bushell speak all at once.

'Have you ever considered moving?' Ned held up his near empty beer bottle to Katie Briggs.

'A few times. I thought about Broome in WA. Kids kept me here though. We had some trouble with a few of 'em.'

'Really?'

'Just silly things kids do. They're not around anymore. They moved all over the place.' Bushell swirled the whiskey and ice around in his glass, the sound of it knocking against the sides had a kind of cooling effect that made the heat more bearable for Ned.

'What do you think of Darwin these days?'

Bushell turned to Ned and huffed, 'This place won't ever change. Hot. Crocs, stingers, fuckin' sharks. Good fishin'. Cold beer. Racist. It's the Territory.' Bushell took a swallow from his glass. 'Mayor Landry. He's a fuckin' crook. He doesn't believe in anything but his money.'

'You know him?'

'I knew his family. I lived in Sydney before the war. I worked as a carpenter for his old man and uncles. They made a fortune building housing commission homes.'

'I didn't know that.'

'Landry doesn't know what it is to look over his shoulder. To scratch around in the dirt for his next fuckin' penny.'

'What was he like as a kid?' Ned took another beer from Katie with barely a look, enthralled by what Bushell was disclosing.

'Same. Always handsome. But without that fuckin' thing he does with his hair.' They both laughed. 'Smart. Ambitious. Why he came here. Opportunity.'

'Not much has changed then.'

'Has a brother no one really knows about.'

'Really? Older or younger?'

'He's older. Their father sent him away to the bush somewhere in New South Wales when he was a teenager.'

'Why?'

247

'I don't know. It was strange. One day he was there, the next he wasn't. I seen him though. He's back here. He's a priest.'

'What?'

'Yeah, he came back. I seen him talking with Mayor Landry a few times at the Darwin.'

'You sure it's him?'

'I know it's him. I spoke to him. Said my hello's and stuff. He didn't seem too glad to see me.'

Ned turned his bottle of beer on the bar and picked at the label, deep in thought. 'What's his name?'

'He don't use his last name. Goes by McKay.'

'Excuse me?'

'Yeah, he's got a parish at some school.'

Ned stood from his stool.

'You okay?' Bushell looked him once over.

'Mayor Landry's older brother is Father McKay?'

'Yeah, that's right.'

'Who else knows? Have you told anyone?'

'Tell someone, why? Who fuckin' cares? I don't.'

'He doesn't want anyone to know. It was real nice talkin' to you, Trey.' Ned laid a one-pound bill on the bar and left.

CHAPTER 28

WHEN CHARLOTTE GOT to the beach, Marcus wasn't there. She looked at her watch as it ticked just past six o'clock. She looked out over the Timor, the water was coffee coloured under the shade of the evening storm clouds that were building. Perhaps Marcus had told someone about their rendezvous, and it had been dismissed as a ploy to take him from what remained of his family. She turned back toward the casuarina trees and thickets of saltbush. She considered calling his name but didn't want to alert anyone else who might be within earshot.

She heard a whistle and from behind the trunk of a casuarina tree, Marcus waved. Charlotte walked toward the scrub. He was smiling. 'You came.'

'Yes. Of course I came. Are you ready?' Charlotte smiled and a wondrous anticipation enveloped her, the same kind of feeling she'd experienced observing someone unwrap a present she'd given them, or watching the first mouthful of food she'd prepared reveal its flavour to a guest.

* * *

The car was parked close to where they exited the bush. It was against a curb in a street with shoulders that were unsealed and gravelly. Marcus sat beside her and watched out the window as dusk fell and the landscape changed. Charlotte looked across at him. 'You can open the window if you like.' Marcus turned to her, as if to ask if she was certain. She smiled again and wound down her own window. A moment later Marcus did the same and the humidity entered the car. It was still across the flat plains of dirt and patchy bush, so there was no wind to rush in and deafen the inside, no gusts that could take their breath away or numb the skin on their faces. Marcus slowly put his arm outside until it was fully stretched, he opened his hand and let his palm feel the speed of the car against the air. He turned to Charlotte and smiled. She put her arm out the window and made like it was a bird's wing, a gentle flap that Marcus copied.

'We're flying.' Charlotte laughed.

'I can smell the storm.' Marcus lifted his nose to the window. 'It's gonna be a good one.'

Charlotte could smell the rain coming and felt the first gusts of wind that were pushing it their way. She closed her eyes for just a moment and took a deep breath. She savoured the smells let out from the earth, the petrichor expanding and rising into the atmosphere signalling the ground was preparing to drink. She felt at ease with herself, and proud.

* * *

When they arrived at the barn they'd already driven through the storm, though they'd only caught the corner of it as it had turned and changed course back toward town. Marcus held his father for minutes without letting go. He buried his head into his chest and occasionally looked up at him, as though to make certain the moment was real. They both cried while Charlotte stood away from them and watched. Then they all sat down over a blanket and ate together; Charlotte made a fuss of them but said little as Michael and Marcus reconnected. She listened as Marcus asked what had happened and Michael filled in only the large pieces that were visible by his injuries. Michael looked at her at times throughout, and she could feel his gratitude along with his own doubt that it might all be unreal and just dreams.

* * *

Marcus fell asleep curled up in his father's form, his head resting on his chest. Charlotte covered him with the corner of the blanket that they were on, and sat opposite Michael.

'He's a beautiful young boy.'

'Yeah. He is. He's always been a good boy, a good heart.' Michael stroked his son's hair.

'I'm glad he trusted me.'

'You must have been very convincing.'

'I don't know. We caught a fish together.' Charlotte let out a laugh that was followed with a sigh. 'Maybe that was it?'

Michael looked directly at Charlotte. 'It's because you're a good person, eh. That's what he saw.'

Charlotte wanted to hold him. To tell him she wanted to go wherever it was he and Marcus were going. She lowered her head to hide the tears that she could feel stinging her eyes.

* * *

Charlotte drove Marcus back to town. He slept most of the way, his meek snore interrupted when Charlotte hit a bump on the road. He woke not long before they reached the mission's border. He looked out the window as he'd done when they'd left. 'I'll miss it here.'

'What will you miss?'

'My friends. Footy. Fishin'. Looking for baby crocs in the swamps. How it smells here.'

Charlotte thought for a moment about what she'd miss if she moved away. 'Yeah. I like the smells too. And the fishing. And storms.'

'I'll come back one day.' Marcus opened the window. 'When I'm grown up. To see my friends and fish here again.'

'Maybe you will.'

* * *

She dropped him off and he walked quickly into the darkness, onto the red dirt path leading to the mission. On her way home she passed Hotel Darwin, and wondered whether Bobby would be there. While the thought was still top of her mind, she saw him. He was leaning against a car, smiling, talking with another woman. As Charlotte passed them, she looked in the rear-vision and saw Kelly Dillon, her head thrown back in laughter. She wondered whether Bobby might have been fucking her. She entertained the idea that he was, and at that moment, in the car, she didn't care.

At home she poured herself a glass of whiskey over ice, and then sat out on the porch. The pushing storm had long passed and the air was still again. The vacant lots of land in front of the house had been mowed, and the openings between the grass and rubble were wider and made the property appear unappealing and severe. She thought about the people who might soon build there and become her neighbours. A young family, or newlyweds, or an older couple.

She could feel the melancholy first around her stomach. She felt a roll of fat overhanging the elastic in the middle of her dress. The fold of flesh began to itch from the perspiration wedged there. Her head became heavier and her neck sore, and she couldn't dismiss or rework her thoughts to something positive. Her outlook had turned dark and, with Michael almost ready to leave, she felt frightened that she may not be able to claw herself back to a consciousness that gave her a reason to stay married and in Darwin. She'd go back to life the way it was before. Stuck in her guilt when she thought of other men, beleaguered by anxiety in a pew across from the confessional box where she'd prepare to disclose her sins to Father McKay. Alone at home during the day preparing dinner for her husband without a single purpose beyond that to look forward to. She looked out over the uneven lots and thought back to being a young girl and the times when she saw her mother in the ruin of depression. How she couldn't get out of bed, barely uttered a word and smelt like sleep the day round. She could understand how it might become like that for her.

* * *

Bobby came home early in the morning, just before dawn. Charlotte was awake, but pretended to sleep. Bobby got into the bed quietly, and he smelt like beer and stale aftershave. But beneath that, Charlotte could smell another woman. It was there, unmistakable. She lay awake wondering what that meant. How it may lead to a different life for her. She wondered whether it might be Bobby who'd leave her. Run off with Kelly Dillon.

She spent the morning packing lunch for Michael and herself, and never bothered to worry about what would happen when Bobby finally woke to find the car gone. She arrived at the barn after midday; the sun was still climbing and the sky was cloudless. It was unlike Darwin for that time of the year. Most days there were collections of clouds on all sides of the sky. People had become well educated about the clouds. Had learnt how to read them and what was to follow, particularly in the cyclone season. Such a clear day let the heat spread freely, not left to sweat and mire beneath bulky assemblies of clouds. Charlotte enjoyed the weather on days like these.

* * *

After eating, Charlotte opened two cold bottles of beer, gave one to Michael and sat beside him, their backs against the barn wall, their legs outstretched. 'I really like the taste of this beer.'

'What's not to like, eh? Barley. Malt. Hops. And alcohol.' Michael laughed.

'Have you decided where you might want to go?'

Michael rested his bottle on his stomach. 'Yeah. Sydney. The city. There's plenty of work there, I know that. I have cousins there.' He looked across at Charlotte. 'I wish you'd come.'

Charlotte let the words run right through her; she closed her eyes and rested her head against the barn wall. A moment later she felt Michael take her hand. She opened her eyes slowly and turned to him.

CHAPTER 29

NED HAD FOUND an address for Lionel Frazier. When he arrived at the house, the empty front yard was overgrown with weeds. He knocked on the door of the neighbouring house and was told that Leila Frazier and her young boy had moved out not long after Lionel's death. The neighbour told him that Leila had wanted to get as far away from the Territory as possible. And that she was *terrified*. When Ned asked of what, the neighbour replied, 'Of being killed.'

Disappointed, Ned turned his attention to the revelation of Landry and Father McKay's relationship. He sat opposite Father Herring in a small room of the parish vestry that was connected to the high school he'd attended. Ned hadn't been back there since leaving. Father Herring was nearly eighty years of age. He was short, thick through the chest and arms, and his neck was almost as broad as his shoulders. He'd been a rugby player of some repute back in England before migrating to Australia after the Second World War. He had a kind face, an almost hairless scalp and a nose that was his distinguishing feature. It was flattened across its bridge and broadened at the edges of the nostrils by the battering it had taken during his time playing rugby.

Father Herring had settled in Darwin after a posting from country Victoria. He'd fallen in love with the tropical climate and had requested to stay. *I've lived all the cold days that were meant for me*, he often told the students. Ned had confessed to Father Herring all kinds of sins while growing up. The typical ones youths might look for to lengthen the duration inside the confessional. Lying was one of them, fighting with his brothers, swearing, and then later anything but the truth. Never a mention of lusting or masturbation, of doubting the existence of God or heaven and hell.

Father Herring told Ned that he'd heard through the *system* that McKay had been expelled from Sydney by his parents when he was fifteen. He'd been sent somewhere bush, to a boarding school. He returned home only when his parents had passed away years after. He'd become a priest by then and had served at parishes in Victoria, South Australia and Queensland. Herring said that he'd been given the posting at St Mary's in Darwin from higher up in the clergy. When Ned asked whether or not he'd ever heard that McKay and Mayor Landry were brothers, Father Herring hesitated before answering.

'Yes. I've heard that.' His brow furrowed. 'A name change. That doesn't sit well with me. Or some others. You do something like that to hide and conceal.'

Ned shared a bottle of red wine with Father Herring before leaving him with an empty promise of coming back to mass.

* * *

Ned followed up Father Herring's information in the days after. He checked school records, Catholic registries of Australia, made phone calls to the parishes he was led to follow. What he was deliberating over was how this new information might be best worked in his favour. He considered going to Mayor Landry and planting it right at his feet just so he could read his reaction. Ned knew there would have to be a considerable reason for the name change, and perhaps it had been insisted upon by Landry to bury some kind of family history. He didn't know where it all fit, and whether or not it concerned his unfinished business, but it felt good to have something on Mayor Landry that very few people knew of.

Ned was rostered off work the following day and he drove to the courthouse to watch the sentencing of Andrew Liston and Dell Sanders for the murder of Clarry Tallis and Lionel Frazier. Both had, as Landry had told him, accepted the plea deals the town had offered them. They would likely escape the death penalty and be given life sentences. When Ned arrived, there was a small press corps gathered at the courthouse entrance. He watched from his car as Riley and Landry stood before them and granted interviews. He watched them both walk the stairs and head into the building, and then he got out of his car. He kept his head down as he walked through the small crowd of people who'd come to hear the verdict. As he approached the press corps a reporter called out his name, 'Constable Potter, a word?'

Ned looked up, and the space ahead closed quickly with reporters.

'Must be a good day for you? To see justice handed out.'

Ned stopped at the foot of the stairs, microphones pushed in the general direction of his face; a bulky wind gag hitting him high on the cheek. 'Um, look it's a case that,' Ned stopped. 'Can you turn off the camera? Please? I have nothing to say. Excuse me.' Ned forced his way through and onto the steps, walking quickly up and away from the questions being shouted at him. He pushed through the doors of the courthouse and immediately saw Andrew Liston. He was sitting in the front row beside his lawyer. His hair had been left to grow and the wild tufts either side of his bald patch had begun to cover his ears. Ned took up a seat in the middle of the gallery. He looked over at Dell Sanders who sat on the other side of the aisle from Andrew. In profile, Ned could see Dell was indifferent, his nose took in air without anxiety and his mouth sat closed and relaxed. Landry sat with Riley in the second row and Ned looked at them from behind. Riley's fat neck pushed up tightly against the back of his buttoned collar, a reddened spool of flesh hung over its edge, pockmarked with acne scars and covered by the sharp ends of finely cut hair. Ned watched Landry flatten out his comb-over, and when he turned to look around, Ned was watching him. Landry offered nothing in his look and faced back to the front.

* * *

It didn't take more than ten minutes for it all to be over. Dell and Andrew received what they'd bargained for. Life. And in the Territory, Ned knew, that's exactly what it meant. Neither of them was ever going to be free again. Ned stood, and when the bailiff walked Dell and Andrew from their seats, they looked at him. Andrew appeared bewildered and nervous, but Dell shook his head when they made eye contact and uttered something Ned couldn't translate. But he knew by the way Dell's face was shaped that it was something accusatory.

'Well done, Potter.' Landry stopped in the aisle of the courtroom with Riley. 'Why don't you go outside like I asked, talk to the press and paint a good picture for the police department and your town?'

'I already told them I don't have anything to say.'

'You get your arse out there and you do as the mayor says.' Riley shoved his finger hard into Ned's shoulder.

'No. I'm not doin' that. Excuse me.' Ned walked between them, and just before he opened the door to leave, he turned back toward them. 'Mayor Landry. I didn't know you had an older brother.' He didn't wait for Landry's reaction, the one he'd imagined, he opened the courtroom door and walked out.

His instinct was to keep on the path. He'd run into a dead end with Leila Frazier, but he could still follow through on the information he'd got from Martha Clay. Ned knew Lionel was employed at one of the local schools as a groundsman and handyman. He looked at his watch and saw it was just on time for school to be let out. He thought about Bonnie, how upset and frightened she'd been made by the threat, and where it might lead if he didn't stop his enquiry. He thought about the consequences of asking a teacher questions from the school Lionel had worked at. Where and whom would Ned's enquiry be directed toward? He didn't know. But he was sure it wouldn't be too long before Landry and Riley found out.

He turned the ignition key, put his car into gear and drove toward the school that was closest to his route home. When he arrived the bus queues that were arranged at the school's front gates were dwindling. The school children chased one another, breaking from the queues with laughter and high-pitched squawking, their faces split with pretend terror and sweaty with determination. Ned smiled as he watched. *How simple their lives are*, he thought. He looked beyond the children to the street adjacent to where they waited for their bus. He recognised the small house and the church that stood beside it. It was the vestry he'd visited and stood before Father McKay. He turned back toward the waiting children and looked among them for an adult. There was a short white man who wore a knee-length grey coat with the word *bus* scrawled in faded yellow across its back. Ned looked in the rear-vision mirror, straightened his tie and then opened his door and got out. He approached the man with a smile. 'G'day.'

The man looked Ned's way and looked him up and down quickly. 'Yes?'

'I'm Ned Potter.'

'Jimmy Paine.' Jimmy took a young schoolboy gently by the shoulder and steered him to the right queue. 'You're this line, Raymond.'

'Are there any teachers about?'

'Staffroom. Over there.' Jimmy motioned toward the school building.

Ned looked across at it, a single-storey brown brick building with a gabled pitch and a bronzed crucifix on top. 'Maybe you can help me.'

'I can try.'

'Ernie Clay. Did you know him?'

Jimmy looked at Ned and then turned away. Ned waited in the silence until he became unsure whether Jimmy had heard him. 'Jimmy?'

Jimmy lifted his chin. 'Who are you?'

'I'm a policeman.'

Jimmy looked toward the school building and Ned could see the question had made him uneasy. 'Yeah, I knew him.'

'And what about Lionel Frazier? You know him, too?'

'He got me my job.'

Ned watched Jimmy carefully while he navigated a pod of chatty younger students to their line. 'Strange they both end up dead and both worked here.'

'Maybe.'

'What do you think?' The afternoon sun was falling, and as Jimmy looked to Ned it fell across his eyes and lit their blue centres.

'It doesn't matter what I think. They're dead.'

'That's true. But what do you believe happened?'

Jimmy took a deep breath, the last part of it quivering. 'I believe what you believe. Or you wouldn't be here.'

'Did they ever talk to you about things?'

'What kind of things?'

'Things they may have seen.'

Jimmy turned his mouth in a way that read as contemplation, and then something caught his attention across the playground. Ned watched his face alter, the answer he was considering in the screw of his mouth swallowed up and digested by fear. 'I got nothin' else to say to you, sir.' Jimmy walked away from Ned and reorganised a bent line of children.

He replayed the look of fear that had overwhelmed Jimmy Paine, and then thought about Bonnie. But he pushed it away. His instinct told him there was something *here* to unlock. He walked across the playground, over the small grassed patches that broke up the asphalt. He got to the little run of stairs leading to the front doors of the building when a man emerged, sullen faced and agitated. 'What do you want? School is out for the day.'

Ned smiled, extending his hand. 'I'm sorry, I wasn't sure what time school finished. I'm kinda new here. I have a son. I was hoping to talk with the headmaster or a teacher about the possibility of sending him here.'

The man's posture loosened, he smiled and then shook Ned's hand. 'Of course. This is a wonderful school. I'm the headmaster. Phillip Ward.' Ward walked down the last steps. 'And you are?'

Ned stumbled without an alias ready. 'Peter.' He followed the name with a smile.

'Nice to meet you. How old is your son?'

'He's four. Turning five.'

'We have lots of children in that bracket. So what brings you to Darwin?' Ward folded his arms, his short-sleeved shirt tight around their fleshy middles.

'Work.'

'Oh. And what do you do?'

Ned took a moment, he could feel the lie getting out of control, and a reprimand from Riley and indeed the town would be warranted and justified if he continued. He cursed under his breath for beginning it in the first place.

'I'm a police officer. And I don't have a son. My name is Ned Potter.'

Ward unfolded his arms. 'Why would you lie like that?'

'Because I believe there's some kind of a conspiracy going on in regards to the murder of three men. Two of them worked here. I want some answers.' Ned stepped forward so he was on the same landing as Ward. 'Jimmy, over there.' He pointed at the bus queues where Jimmy Paine stood. 'He knew both of 'em. And he's scared to talk. Why?'

Ward turned around and headed to the front door of the building. Ned followed him. 'Where you goin', Mr Ward?'

'I don't have anything to say.'

'Did you know David O'Shea? He drowned. Do you know his wife?'

Ward turned around and looked at Ned with the same amount of fear Jimmy Paine had. 'Please just leave me out of this. I don't know anything.' He ran the last five steps and pushed through the front doors of the building.

Ned stood, his stomach rolling, his limbs prickling, as though a swarm of insects had gathered beneath his skin and dug at his flesh. It was pure adrenalin.

CHAPTER 30

WHEN CHARLOTTE NEXT saw Bobby, she considered asking where he'd been to have come home so early in the morning. But he was hungover and complaining that she hadn't filled the car with petrol after using it. And she never expected an honest answer from him. Confronted with her whereabouts and holes in time while she tended to Michael, she wouldn't have replied honestly either. She was in a stalemate and there were just too many things that were more appealing to think about than the painful unpacking of her marriage. She let the query go and instead thought about what lay ahead for Michael and Marcus in Sydney. The city. The new smells. The different climate and the new mass of people. It was so very exciting, even though it was vicarious daydreaming.

Bobby left for work and, after doing the laundry, Charlotte opened all the windows inside the house and let the smell of the oncoming storm fill up every space. She could smell the earth, the rain on its way and the breath of opened flowers. She pulled the hem of her cotton dress up and fixed it under the elastic edges of her stocking. She outstretched her arms and let the breeze inside swirl around her, to touch the insides of her arms and tickle her thighs. She felt light on her feet.

* * *

It was past five o'clock when the phone rang, and Charlotte had woken from an hour's sleep. She answered it in dazed shape, her high replaced by the sticky melancholy that came after an afternoon nap. The news was of her father. He'd had a stroke and was being transferred from the aged care home to Darwin hospital.

Charlotte turned off the stove, put Bobby's dinner and the apricot pie she'd made in the refrigerator, and then walked to the nearest bus stop and connected until she arrived at the hospital. She walked inside and immediately felt light-headed from the smell of disinfectant. It was an aroma that provoked memories. Of visits to see her mother when she'd been unwell and bedridden, and her father had insisted she be looked at by doctors.

When Charlotte arrived at the ward, her father was in bed, his eyes closed, his arms resting by his sides. Charlotte thought he was dead. When she looked over him, she saw that one side of his face had collapsed. His brow had sunk and caved in over his eye socket, and the rest of the flesh on that flank had fallen as though it were faltering under the weight of something. She could see the bloody rim of his lower eyelid, and his mouth was ajar, as though it had been made inert while taking in air on one side.

She spoke to two doctors, both of whom said that her father was not going to recover and would likely die in the coming months, probably of pneumonia or some other kind of infection he'd contract from being in the hospital. They told her that it was pointless to have him moved, and that without a full-time nurse, trying to care for him outside of hospital would be problematic and lead to more complications. She stayed by his bed and held his hand. She watched his chest rise and fall as he breathed. He looked peaceful, she thought, and she wondered what might be playing through his dreams as he lay there. She figured he'd rather be dead than like he was. Already in a struggle with a decomposing mind, and now left without speech. She wished openly, and without guilt from her religion, that she had the power to let him go beyond wherever it was he was at.

* * *

Bobby was drinking with Danny Lewis in the living room when she got home. They were watching the news on television. Bobby smiled at her as she walked past and asked, 'Where have you been, love?'

'At the hospital. My father had a stroke.'

'What? When?'

'Early this morning.'

'He okay?'

'No.'

'How bad is it? Is he …?'

'Yes. He will.'

'Oh, love.' Bobby stood and walked to her. He kissed her atop the head and then stood behind her and draped his arms across her shoulders. 'I'm sorry.'

'Thank you.'

'I mean, I told you he was better off gone than the way he was. And now this? Humane thing would be to let him go.'

Charlotte stared at the television, the black and white picture blurring and turning to a grey fizz. 'I agree. He'd be better off dead. I'll heat your dinner up.' She stood and walked to the kitchen.

She listened to Bobby and Danny Lewis while she finished preparing the food. Their talk was loose, and they didn't think to quieten their volume. They were ranting about something they'd seen on the news. She sat with them at dinner, their conversation changed to rodeo and fishing, though by then she'd switched off and was thinking about her father and what funeral arrangements she'd need to make when he did pass. She was brought back to their dialogue when she heard one of them utter the name Michael Roberts. She looked at her husband and Lewis for where their attention lay, and when she saw that neither were aware that she'd heard the name, she sat as still and as quiet as she could to lessen any chance that they'd realise she was listening.

'Don't worry. He's never gonna turn up.' Lewis dug a toothpick deep into the diastema between two molars on his lower jaw.

'What a fuck-up.' Bobby said it flatly.

'Yep. Big Jack, eh?' Lewis smiled at Bobby.

'It's not funny. Shouldn't have happened.'

'Sorry.' Lewis's smile flattened.

Bobby shifted on his chair and took a breath that quivered at the end. 'I got robbed, ya know? I won that fight.'

'That's the truth.' Lewis looked at the dug-out piece of meat on the end of his toothpick, put it back in his mouth and chewed on it with his front teeth.

Charlotte stood without thinking. Bobby turned around. 'Sweets, love?'

'I'm just goin' to the bathroom. I'll be back to serve it up.'

In the bathroom Charlotte knelt on the floor with her head over the toilet bowl. She vomited until all that was left to come up was the dark green gall from her liver.

CHAPTER 31

BONNIE WAS AWAKE early, before little Rose was woken by her growling stomach and asking to be fed. Bonnie listened for a moment, waiting for the first chortles from Rose that signalled she had another ten minutes of sleep before her daughter's laughter turned to a whine and then a whole-hearted bawling. She nudged Ned. 'Hey. She's still asleep.' She ran her hand down to his crotch, and he rolled over almost immediately. They made love for as long as they could before Rose demanded to be seen to. Bonnie fed her and when she'd finished and put her back down, all full of milk, weary-eyed and relieved of all trapped wind, she sat with Ned and ate the breakfast he'd cooked them.

'Perfect start to a Saturday.' Bonnie looked over the table to Ned, a puckish smile lifting the corner of her mouth. 'You are a stallion, Ned Potter.'

'Well thank you.' He pointed a stacked fork of food back at his wife. 'And you're not too bad yourself.'

Bonnie showered, got dressed and placed a sleeping Rose in her pram and set off for a morning walk. Ned stayed at home,

mowed the lawn and pruned back the overgrowing shrubs at the
foot of their front porch. Bonnie enjoyed Saturday mornings no
matter the weather. Rain or shine, she felt a relief for another week
beneath her and Ned, one from which he'd come home safely, and
another that had seen Rose flourish some more. The morning was
warm, the heat drier than usual with the only clouds visible further
north. But they were building out over the Arafura Sea and there
had been a cyclone warning in place for two days. Bonnie hadn't
thought too much about it, though. From what she'd heard on the
local news it was likely to dissipate before making landfall. As she
walked, she looked down at her arms that pushed the pram. They
were dark, bronzed by the sun and the fine black hair over them
had turned to blonde. She liked how they'd changed colour, was
fascinated by the metamorphosis when she'd been a young girl and
first noticed it. It was as if one day the hair had been dark, the next
flaxen and shining in the sun. It made her feel exotic. She adjusted
her hat and walked toward the trees lining the beach.

'Bonnie? Bonnie Potter?'

Bonnie stopped pushing the pram and turned to where the
voice had come from. Across the street, his head out a car window,
was the same man who'd come to threaten her weeks ago. His hair
had grown, and he had some colour from the sun, but she knew
it was him. She was about to keep walking when the car did a
u-turn, pulled up beside her and skidded to a halt.

* * *

Ned finished the lawn, raked up the loose clippings and bagged
them in a hessian sack. He was midway through thinning the
shrubbery when he looked at his watch and felt the first twinge

of concern. It had been over an hour and a half since Bonnie had left and she never usually walked much longer than an hour. Rose would wake and need to be fed, and Bonnie had it all down to a well-measured excursion. Just as she'd turn into their street, Rose would be stirring and ready to feed. Ned had watched it unfold weeks in a row with a kind of delight. Impressed and proud of Bonnie and Rose's coordinated existence.

He finished his work and then decided to shower, thinking that perhaps Rose had woken and Bonnie may have had to stop mid-walk and breastfeed. He liked the scenario, the image of his wife and child nestled somewhere discreet as the world went by about them.

* * *

It was lunchtime and three hours since Bonnie had left before Ned set off to look for them. He walked the path he knew she'd taken and, when he found no sign of them, he circled back along the route and poked into the wide adjacent streets to see if she might have decided on a detour. He arrived back at their house and ran inside calling Bonnie's name. He checked every room and in his panicked state, which had stripped layers of practicality from his judgement, looked under his bed and in the wardrobes. He sat down on the lounge in the living room, his head fell into his hands and he became paralysed with dread. His first thoughts were that they may have been hit by a car and were in the hospital. But he was certain by that stage he would have been telephoned by someone from the hospital. Bonnie had her purse with her that carried her driver's licence. The next thought was that she may have gone to her father's house. It wasn't likely but it was possible enough to charge him with a bolt of hope and get him off the lounge to call Graham.

* * *

When Graham arrived at the house the first thing he asked Ned was whether he had continued to investigate after the threat. Ned dodged the question with an ambiguous answer. 'I haven't followed up on anything that would cause somethin' to be done beyond that threat.'

Graham looked at Ned in a way that made him feel guilty. It was only then that it occurred to him that Bonnie and Rose's disappearance could be connected to his further investigation of what he'd been told to leave alone. His mind raced. The visit to the school and the questions of Jimmy Paine and the headmaster Phillip Ward.

'Where's your gun?' Graham's voice had an unsteady tone to it. Ned could hear that he was nervous and afraid.

'In the bedroom.'

'Get it.'

Ned stood still. 'And do what?'

'Something! We have to do something!' Graham shouted at Ned, his cheeks trembled, and his eyes lit bright blue behind the glass of his tears.

'Okay.' Ned retrieved a revolver he kept beneath his side of the bed and the two of them ventured out into the street and began down the path Ned told Graham Bonnie would have walked. At the end of the trail, and with no sign of them, Graham clasped his hands across the top of his head. He slowly spun 360 degrees, the sweat from his scalp falling in long thick streams down into his eyes, making him squint. 'Where the fuck are they?'

They stopped in at the local shops around Casuarina and Nightcliff. No one had seen a woman matching Bonnie's description walking with a pram. The sun was falling and the storm that had been moving up from the Arafura Sea showed its looming arrival in a spectacular formation of backlit mammatus clouds. Ned had seen them many times before, and they were recognised in the Territory as an omen of massive storms. They appeared as rounded pouches and bulges hanging from the base of the cloud. Ned looked skyward. 'This is a bad one comin'.'

'Fuck the weather.' Graham scowled at Ned. 'Keep lookin'.'

'Okay.' A gust of wind swept past Ned and carried the bouquet of all that it had picked up and carried on its way to Darwin. Ned smelt the mist from saltwater, the earth, the trees and flowers, the road and the garbage from hundreds of households and streets that the storm had already torn through. The wind went by quickly and then the first drops of rain fell and landed atop his head. Ned could feel their weight over his skin, the drops were fat and when they landed left a splash pattern over his clothes and skin. Hail, he knew, was coming. The wind picked up quickly the same time as the pouches and bulbs of mammatus clouds dissolved and were swallowed by plumes of rolling cumulonimbus. It turned dark and the streetlights flickered on. And then the hail came, stones as large as golf balls that were thrown from the sky with such force that Ned and Graham took cover inside a petrol station and watched wide-eyed as the stones punctured car windshields and broke through shopfront windows. The sound was deafening, and in all Ned's time in the Territory he couldn't remember a squall so violent and hail was rare. The cyclones he'd been through bore stronger winds, but the hailstorm and the noise were terrifying.

He thought of Bonnie and Rose; if they were caught outside in the storm they'd be in trouble.

The hailstorm passed, and was replaced by pelting rain that changed angles in the directions of the wind that pushed it. Strong gusts forced the drops horizontal and blinded Ned and Graham as they walked west away from the house. The roads and footpaths quickly turned to torrents, and twice Ned had to help Graham up after he was swept off his feet. They walked another two miles, the streets deserted. Debris from the streets tumbled past Ned and Graham like tumbleweed. They stood not far from the coastline, exhausted and beaten.

'Let's go back. This is pointless!' Ned yelled over the storm to Graham.

He didn't reply but followed Ned as he set off. When they got back to the house, they both called frantically for Bonnie and the baby, checked the rooms and every crevice and nook. The phone rang just as Ned had collapsed on the lounge in despair. He leapt up, looked at Graham who stood still in the middle of the room, his face elongated, his mouth open and struggling to take in air.

'Are you okay?'

'Answer the fuckin' telephone.'

'Hello.' Ned didn't recognise the voice on the other end, but by its tone he knew to stay quiet and listen. 'Yes, I understand.' He looked at Graham and nodded. 'Okay.' He hung up the phone and sat back down on the lounge.

'What?' Graham shouted.

'They have 'em.'

'Who?'

'People who wanted me quiet.'

'Jesus, fuck! Why?'

Graham stood over Ned, his mouth tightened around a clenched jaw and his words came from between his teeth, 'If somethin' happens to 'em, I'll kill you.'

'Yes, sir.'

'How do we get 'em back?'

'I have to walk away. From the job. Resign.'

'Then you do it. Now.'

Ned nodded and then began to cry. 'I'm sorry. I'm so sorry.'

'Save your tears, boy. Do what you have to, and it'll be okay.' Graham sat on the lounge beside Ned.

* * *

Bonnie and Rose were let out from the same car they'd been snatched by. The storm had passed but the streets were black, not a single working streetlight, not a single room lit and showing the insides of a house. The electricity grids had failed and every suburb was in darkness. When Bonnie arrived at the house she collapsed into her father's arms. Ned went to the sodden pram, took Rose from it and held her against his cheek.

'Ned, please. No more.' Bonnie looked to her husband, the flesh around both her eyes swollen, her nose broader and engorged, hours of crying distending her features to a point she looked almost unrecognisable.

'No more.' Ned walked to her with Rose in his arms. Bonnie let go of her father and fell into Ned's chest.

* * *

274

Bonnie put Rose to bed, showered and then joined Ned and Graham in the living room. Ned opened a bottle of beer for her and one for her father.

'You're not havin' one?' Graham lit a cigarette.

'No.' Ned stood in front of them as they both sat. 'Who was there?'

'It doesn't matter, Ned.'

'Just answer the question.'

'She doesn't have to.' Graham glared at Ned.

'Graham, she's my wife. I'm her husband. They took her and my daughter. My family. Mind your own fuckin' business.' Ned stood taller with his hands clenched in tight fists. He watched as Graham looked at his hands, and he could feel the blood dispersed from his veins across the tight balls he'd made. Graham looked back to him.

'Okay.'

'Who was there?'

Bonnie looked at her father and he nodded for her to continue. 'Tell him.'

'The same man who'd come here. Short blond hair.' Bonnie stopped and a tear fell down her cheek.

'And what exactly happened?'

Bonnie straightened her back and lifted her chin, and when she spoke the words came out forcefully. They were not negotiable. 'I'm never going to tell you. You don't want to hear it.'

* * *

On Monday, Ned walked into the station and straight into Riley's office. Riley leant back in his chair, lit a cigarette and said nothing. Ned threw his badge on the table. 'You fuckin' low dog.'

'Don't be like that, Potter. You'll land on your feet. You're like a cat. But your nine lives here are up.'

'What was it? Goin' to the school?' Ned folded his arms.

'All I know is I get a call sayin' you made out to someone there that you weren't a police officer. And then you were. Now that's as bad as sayin' you are one when you're not. So, I was prepared to put you on leave, which woulda been a suitable punishment. Then I get another call sayin' you're comin' in here this mornin' to resign.'

'Someone took my wife and little girl. You know that?'

'Nothin' to do with me.'

Ned huffed laughter. 'The only difference between you and him is you're not dumb enough to be involved in a crime. And that's what it was. Kidnapping.'

'You can join those dots if ya like, Potter.' Riley sat forward. 'I don't care. All I was told is that you were comin' in here to resign. In my opinion it's a good move for you. That's all I'm gonna say.'

* * *

Ned had told Bonnie that, after he handed in his resignation, he was going to see his brother, Fraser. He drove out to the Adelaide River and sat with him on the porch overlooking the water. It was just gone midday, and the sun was high over the river, the pandanus trees on the bank looked like Hawaiian ladies dressed in ceremonial garb ready to dance. Ned looked over at them, a can of beer in his hand. 'What the fuck am I gonna do, Fraser?'

Fraser pulled another can from the esky he'd stacked full of crushed ice and beer for Ned's visit. He pulled the ring from his can and slurped at the froth that came too quickly from the opening.

'Work. You got a family.'

Ned turned to him. 'I'm not afraid of hard work, you know that.'

'Yes, I do. But you might not get to choose what it is that comes next.'

Ned turned back to the water and belched. 'Maybe the army?'

'Yeah. I wouldn't be rushin' off to do that. They'll have you over in Indochina quicker than you can fuckin' blink. The Americans are there, and soon enough we'll follow 'em.' Fraser dropped his ring into the beer.

'No. The Yanks are gonna pull out. I heard that just last week.'

'They're not gonna do that.'

'Who's not?'

'The government. War's money, Ned. That's a big ol' mess over there and it's gonna get worse. If it keeps goin' lot of boys are goin' over there whether they like it or not.'

Ned wondered for a moment what war would be like. He pictured himself in the jungle greens he'd seen the men who were already over there wearing. The SLR rifles they carried and the webbing that held water bottles and magazines, hatchets and small spades. 'What do you think it'd be like? War?'

'I don't know. Don't want to know either.'

'No.'

'I'll tell you this though. Military is military. I was in the air force and I'm tellin' you, Ned, it's not for you.'

Ned laughed. 'Because I couldn't stand the orders?'

'Look at you here right now. Here because you wouldn't obey orders.'

'That was different.'

'No, it's the same. You don't like being told what to do.'

Ned thought a moment. 'I have to be my own boss then.'

'Yep. Good luck with that.'

Ned smiled without looking back at his brother. 'Hey, you still got the place in Townsville?'

'Yep. Sittin' there doin' nothing.'

'Maybe we'll move over there. I'll buy it off ya. Get a job on a trawler or somethin'.'

'Well, better be your boat.' Fraser winked at Ned, put his feet up on the porch balustrade and then looked back out over the river. 'There's Marilyn.' Fraser pointed with the hand holding his can of beer. Marilyn the croc had her snout on top of the water, her eyes still submerged, the last jagged peaks of her tail curling slowly through the water.

Ned laughed. 'She thinks we can't see her.'

'She's got a whiff of you. She's curious. I think she's gettin' old, lookin' for easy food. Somethin' already dead. I tossed her a couple of chickens last week. Big girl took 'em both under, never saw 'em again.'

'I don't know how to let this go, brother.' Ned watched Marilyn winding slowly closer to the bank.

'Yep. Always had to finish what you started. Walk away, Ned.'

* * *

Ned drove back to town, parked the car at his house and stood on the street and looked up at his home. He wasn't nearly ready to come home. And though Bonnie was rattled to her core and didn't feel safe alone, it wasn't enough to stop him from turning from the house and heading to the Victoria Hotel. On his way there he turned his guilt toward the justifications that were flowing and easy to conjure. *I've just lost my job. My family was abducted. This isn't fair. I should be doin' this.* But without more alcohol, his guilt could not be silenced. *Fuck!* When Ned got to the pub, he ordered three shots of whiskey and a cold beer from Katie Briggs. By the time he was halfway through his schooner, the whiskey had clipped his guilt and sent it to a corner of his mind that he'd soon cover completely and render voiceless.

'You're on a mission, Ned Potter.' Katie's voice was particularly rough.

'I resigned from my job. No longer a cop.'

'What? Why?'

'No choice. I can't say anything else.'

'Okay then.' Katie walked away, and Ned looked through his schooner to the photographs and lights behind the bar. The image was blurry and colourful, and through it all, the stain of amber from the beer. He stared into the image until the colours weakened and all he could make out was the whitish froth in the middle of his glass. *My life,* he thought. *I know it's there, I can see it, I just can't make it out. Fuck Landry. Fuck Riley.* Ned drank and he drank. Until it was dark and the stool next to him had been sat at and left by people he could no longer remember being there. Katie Briggs looked after him, but never cut him off. When he stood to leave, he stumbled over the stool and fell forward onto his front. Nothing he looked at from where he'd fallen had a sharp line or edge. The legs of men and women were bulbous, the stools like long-limbed creatures, and when he turned onto his back, the ceiling looked as though it was falling in on him. He stood and shook his head, as though to erase the images that unnerved him.

When he arrived at Hotel Darwin he sat and ordered a beer. He looked down from where he was and closed an eye in an effort to sharpen his vision.

'Riley!' he yelled from his stool. 'You weak cunt!'

'Hey, mate, take it easy, huh?' The barman put his hand gently on Ned's forearm.

'It's Senior Sergeant Riley!' Ned howled again.

'He's not here tonight, fella.'

Ned slapped the barman's hand away from his arm. 'Fuck off.'

When Ned woke on the floor, he could taste his own blood.

'Stay where you are, mate, an ambulance is comin'.'

Ned looked up at the barman who knelt over him. 'I'm okay, I'm okay.'

'No, you're gonna need stitches.'

Ned found his elbows, then turned to his front and pushed himself off the floor. When he stood up, his head spun, and a moment later his stomach emptied from his mouth and over the floor. 'Sorry. I'm sorry.'

* * *

When he woke in the morning he was on his front and naked. He lifted his head slightly and saw the redness spread out over the white sheet in asymmetric shapes. He got out of bed and stumbled to the bathroom. He looked at himself in the mirror over the vanity, his left eye was closed with swelling, and a long open falcate gash gouged through the edge of his cheekbone. Bonnie and Rose weren't there, and there was a note left on the table saying they'd gone with her father. To where it didn't say. Ned showered and tried to piece the night together, but it was useless.

It was just moments of disconnected recollection that were without chronology or reason. Faces came to him, of people he didn't know, small threads of conversation that he couldn't find the ends to. He knew he'd been at the Victoria and figured Hotel Darwin. His body became wrought with anxiety, his stomach churned and growled for food, but his mind was too consumed by the black holes in time his drinking had left.

He bathed the cut under his eye with antiseptic and put a plastic bag of frozen green peas across the swelling. He washed the sheets and his clothes, and hung them on the clothesline in the backyard. The sun was in and out of the clear patches left between the rolling columns of clouds that moved quickly. The air was sticky and thick, and Ned, demoralised and uncertain of anything, wanted to drink.

CHAPTER 32

CHARLOTTE CAUGHT THE bus to Palmerston where the train left Darwin and travelled south to Katherine. She bought two train tickets, one adult and one child. She spoke to the young lady at the counter and asked about the journey, the length of time, the stops on the way, and what the scenery might be like. She felt excited, as much as if one of the tickets had been for herself.

On the bus on the way home, she brought the tickets to her nose and took in the scent of fresh biro and stencilled paper. She went to bed early but found it hard to sleep, like a child wrought with excitement the night before Christmas. She'd counted twenty-four stops on the ticket from Darwin to Katherine. Through Rum Jungle, Grove Hill and Pine Creek. They were places she'd never heard of, and she wondered who might live there, and what their lives at such places would be like. '*Remote*,' she whispered to herself.

Bobby came to bed and she made as though she were asleep, complete with a gentle snore that was put there to keep him at bay. She dozed and dreamt about Michael. It was an abstract set-up, somewhere in a pine forest with lots of children climbing in the triangular-shaped trees. Michael stood at the base of the trees, his arms open, inviting the children to let go of the branches and fall into his grasp. They dropped and he caught them, and they all laughed. The thread veered from the forest, and Charlotte watched from somewhere behind, as Michael and Marcus ran across a highway down an embankment and out of sight. She woke with a fright and stayed awake until she was ready to leave. She was as quiet as she could be, though she'd planned well enough so that her exit from the house would be fast.

* * *

Charlotte got to the boundary of the mission at dawn. The sun was lifting from the horizon, its broadening arc hidden by cloud cover, its glow dulled and struggling to push through a single ray to brighten the morning. Packed and ready, Marcus had hidden himself in the scrub. His father had told him to tell no one other than Timothy Mitchell about what was planned. He moved quickly from the bush, got into Charlotte's car and they drove to the barn to pick up Michael. Charlotte had bought him clothes and shoes from a charity store, and before she'd left on her last visit she'd given him a small mirror, a sharp razor and soap. He walked from the barn with a discernible limp, and a small smile. When he got in, he closed the door and the aroma of the soap Charlotte had given him overwhelmed the inside of the car. She closed her eyes for a moment and took a deep breath.

They drove to Palmerston where the North Australia Railway began. In the car Michael told her that he'd write when they were settled and safe. Charlotte had set up a post office account where she could collect his mail without it being seen by Bobby or anyone else. At the station there were only two people waiting for the train. A young couple with a stack of cases at their feet, a relocation more than a holiday seemed to be planned. When Marcus spotted the front engine of the train pushing through the watery mirages and taking shape, he leapt in the air and howled. It had come way too fast for Charlotte, and an abject sadness overwhelmed her. She began to cry without first registering the sting through her eyes, or the waver of her chin.

'Please be safe.' Michael pulled Charlotte into an embrace and she leant her cheek against his chest. 'Thank you. You have saved my life.'

Charlotte looked up at Michael and a tear fell from his eye, splashed over her cheek and ran down to her top lip. She felt its warmth and took it into her mouth with her tongue. They let go of one another, and Marcus hugged Charlotte and then stood at the edge of the platform, the train's brakes squealing, the carriages slowing as they passed, finally coming to a halt. The doors opened and a conductor stepped onto the platform. 'Next stop, Noonamah.'

Marcus turned to his father and looked for permission. 'In ya go.' He leapt across the void between the platform and the train and into the carriage. Michael faced Charlotte and the conductor blew his whistle.

'All aboard for Katherine.'

She took Michael's hand and held it tightly. 'Bye.'

'You know where to find me if you ever decide to leave.' He let her go and climbed aboard the train. The doors closed and Michael and Marcus looked out to Charlotte standing on the platform. Their smiles ripped across their teeth as far as they could reach. She waved them goodbye and then slowly walked back to the car.

She opened the door and sat behind the steering wheel and looked out the windscreen in the direction the train had gone. She'd never felt heartbreak before. She'd mourned her mother's death, but it didn't feel anything like this. It was as if all the purpose of her life had been pulled out from her being in an instant. As if something had reached inside and found every small amount of spark she had left, and then tore it from her. She felt listless, and though she didn't know how she looked, she felt ugly and overweight. She cried until her head thumped, and she could feel the blood warming her cheeks. Her breath was hot; and she could smell the mucus through it. She lay down on the bench seat of the car and fell asleep.

CHAPTER 33

NED HADN'T HAD a drink for four months when Bonnie and Rose moved back into the house. He'd taken a job as a labourer on a building site near Darwin Harbour. He worked five days a week, eight hours a day, had half an hour for lunch and twenty minutes for morning tea. He dug holes for the plumbers laying sewer pipes on the ground level, tied steel for the builders and helped them form the beams and floors that were poured with concrete. He liked his job. The rudimentary nature of it, and the simplicity of life that occupied his mind when the day was over. *What to eat, what to watch on television, what time to go to bed.* Life was simple.

Bonnie had told him that another drink like that would send her away for good. That she'd take Rose and move from the Territory and never come back. She'd moved to her father's the day Ned resigned from the police force and came home drunk and beaten. She had wanted to leave the Territory then, was terrified he wouldn't settle, and would one day meddle again in the mess that had gotten herself and Rose abducted. He had got the job as a labourer quickly and convinced her to stay. But it took her all of the four months at her father's house before she agreed to move back in with him.

Back in the house, young Rose had found her feet and was slowly moving from one piece of furniture to another. She wore a constant bruise on her forehead from thumping it over whatever ground she was on when not getting her way. *Spirited* is what Ned called her; *a fuckin' brat* what her grandfather Graham called her.

* * *

Ned worked the whole of the dry season on the same building site. He woke early on a Friday morning, cooked breakfast for Bonnie and brought it into the bedroom on a small table. He'd had trouble sleeping the night before, and when he got to work felt lackadaisical. At every moment he opened his mouth a yawn formed, and though he did his best to keep it inside and from overwhelming the rest of his body, he couldn't. It happened incessantly. His sleep had been interrupted by a dream that he couldn't dismiss. The dream was of Michael Roberts fishing in a billabong out by Tabletop Swamp. He was chasing fish in the shallows, and when he saw Ned on the bank he smiled and then laughed.

Ned lay awake after the dream, pondering if it were to be interpreted as Michael still being alive and letting him know, or Michael dead and showing him he was somewhere in a better place. Or if it meant nothing at all.

By lunchtime he'd regained his enthusiasm and was buoyed by the weekend only three hours away. It was just after twelve-thirty and Ned was about to restart work when word made it to the lunch room that the President of the United States had been killed. The details were vague, and so Ned followed the rest of the men after work to the nearest place with a television, which happened to be Hotel Darwin. They clambered among the usual drinkers and nearby workers from other building sites, and looked up at the small television above the bar. The volume was turned up as loud as possible, and not a person inside made a sound. They watched the commotion that had unfolded in Dealey Plaza, men and women interviewed about what they saw and heard, and if someone in the bar spoke, they were shushed quickly. At one point, Ned looked across and noticed Charlotte Clark. She was ruddy across her face and looked fuller through her cheeks. She took a step sideways to resettle and Ned saw that she was pregnant. They made eye contact not long after, and he smiled at her through a tight mouth.

When he arrived home not long after, Bonnie was sitting in front of the television with Rose asleep on her lap. Ned sat down beside her. 'This stinks.'

'I can't believe it. I just can't believe someone would do that to him.' Bonnie shook her head. 'Why?'

* * *

Over the weekend, Ned and Bonnie stayed tuned to the news unfolding in America. They watched the delayed coverage of the FBI walking the alleged assassin out to a throng of media to be interviewed. He denied any involvement and claimed that he was a patsy. The lid of his left eye was swollen, and he appealed for legal aid.

Bonnie asked dozens of questions in between feeding Rose and cooking meals. Ned said little in reply. He had no answers for her.

But he didn't completely believe the story that was being fed to the American people. To him it seemed just too convenient, the story on the assassin and his links to communism were served up almost immediately. That he was a defector and an active propagator of Marxism. Ned had been left with a bad taste in his mouth from what he'd been coerced into doing by a threat. To walk away and shut up. To leave the trail cold. To let two men wither away in prison for something he knew they didn't do. To be complicit in another man's deconstruction of hope and worth.

They watched in horror the pictures of the assassin being shot live on television in the bowels of the Dallas Police Department. The shooter a known Mafia associate. Ned's police instincts prompting to ask why. *Why* kill Lee Harvey Oswald? *Why? To shut him up.* That was the only intelligent reasoning Ned could rest over.

For weeks after the assassination, Ned became consumed by the news from America that painted Oswald as the lone assassin. He called his friend and former police officer Damien Clooney to ask his take. Clooney didn't say much, and he advised Ned to do the same. He told him, *It's not our business. We got our own problems.* Ned became restless and angry. He snapped at Bonnie when she got to asking about his day and what his plans were career-wise. He felt voiceless and stuck. He talked incessantly to her about what his conclusions on the assassination were, and when she didn't bend and conform to his explanations, he lashed out at her, calling her *dumb* and *naïve*. He couldn't shift or even temper his instinct to investigate. He slept only in naps, and when he woke his mind was clear and ready to continue the discussions and deliberations of Kennedy's assassination. It was as though the event had given him opportunity to surmise and suppose, to join dots and make assertions that might lead to fact. Kennedy's assassination had replaced the investigation he was no longer allowed to follow or even speak of.

* * *

On his way home from the building site one afternoon, he saw Charlotte Clark again. She had a bag of groceries under each arm and a basket of bread hooked over her elbow. He stopped his car, took the bag of groceries for her and walked her to her car. 'So. How far are you along?' Ned motioned to her growing belly.

'Oh, about seven and a half months.' Charlotte's shoulders had broadened, her breasts had become larger and the flesh around her joints thicker.

'Congratulations. You look a picture of health.'

'I don't often feel that way. I've been sick.'

'My wife was the same. It passes.'

'So they say.' Charlotte laughed and pointed toward the car. 'It's just over here by the curb.'

They walked quietly beside each other the remainder of the way. She opened the boot and then asked, 'I heard you quit being a policeman?'

'Yes. I figured I'd try something else.' Ned placed the grocery bag carefully into the boot.

'Oh. Okay.'

'I just,' Ned paused, 'I just needed a change.' He closed the boot. 'How's your husband?' Ned folded his arms.

'He's good. He's ...'

Ned filled in her hesitation. 'He's happy about the baby I'll bet?'

'Oh yes. Very happy. Wants a boy. A cowboy.'

'Ah, don't all men.'

'It was such a shame about the President of America, wasn't it?'

'Yes, awful.'

'He was a good man, I think.'

'Yes, he seemed it.'

'And his poor children and wife.'

'Tragic.'

'I'm sorry, I just haven't been able to get it out of my head.' Charlotte leant over her hip, the joints in her ankles had begun to ache and she felt the urge to sit.

'That's okay. Neither have I.'

'Do you think he did it?'

The question took Ned by surprise. 'Beg your pardon?'

'That bloke, Oswald? You used to be a policeman, what do you think?'

Ned had that answer constructed and on the tip of his tongue ready to be fired at anyone who'd ask him. It had been that way for weeks. He'd played out the set-ups whereby his brother Fraser and his father-in-law, Graham, had asked him the same question, *What do you think happened?* In those scenarios, Ned had let out a perfectly considered explanation, complete with side notes that, if needed, would keep them quiet until he'd finished. 'What do you think, Charlotte?'

Charlotte took a breath and looked over her shoulder, and then back at Ned. 'I guess he did it.'

Ned smiled at her and when Charlotte unlocked her door, he pushed forward and opened it for her.

'Thank you. You're a gentleman.' Charlotte lowered herself into the car and looked back up at Ned. 'Take care now.'

'And you too.' Ned gently closed the car door and watched Charlotte drive away.

CHAPTER 34

CHARLOTTE LOOKED AT herself naked in the mirror tacked to the inside of her wardrobe. Her belly was round and there was a vertical band of skin from her navel to the pubic bone that had turned brown. Her thighs were thick and rested against each other. Her breasts maintained their roundness but hung lower, and her nipples had begun to leak milk. Her face was constantly flushed at the sides, and her lips felt fuller and stayed a deeper shade of red all day long. She liked the way she looked pregnant. And she liked the way she felt. The softness of her skin, the extra flesh on the underside of her arms that she tickled with her fingernails. The firmness of her stomach. She looked at herself a while longer and wondered, *When would it come, and how?*

When she'd first learnt from her doctor that she was pregnant she'd kept it a secret from Bobby. It was early, only a month into it, and she considered some way to rid herself of the baby. She knew of abortion, though it was illegal and the stories she'd heard of the outcomes made her frightened. She'd read about herbs that, if eaten, might bring on a miscarriage. But she didn't entirely

292

believe in that. She eventually told Bobby after three months, her opportunity to abort had passed and she had begun imagining being a mother. Of feeding and nursing, of giving unconditional love and earning the same back. It became important to her to have the child.

Bobby was ecstatic. From the moment he'd found out he walked taller and took every opportunity to proclaim the imminent birth of his child. He treated Charlotte with overt kindness and was gentle with her when they were among other people. Though Bobby had never been especially religious, he asked her to pray with him each night that the baby be born healthy, and a boy. She did, and there were moments where she felt a kind of happiness beside him. On occasion he'd even cooked dinner and breakfast for her, and once had massaged the joints in her ankles that had grown so swollen and sore that she'd cried.

Initially there had been another reason to be reluctant to have the child, but she'd managed to assuage that concern by reasons of her cycles. The anxiety wasn't altogether gone, and whenever she revisited the issue, she became scared and uncertain. She had received word from Michael that he and Marcus had made it to Sydney by hitchhiking, and also train when they found themselves in a place that could connect them further south. He told her they had settled in Redfern. He wrote her a letter every fortnight and she collected it every Friday morning from the post office. She'd take the letter and walk a half mile to where she had a clear view of the Timor Sea. She'd sit down on a small dune beyond the saltbush thickets and casuarina trees, and read. He told her that they were living in a small two-bedroom house, and that he was working as a labourer on a building site in the Eastern

Suburbs. He wrote that Marcus was at school and had made friends, and that he had a local pub that he went to after work on a Friday. He said that he missed fishing and hunting, and the heat *up north*. He wrote that he planned to play rugby league for a team in the local competition when the winter arrived again. Charlotte had begun to write back, and sent a letter most weeks, though it was hard at times to find the space to pen them. Bobby had taken leave for a month and was at home with her. She found excuses to leave the house and write, but it often took more than one lie to afford herself the time to complete what she wanted to say in the letters.

* * *

On this Friday, she got dressed, left the house and walked slowly to the bus stop. The weather had turned muggy, and the first storms of the wet season had arrived. Charlotte could smell the baking tar through the road where she stood waiting for the bus. She took a deep breath and held it for as long as she could before exhaling. The bus arrived on time and she sat close to the front. It had become routine every Friday to visit her father. He'd lasted longer than doctors had expected and had at times seemed to improve. Charlotte looked forward to the half-hour bus trip there where she'd wonder about Michael and Marcus in Sydney and what they might be up to. She pictured them eating breakfast every morning together, and then Marcus walking to school. She liked to think of Michael at the local pub surrounded by new friends, laughing and telling some of the same stories he'd told her. Once off the bus, she had a half-mile walk to the hospital where she passed a pub with a ladies' lounge that she stopped off at after her visit. She'd buy a cold glass of beer and sit at a table and remember leaning up against the barn walls with Michael.

At the hospital she spoke with the nurse in care of her father, and though there'd been no significant change in his condition, he'd managed to shake off a chest infection that had Charlotte worried. She stayed at his bedside and read pieces from the newspaper, and took his hand and guided it over the curve of her hard belly. She spoke to him quietly about Michael and Marcus, and added a little more to the story she'd begun to unveil to him months before. She was almost at the end, explaining how she'd taken them to the train station.

On the way home, she stopped at the pub and ordered her beer. She drank it slowly and blew air from her mouth up toward her nose so she could smell the beer on her breath. On the bus home, the first sharp pain through her abdomen almost made her yelp. She shifted in her seat and straightened her back. It came again quickly after, and this time she let out a small cry. The passenger beside her asked if she was okay. Charlotte smiled and replied that the baby was just restless. From the bus stop back to the house she began to perspire, she mopped up the drops that formed quickly over her top lip with a handkerchief, and the insides of her thighs tickled with the beads of sweat that ran down in long trails to her feet.

By the time she reached the house, the first wave of pain was crowning. It was different to the piercing pain she'd felt on the bus; it was dull and throbbed through her stomach and around to her kidneys. She bent herself at ninety degrees hoping for relief, but it only came minutes after the climax of pain. She took off her shoes and lay down on the lounge. She took deep breaths and looked toward the telephone that was hidden behind the corner leading to the front door. 'I need an ambulance,' she said out loud. She smiled as the relief overwhelmed her and she relaxed completely, the back of her hands lank and resting across her brow.

She closed her eyes and the start of a dream materialised across the blackness of her eyelids. She heard herself talking, but only saw plates of food being placed on a table, potatoes and greens, and a whole fish. It was as if she were watching from her own point of view. She fell asleep and a moment later the pain began again. She woke and pushed herself to her elbows, and without thinking opened her legs and let them fall either side of her. Her water broke and saturated the coarse cloth that covered the lounge. She sat up, pulled off her underwear and lay back down. The pain intensified and an overwhelming impulse to push down through her abdomen overcame her. She cried out in pain at the same moment she felt the head of the baby push through her. She looked down between her legs and saw the matted dark fringe of an infant. She took a breath and gritted her teeth as she waited as long as she could until the urge to push again was no longer preventable. She bit down on her bottom lip and pressed as hard as she could. She felt the baby leave her wholly and she pushed off her elbows and straightened her arms. She looked down at the body, on its stomach and still. There was no sound, no movement. She looked at it, and then at the sac it was fastened to. It was bulbous and purple, and the cord that was attached to the baby was part bone-coloured and part transparent. She picked the child up under its arms and turned it toward her. Its head fell loosely to its side and she cradled it. Its eyes were closed its mouth gooey with blood, its skin bluish. She looked at it, not knowing what to do, and then the child became rigid and it coughed and began to cry. Its tiny legs began kicking, its arms stiffened, and it wriggled as though to break free of Charlotte. She brought the baby close to her breast and watched it nuzzle forward looking for her nipple. 'Ah, so that's what you want.' Charlotte took a breast from her dress, offered it to the baby, and it opened its tiny mouth and attached itself.

Charlotte watched it as it fed, felt it jostle in her arms and pull harder through its mouth. She looked over the naked body and watched its bluish hue dissolve as blood began to flow through it, turning the skin dark brown. She began to cry. She stood and the baby let go of her nipple and began to scream. The placenta fell away from the umbilical cord and dropped from the lounge and split open on the floor. Charlotte reattached her baby and stood rocking it. Her mind raced, her only thoughts of how to save her child. *Where to go? Who to give it to?* And then her thoughts began to fall away and dissipate without effort, and she gave herself over to what was happening in her arms. She looked down at the young boy, his feeding slowing, his jostling and wriggling more intermittent until he was still. Asleep in Charlotte's arms.

* * *

When Bobby came home from work, Charlotte hadn't moved from where she'd fallen asleep. The child was awake. Bobby, overwhelmed and panicked, gathered some towels and poured a glass of water for Charlotte to drink. When he first looked down at the child, he didn't see colour. He took it gently from Charlotte's arms, covered it with a soft blanket and nursed it. He spoke to it, smiled, and offered it back to Charlotte when it began to cry. It was when the baby was back with Charlotte that his exhilaration waned. He looked at the baby, then at her. He walked around the living room, pulling at his hair, a sound split with anger and disbelief growling from his clenched jaw. He left the house and didn't return until the next evening. While he was gone, Charlotte cut the umbilical cord, laid her child in the bassinet she'd bought weeks before, and cleaned up the remnants of her birth that lay on the floor. The baby was asleep when Bobby got home. He was drunk, the colour in his eyes dulled, the whites yellowed and stippled with jagged bolts of leaking red. He yelled at Charlotte, called her a whore, and demanded to know who the father was. When she refused to tell him, he took her by her shoulders, pulled back his head, and then thrust it forward into her forehead. She fell to the floor unconscious and bleeding from a cut across her hairline.

When she woke, the baby was wailing. She got off the floor and ran to it, picked it up from the bassinet and held it. Bobby was gone again. Charlotte wanted to run, take the baby and leave. But she had nowhere to run to, no money, and no way of getting someplace except to walk. The next morning, Bobby returned, sober and quiet. His face looked years older, the lines scored from years of expression, deeper and wider, sunken and spread looking for moisture beneath his skin. He looked at Charlotte while she held the baby, forlorn and then incredulous. He walked over to her, his mouth tightening, his eyes lit by a rage. He pulled the child from her, pushed her to the floor and stormed from the house.

CHAPTER 35

IT WAS EARLY Sunday morning and Ned was driving with Rose in the back seat, en route to the Esplanade on the Darwin foreshore where he'd push his daughter in the pram. It had become a necessity to get her off to sleep after her morning of bustling around the house. From the moment she woke, she was on the move. Walking from distraction to distraction, dismissing the spoonfuls of food that would have slowed her down. Ned had given her a water biscuit to gnaw on while he did the three-block lap from the Esplanade and then south along the suburban streets. Halfway through the last straight, Rose would be asleep.

Ned was already thinking about the next day of work. He hated Mondays. Never before had the days of the week had such a distinct feel for him. As a policeman, he'd enjoyed his Sunday nights, looking forward to the beginning of his working week. Monday through Friday all felt the same. Now, it was different. Monday was just so far from Friday, and Saturday so close to Sunday. It wasn't the job he hated, it was physical and honest, it was the uncomfortable response it had fashioned about how he saw himself. He felt he was underachieving. That he had run away from something he knew he was good at and, above all, wanted to do. He'd stopped talking to Bonnie about it; her response was always to find something else, *You don't have to work on a building site, you can do anything.* When she said it, it was always with enthusiasm and belief, and sometimes her fervour encouraged him. He wanted to please her and provide for their family. But the motivation would quickly wane, and he'd be left playing out the probabilities of a life as a labourer. None of them was appealing, and by Sunday evenings, Ned's melancholy was so profound, it reduced him to one-word responses and had him in bed before his daughter.

He walked with the pram along the street adjacent to the coastline, and from the other side of the road he saw the flock coming from St Mary's Cathedral after mass. Ned looked across and saw Father McKay. He was still wearing his vestments and was talking to a lady whose back was to Ned. McKay threw his head back and his mouth opened, and a second later his laughter, carried by the breeze, made its way to Ned. The lady then turned around and he recognised her immediately. It was Cassandra O'Shea. Ned could see her ginger hair falling from beneath the side of her hat. He looked closer to make certain, and she waved farewell to the priest and walked in his direction. The shape of her face sharpened as she strode from the shadow of a cloud, and Ned could make out the freckles across her nose and cheeks. His hands tightened around the handles of the pram, and he could feel the muscle in his jaw begin to pulse. *He told me he didn't know her!* Ned yelled it through his mind. Mayor Landry wasn't protecting her, he was protecting his brother.

He began walking quickly, turning down a street that wasn't part of his route, and when his frustration reached its crescendo, he walked onto the middle of the road, stopped and let out a roar. People on either side of the street stopped what they were doing and stared at him. Rose, woken by the outburst, was trying to flip to her stomach to gain the purchase she needed to stand up. Ned walked back onto the footpath, leant over the pram, picked up Rose and put her on his hip. He walked back toward the church, and back onto his route. He stopped where he'd seen Cassandra O'Shea. Rose began to cry.

'C'mon, sweetheart, please. Not now. Daddy's not feelin' too strong today.' He held her close and began to rock her side to side where he stood. He closed his eyes and rested his cheek against his daughter's. 'Shhhh. That's my girl. I love you, my little girl.' Rose settled and when Ned opened his eyes, looking at him across the street was Charlotte Clark. It was a peculiar sight, and he could tell she'd been watching him for a while. He smiled and waved. Charlotte did the same, and then lowered her arm and stayed watching Ned as he put Rose back into the pram. When Ned looked up, Charlotte was crossing the road and walking toward him. He took a step back, something about Charlotte's pace and the length of her gait made him instinctively uneasy. She stopped in front of the pram, lifted the brim of her hat and smiled. 'Hello, Ned.'

'Hello, Charlotte.'

'This must be your little girl.'

'Yes, that's right.' Ned watched Charlotte bend forward to look at Rose.

'She's beautiful.'

'Yes. She's a handful as well.'

Charlotte straightened and readjusted the brim of her hat. Ned took a moment, his expression turning toward pity. 'I'm so sorry,

Charlotte. I heard what happened. It's just awful. I don't have any idea what you must be goin' through.'

Charlotte smiled through her pain. 'Yes. It was very unfortunate. A stillborn birth is not an easy thing to endure.'

Ned looked down at Rose, almost asleep. 'Would you like to hold Rose? She's not a newborn but she does love a hug.'

'Oh no. No, I just. I just wanted to see her. And say hello.' Charlotte leant back over the pram and offered her hand to Rose. She took two of Charlotte's fingers and pulled them to her mouth.

'She's got some more teeth comin'. She tries to bite everything.' Ned laughed.

Charlotte felt her fingers in the child's mouth, her new teeth and bare gums biting down on her, her eyes steadfast at her father, as if checking his disposition to gauge whether she was in trouble.

'She's beautiful.' Charlotte took her suckled fingers away from Rose and smelt them. Something Ned noticed and thought strange.

'How are you coping?' Ned asked softly.

'I don't know to be honest. Days seem to blend into each other. I only know it's Sunday because I've just come from mass, and I only knew to do that because my husband told me.'

'And how is he? It must be hard for him too?'

Charlotte let out a small breath and then looked at Ned. It was a face he'd never seen anyone make. It was agony, split with fear. And desperation. He thought, while she looked at him like that, that she was going to speak, to tell him something. But the face collapsed, first over her eyes, and then across her cheeks and down through her mouth, which became loose. And she began to cry. 'Goodbye, Ned.' She looked him directly in the eye and took off her hat. She brought her hand up and pulled back her hair as though to readjust it comfortably.

Ned saw it. A new scar in the middle of her forehead. It was thickish and raised, and it looked as though it had healed without much care. She saw him look at it and watched his face chew up into an expression of pain. She put her hat back on, turned around and quickly began walking in the opposite direction.

* * *

When she got home, Bobby was with Danny Lewis in the lounge room and they'd begun drinking. They were sitting on the lounge watching a boxing match. Charlotte passed them silently on her way to the bedroom to change her clothes. There had been little talk between Charlotte and Bobby, only the essential day-to-day banalities that were asked about and answered with few words. She had begun to sleep in the second bedroom on a fold-out bed. She was desolate. Without purpose. She'd stopped hoping, stopped her dreams of another life. The fight she had within her was gone. And though her husband demanded less of her, she never stopped moving throughout her day. She created chores for herself without thinking, ironing underwear and washing clothes twice before hanging them to dry. She'd begun drinking in the afternoon while she prepared dinner, and by the time it was finished and tidied up, she was dizzy from the alcohol and ready for bed. She'd wake with a dry mouth and a headache every morning. She took Disprin for the headache, and for her thirst she drank litres of water laced with lemon juice.

She thought of suicide, and entertained the methods of getting it done. She didn't have the energy to run and had nowhere to go. She couldn't face Michael and tell him, and she didn't want to. She'd stopped collecting his mail and hadn't written to him since the birth. The moments she found herself with nothing to fill the time with, she thought about her mother. And how she'd told the rest of the world that her first daughter was stillborn to conceal the child's Down syndrome. The shame Charlotte felt when uttering that same excuse was so profound that, every time she'd said it, she'd felt part of herself wither, as though she'd shed layers of skin and her bones had narrowed. She felt feeble afterward and would often have to lie down. She'd visited her father only once since the birth; and wasn't certain she could go back again. The disgrace she'd felt sitting beside him she didn't want to endure again.

She'd watched Bobby cry night after night, a wailing she'd never heard, and if she hadn't have been there to see him crying, she would have supposed he was in the greatest of physical agony. She considered leaving, but was held back by the fear of it all somehow coming to light. She wasn't confident that Bobby, in his grief and anger, wouldn't turn it on her if she left. Have her branded a *whore*, the mother to a *half-caste*. She even wondered whether he'd accuse her of doing away with the child out of shame. She was stuck. And she knew, for similar reasons, he wouldn't leave her. In case she spoke. To have it known she cuckolded him, with a black man.

She never contemplated throwing her husband's own infidelity at him as a defence of her own. One had nothing to do with the other.

* * *

Ned walked another hour after seeing Charlotte Clark. He wheeled the pram through two suburbs and stopped across the street from David O'Shea's house. He saw Cassandra O'Shea moving about inside, and one of her boys came from the house and played jacks on the sidewalk.

Ned stopped by the church where he'd seen her talking with Father McKay and looked up at the small belfry that was part of the steeple. On the way he stopped at a telephone box and made a call to Fraser. The conversation lasted no more than a minute. When he got home, Rose was stirring from sleep in the back seat of the car, and Bonnie was on the porch reading a novel.

Ned got out and looked up at her. 'Sorry, we got sidetracked.'

Bonnie got up from her chair and leant over the balustrade. 'She still asleep?' Ned turned from her. 'What's wrong?' Her smile fell away, and Ned could feel her anxiety from where he stood. It was an energy that he'd come to know; it swept across him in a wave that often prompted him to assuage her worry immediately. But he didn't do that today.

'You look beautiful,' he said with sincerity, but with a face that Bonnie knew carried imminent bad news.

'What?'

'You and Rose need to leave Darwin. There's a place you can go. It's safe.'

'What?'

'I can't do this anymore.' Ned took Rose from the car and held her against his chest. He walked the stairs onto the porch and faced Bonnie. Rose smiled at her mother and reached for her. Bonnie took her.

* * *

Ned sat on the edge of the bed, his pensive frown kept Bonnie in the doorway. She was nervous and uncertain. 'What happened?'

305

'I can't let this go. I can't.'

'Ned, they'll kill you. He told me that. That's what he told me when they took me and Rose.' Bonnie walked from the doorway and sat beside her husband.

Ned turned to her. 'That won't happen.'

'How do you know that?' Bonnie's voice lifted.

'Because I'm no longer a cop. They're not looking for me to investigate. I have leads. Information. I can't, as a human being, just walk away from this.'

'As a human being? Ned, you're a father. Your responsibility as a man is to take care of your family. Of us.'

'There are two men in prison. For life. And I mean life. They're innocent. And I put 'em there.'

'Ned, there's nothin' you could have done about that.'

He stood, put his hands on his hips and turned away from Bonnie.

'Ned, look at me.' He turned back to her, took his hands from his hips and folded his arms. 'Please. Don't do this.' Her eyes reddened and then became glassy. Tears fell.

'I don't know how to do anything else, Bonnie.'

'You haven't tried.' Bonnie sounded desperate.

'If you want the best of me then I can't turn away from this. I'll never be what you want me to be. I'll never be who I am. Never again.' He watched as Bonnie's head fell to her chest and her crying became audible.

'Where are we going?' she yelled. He flinched, and for a moment his determination to get his way vacillated. 'Please, Ned, don't do this.'

He looked at Bonnie and, in a conscious bid to regain his resolve, thought about what might have been done to her and Rose had he not obeyed what was put before him. 'You're going, Bonnie. You and Rose. My brother Fraser still owns a place in Townsville. You'll go there.'

He left the room and walked the mile and a half to Bonnie's father's house. He told Graham what he was doing, and that Bonnie and Rose needed to leave Darwin as soon as possible. He was resolute and explained the situation with an economy of words that left Graham without doubt that he'd made up his mind.

Later that afternoon, he helped Bonnie pack. There wasn't a single word between them referring to anything other than the job at hand. What clothes to take, and how many cases were needed. What of Rose's things needed to be taken with them, and whether or not they were going to need clothes for a change of season. Graham arrived at the house on dark and took Ned aside. He looked at him in a manner that made Ned uneasy and prompted him to take a small step backward. Graham's body stiffened and he clenched both fists, and Ned prepared himself to be hit. 'This man. The one that took them. Do you know him?'

'No.'

'I've been speakin' to my daughter. She told me what he threatened her with when they took her and the child.'

'What? What did he say?'

'She'll never tell you. She shouldn't have told me.' Graham craned his neck forward, shortening the distance between the two of them. 'Find out who it is,' he snarled and walked away.

Fifteen minutes later the boot of Graham's car was packed, and they were gone.

CHAPTER 36

NED SPENT THE night over a legal pad piecing together what he knew and where it all could lead. And then, beside that, what his assumptions were and how he'd arrived at them. When he finished, the sharp angles of the pen he'd used had embedded their shapes in the soft insides of his fingers. He made a plan, and settled over a first move. When he went to bed, he felt electrified. Never had he felt more alive and certain.

* * *

In the morning he made a call to check that his family had made it safely to the place he'd sent them en route to Townsville. He drove out to the Clark house that bordered the next suburb from his. He had the address from a directory that was given to him when he'd become a policeman. It had the details of the town's heads of department and emergency services. Riley was on it, and so too Clark. He parked the car across from the house and looked over the small plots of land that were stripped bare and ready to build upon. He saw Bobby's car, and waited until he left the house and drove off. Bobby wasn't wearing his fireman's garb, which told Ned he wasn't going into work, and could be home anytime soon after he left.

Ned was unsure of where to begin and how. His instinct had led him to Charlotte Clark but it wasn't a credible line of enquiry. She was married to Bobby Clark, who was tight with Riley, who was in the thick of the stink but was off limits. Ned had seen her the day before, and the keloid scar on her hairline had poked some strain of suspicion. He'd remembered his brother Fraser's concern. Maybe, he thought, talking with Charlotte about her welfare, a crumb might be dropped for him to follow.

He was about to get out of his car and knock on the front door of the house, when Charlotte walked from the porch and onto the footpath. He considered approaching her, but instead waited and watched her walk a quarter mile to the bus stop where she was picked up not long after she arrived.

An empty house might actually offer up secrets and clues that otherwise would not be found or interpreted through interrogation. He was around the back of the house quickly. He looked beneath the raised floor of the house and across the freshly mown lawn. The corner of the small backyard housed a little shed made from corrugated iron pockmarked with rust. He walked over to it, pulled at the makeshift doors that were threaded by a thick chain either side of uneven holes. He pulled on the chain and fed it through one hole until a door was free. He opened it slowly and walked inside. It was clammy and smelt of gasoline. The ground was just earth, and in the corners it was muddy from where rainfall had leaked through the gaps in the metal trusses. There were shelves made from timber that sagged from the weight of the tools that were spread evenly across them. Claw hammers and lump hammers, planes and chisels, drill bits and piles of different-sized nails. Ned looked on all four sides of the shed, and nothing looked out of place. On the back wall, hanging from a galvanised spike, was a whip. He walked over to it, took it from the spike and let it unspool. *Fucking cowboy.* The handle was worn, and Ned could feel the notches in the leather made from someone's hand. There were discernible indentations shaped as fingers, and a groove where the thumb had fastened the grip.

Ned picked up the whip's thong and looked at it across his palm. It was broader than any whip he'd seen, and its thickness made it uncommonly heavy. He closed his fingers gently over the thong and pulled it through his hand. He stopped when he felt the edges of the whip roughen. Through the centre of the whip's thong, on both sides, the hide was torn and spiny. He looked closely at the roughened pieces and saw tiny shavings of dark thin matter stuck to the sharp edges. He rolled the whip up and took it with him as he left the shed. He threaded the chain back through the door holes, got into his car and drove away quickly.

* * *

The coroner, Ron Thompson, held a small tape measure across the widest part of the whip's thong. '1.3 inches.'

'Does that match?'

Thompson looked down at the photograph on his desk. It was of Clarry Tallis's back, the intersecting wounds that were left from his lashing. Thompson took another photograph from a large yellow envelope and placed it on the desk. It was a magnified photo of one of the wounds with a measurement written across its width. It read 1.6 inches.

'Is that too wide?' Ned looked disappointed.

'No. By the time I measured this, Clarry Tallis had been in the marsh a long time. The flesh had swelled and the wounds were stretched.'

'Could this have done it?' Ned pointed to the whip's thong and the rough edges along its length.

'If used by a heavy hand. Probably. But is it the one that was used? I can't say.' Thompson took off his round glasses and cleaned the lenses with the sleeve of his lab coat.

'And what about the stuff on the leather, could that be skin?'

'It's hard to tell. Could be animal hide.'

'He doesn't have any animals.' Ned picked up the photograph from the desk.

'But it could have been used before on livestock. We'll never know.'

'But what do you think?' Ned placed his hands on his hips.

Thompson put his glasses back on, adjusted them so they were comfortable over the bridge of his nose and behind his ears, and looked once again at the photographs. 'I think he was whipped to death. You have a whip. But is it *the* whip? I don't know.'

'Fuck.'

Thompson turned and faced Ned squarely. 'I did this as a favour. But I can't help you anymore. You're not a cop, and the case is closed. I'm sorry.'

'It's okay. I appreciate it. Thanks, Ron.' He took the whip and left Thompson's office.

* * *

Ned tossed the whip through the open window of his car. He leant against the driver's door and looked toward the beach. He could see two fishing boats laden with netting and bait pushing against the incoming tide. He smiled when registering the similarity of the boat's struggle and his own. *Against the current with no help.* He thought about his next move. He considered going back to the Clark house and waiting for an opportunity to confront Charlotte when she was alone. *But ask what?* he thought. *Did your husband kill Clarry Tallis? Is this the whip he used?*

He drove out to the mission he'd visited months earlier and stood on the red dirt path leading to the housing. He waited for an hour before he decided to walk toward the tent where he'd seen Marcus. When he got there, Timothy Mitchell was sitting on the ground gutting a catch of red bream. He was the older man Ned had seen in the company of Marcus Roberts in Riley's office.

'What do you want?' Timothy looked older than Ned remembered, and close up he had green-coloured eyes that were masked in either corner by long lumps of thick scar tissue. Ned knew immediately that Timothy had been a fighter.

'G'day. My name is Ned Potter.' Ned realised he wasn't at all prepared. Without the mantle of policeman, he felt naked and realised his enquiry could be read as inappropriate. He knew he had to make an impact. 'I knew Michael Roberts. I know he's missing.'

Timothy's eyes held firm on Ned. 'Yeah?'

'I met his son here once. I was a policeman not long ago and was investigating the murders of two men. You might know them, Clarry Tallis and Lionel Frazier?'

'I didn't know those men. I knew they were killed. That's all.'

'Okay. Is young Marcus here?'

Timothy's eyes narrowed and his jaw tightened. 'Nup.'

'Ah, shit. When will he be back? You see, I told him I'd help find his father and I have some news.'

'Marcus won't be back.'

Ned paused. 'I see.'

'You should go.' Timothy put the cleaned fish into a bucket, picked up the scraped entrails and threw them to a brolga that was waiting a safe distance away.

'Hang on, mate. You're Timothy Mitchell, correct?'

Timothy turned around. 'Yes, I am.'

'Look, Timothy, I'm not tryin' to fleece or hurt anyone here, I'm just tryin' to get to the bottom of something. Something bad that happened. I knew Michael, not well, but I knew him. And I promised the boy I'd help.'

Timothy looked into Ned's eyes and then across the top half of his body, as though he were taking an inventory on what parts he measured to be honest. 'I don't where the boy is. He told me he was goin' with his father. That he'd seen him. That a lady was takin' him there.'

'Okay.' Ned took a breath, knowing the answer to his next question unlocked the pieces he needed to continue without alerting Landry or Riley. 'Do you know who she is?'

'I never met her. He just told me she was a good lady. And that her name was Charlotte.'

'Okay. Can you tell me, was she a black woman or white?'

'White. That's all I know.'

Ned's body straightened involuntarily, and he felt the muscles and ligaments around his joints stiffen as though he'd been given a fright. 'Thank you so very much, Timothy.'

Ned put out his hand for Timothy to shake. Timothy looked at it and then back at Ned. 'Like I said, I don't know where they are. If anyone else asks, I'll say the same.'

'Okay, Timothy.'

Timothy took Ned's hand and shook it firmly.

* * *

Driving away from the mission, Ned couldn't put a reasonable scenario together whereby Charlotte Clark had somehow become involved with Michael Roberts and the boy. *Could be another Charlotte*, he thought. He was almost certain that Bobby Clark was present for the murders of Clarry Tallis and Lionel Frazier, and the whip he'd found had been used. He closed his mind from entertaining any more set pieces on how it all fit, and drove to the Clark house.

When he arrived and parked on the street across from the house, Charlotte was standing on the front porch, drinking from a tall glass. Ned looked at her carefully. From where he was, he couldn't work out what state of mind she might be in. Her stature was masked by the long dress she wore, and the choppy wind blew it out so he couldn't tell if her body looked tired or injured. Bobby Clark's car was still gone, but Ned had no idea when he might be back. He looked at the sky to check how much light was left in the day. The sun was dropping quickly and about to fall into a murky band of low-lying cloud that stretched the length of the horizon. Ned's stomach fluttered as he played with the idea of making his approach. He was so keen for answers that he couldn't stand the thought of waiting another night knowing how close he was to unlocking the puzzle.

Fuck it, if Bobby Clark comes back, he comes back. Ned took a breath and held it until he could feel the air in his lungs rise up and fill his mouth looking for a way out. He let the breath out slowly, took the whip from the passenger seat, opened his door and walked across the road.

She spotted him just as he stepped from the road and onto the footpath. She was startled and felt a surge of uncertainty brought on by the speed and tenacity with which Ned was approaching her. 'Ned.'

Ned stopped just short of the porch and looked up at her. 'Where's your husband?' He said it quickly and without tone.

'He's at the pub, I think.' Charlotte took a step back.

'Michael Roberts.' Ned looked directly at Charlotte and knew immediately it was her. 'Charlotte, listen to me very carefully. You need to come with me. In my car and we need to take a drive and talk.'

'I'm sorry I can't do that.' Charlotte began to turn.

'He was there!' Ned let the anger run through his words. Charlotte turned back to him and Ned held up the whip. 'Did they use this to flog Clarry Tallis to death? Michael was there, wasn't he?'

Charlotte's face grew longer, her mouth fell open and her bottom row of teeth showed. She felt faint and her face lost its colour.

'They killed two men. I need to know why, Charlotte. Did he tell you? Did Michael tell you what he saw, or what those men saw?'

'No. He never did. Please leave, Ned.'

'I saw that scar on your forehead. What happened?'

'Nothing. I fell.' Charlotte instinctively checked her hair to make certain the scar was covered.

'He did that to you. Bobby did. Why? I need to know where Michael is, Charlotte.'

'No. I won't tell you or anyone!' Charlotte turned from Ned quickly and walked through the front door and slammed it closed. Ned stepped up the first stair to the porch and heard the door lock from the inside.

'Fuck.' The word came out on his breath and was barely audible. He looked up to the front door beyond the small deck and then back toward the street. He resolved, as he stood there, that Charlotte wasn't going to let him in the house and that it was better he leave. Before he walked across the street and back to his car, he stepped onto the porch quietly, and left the whip coiled tightly at the front door. He waited in his car as the sun fell beneath the horizon and night took hold. He saw the light to the front porch flicker on, and Charlotte's blunt shape bend and reach down. She cut through the light, became a sharper figure and Ned could see she held the whip. She walked forward, looked out over the porch and across the road to Ned's car.

CHAPTER 37

NED WALKED INTO Hotel Darwin just after seven o'clock that night. He wanted to see if Bobby Clark was still drinking. When he arrived, the first person he saw was Danny Lewis, and with him a brutish blond man who matched the description Bonnie had given of the man who'd first threatened her outside their home and later abducted her and Rose. Ned's stomach fluttered and a nervous squirt of adrenalin weakened his legs. He took a seat at the opposite end of the horseshoe bar, and when he was served his beer, he held it aloft and looked toward them as if to offer some kind of good will. Not a minute later Danny Lewis approached and sat down on the stool beside Ned. He was still in police uniform though it was untidily put together. His shirt was out on one side and the buttons undone to the middle of his chest. Ned could smell the alcohol seeping from the pores of his skin and through his exhaled breathing. 'Potter. You look good in civilian clothes. Suits you.' Lewis slurred his words and his eyelids were lazy, obscuring the top half of his irises so he looked as though he were about to fall asleep.

'You look tired, Danny. Go to bed, huh?'

Lewis smiled and shook his head. Ned looked down the bar to where the brute was standing. 'Who's your friend?'

Lewis followed Ned's look. 'Oh, you don't know him. You don't want to know him.'

'Oh yeah. Why's that?'

''Cause he doesn't fuckin' like you.'

Ned nodded and played dumb. 'Oh, what did I do to him?'

'I'll call him over and you can ask him if you like. He's big, isn't he?'

Ned looked at the brute for just a moment and then turned back to Lewis. 'You're a fuckin' idiot, you know that?' He sat straighter on his stool and turned so he was completely square opposite Lewis. 'You're a dumb cunt, Danny. And, like I said before, you're a fuckin' liar. You've always got a better story. I don't believe you. Riley and Bobby Clark? They've been laughin' behind your back. I've seen 'em. They tolerate you because you'll do whatever it is they tell you to.' Ned shifted his schooner, his eyes directly set on Lewis.

'Couldn't let it go, could ya?' Lewis smiled, as the brute approached from the other end of the bar. He settled next to Lewis and folded his arms.

'Jack Taylor meet Ned Potter.' Lewis signalled to the barman and raised two fingers.

Taylor glared at Ned and tightened the fold of his arms to inflate his biceps. Ned held eye contact until he shifted his look lower to Taylor's broad even mouth. He got caught looking at the fullness of his lips and the flaking skin either side of them. Ned huffed, it reminded him of a child's mouth, battered from a licking to keep it moist against a dry wind.

'I know you.'

Ned laughed.

'Somethin' funny, mate?'

'Your voice. It doesn't match your muscles.'

Taylor looked at Lewis as if to ask how to respond.

'Jesus Christ, you're as fuckin' dumb as he is.'

Taylor unfolded his arms and grabbed Ned by the shirtfront. 'You listen to me, cunt, all I need is a reason to follow through on what we had planned for your wife. Just give me that fuckin' reason.'

Ned looked down at Taylor's fists chewing up the collar of his shirt. 'You got big hands, don't ya?'

Taylor pushed Ned as he let go of his shirt, and Ned wobbled on the bar stool.

'Fuck off, Potter,' Lewis slurred and a spray of spittle landed on Ned's collar.

Ned wiped it away with the back of his hand, looked at both of them and then left without another word.

* * *

He drove past Charlotte's house on the way home and saw that Bobby's car was parked outside. He barely slept that night, considering his next move. There was no angle he could manipulate without knowing where Michael Roberts was, and the only person with that information was Charlotte. The next morning, certain that Charlotte would be wary of his presence, he followed a hunch and visited Darwin hospital. He approached the reception area, and politely complimented the young lady out front on her hair. He shared a story with her from his past, and without too much exaggeration had her interest. He then asked her whether or not she remembered a lady by the name of Charlotte Clark ever giving birth at the hospital. He explained that he was asking only as a follow-up to his superior's request. He didn't tell her what kind of work he was in, and after the exchange of pleasantries, she checked her records and gave him the information.

Without any record of the birth, Ned visited the Darwin library and checked the public records for recent funerals. There was no burial or cremation recorded for a child with the last name Clark.

The next morning, Ned parked his car out of sight from the Clark house, and walked a block to a position where he was hidden behind the stacks of timber that had begun to accumulate at the vacant lots across the road. He saw Bobby leave dressed in his fire and rescue garb, and watched as Charlotte left the house shortly after, holding a small wicker basket. Ned moved out from behind the timber stacks and followed her. She visited the local grocer and then the butcher, Ned staying a good distance behind her the whole time. She continued on and stopped at the entrance to the post office. Instead of going inside, she stood still.

Ned hid in a nook of the building. He watched as Charlotte took a step forward, and then another back to where she'd stood. Finally, she entered the post office, her head toward the ground, her gait wide and pace quick, as though she were preparing to push through an obstruction. Ned thought about the peculiar nature of what he'd just witnessed. *She's not right in the head* is what he thought, and wondered whether anyone else had seen her odd behaviour. She came out not a minute later holding a stack of envelopes and turned toward where Ned was partially concealed. He followed her down toward Nightcliff Beach. She crossed a road, walked over the footpath and sat under the shade of a casuarina tree. Ned stood behind a parked car and watched her unfurl the envelopes from the rubber band that held them together. She took out the first letter and began to read. Ned could hear her laugh carried on the wind, and though he couldn't see her face, he could tell by her posture that she was in a moment of glee. He watched her frame wilt a moment later, and then heard her crying. He counted twelve letters that she read, and at the end of the last one she gathered the envelopes and held them firmly in her hands. She brought the stack to her nose and inhaled.

Ned crossed the road and walked slowly toward the tree she sat beneath. He stopped a foot away from her. 'Tide's on the way out, the whiting'll be biting.'

Charlotte turned to the voice, and Ned took a step forward. 'How are you, Charlotte?' She looked up at him and then back toward the sea.

'I'm okay.'

'Really?' He sat down beside her, leant forward and hooked his arms across his knees.

'I am right now. Today. I'm okay.'

'Those from Michael Roberts?' Ned looked down at the stack of envelopes next to her.

'Yes.'

'He's safe and well?'

'Yes. He's away from here.'

Ned held the next question in his mouth, he contemplated swallowing it and replacing it with a banal observation or enquiry into something relating to anything but this. He was afraid of the answer; and wondered, while looking out over the Timor, whether there was another approach. He took a breath, and moved forward.

'Charlotte, I did some checkin'. You didn't give birth to your baby in a hospital.'

Charlotte's face flushed red.

Ned took the next step delicately. 'I'm so sorry.'

Charlotte looked at the ground.

'Charlotte, the baby wasn't given a funeral either.'

She slowly lifted her head and turned to Ned, her eyes glassy. Her nose had begun to run.

'What happened to the baby, Charlotte?'

Her chin wavered, and she started crying. 'I don't know. Bobby took it away.'

Ned let his head fall forward into the space between his knees. He could feel his face twisting its shape toward pity. He looked up at Charlotte and watched her whole being loosen and falter until it collapsed. She lay on her side crying. He felt his own tears sting his eyes as he gently placed a hand across her back. 'I'm so sorry, Charlotte.' He could feel the vibrations of her sobbing, it was as though her organs trembled and her ribs absorbed their trauma and rattled as they tried to keep from breaking apart.

'Charlotte, I need your help. Michael knows why those men were killed. Help me, Charlotte.'

She reached behind and took Ned's hand. 'You can't tell Michael about the baby. That it was his. Please.'

Ned's eyes widened, the revelation making his heart thump. She turned to him, her voice deepened and slow. 'You can't tell him.'

Ned nodded. 'Okay.'

They stayed on the beach and spoke until Ned had no more questions to ask. She told him about how she happened upon Michael and that he'd managed to escape. Ned pressed her again on whether Michael had told her why Clarry Tallis and Lionel

Frazier were murdered. She told him the truth, that Michael had said she was *better off and much safer not knowin' a thing about it.*

She told Ned with joy about the moments she and Michael had spent together learning about one another while she nursed him back to health at her father's old property. Ned told her he knew where the barn was and that he'd passed it many times driving out to fishing spots with his father and brothers when he was much younger. She explained how she'd found Marcus and, with Michael, planned their escape. He told her about the abduction of Bonnie and Rose, and that he believed Bobby was there during the murder of Clarry Tallis and Lionel Frazier. He explained that he'd been complicit in the conviction of two men he knew to be innocent. They walked back toward Charlotte's house on the footpath, side by side. A block from her house, they stopped. They hugged each other without saying a word, and Ned watched her walk the rest of the way home.

CHAPTER 38

NED GOT IN his car at midnight and began driving. He figured the two and a half thousand miles to Sydney would take him just under four days. Driving directly south to Katherine, he turned east, drove through Mataranka and crossed into Queensland where he stayed at a roadhouse in Mt Isa. He slept four hours and continued through the night until he reached Townsville on the east coast. He swam in the Pacific Ocean at dawn, checked into a motel, slept until midday and then followed the coastline down toward Sydney. He drove past the Whitsunday Islands and onto the Sunshine Coast and crossed the border into New South Wales at Tweed Heads at midnight. Pulling his car off the road and onto a broad shoulder of gravel, he fell asleep until dawn. At five o'clock in the evening, seven hours short of four days since leaving Darwin, Ned arrived in Sydney.

He drove across the Sydney Harbour Bridge, looked out across the water and saw a ferry cutting its way through the gentle chop toward Circular Quay. He opened his window and took in the fragrance, it was tart with petrol and briny from the harbour water. He drove further south into the belly of the city and was overwhelmed by the mass of people walking the footpaths and driving cars. The buses blew black smoke in thick plumes from dirtied exhausts, and car horns parped in disparate lengths that signalled all measure of agitation. Ned smiled in wonder, it was almost unrecognisable in size and activity since he'd left as a six-year-old. As he approached Redfern, the scent of fermenting beer filled the car and he was jolted back to his childhood. Living in the small terraced house in Redfern where, when the wind blew the right way, it filled with the brewery's attar. *Apple pie*, Ned thought.

He booked into a room above a local pub and then went downstairs into the bar. It was crowded with mostly working-class men. Ned ordered a schooner of Carlton and stood alone at a tall table by the entrance. The men looked different from those in the Territory. Their hair was longer, sideburns thicker and they were heavier set. Their accents were different from those in the North too, they were more rounded in the middle of words and without a twang. The sound of the bar was the same, however, the garbled hum of drunks. For a reason he didn't look for, he felt more masculine than these men. There was a soft edge to them, and he smiled while contemplating the hardiness that came with being from the Territory.

Midway through his second glass of beer, a fight broke out and he watched as pool cues were swung at faces and broken bottles thrust at bodies. He retreated to a corner, horrified that a pub fight could be anything but men with arms raised swapping punches. He went back upstairs to his room, lay on his bed and wondered if such ferocious violence was driven by the density of a city like Sydney, and the strain that came with living so closely to one another. He listened through the open window of his room to the rattle and hum of life on the streets outside. *Cars, so many cars.*

He drifted off to sleep and woke at dawn. He got dressed and went for a walk. He connected landmarks he could remember, the rugby league oval and the milk bar across the road from it, and within twenty minutes of leaving the pub, he was outside the old terrace house where he once lived. He stood beneath a small eucalypt and watched a young family come from the home, the youngest child eager to get going, pulling hard against the plastic reins he was harnessed by.

Ned walked back to the pub, showered and got dressed and then asked a young woman with a pram directions to the address Charlotte had given him. From where he was it was half a mile to Michael's house. He walked quickly and relished the drier heat, though there was a stiff westerly wind that was warm and smelt like a campfire. Summer had just arrived and there were bushfires west of the city burning in the Blue Mountains.

When he arrived, he stood out front of the house and looked at the pair of football boots on the small front porch. They were a size to fit a boy and dusty with brown earth. Ned found it strange to see dirt another colour than ochre. He opened the small iron gate and walked along a short footpath, up a flight of stairs, and landed at the front door. He was about to knock when he heard the rumble of a voice and the rustle of clothing. He took a step back and listened as the door was unlocked. It opened quickly and before him were Michael and Marcus Roberts. Michael put an arm across his son's shoulder and moved him away from the door. 'Ned?'

Ned smiled. 'Hello, Michael. Hello, Marcus.'

'How'd you find us?' He turned to Marcus, 'Go back inside.'

Ned raised an eyebrow. 'I know what happened. Charlotte Clark told me.' Michael's face shifted to what Ned recognised as disbelief. 'I'm not here to arrest you for anything. I'm not a cop anymore. I'm here because I need you to come back with me and help me put these blokes away.'

'I don't believe you. Charlotte wouldn't have told anyone where I am unless someone's squeezin' her. Like the police. Like you.' Michael's nostrils flared, his eyes narrowed, and his jaw tightened before he growled through his clenched teeth, 'Now get the fuck out of here and leave us alone before I flog ya.' He stepped over the threshold.

Ned stood his ground and looked directly at Michael. 'I'm not goin' anywhere, Michael. They've threatened my life, kidnapped my wife and my child. They forced me to resign because I wouldn't let this go. There are three men dead, and two men in prison, who I put there for something they didn't do. I got Bobby Clark. I know he was there when Clarry Tallis and Lionel Frazier were killed. I know you were there. I know you got away. I know Charlotte nursed you back to health and got you and your son out of there. So I know a lot. Much more now than they think I know. What I don't know is why. Why were Ernie Clay, Clarry Tallis and Lionel Frazier murdered? And why were you there? Why?'

Michael glared at him, his jawline throbbing with two knobs of muscle as he bit down on his molar teeth. 'They'll kill me before I get a chance to talk. Soon as I'm back there, they'll know it, and they'll kill me.'

'I won't let that happen.'

'You can't protect me. You were one of 'em.'

Ned's hands relaxed and fell by his thighs. He felt a hopelessness overcome him. The solution to this situation was too much to ask of anyone. Michael was right. He couldn't protect him. He couldn't walk him back into Darwin and sound out the allegations of murder before Landry and Riley. He didn't have authority; he wouldn't have anything but Michael's word on why the men were killed. It'd be dismissed, swept under the carpet, it'd never make a news story or be spoken of again. He stood silently, and looked away from Michael and over the porch landing that shimmered with the shiny ends of reinforced steel under the spots of worn-out concrete. He had one last piece of information he'd not revealed to Michael. It was pain, pure pain, but as he stood looking over the worn concrete, he weighed the hurt he'd unleash against the probability of no one ever being made accountable for the horrors that had been committed. Betraying Charlotte, he reasoned, was something he'd have to live with. 'Help me.' He looked back up at Michael.

'I'm not goin' back, I'm not sayin' a word.' Marcus poked his head between the door frame. 'Go back inside.'

Ned watched as young Marcus did as his father told. 'Charlotte had a baby. A little boy. He took it from her.' Ned put his hands in his pockets. 'Do you know why he took it?'

Michael shook his head.

'Because the boy had colour. She told me not to tell you that. And I wasn't goin' to tell you. But I need your help. Now, you wanna do somethin' about that? You tell me everything you know, and I'll find a way to protect you, and Charlotte. You have my word.'

Michael left Marcus at the house and took Ned a quarter mile to a small park with a single bench. It was by a train station and the grass had turned brown from lack of rain. They sat down and Michael rested his elbows on his knees. 'I like it here. I'm gettin' used to the different heat. My boy likes his school. I got cousins. Friends.'

'Michael, you can come back here anytime you like.'

Michael sat straight up and looked out across the park before taking a deep breath. 'Ernie Clay. I used to box with him when he came from Townsville. He was taken from his mum. I used to see him all the time when I wasn't travellin' with the boxin' tent. Before I left the last time, me and Clarry Tallis were with him. We were fishin' the beach. He told us he was workin' for a white fella at a school.'

'Lionel Frazier,' Ned said flatly.

'He gave Ernie a hand. He needed work. Cleaned the classrooms. That sort of thing. Anyway, Ernie told us one day he was told to go and clean the place the priest was in. I don't know what it's called.' Michael looked at Ned and shook his head. 'The Father. The priest was, he was with a young boy. Ernie saw it. He was afraid. Didn't know what to do. Didn't tell the white fella 'cause he didn't want to lose his job. The priest saw him though. Ernie said they looked right at each other. Then one day, I heard he was dead. I knew somethin' was foul. I saw his wife, Martha, we spoke. Ernie told her the same thing he told me. Saw what he saw. Priest saw him. Then she told me that that mayor fella had come to see him 'em both. He asked flat out what Ernie had seen. Ernie thought he was there to help, so he told him. Not long after that they found his body.'

'I was the first cop at the scene.'

Michael looked at Ned, shocked. 'That was you, eh?'

'Yeah. You know the priest's name?'

'Nuh.'

'What about the school he worked at?'

'Kid's school. St Mary's. Not far from the mission.'

Ned's jaw pushed forward involuntarily in rhyme with his anger. 'McKay,' he whispered. Michael didn't hear him and Ned continued, 'The white fella, Lionel Frazier. He was with you and Clarry that night they were killed?'

Michael nodded. 'After the show, we had a drink. Played cards. He found his way there. He liked a bet. He was ramblin' about stuff. But he said somethin'. Wasn't right. I bailed him up. Pretty aggressive I was. He shit himself. I told him to keep talkin'. He told me and Clarry he'd seen somethin' over at the priest's place. Was the same thing Ernie saw. He told us he shouts at the priest and stops it. Little fella runs to him and holds on for his life. This bloke goes to the police. Even goes to see the child's parents. Tells them what he's seen. He tells us all this. Nothin' happens though. The boy's parents don't do a thing. Said he went back to see the cops. Tells them he wants to swear on God what he saw. Said the mayor fella came to see him too. Me and Clarry didn't say anything about Ernie.'

Ned took some time before his next question. 'What happened?'

'Someone musta been watchin' him. Cops. There were other white fellas at the card game. Lots of people. They musta heard him talkin' to us. A day later a couple of fellas grabbed me and Clarry. We were packin' up the tent. Put us in a car. Took us to a place. The Lionel fella was already there when we got there. They held a gun to us. And a fella was there I knew. I boxed him at the show. Charlotte's husband.' Michael stopped and looked at Ned. 'I didn't know that he was her husband until I was nearly better. I never told her.'

'I saw that fight.' Ned half-smiled.

'Yeah? Well, I beat him. He didn't like that. He started on me. "Abo this, Abo that." I think they were just gonna scare us. But it went bad. Clarry jumped in, we got to fightin'. They pulled a gun. Lionel tried to run. They shot him. He was dead. Then they had to kill us, I reckon. We tried. We fought. They shot Clarry, but didn't kill him. They set upon me. There was three of 'em. One real big fair-headed fella. He was the one shootin'. Anyway, they musta knocked me out. When I woke up, the big fella had a whip. He was into Clarry. I ran away. I left him.' Michael's voice wavered and he began to cry. 'I ran into Charlotte on a back road about three miles from where they had us.'

Ned put his arm around Michael's shoulder. 'I'm sorry, Michael.'

Michael said nothing though he tried to muffle his crying in the crook of his elbow. Ned brought his arm away and they sat looking over the park in silence. Ned watched a grey bush rabbit come from behind a small mound of unkempt grass. He thought it stuck out among the brick and mortar of a city.

'When he was ramblin' at the card game. Lionel. He said the name of the boy.'

'The boy?'

'The boy he seen. With the priest.'

'What was his name?'

'Can't remember his first name. But he said O something.'

'O'Shea?'

'Yeah. Might have been. He got the worst of it from what the Lionel fella said. Just a kid. Like I said, Lionel went to see his mum and dad.'

Ned brought his hands to his face and rubbed his eyes as though to wake himself from a nightmare. 'Thank you, Michael.'

* * *

Later that evening, Ned took Michael and Marcus to dinner. He drove them to the Rocks neighbourhood that lay in the shadow of the Harbour Bridge. They ate in the beer garden of a pub, Ned and Michael drank a beer and spoke of what was to come. He dropped them back to their house at Redfern and set off back to Darwin.

As he drove, he put together his next moves while occasionally looking from his window at the blunt outline of bushland in the darkness. Michael had agreed to come back, to say what he saw of the kidnapping and murdering of Lionel Frazier and Clarry Tallis. He would also swear that Ernie Clay and Lionel Frazier had told him the same story. That they'd both seen a priest raping a boy in the vestry of St Mary's Cathedral. It was all hearsay though, and wouldn't hold up, and Ned knew with the legal power the town would bring to bear to defend a priest, it would be improbable that allegations such as these would be properly held to account. He needed more evidence to make that stick, and he needed the backing of some proper authority to lay charges. He knew no one in the Northern Territory Police Department was going to listen to him.

CHAPTER 39

NED PARKED OUTSIDE Cassandra O'Shea's house and looked through the semi-draped curtained windows for activity. He saw her in the kitchen, and then walk through to the living room where he'd sat talking to her months before. *Do you believe in God?* Ned recalled her asking him. He walked the stairs to the porch and knocked on the door. He heard Cassandra O'Shea call to her son not to answer it, but in front of Ned, peeping at him through the wedge he'd opened, was a young boy.

'You must be Aaron?' Ned asked in a soft tone and smiled.

A moment later a forceful hand moved the boy from the door and it opened completely. Cassandra O'Shea looked different, her face haphazardly made-up, the brown freckles across her nose and her cheeks barely visible beneath the chalky foundation she'd applied. Ned thought she looked ten years older than when he'd last seen her just months before.

'Yes?' She stepped outside onto the porch and closed the door behind her.

Ned thought for a moment about how to proceed. He could feel her distrust and her defensive candour in her posture, she folded her arms tightly and stood tall, her legs straightened at the knees and her shoulders back.

'Your son Aaron?'

'Yes?'

'He was sexually assaulted by a priest.' Ned looked directly at her. 'You know that, though.'

'You can leave right now, or I'm going to call the mayor.' Cassandra turned her back on Ned and reached for the doorknob.

'Mrs O'Shea, do you know that Mayor Landry has a brother?'

'I don't care. Now leave.'

Ned took a step across the threshold and into the house. 'His brother is Father McKay.' Ned began speaking louder. 'How much did Landry pay you to keep quiet?'

'Can you please lower your voice?' Cassandra whipped past Ned and peered at the houses either side of her own. She stepped back inside and closed the door.

'I saw your husband in a bar, drunk, and you know what he told me? He told me he abandoned his son. He was crying.' Ned raised his voice again. 'And I was the one who took his body to the morgue to be examined.'

'Enough!' Cassandra O'Shea cupped her hands and put them over her ears.

'He committed suicide, Mrs O'Shea, because he couldn't live with the shame of turning his back on what had happened to his son.'

Cassandra pulled Ned by the shirt and slapped him across the chest. 'Stop it!'

'He was raped by your priest!'

Cassandra O'Shea fell onto the carpeted floor and began to cry. Her body convulsed as she sobbed, and Ned sat down, pulled her in close to his body and held her tightly.

'God wouldn't do this to me.' She put her hands over Ned's forearms and squeezed.

'It wasn't God, Mrs O'Shea.'

The front door opened, and young Aaron O'Shea stood looking down at Ned embracing his mother on the floor. His eyes were listless, his face pallid. He got down on the floor and sat cross-legged in front of them. 'Is this because of me?'

'No, son.' Ned shook his head.

* * *

Ned took Cassandra and the boy into the living room, and when Cassandra settled, they talked. She told him that Lionel Frazier had come to see her and her husband, and told them what he'd seen Father McKay doing to their son. She then told him that Mayor Landry had also come and explained that Lionel Frazier was a convicted criminal and a drunk, and shouldn't be believed. And that having any such allegations out in public would be disastrous for the parish. Before he left, he handed her an envelope and told her, *This is for my peace of mind*. She opened it later and inside were ten twenty-pound bills. David, she said, wanted to go to the police, but she had stopped him by threatening to leave and take their sons. She said she was afraid that if it had come out in the open, no one would have believed them.

Before Ned left, she looked at him in a manner that was so wrought by pain and guilt that he wondered whether she'd ever be able to reconcile with herself. The last thing she asked him was, *Do you believe in God?* He answered yes, and he saw her anguish abate.

* * *

Ned left the house and travelled south to Katherine. He arrived at Damien Clooney's house just on dusk. The house was new, elevated from the claggy earth and on the banks of the Katherine River. Damien Clooney had moved there from Darwin when he'd retired from the police force. He'd built the house, and bought an old fishing boat, cut away the rotting fragments of the aluminium hull and welded new pieces to make it watertight. He'd ground the joins smooth, repainted the rim in sky blue and attached a new chunky outboard motor. He sat on the small deck of the house most afternoons and peeled the cherabin prawns he'd caught in the early morning.

Ned knocked on the door and Damien's wife answered. Fran was a short woman, her hair in a bunch of broad curls.

'Ned.' She smiled and opened her arms. Ned hugged her, walked inside, and a moment later he was sitting across from Damien Clooney for the first time in three years. Ned didn't mince his words, he laid out the evidence he had, the testimonies that had been volunteered and the collusion from the mayor's office that had covered up the crimes. He asked Damien to light a path to follow so that he could make a case that would stick. Without a badge, Ned couldn't see a way in without his revelations and accusations being dismissed as ramblings designed to get back at Riley and Landry. Clooney told him that to *untie the knot* he needed to be *invisible*. To have the foundations of conspiracy displaced by someone else. Then he said, *It can crumble. You can't be in the frame, they'll bury it otherwise.*

Later, Clooney walked him to his car, and they looked out over the Katherine River, the lithe shape of a freshwater croc winding through the broad white stripe from a reflected half-moon over the water.

Damien extended his hand. 'Good to see you, Ned.'

'You too, Damien.' Ned shook his hand.

Damien gently placed a hand on Ned's shoulder. 'I'm gonna tell you straight up. This could be dangerous for you even when you're keeping yourself invisible. This is government. Some people and their friends aren't gonna be happy with what's about to go down.'

'I don't care.' Ned shook his head.

Damien moved his hand from Ned's shoulder, and stuck a finger in his chest and poked it as he spoke. 'Listen, don't be a fuckin' idiot here. You're not a cop. Find a way to shake the tree. The rotten fruit will fall. Let the investigation find you. Be smart. Sit back and watch it fall.'

* * *

Driving home, Ned thought about what Damien had said. He went back and forth deciding his approach. There was such satisfaction to be had having Landry and Riley know that he was the one to uncover it all. As the pieces began to fit and the magnitude of the deceit and the vile nature of the crimes materialised before him, he'd fantasised about the moments he'd have watching Landry and Riley squirm as they were pressed with questions and asked to explain the allegations. He wanted to be present to see that. To see them see him. But he thought about Bonnie and Rose, and also Charlotte. He decided no connection was safer for all.

CHAPTER 40

CASSANDRA O'SHEA, DRESSED in a knee-length cream skirt and powder blue blouse, clutching a set of cedar rosary beads in her hand, walked into the Darwin Police Station, her son Aaron by her side, and asked to see Senior Sergeant Joe Riley.

The moment he saw her, he quietly ushered them into his office. He pushed back and made a veiled threat that her allegations could see her family *possibly harmed* and *ostracised by members of the community.*

After her visit to the station, she went to the office of the *Northern Territory News*. A story about police negligence to investigate a crime broke three days later and Riley was stood down by the police commissioner the same afternoon. His replacement to head up the investigation came from North Queensland and arrived in Darwin at the end of the week. Tommy Butler had been an infantry warrant officer in the Second World War. He was seen to be doggedly determined and unapologetically impartial as an investigator.

Before the story broke in the newspaper, Riley had phoned Landry intending to let him know a thread had been pulled that would leave their conspiratorial allegiance exposed. Landry hadn't answered, and Riley, quickly becoming panicked, called Bobby Clark and told him to meet him. Bobby Clark was nervous and already drinking at Hotel Darwin when Riley walked in, grim faced and pale. He ordered a schooner of ale and sat down next to Bobby. 'We're fucked. This could blow right up if they join the dots.'

Bobby turned his glass of beer over a sodden coaster, his breathing quickened and his face drained of colour. He and Riley looked like a couple returned from the Northern Hemisphere after a month-long holiday with no sun. Bobby took a deep breath, exhaled through his mouth and looked directly at Riley. 'Fuck that. I didn't shoot anyone. I didn't kill anyone.'

'You're an accessory, Bobby. You were there.'

Bobby gritted his teeth and took a step toward Riley. 'Because you told me to go.'

'You wanted to go, Bobby. As soon as I told you that bloke Michael Roberts was going to be picked up, you couldn't wait to get there to get even.'

'To belt him. Not fuckin' kill him! And I didn't know why you wanted them kept quiet! Why? What was it about?'

'None of your business.'

'Fuck you. I had nothing to do with this.'

'Keep your voice down.'

Bobby dug his closed fists into his pockets. 'I'm not goin' down for this. You told me it'd be okay.'

'Well, now it's not.'

Bobby cursed himself and then turned to face Riley. He didn't give him an inch of warning before he unloaded a left hook on Riley's chin that left him on his back and unconscious at the end of the horseshoe bar.

* * *

When Bobby arrived home, Charlotte was on the porch reading a novel. He barely looked at her, but she could tell he was rattled. His lips were dry, his mouth open, as though his mind was on other things. The next days, as the story broke in the newspaper, Bobby became more uneasy. He didn't go to work and drank instead. Late one evening, he collapsed drunk on the kitchen floor and started wailing. It was a surrender and a confession, though from where she lay in her bed, she couldn't make sense of any of it.

* * *

Tommy Butler interviewed Cassandra O'Shea and her son, and Aaron told the policeman what had happened. And that it hadn't happened just once, but numerous times. Aaron wet his pants during the testimony and cried when Butler told him the priest would be going to jail *for the rest of his life*. Cassandra O'Shea told Butler about Landry's visit and the money paid to *give him peace of mind*.

The next story that broke surrounding the investigation was the crime Riley had failed to investigate. The revelation shook the Catholic community of Darwin to its core. Ned watched across the road from Father McKay's house as three policemen led him onto the street. Two photographers clambered between the officers trying to get the shot that would go with a front-page exposé. Ned got a glance of McKay as they turned him toward the street opposite, and led him to the back passenger-side door of a paddy wagon. He looked dazed and childlike, Ned thought. There was no strength in his posture, no weight against the pushing and directing of policemen. It was as if the heft of his body had left him and he was the mass of a small child. Ned watched as they drove him away, and he wondered what lay ahead for McKay in a jail. A cell shared with someone. Someone who'd soon know why his new cellmate was incarcerated. 'So be it,' he said quietly.

* * *

It was the following day when Landry answered his door to Butler.

'Yes?' Landry stood tall.

'You know who I am?'

'No. But I know what you're here for. Riley. Nothing to do with me. And I'm sure he would have told you that.' Landry smirked.

'I haven't spoken to him yet.' Butler's eyes narrowed, a frown across his forehead. 'But I will.'

'Good. Go talk to him.' Landry shovelled his hands into his pockets. 'Like I said –'

Butler interrupted, 'I spoke with Cassandra O'Shea.'

Landry's mouth opened, his face lengthened and a sound followed but no word formed; it was an involuntary noise squirted from the anxiety that had instantly ballooned and twisted his insides.

Butler, nondescript and patient, waited a moment. Nothing followed from Landry. 'You paid her.'

'That means nothing. It was a gift.' Landry regained some semblance of arrogance. 'I told Riley what she told me. She didn't believe it. But I'm not a cop. Not my job to investigate and charge.'

'No, that's true. But I was curious as to why you'd take an interest in that matter. Why go see her?' Butler raised his eyebrows.

Landry took his hands from his pockets and the timbre in his voice shifted higher. 'Look. Someone told Riley they'd seen something at the vestry. I was concerned. It's my parish. The Catholics in this town are my base. We're one. I don't know where the story came from, but I went to see her and she didn't believe it.'

Butler nodded and then shrugged. 'I did some digging anyway. Because I was curious. The priest. McKay. He's your brother.' Butler watched silently as Landry's face reddened and he took a step backward.

'I'm not saying anymore.'

'That's your prerogative, Mayor. But I have cause to believe that you were there seeing that lady not for the wellbeing of your parish, but to protect your brother in regards to a matter that, if investigated, would severely impact your standing politically and socially. So I'll need to talk to you again in a much more formal situation. I'd suggest you bring a lawyer with you when that occasion comes around.'

***

While McKay was the first to fall, no one in the town could imagine, other than Ned, what was about to unravel. Butler, following Cassandra O'Shea's trail, arrived at Ned, the former policeman who'd investigated the death of David O'Shea. Butler called Ned and they arranged to meet at a steak restaurant on the promenade.

Getting dressed for the meeting, Ned wondered what Butler knew. Whom he'd spoken to. He didn't want to get dragged into the investigation where he may one day be called to give testimony. Butler was already seated and drinking an iced tea when Ned arrived. Ned sat opposite, and before he got to order a drink, Butler began, 'What do you think?'

Ned took a moment, rolled his tongue across the inside of his cheek. 'What do you know?'

'I know a lot.'

'Well, there's more.'

Butler took a mouthful of his iced tea. 'You quit. That's what I heard.'

'I did.'

Butler took a long look at Ned and then sat forward. 'I don't think so.'

Ned raised his hand and summoned a waiter. 'You spoken to Landry?'

'Maybe.'

The waiter arrived and wiped the sweat from his forehead with the back of his hand. 'Fuck it's hot. Want a beer?'

'A draught, please.' Ned waited for the waiter to leave and then sat back in his seat. 'It's bigger than the priest, the mayor and the cop.'

Butler smirked. 'That's pretty big. That's collusion, blackmail.'

'You spoke to Cassandra O'Shea then.'

Butler let out a laugh through his nose. 'Must have been hard for you to walk away.'

'Not really. Not with what was at stake.'

'So what is it then?'

Ned sat forward, rested his elbows on the table and clasped his hands. 'Ernie Clay. He'd been killed. Riley dismissed it. There were two other men, Clarry Tallis, Lionel Frazier. I sent two men away for their murders. They didn't do it. Riley and Landry set it up.'

'But they were convicted? These other men?'

'Yes.'

'I'm not here to make a case for the retrial of two murders.'

'Ernie Clay worked for Lionel Frazier. At the school the priest presided over.'

Butler's eyes narrowed. 'They knew.'

'Ernie saw. Frazier saw. Tallis was in the wrong place at the wrong time.'

Butler took a laboured breath and shrugged. 'I can't interview dead men, Mr Potter.'

'No. You can't.' Ned sat straight. 'There was another man. He got away when Tallis and Frazier were killed.'

'Right. And what's he know?'

'Everything.'

Butler left before Ned finished his beer, and caught the first plane to Sydney.

* * *

It was the afternoon and Bobby Clark was sitting watching television and drinking beer from a dimpled glass mug when Charlotte answered the door. Tommy Butler stood before her, hands on his hips and a staid expression on his face. He asked to speak with her husband and when she welcomed him into the house, Bobby called from his lounge chair, 'Who's there, Charlotte?'

'A policeman.'

Bobby stood from his chair and when he turned toward the front door Butler was walking into the living room.

'Can I help you?'

'Bobby Clark?'

'Yeah.'

'I need you to accompany me to answer some questions.'

'About what?'

'The murder of two men.'

Bobby stood perfectly still, his mouth ajar.

'Mr Clark? Did you understand what I just said?'

Bobby looked at Charlotte, his eyes glassy, the acne scars on his chin accentuated as it trembled.

'I was there but I didn't do anything. I didn't kill anyone.'

'Mr Clark, you need to come with me.'

Charlotte knew then definitively that Bobby had been part of the assault on Michael. She walked from the room and pushed through the front door to the porch. She strode to the balustrade, leant over it and looked across the road to the plots of land that were now occupied by bare timber frames being clad and braced by plywood. She never turned back as Butler brought Bobby from the house and passed her to his car.

***

Ned had received a call from Graham asking whether he'd found the identity of the man responsible for Bonnie's abduction. He told him that he had though he didn't know where he was. As the story continued to unfold, Jack Taylor had been conspicuous in his absence. Ned knew he'd have gone underground, possibly left the Territory to avoid being arrested. He almost stopped looking for him. Almost.

A month after Graham's call, early one morning Ned was driving out to go fishing for flounder and whiting at low tide down the western end of Lee Point Beach. As he drove by a small local store he saw a man step out, with his head down, walking to a car carrying a brown paper bag of shopping. The first thing he noticed was the man's short flaxen hair. He slowed and watched the man get into his car and drive away. It was an easy follow and he clocked the dirt track the man's car turned down that led to the water. Later, Ned checked the area out from the waterline while he fished. He looked back into the scrub and noticed a crudely built shelter thatched with yellowing palm leaves. He'd seen the place before and had thought the shelter was a fishing cover that had been put there by some local boys, used to sleep in when the tide was too full and when the sun was too hot. As Ned fished, he kept an eye on the shack and after an hour or so he saw Jack Taylor walk from the scrub and onto the beach for a swim. Taylor never turned Ned's way and, while he was in the water, Ned left.

Ned went to bed that night but didn't sleep. He changed his mind by the minute, and when morning broke he was exhausted and still uncertain. He gutted the whiting and flounder he'd caught the day before, floured them and fried them in a shallow pan. While eating, he thought of Michael Roberts and what he'd told him of that night. How there was a *big fair-headed fella with a whip taking to Clarry.* He then remembered the smell of formaldehyde in the morgue while he looked over the torn back of Clarry Tallis.

He finished his fish, drank a bottle of cold beer and then, without hesitation, phoned his father-in-law. A day later he drove to Darwin Airport and waited at the arrivals lounge for the plane from Townsville. Graham greeted him with his brother Callum. They shared the same long face and when they spoke it was hard to tell one voice from the other. Only Callum's thicker Irish brogue distinguished him from Graham.

It was just before dusk when they got into the car. The sky ahead of them was grey and purple, the clouds sinking lower to the earth as they rolled forward, hauling a storm that held rain and hail. It was dim when they pulled up at the edge of the scrubland beside the western end of the beach. Ned told them where the thatched shelter was and, without another word, Graham and Callum left the car and walked side by side into the bush. It wasn't five minutes later that Jack Taylor, bleeding from his head and limping, was forced into Ned's car.

'Drive!' Ned couldn't tell who had said it.

Taylor fought hard with elbows and fists when he was able, but the brothers kept him covered up, their punches and their lunging heads sounded like claps of thunder off Taylor's bone. In a moment where Taylor could look between his cover, he made out the profile of Ned.

'I know you.' There was a final dull wallop muffled by the thickness of Graham's hair, and then it went quiet.

'Fuck. That hurt my head. He's out cold.' Graham pushed Taylor's head to its side, and blood flowed from a cut above his brow.

There wasn't another word said as they drove out toward the barn where Charlotte had nursed Michael Roberts back to health. Every time Jack Taylor roused and regained some consciousness, Graham and Callum took turns to turn out his lights again. Ned parked close to the entrance and stayed in the car while Graham and Callum dragged Taylor into the barn. He didn't hear a sound coming from behind the raking doors, and though he knew what was happening, he didn't once think about it.

* * *

It was dawn when they all got into Fraser Potter's boat. Taylor's body had begun to stiffen and his bleeding had stopped hours before. His face was unrecognisable, and Ned couldn't look at it.

Fraser stood at the bow, his hands limp over the steering wheel. Ned sat in the middle, Graham and Callum aft, with Taylor lying horizontally at their feet.

'Where is this thing?' Graham lit a cigarette and pulled back hard.

'She's here somewhere.' Fraser shut off the throttle and looked carefully over the still water. It was pond-like and the breaking dawn showed itself in soft yellow ribbons across the river. 'There she is.' Fraser pointed ahead. 'You see her eyes? Glowin'?'

Graham and Callum stood up. 'That's a crocodile?' Callum let loose a small childish laugh.

'No, that's Marilyn.' Fraser pushed the throttle gently forward and the boat slowly made its way toward Marilyn. He shut off the engine and they glided in beside the croc. 'Okay. She's curious, but she'll disappear if we don't give her somethin' quick.'

'She gonna eat him whole?' Callum began to reach for Taylor's body.

'No. She'll take him somewhere she knows good, put him under a tree root nice and tight, wait for him to soften up and eat him bit by bit, bone by bone, until there's nothin' but his dead stink left in the water.'

'Clothes and all?' Callum hoisted Taylor up from the bottom of the boat by his armpits.

'Yep. She'll eat everythin'.' Fraser pulled an oar from the side of the boat, thread it through a gunnel and paddled their way closer to the croc.

Graham took Taylor's legs, and he and his brother moved the body so that it was lengthways in the boat.

'Okay. When I say, drop the body in.' Fraser pulled the oar from the gunnel and laid it down. 'Okay, lift it up.'

Graham and Callum hoisted Taylor's body so it rested on the thin edge of the boat. Ned looked at his brother as he leant over into the river and thrashed his hand around in the water to alert Marilyn.

'Okay, put him in.'

Graham and Callum pushed the body into the water, and it entered with barely a splash. Taylor's body floated on its front for just a moment before rolling onto its back. In that instant Ned saw the horror of what had become of Taylor's face. His mouth was open, and he was missing teeth from both his top and bottom gums. His lip was split in the centre and the cut widened through the flesh where he'd begun to grow a moustache. The bridge of his nose was bent, and a knot of broken bone whitened through the skin like a knuckle on a clenched fist. His cheekbones were smashed and concaved, depressed at the points of impact. The swelling on both sides had covered his eyes and all that could be seen were the tiny ends of his lashes. Ned watched the body curl over onto its front, and air inflate the space between his back and the shirt he was wearing. It reminded Ned of a parachute opening.

'Here she comes.' Graham said it evenly and without emotion.

Marilyn wound her shape slowly toward Taylor's body, her eyes looking over to the men in the boat.

'She's lookin' at us.' Callum laughed.

As she approached Taylor, she slowed and became still, her eyes unblinking and looking directly at the boat. She then submerged without creating a ripple across the water's skin. Moments passed and Graham looked to Fraser. 'Where'd she go?'

'She's underneath us.' Fraser smiled.

'Fuck me.' Callum's Irish brogue thickened with panic.

And without warning, and barely a disturbance across the water, Taylor's body was dragged beneath and gone. The men looked across at each other, and Ned sat back down. 'Let's get outta here.'

'Wait a minute.' Graham dug a hand into his pocket, pulled it out and held a bunch of teeth across his palm.

'What the fuck are they?' Fraser stood taller to get a better look.

'They're his teeth.' And Graham threw them as far as he could across the water, like a child throwing a heap of stones from the bank of a river. He sat back down on the boat's edge and looked at his brother.

'Thank you.'

'Welcome.'

He then looked at Ned, his chin tucked close to his chest, his forehead furrowed, like a fighter looking at an opponent. 'I won't have a threat like the one I heard from that cunt hangin' over my daughter's life and her child's. Not ever.' He turned away from Ned and looked back over the river. 'I'm proud of you, Ned. Should be proud of yourself.'

* * *

Graham and Callum got a taxi from Fraser's house back to the airport. Graham flew back to Townsville, and Callum directly back to Brisbane.

Ned and Fraser sat out on the porch and looked over the river, watching the sun in the middle of the sky, colouring the water a shiny bronze that flickered and sparkled when the wind pushed tiny ripples across its surface. For almost an hour not a word was said. It was Fraser who waded gently into the murky psychology of what they'd both witnessed and participated in. 'What did he say he was gonna do to Bonnie?'

'I don't know. I don't ever want to know.'

'Fair enough.' Fraser got up and walked inside the house leaving Ned alone. Ned rubbed the thick stubble that had been growing for a week and had begun to itch. He thought about Jack Taylor's moustache and how it looked while torn in half. *They must have kicked him there*, he thought, *kicked him to death.*

He didn't feel sympathy nor sadness for Jack Taylor, though he wondered if he should. He supposed Taylor had been hand-fed his attitudes since he was a boy. Ned knew he was no different from many of the people he'd grown up with. But Ned couldn't forgive the brutal murder of innocent men in the face of even the most bent and thwarted development.

He took a breath and stood up, scratched the patchy growth of whiskers across his jawline, and leant over the porch balustrade, looking to the spot where Marilyn had pulled Taylor under. *Hell of a way to die.*

CHAPTER 41

BEFORE SHE WENT to Fannie Bay Gaol, Charlotte visited her father in hospital. She sat by his bed, held his hand and read from the new novel she'd just begun. It was about an Irish horse wagoner, Paddy Doolan, and his young son hauling freight across the Gulf Country in the 1920s. Charlotte had started narrating it to her father the month before, and on the three readings she'd had by his bedside, at some point during the delivery, a smile had formed from the corner of his good side.

Charlotte wondered, when driving home from those evenings, what may have prompted her father's delight. Perhaps, she thought, the descriptions of woodland and savanna grasslands in the Gulf Country where her father had cut sugar cane as a young boy with his brothers. After an hour of reading, she put the book down on his bed, and then bent in close to his ear. 'All hell broke loose here, Dad. And I'm in the middle. I wish you were with me.' She took the novel from the bed, and gently opened her father's hand, which was flaccid and half closed. She placed the spine of the novel against the loose webbing between her father's thumb and forefinger, and then locked his fingers over the cover. 'I love you.'

* * *

Charlotte had taken more than a dozen phone calls from the Fannie Bay Gaol, the operator on the other end politely asking whether she'd agree to the charges. She'd refused on every occasion but the last, where Bobby begged down the line for her to come see him. The conversation was short, and when she spoke to him she could feel the curt, clipped cadence of her words through her throat. When she arrived, she signed a thick hardback register that was years old, thousands upon thousands of names and addresses entered in blue biro, the flow of the cursive and the pressure in the print a gaze into the mood of every visitor. Fear, anxiety, uncertainty and anger. Charlotte could smell the ink from the pen while she wrote her name and for a moment became light-headed.

'This way, ma'am.'

She was led from the registry to a small internal room without windows; the walls uneven and in parts bulky from the crude cement bagging job over the brickwork, the paint colourless and applied heavily. She sat on a small timber chair and waited. The first thing she noticed when Bobby entered the room was the grey hue of his skin. He sat down opposite her and reached for her hands. Charlotte pulled them away.

'I didn't kill anyone.' Bobby leant forward.

Charlotte clasped her hands and squeezed them, as if the pressure may help to force her words out. Her mouth opened, but only her breath was let out.

'I didn't know why those men were … I didn't know why I was supposed to frighten them. I didn't know about the priest. I didn't.'

'Why were you there then?' The question was toneless and came quickly.

'One of the men. I boxed him. At the show in the tent. He beat me. Well, he didn't, but they said he did. I was just told he would be there and that …' Bobby stopped. 'I shouldn't have been there. I would never have been there had I known about the priest.'

'Why are you telling me this? It doesn't matter to you, surely.'

'It does matter.'

'Why?'

'Because. You're my wife. And despite everything, I love you.'

Charlotte unfurled her hands. 'I know, Bobby. About the other woman. I know.'

Bobby's eyes caved in, his head fell. 'I'm sorry.' A moment later he looked up at Charlotte; he raised his brow and spoke softly, 'I can forgive you. You forgive me.'

Charlotte thought a while. Bobby's mouth opened slightly and the airy breath he took in gave away his hope.

'I'm not sure the judge and jury will forgive you. That's all you should be worried about.'

'I didn't do anything.' Bobby's voice rose.

'You took a whip there.'

'To make noise. To scare them. I didn't use it, that wasn't me.'

Charlotte closed her eyes and rubbed their sockets with her thumb and forefinger. She stood quickly. 'I have to go.'

'We've still got time.' Bobby sounded desperate.

'No.' Charlotte walked away from him and toward the prison guard who stood at the entrance to the room.

* * *

Tommy Butler set an interview with Landry in the office once occupied by Senior Sergeant Riley. Landry arrived, this time with his lawyer present, and started in a combative manner. 'This going to take long?' He took a soft packet of cigarettes from his suit pocket and tapped the end to loosen a smoke.

'Don't smoke in here.' Butler glared at Landry.

'No law in smoking.'

'It's my office. In here, I'm the law of everything. Light it up and I'll put it out.'

Landry huffed, glowering at Butler. A moment later, unnerved and uncertain, he returned the packet of cigarettes to his suit pocket. 'Whatever you say ... what do I call you?'

'I'm a detective. So you can address me as that.'

'Okay then, Detective. You can address me as Mayor, or Mayor Landry.'

Butler nodded, turned a page to a notepad and began to read silently.

'Mayor. Do you know a man named Jack Taylor?'

'Yes. I do.'

'He's been renting a house, the agreement has your name on it.'

Landry shifted in his seat. 'Yes. He's a friend. A family friend from down south.'

'From Sydney?'

'Yes. Where I'm originally from.'

'He seems to have disappeared. Do you know where he is?'

'No.'

'He work for you?'

'No. Like I said, just a friend who needed a bit of a break. A hand.'

'Did you know Ernie Clay?'

'No, never heard of him.'

'Why then did you visit him and his wife?'

Landry glanced at his lawyer and before he could answer Butler kept at him. 'Why did you see Lionel Frazier and his wife, Leila? Why Cassandra and David O'Shea?'

Landry stood, reached for his comb-over and flattened it. 'Listen, Detective –'

'Sit down, Mayor.'

Landry, ruby faced and beginning to sweat, sat slowly.

'Do you know who Michael Roberts is?'

Landry clenched his jaw firmly and shook his head.

'He got away. I spoke to him. He knows why these men were killed. What they saw. You see where this is headed, Mayor?'

'I want a deal.'

Butler shrugged, and twisted his expression in a way that gave Landry just enough optimism that a transaction could be made.

'Jack Taylor killed Ernie Clay,' Landry said quickly. 'I didn't tell him to do that. And I specifically told him not to kill the others.'

Butler sat back in his chair, stayed silent and invited Landry to continue with a restrained nod.

'Riley was in on it. I paid him to quieten those men. But not to kill them. Taylor, he's a criminal. He's the one you want.' Landry took a breath, looked at his lawyer as if to solicit praise for his unnegotiated testimony. 'What do I get for that?'

'Probably another ten years added to your sentence.' Butler winked at him and then called in a constable to arrest Landry there in the office. As Landry stood to be led away and processed, Butler asked, 'The cop. Potter. Why'd he quit. That you?'

Landry shook his head. 'His wife was spoken to. He walked away.'

'By whom?'

'You can join the dots on that one, Detective.'

* * *

When Ned was told of what happened, he could only think about what it might have been like to be in the room as Landry unravelled. He wanted so badly to have the mayor know that it was him who'd put it together, piece by piece, without help, shackled and thwarted whenever a lead presented itself. He saw the photo of Landry as he was led handcuffed from the police station. He looked diabolically dishevelled, his comb-over loose from his scalp, the long broad band of overgrown hair, resting on his shoulder. The collar to his business shirt sat unevenly, one side left unturned, the other flat.

Danny Lewis was interviewed and, from what Ned heard, caved almost immediately. He told Butler he had shot Lionel Frazier and Clarry Tallis only after they were already dead. He cried as he told them that he'd been forced to do it by Jack Taylor. Ned remembered clearly what Ron Thompson had stated, that the post-mortem gunshot wounds signalled *pack behaviour, usually by a subordinate to earn his stripes, so to speak.*

* * *

Butler went after Riley aggressively. As complicit as the senior sergeant was, he was never present at the murder sites, and so what

Butler had him tied to was neglecting to investigate. There was no paper trail of money from Landry to him, and none from Riley to his attack dogs. It was his word against Landry's as to who ordered the coercion of the men who ended up murdered. He lost his job, and escaped a custodial sentence abetted by his previously unstained record as a policeman.

In an attempt to win favour and keep himself out of jail, he did offer up the reason why Landry had asked his priest brother to come to the Territory. He told Butler that Landry had told him the complete story one evening while he was drunk. Until then, Riley said, he never knew of the connection or even that Landry had a brother. He said that, *There was a political angle to be played to have his brother in town. To have a priest in his corner. To spread the word of what a good Catholic man he was among the Labor voters that were his base. That his intentions were wholesome and the essence of a truly God-fearing man's principles.* Riley said Landry told him that, *Father McKay could paint him the way he wanted to be seen. To be revered. And there was never a chance they'd be recognised as brothers.* Landry gloated when saying, *His brother was shorter, had a beard, was plain ugly and bald.* Riley belly-laughed when telling Butler, *I've seen the long side of Landry's hair hang from his head, he's got fuck-all hair up there.*

* * *

One afternoon not long after Ned had learnt Riley had escaped a jail term, he walked purposefully into Hotel Darwin. Riley was, as he'd always been, down the end of the horseshoe bar furthest from the entrance. He was alone, dressed in ill-fitting civilian garb and drinking schooners of ale. Ned approached and sat at the stool beside him. Riley kicked the knot of tobacco flakes stuck at the corner of his mouth with his tongue, and spat them on the bar in front of Ned.

'You look well, Joe.' Ned held up a finger toward the barman. 'A beer over here please.'

'Fuck are you doin' here, Potter, but ruining my afternoon?'

'Just came by for a drink.'

'Bullshit. You came here to rub it in my face.'

'No. I couldn't care less about you, Riley. You're an insignificance of a man. A pig. Ignorant. And dumb. I've wasted too much time already thinkin' about you.' Ned took his schooner from the bar. 'You're lucky, Riley. You should be in jail.'

'In jail for what? That detective had fuck all. I'm still here, aren't I? So I'm not that dumb, am I, Potter?' Riley smiled, pulled a packet of cigarettes from his trouser pocket.

'Well, not that way it seems. You're dumb in another way, Riley. The way it counts. You're no more than what you were as a child. You haven't changed a single opinion of what you got told by your people when you were a kid. Not one. Never asked why, never asked how.' Ned took a swallow from his glass. 'In my estimation that makes you dumb.'

Riley stayed quiet for a moment, processing what he'd heard. 'Fuck you, Potter.' Riley laughed. 'I got everythin' I want. I was gonna leave the job anyway. And let me tell you, son, there are a lot more here like me than there are of anyone else.'

'You believe that, don't you, Riley?' Ned met Riley's smile with his own.

'Yes, I do.'

'Answer me this then. Why are you out of a job? Why's Landry in jail? Why's Bobby Clark in jail? Where's Jack Taylor?' Ned smiled more broadly. 'Days are gone of sweepin' your shit under the mat, Riley. People have had enough.'

'You tell yourself whatever you want, Potter. If things are so different why were you forced to quit then? I made that happen.' Riley reached for his crotch, adjusted himself, and then moved closer to Ned. 'I'm insignificant? You're a bum on a buildin' site. You come here and gloat to me about what's gone down in this town? You tried and failed, Potter. You're no cop. You couldn't find your own arsehole with a flashlight.' Riley glared at Ned, his eyes narrowed and lit, joining the contemptuous grin that had split his mouth so broadly that both rows of teeth were showing.

Ned stayed silent, but looked directly into Riley's eyes while contemplating whether to let it all out. It was right there held in his mouth, chronologically prepared and ready to be delivered without pause or infraction of truth.

'What? You got somethin' to say, Potter?'

Ned's mouth opened, the bow pulled, the arrow of truth ready to be let go. How he'd uncovered it all. But no sound came, and no words formed. Instead a smile slowly took shape and settled. 'No, I got nothin' to say, Riley. I'll see ya around.' Ned winked at Riley, got off his stool and walked out.

* * *

Bonnie, Rose and Graham returned from Townsville just before Christmas. Rose was walking, Bonnie had lost weight and there were ribbons of blonde through her dark hair that had been bleached from sun and seawater. She told Ned that she liked Townsville, and that perhaps a new start there might be *good for all of them*. Ned didn't disagree, and wondered, without speaking of it, whether a life in North Queensland could see him back to being a policeman. He and Graham never once spoke about Jack Taylor, though there was novel depth to their relationship now. Ned felt a new respect from Graham, it was manifest in the way he spoke to him, and the way he heard his father-in-law speaking of him to others.

* * *

One afternoon, Ned went to the Victoria Hotel, ordered a schooner of draught beer from Katie Briggs and sat alone at a table by an open window. He looked toward the coast and watched a rolling column of black and purple cloud turn over itself, headed toward land. It folded and churned but the gloom of colours brightened when the sun came out. Ned smiled and closed his eyes when the first fragrance of rain pushed by the storm's frontal winds floated under his nose.

'Smells different in Sydney.' Ned opened his eyes and before him with a glass of beer was Detective Tommy Butler. 'Not as muddy.'

'It's the soil here. That's why.'

'How are you, Mr Potter?'

'I'm okay.'

'You've been watching, reading?'

'Bits and pieces.'

'House of cards.'

'Yep. House of cards.'

'Mind if I sit down with ya?'

Ned shook his head and Butler sat in the chair opposite. 'It must have been hard to choose what thread to pull.'

Ned smirked. 'Yeah, well, I guess I got it right.'

'Cassandra O'Shea.'

'Good woman.'

Butler took a long swallow from his glass, wiped the froth left on his upper lip away with the back of his hand. 'I drink too fast up here.'

'Goes warm otherwise.'

'Well, I drink more, but sweat more. So it evens out. That's what I tell myself anyway.'

Ned nodded.

'You don't say much, do ya?'

'Depends what we're talking about. You're not here to talk to me about beer and rain.'

'No. I'm not.'

'And the things you want to talk to me about then, I really don't have much to say. I told you what I could.'

Butler leant over the table. 'Jack Taylor. You know who he is?'

'Yeah, I know who he is. I met him once with Danny Lewis. Big prick.'

'That's right. But, you see, I can't find him.'

'What's he done?'

'Well, according to Mayor Landry he killed Ernie Clay, Clarry Tallis and Lionel Frazier.'

Ned folded his arms, sat back in his chair and half-smiled. 'I heard Landry sang like a bird.'

'He did.'

Ned shrugged. 'Like I said, I only met him once.'

'You also said to me before it wasn't hard to walk away considering what was at stake.'

Ned stayed still, tightened the fold of his arms.

'I was entirely impressed by what you uncovered considering the obstacles put in your way. So I was intrigued as to what it might have taken to get you to walk away. I threw it at Landry. Someone got to your wife.' Butler met Ned's glare and remained quiet.

'And daughter.'

'Must have been a serious threat made.'

Ned unfolded his arms and reached for his beer. He looked directly at Butler, then finished what was left in his glass in one swallow. 'I gotta go, Detective. I'm cooking my family dinner.' Ned stood.

'Well, you enjoy that. I don't think I'll see you again. But, you know, you should consider going back to being a cop. You're very good at it.'

CHAPTER 42

NED WAS PRESENT in the courtroom when Landry was found guilty on all charges. It took the jury less than two hours to make their decision. Ned stood at the back with the dozens of others who'd missed out on a seat. Every major newspaper in the country and their reporters were there covering the verdict and sentencing. Ned watched as Landry was asked by the judge to stand. Even from behind he could tell Landry had lost weight. The top corners of his jacket were left unfilled by his shoulders, and as a consequence the sleeves hung down past his wrists. It looked like a borrowed suit, a vagrant's hurried effort to appear respectable before the court while on trial for petty crime. Landry got life. And after reading him the verdict, the magistrate sat forward and pointed his finger at Landry. 'You are a disgrace to yourself, and this city. The murders, and the part you played in them, are abhorrent enough, a puppet master of the most vile intentions. But to have brought your brother here, to know what he was, and to put him in the company of children, all for your own political gain and good opinion within the town, is nothing short of evil. Consider yourself lucky I have not sentenced you to death.'

Sitting in front of Ned was Martha Clay, her head bowed. Ned watched her closely throughout, and when Landry stood to be sentenced, he could see her shaking. Her shoulders trembled and sent shockwaves down her arms.

A week later, Ned was at the courthouse again when Bobby Clark and Danny Lewis were sentenced. Bobby got ten years for accessory to murder, and Lewis was sentenced to death. Immediately after the verdict, Lewis began to cry and begged the magistrate to reconsider, *They were already dead when I shot them, I didn't kill anyone.* He watched as Bobby Clark searched through the courtroom, conspicuously looking for a known face. *Charlotte*, Ned knew. He looked himself. She was never present.

* * *

A month later, Ned didn't sleep a wink one night, contemplating the morning to come. What he would say, how it might feel and whether reconciliation within himself may be possible.

He arrived at Fannie Bay Gaol early, and though without any sleep, he felt more alive than he had in weeks. The news coverage during Landry's trial had made Ned melancholic and lethargic. He had to relive the facts of the whole conspiracy and the violence that was applied and executed to keep it all clandestine. He'd revisited the images he'd seen, of the murdered men, of Clarry Tallis's back, more open wound than held together flesh from having been flogged to death. And he got stuck in remembering the obstructions that were put before him as he tried to investigate. He asked himself question upon question about how he might have better handled Riley and Landry and sidestepped their obstacles to have kept Bonnie and Rose from the line of fire.

It had taken four months for the paperwork to be processed to declare Dell Sanders and Andrew Liston innocent and to set a date for their release. They were waiting in a secure room, dressed in the clothes they'd worn on the day of sentencing. The door opened and Ned walked through.

'Constable Potter?' Andrew's wild hair had been shorn to stubble length and made him appear years younger.

'Hello, Andrew.' Ned smiled and then turned to Dell. 'Hello, Dell.'

Ned could sense Dell's wariness.

'Constable.' Dell put both hands into his trouser pockets.

'Well, not anymore. I resigned months ago.' Ned spoke gently.

Dell simply nodded.

'Why?' Andrew stepped forward.

Ned smiled at him. 'It doesn't matter. And, Dell, you can relax. I'm not here to bring bad news. I'm here to apologise. I didn't do right by you both. I knew you weren't responsible. I knew that. I'm sorry you had to come here.'

Both men stood quietly, and Ned felt compelled to keep talking. 'I can't imagine what it was like for you both in here, knowing you were innocent.'

'Innocent or not. Place doesn't change. In here, we're all guilty. And you're treated that way.' Dell spoke slowly and without much intonation.

'Yes. I guess you're right.' Ned's mouth tightened, his lips hidden and evened out. 'I'm sorry. I'm sorry you were put through this.'

Dell nodded, his brow furrowed, and he looked across to Andrew. 'Well, we were okay. We looked after each other.'

'Dell looked after me.'

'I'm sure he did.' Ned smiled at both of them. 'Anyway. Good luck.'

'Thank you.' Dell said it quickly, and Andrew nodded.

* * *

Driving back to his house, Ned felt a dissatisfaction for how it had unfolded between Dell and Andrew and himself. He thumped the steering wheel, and thoughts of drinking poked their way through his angered scenarios of going back to the jail to lay it out before both of them. How he'd put it all together and been responsible for their freedom.

When he got home, he felt exhausted, the feeling of the morning long gone; his melancholic lethargy returned, exacerbated by his sleepless night. He lay on his bed and went to sleep. When he woke it was the afternoon and the wind that came through the open window and swept across his naked torso was warm. He sat up on the bed, turned his head toward the wind and took in a deep breath. He closed his eyes when he smelt the cooking tar of the bitumen road outside. He breathed through his nose to smell for rain that may have been on its way and determined it wouldn't be until perhaps later that evening when the air would thicken and heat to a point where a downpour was certain.

Ned put on a pair of shorts and walked from the house shirtless and barefoot. He drove an hour south to the beginning of the Adelaide River, to a spot that wound around shallow inlets banked by knotty mangroves. He looked to the setting sun and did a sum of how much light was left and how long he'd be able to be in the water before it was too dark and perilous.

'We got twenty minutes to go at it, fish. Me and you.' Ned smiled as he spoke quietly. He slid down a claggy hillock, walked over the gnarled twists of mangrove roots and entered the river. The mud beneath his feet was soft and cool, and tickled when it spurted between his toes from the pressure of his steps. 'Here we are, fish.'

Ned felt his stomach flutter and lighten, as though about to take the field in some kind of competition. He'd felt the same sensation as a young boy lining up for running races and before taking to the grass for games of football. He enjoyed the way the imminent contest touched his being. He began shifting his feet in the riverbed below. The bottom had firmed in small spots either side of him, though it gave way quickly to softer mud when he twisted his feet and bore down on the surface. He could feel the reeds sway in the strengthening current, their pointy ends and soft edges fondling the broadest spots of his calves and the bony knobs of his ankles. He stayed still, waist deep, and watched the stagnant sheets of water close to the riverbank, hoping for a disturbance that would tell him where his fish was lurking.

When he looked past the inlet to the belly of the river, aware of where a croc might slowly approach from, he felt the thick twisting flank of a fish sweep by his calf. Without thinking he dropped beneath the surface, blindly reaching at a point where he figured the fish might be. He felt along the surface with both palms, and followed a building knoll of muck that peaked and fell evenly to the mouth of a large hole. *You in there?* Ned ran the edge of his wrist around the perimeter of the hole, and then plunged his arm inside as deep as it could reach. He tunnelled an inch further with the tips of his fingers and felt the scaly side of a fish twisting urgently to find more space to hide in.

Ned kicked hard against the water to keep his shoulder flush with the mouth of the burrow. He felt the fish turn again, and its open gill brushed past his thumb, a spot not close enough to the middle of his hand where he could close it quickly and where his grip was the strongest. His lungs began to burn, the first alert to let some air out that would make him less buoyant. The bubbles of carbon dioxide came quickly from his mouth and popped as they rose past his open eyes. The fish swept past his hand quickly and turned, the broad brush of its tail wobbling over Ned's fingertips as it dove deeper into the hole.

Ned pushed hard against the mud floor and felt the ball of his shoulder lift out from its socket and run across the cartilage surrounding it. He yelped in pain and lost a load of air that sunk him flat over the riverbed. *You bastard.* A moment later, the fish turned again and Ned felt the spiny dorsal fin. He bit down on the pain as the ball of his shoulder rolled back over the gristle and into its socket. He closed his eyes and reassured himself that he had enough air left to make a strike. He could feel the thumping of his heart rattling through his ribcage and begin to slow.

Okay, you gotta be quick, Ned. He very slowly began to pull his arm from the hole, and felt the concave head of the fish at his fingertips, following him, giving him the space he needed to grab its gills. Ned stopped his arm from moving backward, and its rubbery mouth swept past his palm. *Okay, now.* Ned dug the toes of both feet into the riverbed, and pushed off it, sending him shooting forward. He felt his hand pass the fish's side, and then brought it back quickly and shot his fingers into the open space between its flank and gill. *Got ya!* Ned pulled as hard as he could. Finding his knees and then his feet, he dragged the fish from the hole and stood up.

He broke through the surface of the river and shook his head like a dog ridding its coat of excess water. He opened his mouth, took a breath, and pulled the barramundi into the atmosphere. Its mouth opened and gills flared, its body turning and twisting, trying to break free. He got his free hand inside the other gill and hoisted the fish further from the water. It stopped fighting for a moment and Ned held it at eye level.

'Look at you. You gotta be sixty pounds. More even.' He looked into the barra's eyes and smiled. 'You'd look good on a wall.' The fish began to fight, its tail thrashing, breaching the surface and blinding Ned. 'Whoa, take it easy.' And the fish calmed. 'That's it.' Ned smiled. 'Can you hear me? You understand what I'm sayin'?' The fish's mouth began gulping as though the undissolved oxygen over land was what it sorely needed. 'You're beautiful, you know that?' The fish twisted and pulled back on Ned's grip, but only for a moment before settling again. Ned first realised he was crying only when he tasted the salty flavour of tears that had fallen into his open mouth. He stopped the instinct he had to thrust his involuntary emotion aside, and he let go. He began to sob. He brought the fish closer and held it above his head, like a father with a young child giving them the first thrills of height. 'Let it all go, Ned.'

He lowered the fish to eye level again, kissed it on the mouth, and then let go of it.

CHAPTER 43

THE MORNING THAT Charlotte read that Father Joseph McKay was found dead in his jail cell, the hospital called and told her that her father had passed away. *Peacefully*, they had said over the phone, *while asleep.* She cried, but beneath her sadness was the knowledge that nothing held her to any place any longer. It was a surreal feeling, a freedom she'd so often conceived and coloured in with scenarios of a new life. Imaginings that if conjured well enough gave her a thrill, and were then stored and built upon during the next round of reverie. It was before her. She was unshackled.

* * *

Before her visit to Fannie Bay Gaol, Charlotte woke at dawn and walked from her house to Nightcliff Beach with the quarter bucket of pipis she'd dredged from the sand at low tide the evening before. She had a new cork reel that she'd fixed with a small sinker and three long shank hooks in a neat row. She arrived at the waterline just as the sun completely breached the horizon and the tide had

371

ebbed to its lowest point. She broke open the pipis with the middle edge of her pocketknife and baited the hooks. She cast out past the slag of small broken waves and waited until she felt all three baits hit before reeling her line in. She caught twelve whiting in five casts, twice with her tackle completely snared with fish. She threw six back, gutted the rest on the beach and left the innards for the gulls and herons.

At home she filleted her catch, rolled them in flour and put them in the fridge ready to be fried for her dinner. Driving out to the jail, she considered turning around and returning home. But it had been her that had organised this visit, and it was only the fourth time she'd seen Bobby since he'd been in custody. She'd visited him Christmas Day and early in January, and then once since he'd been sentenced. It was now June. She had a plan for how the visit would play out, and, in that scenario, she'd leave having made her case, fry her fish for dinner and drink a tall bottle of beer while eating. The next day she'd be gone. Where, she didn't know.

* * *

She sat down at the same seat in the colourless room and waited for her husband. He smiled at her before sitting opposite and then reached for her hand. Charlotte took it and held it firmly. 'I've got something to say.'

'What?' Bobby's smile broadened and showed his teeth.

'I'm leaving.'

Bobby's smile stayed but the sunken shape of his forehead gave away his confusion.

'Here. Darwin.'

'What?'

Charlotte let his hand go. 'My father passed away. There's nothing here for me now.'

Bobby's smile dissipated, his mouth left open.

'I want to move on.'

Bobby shook his head. 'I thought you came here to.' His voice deepened and growled, 'You organised to see me, to tell me you're leaving me?'

'Leaving everything.'

'So what do I do?' Bobby pushed his jaw forward, his lower teeth hooked over their top row. 'Just sit in here and rot?'

'I don't know.'

'You can't just leave. We're married. I know I mucked up, but so did you.'

'It's not about that.'

'What the fuck is it about then?' His face turned red, his pale blue eyes brightened by the sting of un-spilt tears.

'Me. It's about me.' Charlotte stood up.

'Where are you going? Sit down.' Bobby's anger quickly made way for panic.

'I hope you live well, Bobby.'

'I know where the baby is. It's safe.' Bobby wiped a tear that had fallen from his eyelid and down his cheek.

Charlotte's stomach fluttered, her heart palpitated and she felt the hitch in her throat.

'I'll tell you where he is. But don't leave me.'

Charlotte left the jail not five minutes later with an address in Yeppoon in North Queensland committed to memory. She went home, cooked and ate her fish and drank her tall bottle of beer. She didn't wait until morning to leave.

ACKNOWLEDGEMENTS

To Pippa Masson for her unwavering support over so many years. For her guidance, honesty and friendship. Thank you.

To Vanessa Radnidge for fighting for me. For her belief and enthusiasm. I hope I can one day repay such faith. Thank you.

Thanks to Deonie Fiford and Cathy Craigie. Also thanks to Fiona Hazard, Isabel Staas, Jenny Topham, Louise Stark, Ailie Springall, Jacquie Brown, Daniel Pilkington, Graeme Jones, Luke Causby and the whole Hachette team.